KANGAROO
TOO

ALSO BY CURTIS C. CHEN

WAYPOINT KANGAROO

CURTIS C. CHEN

KANGAROO TOO

THOMAS DUNNE BOOKS

ST. MARTIN'S PRESS ≋ NEW YORK

THOMAS DUNNE BOOKS.
An imprint of St. Martin's Press.

KANGAROO TOO. Copyright © 2017 by Curtis C. Chen. All rights reserved.
Printed in the United States of America. For information, address St. Martin's Press, 175 Fifth Avenue, New York, N.Y. 10010.

www.thomasdunnebooks.com
www.stmartins.com

Library of Congress Cataloging-in-Publication Data

Names: Chen, Curtis C., author.
Title: Kangaroo too / Curtis C. Chen.
Description: First edition. | New York : Thomas Dunne Books, 2017.
Identifiers: LCCN 2017009493 | ISBN 9781250081896 (hardcover) |
    ISBN 9781250081902 (e-book)
Subjects: LCSH: Science fiction. | Spy stories. | BISAC: FICTION / Science Fiction /
    Military. | FICTION / Espionage.
Classification: LCC PS3603.H4473 K36 2017 | DDC 813'.6—dc23
LC record available at https://lccn.loc.gov/2017009493

Our books may be purchased in bulk for promotional, educational, or business use. Please contact your local bookseller or the Macmillan Corporate and Premium Sales Department at 1-800-221-7945, extension 5442, or by e-mail at MacmillanSpecialMarkets@macmillan.com.

First Edition: June 2017

10 9 8 7 6 5 4 3 2 1

To my parents,
two immigrants
who get the job done

KANGAROO TOO

CHAPTER ONE

Asteroid belt—undisclosed location
30 minutes after my totally coincidental rescue

The nurse-bot that took my vital signs and continues to monitor me from its charging slot in the corner of this small room doesn't have very sophisticated sensors. Even if it is watching me, all it'll see is a guy with his ear up against the air vent on the far wall. My derelict spacecraft was just towed into this strange asteroid station; of course I want to know more about my surroundings. Natural human curiosity, right?

If only my ears were working better right now.

"—waiting (STATIC) SUPPLY DRONES (STATIC) inner planets (STATIC) TIME—"

My left eye's heads-up display shows me the agency's best available map of this station, overlaid with a diagram of where my ears are tuned to right now. Using custom software, I'm able to focus in on sound sources at specific distances from my current location based on amplitude, frequency, and some other technical jargon I didn't really pay attention to while Oliver, my Equipment officer, was explaining it. I know he's proud of the gadgets he makes, but *I* don't need to know how they work; just tell me what buttons to push, man.

I'm hearing a lot of audio interference, and the volume keeps jumping up and down. I move my eyes and my fingertips in specific patterns to adjust my hearing enhancements. My left eye scanners, which can sense throughout the electromagnetic spectrum, aren't detecting any active jamming or other technological interference. There must be something wrong with my hardware. Unfortunately, I can't get to the actual implants in my body without nontrivial surgery; the best I can do right now is compensate by washing the input through software signal processing modules.

It's nobody's fault. The bionics that enhance my hearing are pretty sensitive, according to Oliver, and the high acceleration I endured while traveling in a military spacecraft out to this mid-belt asteroid must have compressed something important or pushed some component out of alignment, and now I'm not getting a good connection between the audio pickups in my ear canal and the computer core under my collarbone.

"—astronaut (STATIC) clearly isn't (STATIC) new boot magnets—"

I think I've got the volume under control now. And the static seems to be coming in regular waves; maybe I can filter it out. I wiggle my fingertips to try some standard soft-mods.

Hardware repair in the field was one of the problems my nanobots were supposed to address. Last year, Jessica—my Surgical officer—got approval from our government overseers to start experimenting with new software for the microscopic robots in my blood, so they could do more than just maintain a wireless mesh network for all the other tech inside my body. But for whatever reason, the bots either haven't identified a problem in my ears or haven't been able to repair it.

And I admit, there is an outside possibility that this issue is related to my earwax, which Jessica claims is medically termed "intermediate" or "unclassifiable." In genetic terms, that means I have a rich ancestry bringing together multicultural ethnic groups from all over Planet Earth. In practical terms, it means the consistency of my earwax varies quite a bit between "wet" and "dry" and is difficult for the nanobots to deal with algorithmically. But again, that's nobody's fault. You can't blame me for my heritage.

"—murder! Homicide! Robotic manslaughter? What? That's totally a thing . . ."

That's better. I think? I'm confused for a moment because I can definitely understand some words now, but they're not making any sense.

After another minute or so of eavesdropping, I realize I'm hearing a group of off-duty personnel playing a guessing game. One of the players is really bad at it. It's amusing, but it's not what I'm looking for.

Now that I've fixed—or at least mitigated—the input problem, it's time to actually start searching. I probably don't have much time before a human comes back to this medical bay to check on me.

Voices fade in and out as I modify the target distance. It's like I imagine tuning in an old frequency-modulated analog radio signal must have been like—or, at least, how it's depicted in the old entertainment vids I consumed desperately in my childhood. Benefits of being the orphaned child of twentieth-century media scholars who left behind their entire digital library when they died.

". . . oh! Yeah! Harder! Don't stop! YEAH! YEAH!"

I'm momentarily embarrassed, then oddly fascinated, then a little grossed out by the sounds of this erotic interlude. *Moving on.*

". . . catalog those specimens yet?"

Jackpot.

"Doc won't let us handle them until he's done with the isolation study," says a second voice, which sounds much more lethargic than the first.

"And how much longer will that take?" asks the first voice, who I've decided to call Grumpy.

"Your guess is as good as mine," replies Sleepy.

"Shit, man." I hear clinking noises, like laboratory glassware. "I didn't volunteer just to sit on this rock with my thumb up my ass."

"Hey, they're still paying us, aren't they?" says Sleepy.

"I can get paid planetside," says Grumpy. "I came out here to do some actual fucking science."

I've got an approximate distance to the voices, but not a precise location—this software wasn't designed to trace sounds bouncing through ventilation shafts. I add an overlay to the station map in my eye to show what direction the sounds are coming from.

I do my best not to think about how the agency got this map. The last agent we sent out here, code name WOMBAT, had many of the same scanning implants I do, and was able to transmit a few recorded data bursts. But there's a big blank space in the bottom half of the asteroid map—the places Wombat wasn't able to scan before someone here got suspicious and made W disappear. Hopefully into a shielded holding cell and not out into space.

There is an awful lot of shielding in this station. I noticed that as soon as I came aboard and turned on my eye. Even for an off-the-books science facility. What are they hiding? It makes sense to experiment with biotech out here in the asteroid belt, where there's no risk of spreading contagion—hard vacuum will kill most biological specimens before they can reach another inhabited location—but why would you need to hide the rooms *inside* the station from each other?

An alert flashes in my eye. I muted the ear I don't have pressed up against the air vent, but left a separate software process running to monitor its signal input, and the alert is now telling me that it hears footsteps approaching. I push myself away from the wall, sit back on the med bay's exam table, and reset my ears to normal hearing, bypassing the implants.

The door opens and a new person enters. It's not the astronaut who pulled me out of my "derelict" spacecraft after picking up my distress signal, or the technician who met me at the airlock and then brought me to this room—which has a door that locks from the outside, I was interested to discover. Why would you need to lock people inside your medical bay?

"So," the man says, looking over the computer tablet in his hands, "Mr.—Bafford?"

"Baf*ford*," I correct, putting the emphasis on the second syllable. If I need to use an alias, I might as well have some fun with it.

"Baf*ford*," the man repeats. "I'm Dr. Imley—"

"You a medical doctor?" I ask. I hope my fake working-class Belter accent isn't too broad.

He looks at me like I'm an idiot. "Yes. What other kind of doctor would I be?"

"I dunno, some of the guys I met on the way in were saying there's scientists here, doing science stuff."

Imley continues staring at me. "How many 'guys' did you talk to, exactly?"

I shrug. "Who's counting? How many persons you got on this rock, anyway?"

"I was under the impression that you only met one technician on the way here."

"Well, you know," I say, waving one hand, "there was the other guy outside."

The agency couldn't send me in with the same cover that Wombat used, that of a government inspector who mistakenly landed on the wrong asteroid, so I pretended to be a freelancer whose spacecraft malfunctioned near this rock. Nobody in the belt can legally ignore a distress call, and there was enough waste heat coming off this asteroid for a civilian pilot to plausibly detect. It had taken me nearly half an hour of transmitting, with my main radio dish aimed directly at the station, before they responded.

Imley nods. "I'm just going to give you a quick physical exam, Mr. Bafford. To make sure you didn't suffer any adverse effects from drifting in space for so long."

"I feel fine," I say. "Just glad that you guys had a station so close, you know? Who knows how long I might have been stuck out there otherwise. Which company did you say owned this rock?"

Imley turns his back on me and opens a drawer, rummaging for something. "Do you have any preexisting medical conditions, Mr. Bafford? Any allergies that I should be aware of before I begin treatment?"

"Hey, whoa, whaddya mean *treatment*? And in fact, my religious beliefs prohibit me from using certain substances—"

He whirls back around, holding something in one hand and moving it toward me. I can't tell what the thing is. I grab his wrist and push it away, then catch his other arm and twist it down to cause maximum pain.

Imley screeches as I lever myself off the exam table, plant my feet on the ground—this is trickier than it sounds in the low gravity of this asteroid— and pin him against the wall.

Then I get a good look at what he's holding. It's a teardrop-shaped ampule, with a flat honeycomb of capillaries on the underside. An injector slug, and I can guess what's inside: something to put me to sleep.

Not gonna happen, Doc.

"Please, Mr. Bafford," Imley says, his voice remarkably calm, "you're suffering from hypoxia. This is a simple reoxygenation infusion—"

"Sorry, Doc," I say in my normal voice, plucking the slug out of his fingers. "I'm not informed, and I do not consent."

I press the slug against his neck until it hisses and empties its payload into his arteries. He's unconscious within a second.

I lower him onto the exam table and try the door handle. Still locked. *Dammit.* I blink my eye into EM scanning mode and examine the lock. Good news: it looks like it's purely mechanical, and not wired into any type of alarm system. But I will need a tool to break it.

I press my ear against the door and tune my audio sensors to detect breathing, just in case there's a guard standing outside. After a few seconds with nothing tripping the sensor thresholds, I turn to face an empty spot in the room and open the pocket.

My code name is KANGAROO. That's the only name I have within the agency. Not because my face resembles a large marsupial mammal, or because I used to be an Olympic hurdling champion—though I have, oddly enough, used both of those ploys in bars to get through some sticky social situations. Well, I tried, anyway. They are both apparently too ridiculous for anyone to believe.

I'm Kangaroo because I have a universe-sized secret pouch. I call it "the pocket" because I named it when I was ten years old; Science Division calls it a "hyperspace shunt" because they don't know any better than I do how it works or why I have this ability. They've been testing me for more than a decade, and we're still no closer to any real answers.

All we know is that I can open a portal into this empty, apparently infinite, parallel universe. I can't go inside, but I can hide just about anything else in there—as long as the item can fit through the circular portal and survive being in deep space for as long as it takes me to travel to wherever the agency wants the item to end up. And when I go into the field on a mission, Oliver packs as many things into the pocket as he thinks I might have an outside chance of needing to use.

Most of the time, it's a huge waste of time to put all those items into the pocket, one at a time, and then have to take out everything I didn't use afterward. The largest load-in we've ever done took nearly ten hours. And that doesn't include the prep time for Oliver to pack all the delicate machinery inside therm-packs to keep it from freezing too quickly.

Other times, though, I'm really glad he makes me bring more toys than we actually think I'll need.

The portal into the pocket appears in front of me: a flat, glowing, white disk suspended in midair, level with my chest. I extend my arm and push my hand, wrist, forearm through the center of the disk. That's the barrier—a "pressure curtain" made of the same exotic energy that rings the outside of the portal. I can open the pocket without the barrier, but then the air in this room would rush through to the empty universe on the other side. The barrier prevents air from escaping into the pocket but is permeable enough for me to push my arm through it.

I visualized a red teapot when I opened the pocket, which placed the portal at a particular location in the other universe. Picturing reference objects in my mind's eye is the only reliable way we've found of targeting the portal to specific places inside the pocket. And every image needs to be unique, to ensure I don't accidentally open the pocket to the wrong location.

I can't see through the barrier, but I can feel when my fingers close around the therm-pack. I grab the insulated bag, pull it back through the portal, and close the pocket. I open the therm-pack and pull out a small but very powerful plasma torch.

It's a bit more than I need for this particular task—a lockpick gun would be faster and less destructive—but I'm not allowed to have a lockpick gun anymore. I blame Oliver. It's really his fault for not securing his experimental robots better. And not labeling his storage lockers clearly. But apparently he's still the "responsible one" and I'm the "loose cannon," so I don't get a lockpick gun.

The plasma torch makes short work of the lock. I kick the melted handle away, push open the door, and emerge into a long, narrow corridor. According to Wombat's scans, this passage meets two different corridors in T-intersections at either end. I do a quick jog from one end to the other to verify. Then I blink my eye into range-finding mode to measure the length of the space.

Finally, I think of a white basketball with red lines and open the pocket again, this time a good three meters away from myself. A tethered line of armed spacemen falls out of the portal and into the hallway in front of me.

The pocket always has to face my body, and once I open it, it's locked to that position in space relative to me. I can place it off-center from myself, but never more than the radius of the portal itself—we just figured this out in the last year, and it's saved my bacon more than once since then. Oliver keeps wanting to backsolve the math for how the pocket works, but I don't really care that much. It's all instinct for me. I don't have a dial in my head to set the portal size when I open it, or an on-off switch for whether I use the barrier; it's just a thing I can do—like closing my hand into a fist. I like to focus on results. I couldn't tell you how all the muscles in my body actually work, but you're going to feel it when I punch you in the nose.

Another trick I can do is pocket rotation—which Science Division still has on the books as "Project Backdoor," I suspect mostly to spite me, since I insisted on that name when I was a teenager, not allowed to do fieldwork, and scientists were experimenting on me relentlessly. You take whatever rebellion you can get when you're fifteen years old and under the thumb of an above-top-secret intelligence agency.

"Backdoor" means I can rotate the portal around an item I previously put inside the pocket—but I can only rotate it exactly 180 degrees. It's handy for getting things in and out of the pocket quickly: throw it in the "front door," then rotate the pocket when I open it again, and the same item flies out the "back door." Conservation of momentum or something like that.

The fourteen spacemen, all wearing armored spacesuits and tied together with a safety tether, land on their feet with remarkable agility. They've had a lot more low-gravity and zero-gee movement training than I have, that's for sure.

My ear buzzes with an incoming radio transmission. The radio implant is separate from the hearing enhancements, so this audio is unaffected by my earlier malfunction. "All clear, Captain?" asks a female voice.

"Affirmative, all clear, Sergeant," I say.

The spaceman at the front of the line—my agency escort for this mission, Leonard "Lenny" Carrozza—removes his helmet and sniffs the air, flaring his nostrils. "Smells like feet."

"Nice to see you, too," I say, then add, "Corporal."

It's tough remembering all these ranks, but Lenny and I need to maintain cover in front of the X-4s. The Outer Space Service's Expeditionary Forces are well known as the toughest bastards in the Solar System, and they probably wouldn't respect Lenny and me quite as much—or feel compelled to follow our orders—if we didn't outrank them in the same chain of command.

Lenny clips his helmet to his life support backpack while I give a quick situation report. None of the other spacemen remove their helmets; they simply undo the tether connecting them all and proceed to check their other equipment. The tether was necessary when I put them in the pocket. Each pocket location only "locks" to one item at a time—"item" defined as a single solid object, either a continuous shape or connected by something. Oliver and Jessica call it a "memory labyrinth thread," and they explain it a lot better than I can.

I finish my report to the squad leader, Sergeant Radcliff, who is identifiable by the triple chevrons and two crossed comet tails etched into her spacesuit's shoulder pads. She gives me a hand signal in acknowledgment, then calls out orders to the other spacemen, who have separated themselves into groups of four.

"Fireteam Red!" Radcliff says. "You will accompany Captain Bafford—"

"Baf*ford*," I correct. It's important to be consistent with your legend.

Radcliff glares at me. "Accompany Captain Baf*ford* and Corporal Carrozza to the top of the station and sweep downward. Do not fire unless fired upon. Use of deadly force is authorized."

Lenny offers me an assault rifle. I wave the weapon away. If we run into anyone in here, I'm going to be better at running my mouth than shooting a gun.

"Fireteam Blue, go to the bottom of the rock and clear upward," Radcliff continues. "Fireteam Green, hold position in this med bay until you've secured all automated systems, then meet us at the central hangar. Any questions?"

"I'm sorry," I say, "can I just add one thing?"

Radcliff turns to look at me. "Yes, Captain?"

"Just wanted to remind everyone that we are also looking to extract a prisoner. One of our field agents. And retrieve any scientific specimens we can—intel says they're live animals, probably reptiles." Wombat's last message wasn't very clear. "Sorry, that's actually two things. Prisoner and specimens. All the info should be in your mission computers. Don't shoot those things. Okay?"

"Copy that," Radcliff says. She turns back to her spacemen, who are tapping at the wrist-mounted control bands in their spacesuits. I see information displays lighting up their helmet visors. "You heard the captain! Neutralize resistance, extract the prisoner, seize any specimens. In that order. Your priority is taking control of this station, using all necessary force." She pauses, I suppose to let that last bit sink in. "Good to go, X?"

"Oo-rah!" the spacemen respond in unison.

"Let's do it!"

Radcliff hustles down the corridor. Blue team follows her and sweeps around the corner, heading for the nearest stairwell. Green team ducks into the medical bay and closes the door. Red team forms up around Lenny and me.

"Your show, Captain," says the corporal leading Red team, a woman named Stribling. "Lead the way."

I turn to Lenny. "Ready?"

He cocks the assault rifle. "Right behind you, Cap."

"Just watch where you aim that thing," I say. Then, in a Russian accent: "Most things in here don't react well to bullets."

Lenny frowns at me. "Why are you talking like that?"

"Come on," I say. "We watched the vid on the way out here. The one with the Soviet stealth submarine?" I'm always trying to educate my colleagues about twentieth-century entertainment, mostly so they'll get my jokes.

"What's a Soviet?"

"Never mind." I give up. "Just don't shoot any windows."

Intel estimated there could be anywhere from thirty to fifty people in this asteroid. So far, based on the X-4s' radio reports, we've only found about a dozen, and the corridors feel eerily abandoned. Where are the rest of the station personnel hiding?

"Green Leader, this is Ajax," Radcliff says over the radio, using her call sign. "Where's my internal sensor tap?"

"Working on it, boss," Green Leader replies. I don't remember his name. Huffman, maybe? "So far all we've got is visible-spectrum in the hallways, and nobody's walking around but us."

"Nothing in the rooms?"

"Found the data streams, but they're encrypted." That seems pretty paranoid. Huff*ton*? What *is* his name? It's going to bug me until I figure it out. I pull up our mission roster in my left eye.

"All right. Keep me posted," Radcliff says.

Huffley! That's it. Now I'll be able to sleep tonight. "Green Leader, Bafford," I say. "Did you search the unconscious guy in the med bay? The doctor?"

"Negative. We put him in restraints and moved him out of the way," Huffley replies. "What are we looking for?"

"Check his pockets for a tablet. Maybe a notebook. Something he might have saved his access codes in."

There's a pause. "You think this guy *wrote down* his password?"

"He's a doctor," I say, "not a security specialist. People hate remembering passwords. Look in his wallet, I don't know."

"Wait one."

"Hey, Cap," Lenny says. "Is this the place?"

I stop and look where he's pointing: a door marked LABORATORY J-47. I switch my left eye back to the overlay map I'd marked while eaves-dropping through the air vents. This is where I heard the two lab techs talking about specimens. I didn't share this map with the X-4s; I still don't quite trust them not to shoot first and ask questions later. I do trust Lenny to know his job.

"Looks like it." I adjust my eye sensors to check if I can see through the door. No dice. "Shielded. A little help here, Stribling?"

The X-4s take position around the door as Lenny and I step back. Stribling directs one of her team—the name tag floating next to the hel-met in my eye's battlefield overlay says "Yu"—to step forward with a more powerful scanner than the one I have implanted in my skull.

After a moment, Yu shakes his head and gives a thumbs-down sign. Stribling waves him back, then flashes a series of cryptic hand gestures at the other three X-4s. I should probably learn those at some point, maybe. Lenny seems to understand what's going on. I figure just staying out of the way will be good enough.

My left eye tells me that the two X-4s setting up in front of the door are Graham and Tullis. Stribling and Yu take up positions behind them. After they all check their weapons, Tullis attaches a device to the elec-tronic lockpad by the door. The lights on the device flash red for a few seconds, then go solid green, and the door slides open.

A lot of stomping and shouting follows. The X-4s make sure Grumpy and Sleepy are unarmed and then herd them into a corner. Lenny and I step inside after it quiets down, and I start looking around for anything specimen-like.

When Wombat stopped reporting in last week, agency analysts back on Earth took a harder look at the intel that had led us to investigate this part of the asteroid belt. The agency has been watching the belt for un-usual activity since last summer—when our director of intelligence com-mitted high treason and then disappeared into the belt—and there were some discrepancies in the documented location of one of Rubinaxe LLC's asteroid bases and the navigation data that actually appeared on FDA audit logs from the facility.

It turned out that Rubinaxe was maintaining two rock bases in close proximity, one on the books and one not, and that's more than a little suspicious. It got even more suspicious when the agency sent Wombat to look into it, and W disappeared. Trained operatives don't just disappear. Something happens to them—usually something bad.

My handler—who also happens to be the agency's director of operations—decided not to pull any punches with his follow-up. He called up a full squad of X-4s, hid them in my pocket, and sent me to retrieve Wombat and take control of the asteroid. You don't mess with Paul Tarkington or his people. There's a reason D.Ops's code name is LASHER.

My eye's biochem scanning mode isn't showing anything unusual. I cycle through some other sensor modes and see a patch of color pop up in infrared, at the back corner of the room. I point at the heat signature there. "What's that?"

"Checking," Lenny says, walking up to the corner. "How about that. There's an access hatch here."

"That's just a service tunnel," says Grumpy. "Wiring, plumbing, other boring stuff."

Definitely not trained in security. "Well, then you won't mind if we take a look inside." I kneel down and feel around the hatch, but I can't quite get a grip on it. "A little help here?"

"I am helping," Lenny says. "I'm ready to shoot any bad guys who jump out of there."

"Thanks."

I pry the hatch open. Nothing jumps out at us.

I peer inside what appears to be a service crawlspace. It goes straight back for about two meters, then makes a right-angle turn to the left. Boring as advertised. There's a fading trail of body-heat blobs leading down that way, but I can't see through the sides of the crawlspace, either—whatever this asteroid is composed of, it naturally interferes with scanners. I report all of this to Lenny.

"Does that tunnel get any smaller inside?" he asks.

I put a three-dimensional wireframe in my eye, then lower the brightness of the overlay so I can see how it matches up with the surface of the wall. "Looks like it stays the same. About a meter across the diagonal."

"So we'll fit inside."

"I will. You won't, not in that spacesuit."

Lenny stares at the wall for a moment. "Fuck it. Let's go." He unlatches his chestplate and starts taking off his armor.

"Recommend against that, Corporal, Captain," Stribling says. "We can't follow you in there."

"We'll be fine," Lenny says. "You just keep an eye on those two."

"It's dangerous in there!" says Grumpy.

I stare at him. "How so?"

He stares back at me. "There are snakes in there."

I blink. Sleepy looks horrified, which signals to me that Grumpy isn't lying. "Snakes."

"Yeah," he says. "Venomous snakes. Like, super poisonous." He might be exaggerating. He really doesn't want us to go in there. Which means we definitely should.

"Thanks for the warning," Lenny says. "We'll take our chances."

My radio buzzes as I'm getting into the service tunnel behind Lenny. Sergeant Radcliff's voice comes through. "Bafford, Ajax, please respond."

"Copy that, Ajax, Bafford here," I answer. "The corporal and I are clearing a crawlspace in section J-47. What's your status?"

"Blue team has recovered Wombat," she says.

"Is Wombat injured?" I ask.

"Unconscious but stable."

"What happened?" Lenny asks. He doesn't have a comms implant, so he's not hearing any radio chatter now that he's doffed his spacesuit. The only equipment he's carrying is his assault rifle. I opted for a stunner, myself. If I have to shoot something, I'd rather not kill it immediately.

"Blues got Wombat," I say with the radio muted.

Lenny nods. "Oorah."

"Sure." I unmute myself. "Ajax, Bafford. Red team has detained two lab techs in this section, and Carrozza and I are running down a possible third."

"Copy that. Be advised, Blue team also reports they caught some station personnel releasing lab animals into a service tunnel."

"Were they snakes?"

"Unknown," Radcliff says, not missing a beat. "Blue team found empty crates next to an open access hatch. Station personnel are not cooperating."

"Yeah, I'm shocked," I say. "Let us know if Wombat wakes up. We'll tell you what we find in here as soon as we find it."

"Wilco. Ajax out." I return my attention to crawling.

The service tunnel looks like it was carved out of the solid rock of the asteroid, and the walls are still rough and sometimes jagged where they didn't need to be smoothed or grooved in order to run conduits or attach equipment. Lenny points out jutting edges or sharp points as he passes them, which I'm grateful for, since I'm still scanning for targets. If Lenny is irritated by the high-pitched tone I'm generating with my shoulder-phone to get a sonar picture of the area, he doesn't show it.

We approach the turn leading to the left, and my sonar starts pulsing. I turn up the audio reception in my ears to verify what I'm hearing, then tug on Lenny's boot to stop his forward motion before he turns the corner.

He stops and turns to give me an annoyed look. I tap my chest quietly with one hand and mouth the word "heartbeat."

Lenny stares at me, then nods. He makes a series of hand gestures I don't understand. I shrug in response. He rolls his eyes, points at me, points at the floor, and mouths the word "stay."

I grip my stunner in both hands and watch as Lenny turns back to face the corner, coils his body, then launches himself forward in a tight roll, coming back up with his back flat against the far wall and his assault rifle pointed down the tunnel past the curve. He stares in that direction for a moment, at something I can't see.

"Do not move!" he calls down the tunnel. Then, still aiming his rifle there, he raises one hand and waves me forward.

I move to where Lenny is with considerably less style, shuffling on my knees and elbows, struggling to keep my stunner pointed and steady.

I round the corner and see a portly man with thinning brown hair, wearing a white jumpsuit. He's slumped against the side of the tunnel, about a meter and a half away from Lenny. In the man's lap is a clear rectangular box containing a writhing mass of—tentacles?

No. It's snakes.

The man's holding a whole box of goddamn snakes. Grumpy wasn't lying. One of the snakes pokes its head up, studies me with beady black eyes, and extends a forked tongue.

I don't like snakes. But at least they're contained.

I lower my stunner. The man doesn't present much of a physical threat.

And Lenny's got a good bead on him with that assault rifle. Then I think again and raise my stunner again. It might not be the best thing for Lenny to shoot to kill if this guy makes any sudden moves.

"I got this, Corporal," I say to Lenny. "You can stand down."

Lenny frowns without looking at me. "I prefer the redundancy."

"Then switch to nonlethals," I say through clenched teeth. "Our friend is likely to be more cooperative if he doesn't think we want to kill him."

"Don't you?" the man in the lab outfit says. "You're only interested in the animals, aren't you?"

"Our assignment is to secure this station," I say. "We'd like to keep as many people—and animals—alive as we can."

"But we will defend ourselves if necessary," Lenny says. He still hasn't put away the firearm, but I don't want to tell him again. It's not good to disagree with your partner in front of hostile forces.

The man with the snakes shakes his head. "I will cooperate. I never wanted to come out here in the first place."

My initial relief—*he's cooperating!*—almost immediately turns into suspicion. Why is he volunteering so much information? Nobody whose workplace gets stormed by commandos wants to cooperate that much. I didn't trust Grumpy, and I don't trust this guy.

But if he wants to talk, I'm going to let him talk. He can't lie with his mouth and his body at the same time—that's one of the first things the agency taught me, when they finally agreed to give me field training. People betray themselves all the time, if you know how to read the signs.

I lower my stunner ever so slightly. "What do you mean by that, Mr.—?"

"My name is Klaus."

"So is that your first name, or . . . ?"

"Dr. Stefan Klaus," he says. "They promised me a facility of my own. They never said it would be on an asteroid. But I could not argue with their reasoning."

"Which was what, exactly?"

Klaus looks at me for the first time, and I study him with my left eye's medical scanners. He doesn't seem all that agitated, which is a bit odd. Pupils slightly dilated, which might indicate he's on some kind of drugs. I can't test for that, but if he's not thinking straight—

Of course he's not thinking straight, Kangaroo. He brought a fucking box of snakes into a small, enclosed space.

"Isolation," Klaus says. "Privacy. Absolute security. Limited risk of escape or contagion."

"Contagion?" Lenny says, shrinking backward. "What's wrong with the snakes?"

Klaus chuckles hoarsely, his head bobbing from side to side. Okay, I'm pretty sure he's on drugs at this point. "One could argue they are not snakes anymore. Not really, you know. Not genetically."

Great. They're doing unregulated gene editing out here. Probably trying to get even deadlier neurotoxins out of these animals, attempting to twist Mother Nature's design to suit human purposes. That never goes well.

"A new species," Klaus continues. "I should name them. Yes, that needs to go on my to-do list." He reaches into one of his jumpsuit pockets.

"Put it down!" Lenny shouts, raising his assault rifle and bracing it against his shoulder. "Open your hand and drop what you're holding!"

Klaus opens his hand. Then the box of snakes sails toward us. We were so focused on the hand reaching for the pocket, we didn't notice that his other hand had braced the back of the transparent cage, preparing to launch it at us.

I open the pocket at the same instant I have the thought: *Lenny's going to shoot.*

The portal pops into being on the other side of the snakes, without the barrier, a black hole sucking air—and, hopefully, bullets—into an alternate universe. At least two deafening thunderclaps fill the tiny crawlspace. The sound reverberates horribly, so I'm not sure exactly how many times Lenny fired.

I don't know if I was fast enough. I close the portal before the snakes get sucked in.

The cage tumbles to the ground, falling over Klaus's feet. One hand rests in his lap, clutching some kind of handheld computer. The snakes hiss and slither madly inside their clear plastic box. There are two bright red spots on Klaus's chest.

I wasn't fast enough.

I don't have curses strong enough to express how unhappy I am right now. "Jesus fucking Christ, Lenny!"

Lenny ignores me and dives forward, snatching the device out of Klaus's dead hand and examining it. "Shit. We need to get out of here."

I suppress my desire to strangle Lenny and ask, "Why?"

He shoves the device in my face. "Because we've got three minutes before every airlock on this station blows out."

I grab the device—it's a remote control tablet, tied in to the station's environmental controls—and look at the display. Lenny's right. The three-minute countdown is a safety feature, the only one that Klaus wasn't able to override from this tablet. He turned off the audio announcements and alarm lights. If we hadn't found him in this tunnel, we might not have had any warning before the whole station was opened to space and we all got blown out into vacuum going every which way, and good luck to the X-4 transport pilot for having to decide who to try to recover first before we spun out of radar range.

"Go!" Lenny has the snake cage under one arm and is pushing me back down the tunnel with his other shoulder. "Go! *Go!*"

"Ajax, Bafford!" I call over the radio while scrambling backward. "Abort mission, say again, abort mission!"

I hear a series of rapid, high-pitched tones: the abort signal. "Every X, this is Ajax: abort, abort, abort!" Radcliff calls. The radio clicks as she switches from the broadcast channel to her private link with me. "What happened, Captain?"

"Countermeasures activated! All airlocks blowing in three minutes!"

"Can we stop it?" Radcliff asks.

"Let's assume not!"

By the time Lenny and I get back into the lab, Red team have already put Grumpy and Sleepy into wraparound torso restraints and are marching them down the hallway. I can't get Klaus's tablet to respond to any of my commands.

"We'll meet you on the hangar deck!" Stribling calls. "Station personnel are evacuating in escape pods. Our transport will recover us after the blowout."

I point at the prisoners. "Do you need a rescue bubble for those two?"

"This corridor's not wide enough to inflate a bubble," Stribling says. "We'll do it on the hangar deck." She follows her team around the corner. On the radio, Radcliff is telling all the X-4s to assemble on the hangar deck to prepare for our surprise spacewalk.

"Okay, I guess we need to carry these—what the hell are you doing?" I ask Lenny. He's put down the snakes and is pushing the lower portion of his spacesuit into my hands.

"Suit up," he says.

"We can do this on the hangar deck—"

"Won't make it in time." Lenny grabs one of my feet and shoves it into the spacesuit. "Can't run while carrying all this gear. There's an airlock at the end of the corridor, we'll get blown straight out, just need to get you in a suit."

"We *both* need to—"

"No time! I'm expendable. You're not."

I hate it when people remind me of that, but I can't argue. Being the only person in the known universe with a superpower does come with some limitations.

"Fine." I let Lenny help me into the suit. I look at the control tablet before putting it down. One minute and twenty-eight seconds and counting. I blink a timer into my left eye.

It usually takes a good five to ten minutes to get into a spacesuit by the checklist, making sure all the seals are airtight and verifying that the life support system is nominal. I'll be okay if I'm leaking a little air or still waiting for the life support computer to wake up when the airlocks blow, but I need to have my helmet on.

"At least let me pull a breather mask for you," I say to Lenny. I always have emergency supplies in the pocket.

"Secure the animals first," Lenny says, fitting a glove over my left hand.

"What?"

"Cage got clipped." He elbows the side of the enclosure, and I see a hairline crack radiating out from a bullet hole splinter even more. The structure clearly won't survive being carried while we run anywhere, much less being bounced down a hallway by explosive decompression.

"Please do *not* break the snake cage!" I say. "Fine. I can put them in the pocket. Also? We need to talk about fire discipline in the field."

"Save it for the debrief," Lenny grumbles. "And negative on the pocket. Snakes won't survive in hard vacuum."

"Don't reptiles go into hibernation?"

"Hard vacuum," Lenny repeats, fastening my second glove. "They need air. I'm going to put them in your suit."

He turns his back before my brain can process this information. "*What?*"

Lenny turns back to me, holding the cage in both hands. He's removed the cover, and some of the snakes are already slithering toward the top, anticipating freedom. "It's only until we get back to the transport."

"No no *no no NO*!" I take a step back. "Those are *snakes*! *Poisonous* snakes! You are NOT dumping a whole BOX of SNAKES into my goddamn spacesuit!"

Lenny glances down at the control tablet. "You've got fifty-two seconds to think of a better idea."

We stare at each other.

There are a lot of fucking snakes in that box.

But any number of spacesuit-snakes is still better than explaining to Paul why I wasn't willing to do what was needed to complete my mission.

I look around the lab and grab the first bag-like container I see that seems sturdy enough to stop a snake bite. "Snakes in the bag. Bag in the suit."

Lenny nods. "Hold it open."

"Worst idea ever," I mutter as I watch what must be two dozen snakes cascading into a very thin plastic bag. I grab the spacesuit helmet and walk out into the corridor, looking for the airlock and then standing to face it. If I'm going to be blown out into space, I want to see where I'm going.

Lenny drops the cage in the lab and joins me in the hallway with the bag full of snakes. "Thirty seconds."

"Fuck you." I open the pocket, pull a breather mask, and hold it out. "Don't die."

Lenny holds up the bag. "Same to you."

I close my eyes and try to ignore the squirming as he raises the bag to my face and guides it into the open collar of my spacesuit, down my torso, between the suit lining and my equipment vest. Lenny snaps my helmet on, then uses some kind of a strap or hose and attaches himself to my waist. Finally, he puts on the breather mask.

The bag is still squirming. I hope it doesn't slide down past my waist. Or, if it does, I hope they kill me. I really don't want to have to explain to Surgical why I came home with two dozen snake bites on my crotch.

"Ten," Lenny says, "nine—"

"Stop with the countdown."

Lenny shrugs. "Also, for the record, I hate snakes."

"I hate *you*."

"That's fair."

CHAPTER TWO

Debriefings are my least favorite part of this job.

It took Wombat and Lenny and me a solid sixteen days to get out of the asteroid belt and back to the Moon, even under military acceleration aboard the OSS frigate *Torrance*. The X-4s went back to their nearside Moon base, and Lenny and I transferred through the farside industrial spaceport onto an Earthbound shuttle. We brought Wombat with us, in a life support pod—but W still hasn't woken up.

Lenny and I spent the whole trip back alternating between tag-team interrogations of our uncooperative prisoners, peeking at the snakes to make sure they hadn't died or anything, and checking in with the X-4 medic to see if there was any change in Wombat's condition. All vital signs seemed stable, and if there were toxins still in W's system, the equipment we had couldn't detect it.

Once we got to the Moon, all those things became other people's problems—the prisoners went with the X-4s, and two researchers from Science Division took Wombat and all the snakes into their care. Now Lenny and I need to account for everything we did out in the field before we get back to D.C. An Operations analyst, Ramírez, joined us aboard the Moon-to-Earth shuttle to start processing our after-action reports.

"Tell me about the snakes," Ramírez says for what feels like the hundredth time in as many hours. It's probably only been an hour at most, but it feels longer, especially shut in this tiny conference area inside the shuttle.

"I kind of miss them," I say, just for variety's sake.

"What?" Ramírez frowns but doesn't look up. He's been studiously avoiding meeting my eye this whole time. It's a little impressive and a lot annoying.

"I mean, yeah, I didn't like them much when we first met," I say. Now I'm going for entertainment value. "Too intimate too soon, you know? I usually wait until the second or third date before I let someone get into my space-pants."

"Let me rephrase the question—"

I don't let him talk. *Ask a stupid question, you get the whole stupid answer, pal.* "But it all worked out okay. We came to an understanding. I know people say relationships formed under stressful circumstances never last because everyday normal life can't compare to the thrill of an extraordinary meet-cute, but there are exceptions to every rule, right?"

"Kangaroo—"

"And it was pretty thrilling, flying out into space like that—well, it wasn't great having Lenny tagging along as a third wheel, but he was polite enough to give us some privacy when we needed it. And then it was like we were all alone, just me and the snakes drifting peacefully among the stars."

"Are you finished?"

"Nope!" I say. "It was nice while it lasted, but we all knew it had to end eventually. As you know, my particular line of employment doesn't exactly keep regular hours. Plus I was headed to one place, the snakes had to go somewhere else, and maintaining a long-distance relationship is difficult under the best of circumstances. You know how it is."

"I actually don't."

"Well, it was mutual. No hard feelings on anyone's part. Besides, we had a whole two weeks to ease out of it, traveling from the asteroid belt. You know, nice spacious X-4 transport, separate bunks, we didn't have to keep bumping into each other. It all worked out. And we're still on good terms, me and Felix and September and Kobe—"

Ramírez sighs. "You *named* the snakes?"

"Wow, imperialist oppression much?" I say. "I *discovered* their names. Felix had this very distinctive black-and-white pattern to his scales, just like the cartoon cat—you know, the one with a bag of tricks? No? Just me? Okay. Anyway, that was Felix. Then September was, like the month, the ninth one out of the bag . . ."

After a minute or so, I run out of steam, and Ramírez says, "Please tell me about when you first met the snakes."

"Sure." He's been a good sport. I start recounting the service tunnel incident again.

My debriefs do tend to run longer than most other field agents'. And it's not just because I can't resist messing with uptight debrief officers. Apparently I incur more "variation" during my missions than other agents.

"Variation" is the official agency term for when something doesn't go exactly as planned. But come on, of course things never go precisely as planned. That's why we're all trained to deal with unexpected circumstances, why we all carry emergency equipment, why it usually takes several hours to load up my pocket before I go out. When you've got an infinite amount of space in which to hide things, your superiors tend to want you to be overprepared for every possible contingency.

"Variation" is a catch-all term, and pretty meaningless: it could be something as significant as an agent being killed—which is never expected or desired—or something as trivial as your wake-up alarm not going off in the hotel one morning, which causes you to miss your scheduled rendezvous with a contact on the ground.

Even if you were able to meet with that contact just a few hours later and it didn't affect the mission at all, it's still a "variation" and your debrief officer still has to spend a good fifteen to twenty minutes reviewing why your alarm didn't go off and whether that indicates some kind of subconscious desire to sabotage the mission, which might in turn indicate some kind of deep-seated longing to eventually betray your country. Which, again, is very unlikely and would seem pretty ridiculous to any normal person, but as events keep reminding me: I don't deal with normal people.

I finish telling my story—again—and Ramírez nods, still staring down at his tablet.

"And just to be clear," he says, tapping at the touchscreen, "you do not believe that Mr. Carrozza was targeting the snakes with his weapons fire?"

Well, at least this is a new question. "Why would he do that?"

"Just answer the question, please."

"I don't read minds," I say. "All I can tell you is what I saw and heard."

"You used to be an analyst, Kangaroo," Ramírez says. "I'm only asking you to draw the most reasonable conclusion based on your observations. That's well within the scope of your skills and training."

"Fine. What I *believe* is that Lenny didn't know what Klaus was reaching for, and he reacted as he was trained to by attempting to stop the guy."

Ramírez rubs his chin. "And you opened the pocket—the 'portal'—in Carrozza's line of fire."

"Yes." I'm not sure where he's going with this. "I was trying to catch the bullets. I didn't want him to kill Klaus."

"Is it possible that the vacuum of the pocket deflected Carrozza's shots from his intended target?"

This is the other reason my debriefs take so long. Everyone wants to talk about the pocket. They've always got some technical question about how it works, or why I used it the way I did on this mission and not some other way, or *something*. I wish Science Division would just start sending out an agency-wide newsletter, but of course my ability is classified top secret and "Sensitive Compartmentalized Information," so we can't just go around telling everyone the good news. Sometimes I feel a little too special.

"The muzzle velocity of his weapon was, what, two thousand meters per second?" I say. "No amount of wind would have deflected those bullets significantly in that small a space. Besides, I didn't open the pocket in time anyway. The shots had already connected."

Ramírez looks at me with a blank expression. "And Carrozza did nothing else that could be interpreted as an attempt to harm the snakes?"

I gape at him. "He *saved* the snakes. By putting them in my spacesuit. Did I not emphasize that in my report? The snakes were *inside* my *spacesuit*."

"Understood," Ramírez says. "But you also say that Carrozza advanced this course of action over your"—he taps at the tablet—"'strenuous objections' is how you worded it. Is that correct?"

"Yes. I didn't actually *want* him to put a whole bag of snakes inside my spacesuit."

"Isn't it possible that Carrozza thought you might damage the specimens somehow?"

I'm not sure I'm hearing him right. "*I* might damage *them*?"

"Yes."

"No." I feel like I'm talking to a crazy person. "I was actually a little more concerned that the *mutant snakes* might *bite me to death*."

Ramírez grunts. "I'm just saying, isn't it possible that you might have become anxious and responded physically by thrashing or convulsing?

Which would have smashed some of the specimens up against the inside of the pressure suit, and could have injured or killed some of them?"

I finally understand what he's getting at, but my comprehension doesn't make me any happier. "Well, if that *was* his plan, it didn't work out at all, did it? Everyone's alive and well, except for Wombat. What are we doing for Wombat, by the way?"

"That's outside my purview," Ramírez says. "I'm just here to assess how well you and your partner worked together during this operation."

"We were fine."

"But not optimal."

I frown at him. "Is that what this is all about? You're matchmaking?"

Ramírez puts away his tablet. "I think I have everything I need. We're done here." He stands up and moves toward the door.

"We're not done," I say, stepping between him and the door. "Look, I know I'm not the easiest person to work with. That is not entirely my fault."

"Psych evals are also outside my purview," Ramírez says. He points at the door. "Do you mind?"

"We're stuck together on this shuttle for another couple of hours," I say. "You really want to bring *this* outside?"

Ramírez sighs. "Kangaroo, I'm just doing my job. You know Lasher's been extra paranoid ever since Sakraida flew the coop last year." Terman Sakraida, our former director of intelligence, pretty much nuked his entire division when he bailed, and everyone in the agency is still dealing with the fallout. "I don't know what he wants to do with you. I just write reports. You remember what that's like, don't you? Being compartmentalized?"

"I'm still compartmentalized."

"You know what I mean." He holds up the tablet. "You want to see my report? Help yourself. I'm sure reading all that will make the time just fly by."

I stare at the tablet. I feel like I want to know, but maybe I don't actually want to know.

"Okay, then." Ramírez tucks the tablet back under his arm. "Shall we?"

I step aside and let him open the door, then follow him out into the main cabin, where Lenny's enjoying a transparent drink bulb of what looks and smells like whiskey while pretending to watch a vid on his own tablet. I know he's pretending because he looks up as soon as Ramírez and I walk out of the conference room, and he immediately swirls the bulb even harder, making the liquid look like gelatin in the shuttle's half gravity.

"That is a great idea," Ramírez says, pointing at Lenny's drink. "You find that in the galley?"

"Dream on," Lenny says, pulling a squeeze-flask out of his jacket. "But I'm happy to share."

The lights above us change from flat white to pulsing blue. A synthetic male voice says, "Attention. Delta-vee warning. Acceleration vector changing. Repeat, delta-vee warning. Prepare for acceleration vector change. Thank you."

Then the human pilot's voice comes over the loudspeaker in the ceiling: "Gentlemen, we're coming up on reentry. Flipping in sixty seconds. Please take your seats."

Our path into Earth orbit requires us to burn off some speed, so the shuttle's going to turn around and fire its main engines as retro-rockets. Pretty standard maneuver. This is a private charter, though, so the pilot doesn't know we've all passed astronaut certification and don't need to be warned about basic stuff like this.

"Guess you'll have to wait," Lenny says, putting away his flask and finishing his drink in one gulp.

Ramírez stows his tablet and lunges from one side of the cabin to the other, leaning to look out the small round windows on either side of the shuttle. "Hey, Kangaroo, what's our position?"

I frown at him. "Why don't you ask the pilot?"

"She's busy. Come on, just give me a quick instrument reading."

I don't like being used like a human scanning device, but it's not the worst thing I've ever been asked to do. I blink up my eye scanners and read off some numbers.

The pilot announces that we're at the turnaround point. Gravity goes away, and the floor feels like it's sliding out from under me. I grab a seat and belt myself in. I don't want to be standing the wrong way when the engines kick in again.

Ramírez bounces over to yet another window and whoops. "Yes! There it is."

He's on my side of the shuttle. I look out and see a small, glittering speck in the distance, above the blue-and-white curve of the Earth. My eye, which can interpret all kinds of satellite data via my shoulder-phone and computer implants, identifies it as the Eyrie.

"You don't get out much, do you?" I ask.

"Just never seen it with my own eyes before."

"Not thinking about changing teams, are you, Ramírez?" Lenny asks, spinning his empty drink bulb in the air.

The Eyrie is home base for the other half of our agency, the Intelligence folks who gather data to guide Operations. There's always been some tension between the two halves, and it's been worse since the unfortunate events of last summer, which required the agency to rebuild Intel from the ground up.

"Of course not," Ramírez says. "But I was never in the military. This is the closest I've ever been to a capital ship."

"Wow," Lenny drawls. "Must be your lucky day. Maybe they'll invite you aboard to fuck you over in person." I think he might be a little drunk.

"What's your problem with Intel?" Ramírez asks.

"Seriously?" Lenny says. "Have you been living under a rock for the last eleven months?"

"Just because Sakraida and his inner circle turned out to be evildoers doesn't mean the whole division was corrupt," Ramírez says.

"Assholes or idiots," Lenny grumbles.

"What?"

"Assholes or idiots," Lenny repeats in a louder voice. "Either they knew what was going on and went along with it, or they had no idea because they're bad at their jobs."

"Well, that's insultingly reductive," Ramírez says.

"Yeah? So's your mom."

They continue trading barbs while I settle into a seat and buckle myself in. I really don't want to get involved in their debate. And I haven't seen the new Eyrie up close either.

The agency's director of intelligence has always been based in Earth orbit, aboard a manned space station that circles the planet once every ninety minutes. It's called the Eyrie because, I don't know, eagles or something. But this Eyrie is actually a completely different facility from the one we had last year.

A lot of bad stuff happened last summer. My department got audited. The agency's then-director of intelligence, Terman Sakraida, revealed himself to be a traitor and tried to crash a spaceliner into Mars. Innocent people died before we were able to stop that disaster. Sakraida and his cronies escaped, and we're still waiting for the other shoe to drop.

Right after Sakraida bolted, there was a lot of finger-pointing within the agency, a lot of ass-covering, a lot of passwords changed. It may be impossible to ever know the full extent of the damage he caused—and may still be able to cause. As D.Int, he had access to practically everything in the agency's data warehouse. We have to presume he and his cronies copied every bit of information they could and took it all with them when they disappeared into the asteroid belt, where they're no doubt now working on breaking the encryption of the most secure files.

The agency decided that rather than go over every centimeter of the old Eyrie to make sure the bad guys hadn't left behind any booby traps or other nasty surprises, it was safer to deorbit the entire station and put up a new one. So that's what they did. Evacuated all personnel, fired a few thrusters, then let the whole kit and kaboodle fall out of orbit and burn up in the atmosphere.

Our new D.Int is Admiral Darlene Morris of the United States Outer Space Service, and she brought her own office to her new job—literally. US-OSS decommissioned her former command, the battleship *Waukegan*, and removed its main weapons and refitted it for service as an orbital station. If anyone had previously compromised that vessel—a ship of the line during the Independence War between Earth and Mars—we would have bigger problems anyway. There's been only a little grumbling from the Intel folks about the utilitarian military accommodations.

The shuttle's acceleration alarms sound again, and my seat presses up against me. I watch Ramírez settle into a window seat across the aisle.

Then something explodes beneath us. Red alert lights flood the cabin.

It's got to be the engines, I think as my hands instinctively clutch my seat belt, making sure it's buckled tight and low across my lap. The entire shuttle vibrates more than I feel like it should. The sunlight coming in through the windows slides across Ramírez's face. We're tumbling. *Shit.*

The pilot's voice interrupts the loud alarms. "Gentlemen, we've had a main drive malfunction," she says, sounding remarkably calm. "I'm in con-

tact with OTC and they're working on a recovery plan. Please stand by."
She ends her announcement.

As much as I trust Orbital Traffic Control to do their jobs, I'm not
going to just sit around and wait for that. I put a calculator in my eye and
start doing some math.

"Someone's trying to kill you!" Ramírez points at me. "Who knows
you're aboard this shuttle?"

"Calm down," Lenny says, unbuckling himself and moving to the back
of the cabin. "If they wanted to kill us, they'd have hit the fuel tanks, not
the rockets."

"This can't be an accident," Ramírez says. "Not with Kangaroo aboard."

"We'll figure it out later." Lenny yanks open a storage locker and pulls
out a spacesuit. "First we do our best *not* to die in a fire."

"We've got maybe fifteen minutes before this shuttle starts disintegrat-
ing," I say. If the pilot can't regain control and point the heat-shielded
part of the ship downward, friction with the thickening atmosphere will
start melting parts off the spacecraft.

"Isn't there an escape pod?" Ramírez asks.

"No," Lenny says, inspecting the three spacesuits he's extracted from
the locker. "This is a short-range shuttle. Safety regulations only require
lifeboats on interplanetary vehicles."

"When I get home, I am writing a strongly worded letter to whoever's
in charge of that!" Ramírez says.

Lenny looks at me. "These are vacuum suits. They won't last long out
there."

"They'll be fine in the pocket," I say.

He gives me a wolfish grin. Definitely drunk. "Once more into the
breach!"

"What's happening?" Ramírez asks.

"Good news, Ramírez," Lenny says. "We're all going for a spacewalk."

I put a countdown timer in my eye and remind everyone as the minutes tick
by. It takes two minutes for Lenny to yell loudly enough to convince the
pilot to open the cockpit door, at which point I knock her out with one of
the handy sedative injector slugs from my emergency medkit. You never
know when you'll have to sneakily render someone unconscious.

Then it's five minutes to get all of us into emergency spacesuits, and one more minute for me to tie Lenny, Ramírez, and the pilot together with some plastic wrap from the galley so I can stow them all in one location inside the pocket.

After closing the portal, I'm all alone with eight minutes left. I move toward the airlock and call Oliver on my shoulder-phone. This close to Earth, I can connect to any number of secure satellite relays. I really hope my audio implants are still working.

"Hello, Kangaroo," Oliver says in my ear. Why does everyone sound so calm? "This is Equipment. I was wondering when you'd call."

"EQ, Kangaroo. You know what's happening, then?"

"Semper vigilantes."

"You're always fighting crime?"

"Never mind," Oliver says. "I take it you've secured the other passengers in the pocket and are preparing to abandon ship?"

I'm at the airlock and studying the emergency release instructions. "Great minds think alike. I'd like to get a little altitude once I'm outside. Was hoping you could help me time my jump so I go up and not down."

"Affirmative," Oliver says. "Let me know when you're ready."

"Wait one." I pull the handle on the airlock's inner door and step inside. I close the door behind me and look for something to brace against when I pop the outer door. The air in here is going to blow out, and I don't want to go with it. I need to stay with the shuttle for this next stunt.

I find a tether point for a spacewalk cable—thank government regulations for standard airlock construction guidelines—and hook one glove into it, tugging to make sure I'm secure. Then I hit the egress cycle activation control.

Air hisses out of the compartment for a few seconds. The outer door swings open, then flies completely off its hinges and disappears. The shuttle's still tumbling, but now it's eerily silent after that explosion of cabin air into the thin upper atmosphere. I activate the magnets in my spacesuit boots and slowly, carefully walk out onto the exterior hull.

It takes me nearly a minute to crawl over to a flat section of the shuttle, and then another couple of seconds to steady myself enough to stand. It's pretty nerve-wracking, standing up on a shuttle that's spinning every which way, trusting that my mag-boots will keep me attached. But the agency's standard astronaut training prepared me to at least endure the physical disorientation. Still, it's probably a good thing I didn't partake of Lenny's flask earlier.

I slowly, carefully walk across the hull toward the back of the shuttle, where the engines used to be. I can see part of the hull torn away by the explosion. When I get closer, I see that there are several segmented metal shafts hooked into the hull just above the ragged edge of the blast.

There was something attached to the outside of the shuttle. Something that wasn't supposed to be there. The metal parts stuck into the hull look like they were severed from some other device. I see wires and circuitry inside the hollow triangular shafts.

I can't tell what our stowaway might have been, but maybe someone else can later. I record as much as I can with my eye, in every scanning mode available, then move back to the widest, flattest section of the hull I can find. After stabilizing myself—closing my eyes helps—I call Oliver again.

"This feels oddly familiar," I say, thinking of the last time I stood on the outside of a spaceship spinning out of control.

Oliver ignores my remark. "The good news is, you're in free fall and there don't appear to be any additional thrust vectors at play now. I'm putting an indicator in your HUD."

The heads-up display fused to my left cornea lights up with a horizontal box that fills in with color from left to right—first red, then yellow, then green when the box is entirely filled.

"So I jump when it's green?"

"Affirmative. I've given you as much error margin as I can."

"Okay." I keep my eyes closed—I don't want the giant planet spinning around me to distract me—and bend my knees as far as I can. Lenny was right; these are really cheap spacesuits. I feel like I'm stuck inside a balloon.

"Don't wait too long," Oliver says. "You're approaching the mesosphere."

"Is that bad?" I'm counting to myself as I watch each cycle of the progress bar, finding the right rhythm to time my jump.

"That's where reentering objects start to burn up."

"Okay, let's stop talking now."

"Good luck." A soft beep indicates Oliver's disconnected the call. But I'm sure he's still watching my telemetry, maybe even seeing my image through a telescope nearby. The agency has lots of automated surveillance resources this close to Earth. Analysts in Ops and Intel are probably also monitoring my situation. Because they need to know if I'm about to die.

No pressure, Kangaroo.

The progress bar turns yellow. I tense my leg muscles. As soon as the bar turns green, I slap the control to deactivate my mag-boots. At the same time, I extend both my legs straight as hard and fast as I can.

Then I open my eyes.

It's not strictly necessary, since the readouts in my left eye are telling me everything I—and Oliver—need to know about my course and speed. But it's reassuring to see that there's empty space in front of me and not a huge freakin' blue planet.

I'm just about to breathe an exaggerated sigh of relief when an alert starts blinking in my eye. A red arrow points me to turn my head to the right, and then I see a red circle pulsing around something heading toward me very quickly, according to my eye's short-range radar.

I squeeze my fingertips together to call Oliver again. "Hey, EQ, it looks like there's something pretty solid heading toward me very fast? Am I about to hit some space junk up here?" Centuries of launching satellites and rockets has left a lot of debris still circling the planet.

"No worries, Kangaroo," Oliver says. "You're in range of the Eyrie. That's a Pelican coming to pick you up."

Oh, Lenny is not going to like this.

CHAPTER THREE

Earth orbit—the Eyrie space station
I'm guessing 5 minutes before Lenny throws a fit

"Welcome aboard, Kangaroo," says the officer on the Eyrie's flight deck when I step off the ladder of the Pelican. "D.Int would like to speak to you as soon as you're settled."

I used to get a little miffed when people didn't ask me if I was all right after getting rescued. But I'm used to it now. The reason they don't ask is because they already know: Jessica makes a habit of relaying my vitals, which she receives from my implanted sensors whenever I'm in range and not running silent, to anyone else who might need them. "Privacy" is not a word that exists in my department's vocabulary.

"Regarding what topic?" I ask the officer. I don't generally get debriefed by someone who reports directly to the secretary of state. Well, unless it's Paul.

"I don't have that information," the officer says. "I'll escort you to her office when you're ready."

"Sure. Just one second."

I turn back to look up the ladder, where Ramírez and Lenny are arguing with the Pelican's pilot. I want to make sure they're not going to come to blows, but I also need a moment to collect myself. Because whatever D.Int wants to talk to me about, it's probably pretty serious.

"You two okay there?" I call up the ladder.

"We'll be fine as soon as I get off this station," Lenny says.

"I'm sorry, sir," the pilot says, "even if I had authorization, I can't land you in this vehicle. The Pelicans aren't designed for reentry."

"Just walk across the deck, Carrozza," Ramírez says to Lenny.

"I am not setting foot in this place," Lenny replies.

"You do realize that you're technically aboard already, right?"

Lenny points at the pilot. "We are leaving. You get us a ground-to-orbit shuttle. We'll dock with them in space and transfer over."

The pilot glances at Ramírez, who throws his hands up. "I'll need to get authorization, sir."

"You do that. We'll wait here." Lenny folds his arms.

"Okay, well, you two have fun with that," I say. "I'm going to go now."

Ramírez and Lenny mutter and wave at me. I turn and follow the flight deck officer into the Eyrie.

The official history of the agency says that we built the original Eyrie as a cost-saving measure, to take advantage of the direct solar power always available in Earth orbit. It takes a lot of electricity to run all those information-crunching supercomputers. Unofficially, it's because the D.Int at the time wanted an ultra-secure facility for handling all this sensitive data. It's impossible to sneak up on an orbital space station, and there's no chance any unauthorized personnel can slip aboard without detection.

I'm not saying that all our D.Ints have a tendency to be paranoid, but there does seem to be a pattern, historically.

Admiral Morris's office is near the center of the station—the most heavily shielded location, and the least vulnerable to any outside attack—which means it's not in the large gravity ring rotating around the Eyrie's midsection. I'm thankful for the gradual change to weightlessness as the flight deck officer and I ride the lift into the station hub.

The door to D.Int's office is a half-meter-thick slab of titanium alloy that takes a good fifteen seconds to roll back. I have time to peek around the space while waiting, and it's pretty luxurious, all things considered. Even looks like she has a private bathroom in here. Must be nice to not have to worry about your colleagues making a mess because they can't get the hang of using a zero-gee toilet.

"Come in, Kangaroo," D.Int says.

I pull myself over the threshold, aiming for one of the two chairs in front of her desk. I catch the one closer to the door, pull myself down and close the seat belt around my waist, then wait for her to finish what she's doing.

Admiral Morris has no fewer than six different screens extruded from the clear plexi surface of her desk, displaying a dizzying array of multicolored animated datagrams. Her fingers dance from one screen to another, manipulating controls I can barely see to combine and partition and recombine the data. It reminds me a little of Jessica, my uncannily detail-oriented Surgical officer, reading the raw logs from my implanted body sensors, but this is even a step beyond that—D.Int has already applied some processing to whatever data she's looking at, and now she's doing further transforms on it.

I'm a little surprised that someone at her level would be working directly with intel data like this. Most directors are more managers than individual contributors; Paul doesn't go out into the field, and fleet admirals don't helm their own ships. But all those people must still itch to do the work that got them to where they are now. I guess it's easier for Morris to actually do this analysis herself once in a while, since her job is all about data, and she can study that just as easily from her secure office location.

"Do we know of anyone actively trying to kill you this month?" she asks. Her eyes are still tilted down at the desk screens. Her dark, curly hair bobs in zero-gee as she works.

"It's nice to meet you, too, Admiral."

"Let's skip the small talk."

"If you don't know who our enemies are, we're probably in a whole lot of trouble."

Morris dismisses her desk screens with a swipe of her hand across its surface. The infinitely malleable piezoelectric material melts back into her flat desktop. She looks up at me. "Touché. Science Division is analyzing your scans of the shuttle. I need you to deliver a message to your boss."

This is getting more and more confusing. "Is there something wrong with our communications?"

"Lasher isn't taking my calls," Morris says. "I need you to tell him to knock it off."

I knew Paul was a bit sour on Intel, ever since that side of the agency completely imploded last summer, but I didn't realize he hadn't been talking to our new D.Int. Ops and Intel are still working together, and I don't need to know what goes on with my superiors. That's not my job, and this is not my problem—or at least it wasn't until now.

"Okay," I say. "Would you like to write that down on something, or—"

"D.Ops and D.Int are two halves of the same whole," Morris says, staring at me. I'm not sure she's actually blinked since I came in here. It's mildly unsettling. "Intel and Ops need to work together. That doesn't just mean our people. That means him and me personally. Do you know we haven't even been in the same room since I took this job?"

"Well," I say, "he has been a bit busy."

"*He's* been busy?" Morris scoffs. "I had to rebuild this division from literally nothing. I am doing my best to—oh, forget it. Just turn on your eye."

"Um." I'm not sure what's happening now. "What?"

"Your scanners. In your left eye." She points at my head. "Turn them on, start your mission recorder, and look around my office. Hell, look around this whole damn station. Tell Renwick to give you the grand tour." That must be the name of the officer who escorted me here.

"I'm not sure Lasher is interested in—"

"You scan every centimeter of the Eyrie for eavesdropping devices or unauthorized transmissions or whatever else Lasher thinks might be a security risk up here," Morris snaps. "He needs to trust me. He can't run Ops without Intel. It's not feasible, it's not legal, it's not possible. Whatever he needs to put his mind at ease and make this partnership work, I'm open to discussing. But he needs to talk to me."

I nod slowly until she finishes. "I will let him know."

"Thank you."

"Is there anything else?" I really hope there isn't.

Morris stares at me for a moment, then swivels her chair around to face the back wall. She puts one hand against the wall and leans forward. I see the telltale glow of biometric sensors around her face and palm, and then the wall irises open to reveal a small vault. She reaches inside and pulls out something very small. The safe disappears back into the wall as she turns around to face me again.

"You used to work Intel," she says. "You know what this is."

Before I can correct her—I did work as an analyst, before the agency allowed me to do fieldwork, but I was on the Ops side of the fence—she shows me the thing she took from the safe, holding it between her thumb and index finger. It's a holographic data card, made of translucent red memory crystal. It might be mistaken for a ruby, except for its flat shape and the symbols etched into the surface.

"That's a red key," I say. "Why are you showing me—"

"Take it," Morris says. "It's yours."

I don't move. "Admiral—"

"Take it," she repeats. "That's an order."

I don't think she technically outranks me, since we're not in the same chain of command, but I already have enough crazy stuff to explain after I get home. I don't want to also start an argument with D.Int. I take the red key.

A red key is what the President of the United States would use to activate her nuclear football. It's the ultimate security item within the federal government: a personal decryption device used to unlock highly sensitive computer equipment. The red key won't work unless it can verify the user through biometrics, a subdermal agency transponder, and probably a whole laundry list of other heuristic signals I'm not authorized to know about. Basically, it's a magic opener that grants you access to an incredible secret, as long as you can prove you're you.

Paul's never given me a red key. I've never even asked about it. Why is D.Int giving me this one? What does it unlock?

I'm almost afraid to ask.

Almost.

"So why do I have a red key?" I ask.

"Do you have a problem with me, Kangaroo?"

I would not want to play poker with this person. "No, Admiral."

She smiles, finally, and it's only slightly insincere. "Please, call me GRYPHON. I need to get used to my new code name."

"Okay," I say. "Gryphon. Ma'am." It feels weird not to call her by some kind of title.

"You need Intel to back you up," she says. "And I'm talking about you personally now, Kangaroo. We're the ones who set 'em up so you can knock 'em down, metaphorically. Your ability is unique and invaluable, but to use it for maximum effect, you need a support team. Equipment, Surgical, Science, Intel. We're all here to help you succeed."

"Yes, ma'am." I'm not sure where she's going with this. "And I appreciate everything Intel does. But what does that have to do with the red key?"

Leaning forward on her desk doesn't have quite the same effect in zero-gravity, but she makes it feel significant nonetheless. Probably had a lot of practice during the war and whatnot. "We're here for you, Kangaroo. Lasher's trust issues are problematic, but I don't want his intransigence to affect you." She spreads her hands wide, palms up. "If you ever need anything, Intel is at your disposal. Don't hesitate to call. You now have a direct line to this office. That red key will open a secure channel to me from any agency-owned facility. Any time you need my help, I'm here for you."

I stare at her for a moment. "You do realize I have to tell Lasher all about this when I get back to Earth, right?"

She folds her hands, and her expression hardens again. "You tell him whatever you want, Kangaroo. But that's your red key. I am the only one who can revoke your authorization for that comms access. Is that clear?"

I really don't like office politics. "Absolutely."

"Good."

"Is there anything else you wanted to, uh, talk about?"

She stares at my hand. I'm still holding the red key, because I'm not quite sure what to do with it. "Don't you want to put that away?" she asks.

Of course. You want the show. "Yes, ma'am."

I turn so she'll be able to see the portal, think of a bright red bird with bushy black eyebrows, and open the pocket.

CHAPTER FOUR

Earth—United States—Washington, D.C.
12 hours after this red key started burning a hole in my pocket

Paul doesn't react visibly when I walk into his office and set the red key down on his desk. I watch his profile and reflect on how easily he could dress up like a British monarch. All he'd need would be the ceremonial sash. Maybe some white gloves.

After a few seconds, he glances over at the device and says, "That's from D.Int, I presume."

I grab the red key and put it back in the pocket. "You take the fun out of everything."

Our department's headquarters, where Paul spends most of his time, are deep underground. Surface-level office space in Washington, D.C., is at a premium these days, and Paul claims he gets more work down here anyway—fewer distractions. This facility used to be some kind of mid-twentieth-century bomb shelter, back when atomic weapons were the new hotness and people were afraid of being attacked with little or no warning by evildoers from overseas. Humanity has expanded our horizons a bit since then. Now we're more worried about Earth getting bombarded by unscrupulous residents of other planets in the Solar System.

"There is a very limited number of people who have the authorization to encode and distribute red keys," Paul says, still working on his desktop. "And I'm almost certain you didn't stop at the White House or the Pentagon on your way back from the Eyrie."

I'm surprised and happy that he said "almost." Let's see how long this conversation goes before he uses the word "idiot."

"I haven't tried using it yet," I say. "Do you think I should—"

"Do what you like," he said. "That's between you and Gryphon."

Of course he doesn't care. Paul can talk to D.Int whenever he wants. He just doesn't want to.

"So how long are you going to keep giving Intel the cold shoulder?" I ask. "I think they're starting to get a little annoyed. And, you know, it would probably relieve our workload if—"

"I'll trust them when I know I can trust them," Paul snaps.

"Pretty sure that's not how trust works."

He stops working and glares at me. "Has my cautious attitude with respect to the new head of our Intelligence division adversely affected your work conditions?"

I stare back at him. "Not until today."

"I hardly think one extra meeting presents an unreasonable burden on your schedule. At any rate, Gryphon is the one who chose to inconvenience you."

"Because she couldn't get to you," I say. "She's going to start looking for more backchannels."

"And that will be very interesting to observe." He returns to his work. "Don't leave yet."

Paul can be infuriating at times. Not because he's so stubborn, but because he always knows exactly what he's doing. He just doesn't choose to share a lot. Or sometimes at all.

That's the real problem here: I don't want him to continue juggling however many schemes he's got spinning right now. He may be the agency's director of operations, but he's only human, and it's not pretty when he crashes.

"You're working too hard," I say.

"Have you been talking to Surgical?"

"Does she agree with me?"

"You're not a doctor," Paul grumbles. He turns to the other side of his desk, where a rectangle of plexi is rising from the surface. The programmable material is connected to the office's computer network by secure wireless link, and can be remotely commanded to change its appearance to show information or alter its shape to form appropriate display surfaces.

Once the rectangle has coalesced into the size and shape of a standard reader tablet, the transparent material becomes opaque, and Paul snaps it off the desk and hands it to me.

"You're a field operative," he says. "That's your next assignment."

I take the tablet and look at the screen. It shows an agency personnel record for a white-haired woman named Gladys Löwenthal, code name CLEMENTINE.

"Friend of yours?" I ask.

"Asset." That's the agency's catch-all term for a person we can exploit in some way.

"She knows something about the attack on my shuttle?"

"That's the hope." Paul taps at his desktop, and the tablet display changes to a still image from my eye scan of the damaged shuttle, now with additional readouts overlaid on the picture. "Equipment analyzed your sensor data and identified the remains of an asminder."

"An ass-minder?"

"*Asminder.*" He changes the display again, to an animated schematic of an industrial robot. "Asteroid mining spider. Standard model built by ShanKongRobo. Usually operated by remote control, but they can also be used as autonomous units."

I can see why they're called spiders. Eight multisegmented legs extend out from a bulbous, three-lobed body. The cycling animation shows the legs bending every which way, two sharp triangular leg-tips chipping and drilling away at a rock wall, then manipulator claws attached to the outermost joints collecting rock fragments and depositing them in a cargo hold in the middle of the spider's body.

"Is there some reason EQ isn't telling me this himself?" I ask. Oliver usually loves to make me listen to his highly technical lectures. Especially when they're about robots.

"Equipment's busy," Paul says. "I'm telling you." He taps his desk, and my tablet shows me a grid of what appear to be telescope photos of the same shuttle. "We were able to backtrack your shuttle's trajectory from the Moon. The spider was riding with you the whole way."

"All the way from the Moon?" I say. "But that means—"

"We've already interviewed the maintenance crews on the farside space elevator. They're clean. But any number of people could have reprogrammed the spider to stow away on your shuttle and stab one of its mining implements into the engine when the pilot started your braking maneuver."

My mouth feels dry. "So somebody *was* trying to kill me."

"Let's not jump to conclusions," Paul says. "Nobody outside of Operations knew you were on that shuttle."

"Are we sure about that?"

"I know what you're thinking, and it's extremely unlikely—"

"It was also *extremely unlikely* that the agency's director of intelligence would go rogue," I say. "But that happened. I'd just like us to consider all the possibilities. Especially the ones that involve me being an assassination target!"

"If Sakraida were targeting you, Kangaroo," Paul says, "he'd be trying to capture you, not kill you."

"Not actually making me feel better here."

"Whoever sent that robot knew they were targeting agency personnel," Paul says. "That's all we can be sure of at the moment."

"So let's figure out who sent the damn robot."

"I'm glad you feel that way, because your next assignment will enable us to trace the robot back to its masters."

I touch the tablet to return to Gladys's file. "And how is Clementine going to help me with that?"

"She's not going to help you," Paul says. "She doesn't know you. She's only willing to deal with Jessica Chu."

"That's funny," I say. "We have another asset with the same name as Surgical?"

Paul frowns at me. "No."

I blink at him for a moment. Then I look down at the tablet and search through Gladys's file for known associates. I find JESSICA CHU, M.D., Ph.D. in the list and tap on the name, and it expands into an image of Jessica's face beside a summary of her military service record. One section of that record is highlighted.

"Surgical knows Clementine from the asteroid belt?" I say, skimming the file.

"Clementine is a retired asteroid miner and roboticist," Paul says. "She holds three patents for remote programming features. She's also a former passive source for the agency."

"This nice old lady?"

"As you know, we've never had great HUMINT coverage in the belt," Paul says. Human intelligence assets are still the best way to get reliable information about a foreign land, but the physical isolation of asteroid outposts means it's difficult to keep tabs on their residents. "Clementine enjoyed being a social butterfly. She also enjoyed passing information about her associates back to the agency. For a price, of course."

I continue reading the file while he talks. "And she retired to the Moon."

"Her options were limited after living in low gravity for so long. Bone density loss, muscle atrophy, et cetera. Even on the Moon she's confined to a wheelchair."

According to the file, Jessica was assigned to the hospital ship *Virginia Apgar* and deployed in the belt for several years. I'm starting to get the picture. Then I notice the category flag next to her name. "Wait. This is a surveillance list."

"Yes."

My brain starts to hurt. "The agency had Clementine watching Surgical? Why?"

"Clementine was a passive source," Paul says. "We didn't assign her to monitor anything or anyone in particular. She reported activity she thought might be significant, and maintained a wide variety of contacts for possible future exploitation."

"Like Surgical." Something else occurs to me. "Hold on. You're sending Surge to meet with Clementine? You're putting her in the field?"

"I'm sending you with her," Paul says. "She's the contact. You're the courier."

Of course. I have the pocket. "And what am I smuggling onto the Moon?"

"Gold."

I blink. "Excuse me?"

"You're going to buy some data from our old friend Clementine."

I check the dates in Gladys's file again. "What data? Any intel she has about the belt is going to be years out of date."

"She knows mining robots inside and out," Paul says. "Two of her patents are owned by ShanKongRobo, which is headquartered on the Moon. And she still has friends at SKR."

Paul taps his desktop, and my tablet display changes to a close-up of the stowaway spider's mangled leg. The shell has been cut apart, showing the interior surface, and I recognize the stylized cloud-and-mountain ShanKongRobo logo next to a factory bar code etched into the metal.

"That's a serial number," I say. "Clementine's going to find out who bought this robot? And then we can track down the bastards?"

"Even better," Paul says. "We couldn't risk telling her what specific information we're after or why we want it. But she's willing to get us a data dump from SKR's computer core. Every customer record from the last decade, including sales contracts and technical specifications for all software deployments."

"That's—a lot of data?"

"And it's going to be worth every ounce of gold we pay her. SKR supplies robotic systems to all asteroid mining concerns in the belt. Once we have those software specs, we can design our own code to remotely access the bots' onboard sensors and monitor any outpost within a hundred kilometers of an SKR-built radio unit."

I look up from the tablet. "You're going to hack the entire belt?"

Paul almost smiles. "Only as much as we need to find Terman Sakraida."

"You think he's laying low as an asteroid miner?"

"He's not surviving out there without help. He needs air, water, food. Someone's supplying him. And everyone uses robots in the belt."

This is a pretty audacious undertaking, even for Paul. "Do I want to know how much political capital you had to spend to get this massive invasion of privacy approved?"

"Sakraida is the architect of the worst security breach in the history of the agency." Any fleeting playfulness has abandoned Paul's face. "He betrayed all of us. He stole a mountain of above-top-secret files that he could potentially decrypt and use against us. We will go anywhere and do anything to stop him from doing that, if we can, and we will bring him to justice regardless. Understood?"

"I'm on board," I say. "Damn the torpedoes and all that. I just want to make sure everyone else is, too."

"Let me worry about building consensus," Paul says. "You just get the information."

"Give me the gold," I say, then add: "Arrr!"

Oliver looks up at me. I'm standing in the doorway to his workshop, just down the hall from Paul's office. A tall tangle of wires sits atop some kind of partially disassembled ceramic cylinder, obscuring the lower half of Oliver's face so only his beady eyes and mop of black hair are showing. This is not as unusual a sight as it might seem; as my department's "Equipment Research, Development, and Obtention Specialist," he's always tinkering with something.

"It's not ready yet," Oliver says, ignoring my flawless pirate impression. His voice appears to be muffled by the machine parts in front of him. "Come back later."

"Want to do my check-in now?"

"No."

"I'm on a quick turnaround for the next operation."

"We're continuing your inventory," Oliver says. "I'll call you when I've got your new load-out ready."

That's unusual. Oliver tends to be somewhat anal retentive when it comes to keeping track of the items in my pocket. He's also overly cautious about making sure electronics and other sensitive devices don't freeze inside the pocket—it's hard vacuum, which means objects lose heat slowly but surely. Oliver doesn't like leaving anything inside the pocket for too long.

"Am I getting a Lunar rover?" I ask.

Oliver frowns at me. "Have you not gotten your briefing yet?"

"Lasher says Surgical's supposed to brief me, but I can't find her." I even tried calling her, on the off chance she might answer, but she ignored me as usual. Jessica doesn't like to mix her agency job with her personal life. I know pretty much nothing about what she does outside the office.

"She'll be back soon," Oliver says.

"You know where she is?"

"I know where she went."

I wait for him to tell me, but he's not forthcoming. "Where did she go?"

"You should probably ask her yourself. When she gets back."

If it were actually a secret—a work-related secret—he would tell me I don't have clearance to know. Which means this is something personal, and he just doesn't want to tell me. Because it has to do with Jessica. Which means she'll be even more reluctant to spill the beans.

Oliver is my best shot at getting this information, whatever it is. And really, it's his own fault for not giving me anything else to do.

"Just tell me where she isn't, then," I say. "Is she still on the planet?"

"I'm not playing this game with you, Kay," Oliver says. "Go away and come back later."

"I'm going on this mission with Surgical," I say. "I'll be spending nearly every waking minute with her, probably. And you know she's not going to tell me anything herself. If there's something I need to know—something that might adversely affect our operational performance—you need to tell me."

Oliver sighs and steps out from behind his work bench. He's wearing a face mask, an apron—the material looks like rubber, possibly neoprene—and thick gloves that extend up to his elbows. He takes off the gloves and walks across the room to the sink.

"Um, should I be wearing some kind of protective gear in here?" I ask while he washes his hands.

"Relax," he says, pulling off his face mask and dropping it into a bio-hazard disposal bin. "I sealed the canister already."

"Oh, well, as long as the canister's sealed." I take a step backward.

Oliver removes his apron and hangs it on the wall next to the sink. Then he walks toward me. "Come on."

"Are we going somewhere?"

"Yes." I move back into the hallway, and he walks past me and turns toward the other end of the corridor, opposite the single entry door. I follow him into the conference room at the end of the hall. The lights come on as we walk in. Oliver closes the door behind us.

"Why are we in here?"

"For privacy," Oliver says. "Surgical hates meetings. This is the last place she'll investigate if she's looking for either of us."

"You don't know when she's coming back."

"I don't know how long funerals usually last."

I blink a few times while searching for the most sensitive way to ask my question. "Whose funeral?"

"It was death in the family."

"Now, when you say 'family,' do you mean—"

"Oh, for crying out loud," Oliver says. "It was her mother. All right? Surgical's mother passed away. The funeral was in Baltimore, today. That's all I know."

This is literally the most information I've ever had about Jessica's personal life. "Wait. Lasher knows about this."

"Of course."

"And he's sending her out? Into the field? Tonight?" *Why didn't he tell me my partner was going to be emotionally distraught?*

Oliver frowns at me. "The answer to all those questions is yes."

"That seems extremely ill advised."

"Lasher keeps his own counsel. As you know."

"Yeah, that's another thing," I say. "You know how I ended up on the Eyrie earlier?"

"I sense there's a funny story coming," Oliver says.

I ignore his gibe and tell him about D.Int giving me the red key and Paul not seeming all that concerned about his counterpart trying to subvert his authority. Oliver also seems rather indifferent to the situation. "You're not worried about getting caught in the middle of this . . . whatever it is?" I ask.

Oliver shrugs. "Not much I can do about it from down here."

"You can talk to Lasher," I say.

"*You* can talk to Lasher," Oliver says. "*I* have actual work to do."

"This *is* work!" I know Oliver would prefer to deal exclusively with computers and machines and equipment and not have to suffer all these messy human interactions, but if he's not dealing with Paul and Jessica's not dealing with Paul, that means I'm the only person around here dealing with Paul. "You're going to be the one stuck down here with Lasher while Surgical and I are on mission."

"We have separate offices."

"So you're just going to avoid him the whole time?" I ask. "You're just going to let him continue trying to run the entire Ops division without any support from Intel."

"We're still supported," Oliver says. "Rumblings on Mount Olympus don't affect the price of feta cheese in the agora."

I'm just about to unreel a detailed takedown of his faulty ancient Greece analogy when the door to the conference room flies open. Jessica steps inside, holding a laptop computer and wearing all black. It's a departure from her usual attire of neutral colors. She looks like a ninja. A very angry ninja.

"You're back," I say. "How was the—"

"Fine," she says. Then, to Oliver: "We're continuing his inventory?"

He nods. "Yes. New load-out will be ready by end of business."

"Good. You don't have to stay."

Oliver fast-walks out of the room as Jessica sets her laptop down on the conference table.

"So," I say, "that implies that I *do* have to—"

"Shut up," Jessica says. "Sit down. This is your briefing."

Well, at least the funeral doesn't seem to have worsened her usual mood.

CHAPTER FIVE

"Sorry to hear about your mother," I say. "My condolences."

"Thanks." Jessica doesn't look up from setting up her laptop to talk to the conference room systems. "What did they tell you?"

"Lasher didn't tell me anything. EQ told me he didn't know how long the funeral would last. That may or may not have been slightly racist."

She looks at me like I'm an idiot. "Sit."

I take a seat near the head of the table, across from where she's set up the laptop. Jessica pulls a control wand out of the side of the laptop and taps it on the top of the screen.

"I've read your after-action report and Ramírez's debrief," she says. "We'll run down the nanobot issue later."

"Is there a problem?" I lean forward. "If the tiny robots in my blood are malfunctioning, maybe we should turn them off for now?"

"They're not malfunctioning." Jessica adjusts something on the control wand. "Not technically."

"I'm sorry," I say, "my ears might be glitching again. What do you mean, they're not *technically* malfunctioning?"

Jessica sighs and lowers the wand. "I have been working with Science Division on long-term upgrade protocols for the nanobots. We've been releasing incremental code patches to add functionality, but there have been unexpected interactions between some of the new software modules. Don't worry. We've rolled back the latest changes."

I stare at her. "I used to like talking to you because you didn't sound

49

like Equipment." It's usually Oliver who throws all the computer jargon at me. "And what *functionality* did you add that accidentally destroyed my hearing?"

"I think you're exaggerating. Only the long-range microphone pickups were affected."

"And *why* were they affected?"

Jessica folds her arms. "Do you remember Project Weyland-Yutani?"

"Of course I do." I suggested the name myself, based on an old horror movie about an alien life-form with acid for blood. It seemed appropriate, since the idea behind this project was to harden the nanobots' shells so they could survive outside my body for a short time, and then program them to attack technological targets—basically, I'd be able to bleed on anything electronic and break it. "Wait. You're actually implementing that now?" I stand up. "And you didn't *tell* me?"

"We were adding individual functions," Jessica says. "You've been complaining about your cerumen situation for a while." That's true: my random earwax clogs can be pretty inconvenient, QED. "We didn't expect the nanobots to—"

"Turn them off," I say. "Turn the nanobots off, right now, all of them!"

"Calm down," Jessica says. "We debugged the issue during your return trip and flashed a software update as soon you came within range of an agency wireless hotspot on the Moon. The nanobots have been reset to the last stable version from a month ago."

That's a relief. I sit down again. "I thought making the nanobots purely technological was supposed to avoid these unexpected mutation problems." Most people are still skittish about nanotech because of the Fruitless Year, when swarms of tiny cyborgs destroyed every apple tree on Earth. But my nanobots are software only no biological components. We're supposed to be able to control every aspect of their functioning.

"It's not mutation," Jessica says. "This is a software issue. It's different."

"For the record," I say, "I would like to be *informed* of any further software updates *before* they take effect!"

"You don't have to shout."

"I enjoy shouting! It's a hobby of mine!"

"We're improving the system," Jessica says. "As I said. Science Division is planning for long-term field deployment of nanobots in other agency personnel. Identifying and fixing these minor issues will help us avoid larger problems later on."

"I sure hope so!"

"Are you ready to start the briefing for our new operation?" Jessica asks. "We are actually on a schedule here."

I fume silently for a moment. As therapeutic as it would be to continue yelling at her, we probably don't have time for that. And I don't want to have to deal with Paul if we miss our launch window. "Fine. Brief me."

Jessica waves her wand, and the large screen dominating the conference room lights up with an image of the full Moon as seen from Earth. "Lasher told you we're going to the Moon?"

"Yeah. To talk to your old friend Clementine."

"*I'm* going to talk to her," Jessica says, tapping the wand against her palm to change the display. The screen cycles through various maps and diagrams of the Lunar nearside. "*You're* going to keep your mouth shut."

She does something else with the wand, and the screen changes to a grid of thumbnails. She points the wand at one image. The screen fills with an "X-ray" view of my ill-fated shuttle, reconstructed from a few different scans produced by my left eye. The spider-bot looks like a sinister wireframe glowing in pale blue and white against the darkened outline of the shuttle engines.

"Did Equipment give you the rundown on this thing already?" Jessica asks.

"The ass-spider?" She doesn't react. That's fair; it's not my best material. "Lasher gave me a quick overview."

Jessica turns to frown at me. "Why didn't Equipment brief you?"

"Lasher said EQ was busy."

"Not too busy for gossiping, apparently."

"We were comparing the merits of various management techniques—"

"Equipment needs to brief you," Jessica says. "If someone can program one of these things to stow away on a shuttle and kill the engines, they can program it to do something more sinister. Make sure you have anti-mech countermeasures in the pocket."

"So these bots are autonomous?" I don't like the idea of a whole bunch of robo-spiders running around unsupervised.

"They have soft comms."

"They have squishy radios?"

"Soft as in *software*," Jessica says. "User-configured computer modules. Whoever buys these spiders from SKR can deploy them however they want—as remote-operated units, or semiautomated drones, or use some kind of clustering algorithm."

"Is there any way we can trace the code? Figure out who programmed it?"

"Most of the spider was destroyed when it blew the shuttle's engines." She waves the wand to advance through images until we're looking at evidence photos of the lower sections of two of the spider's metal legs. "That's everything we recovered. Two stalks that were embedded in the hull. No computer memory components, and we don't know what other hardware modifications might have been made to the main body of the robot."

"But we have the serial number."

"Yes. And once we buy that database from Clementine, we'll be able to investigate further."

Jessica advances to the next slide, which is Clementine's dossier. "So you want to tell me about your friend there?" I ask.

"She's not my friend."

"Acquaintance, whatever. Lasher said—"

"We met once," Jessica snaps. "That's all."

"Okay, I'm confused," I say. "We're going to visit Clementine in her retirement home. That means you need to know her well enough that you—your cover identity—would take a trip to the Moon to see her. Right?"

Jessica squeezes her eyes shut and pinches the bridge of her nose. "Fine. Let's start at the beginning."

The Moon is not a place where humans can live, long-term, and still expect to return to Earth every once in a while. That's true for most places in the Solar System, which are either smaller planets or much smaller asteroids or subplanetary bodies, where gravity is significantly less than Earth's one gee. Mars has one-third of Earth's gravity. The Moon has one-sixth.

Spend long enough in any of those off-world environments and your body will start adapting. The biggest problem is you'll start losing the core density in your bones. It'll grow back if you move to a higher gravity environment, but there is a point of no return: if you lose too much bone mass, you'll never get it back to its previous strength, and you won't be able to walk or even stand in one gravity for the rest of your life without mechanical assistance.

People have tried to address this problem technologically ever since living the rest of your life off Planet Earth became possible. A lot of rich folks who wanted new real estate funded research into robotic exoskeletons and gene therapy treatments and biotech implants that promised to either restore or make up for bone loss due to extended stays in low gravity. None of those potential cures has panned out yet. So anybody who leaves Earth has to decide, within no more than two years at the outside, whether they want to stay there for good.

The Moon is close enough to Earth, and still within range for minimal-delay communications, that rotation between the two places makes sense for most people. Industrial workers on farside tend to swap out every six to nine months; nearside's spaceport and space elevator and tourist trap staff usually have longer rotations. Being able to see the Earth is a pretty cool thing. Having nothing but gray rocks and the black void of outer space for scenery all the time is less exciting for most people, even if it's just a short tube ride back to nearside.

A few years ago, the Medical School of Earth's Leland Stanford Junior University—commonly known as just "Stanford University"—received a significant endowment to fund a new research and teaching hospital on the Moon. This was a big deal in the news: not only was it the first private medical institution on the Moon, its charter also included a commitment to treat anyone living there, and that promised to be a big step up from the government-funded and small-scale medical clinics that had previously been established during the colonial period.

Stanford's hospital on the Moon, nicknamed "Lunar General," expanded quickly, and over the years even declined a number of opportunities to collaborate with other medical groups. One idea that made it through their gauntlet of disapproval and actually broke ground was a retirement community attached to Lunar General. In retrospect, it seems obvious—or at least that's what all the pundits say now. The elderly are looking at end of life anyway, and their bodies are deteriorating already. Why not put them in one-sixth gravity, where some of them will actually be able to move around without canes or walkers or wheelchairs?

There's currently a very long waiting list to get into the Silver Circle retirement community. Even with the high price tag, it's a one-of-a-kind living situation with obvious advantages and enormous novelty value. If you're old and sick, there are worse ways to spend the last of your money than going to the Moon.

Jessica Chu got both her M.D. and her Ph.D. degrees at Stanford University. That's her connection, and how we're going to get access to both Lunar General and Silver Circle: she's going to work her Stanford contacts to get us on site, and then we're going to sneak into Gladys Löwenthal's room.

My job will be to follow Jessica around, posing as her personal assistant—that'll be a laugh and a half—and then, once we're in private with Gladys, to open the pocket and retrieve the precious metals we stowed there before leaving Earth. I don't know where Gladys is going to hide twenty bars of solid gold in a nursing home, but hey, that's her problem.

Something's going to go wrong. That's one of the lessons I learned during my field agent training, and it's proven out during my actual missions: at least three unexpected things are going to happen during any given operation. It's just a fact of life. "Variations." The best you can hope for is that nobody dies or gets seriously injured who isn't supposed to.

I don't have a high enough security clearance to see everything in Jessica's and Gladys's personnel files, and the parts I can access don't tell me how they might have known each other back in the day. The curiosity is killing me. Jessica clearly isn't going to tell me, so I guess I'll just have to ask Gladys when we get there.

CHAPTER SIX

"Use the buttons," Jessica says.

"What buttons?" I ask, turning the tablet over in my hands.

She grabs the tablet with one hand and points with the other. "There. Up, down, select."

I shake my head while trying them out. "This is ridiculously slow."

"Get used to it," she says. "You can't use any implanted tech that civilians wouldn't have."

We're in her section of the office, a medical area including a diagnostic bed, a wall of equipment and supplies, and a work desk. Right now we're standing next to the exam bed and she's showing me all the medical equipment I'll be expected to know how to operate while I'm posing as her assistant.

Jessica Chu, my "Surgical and Medical Intervention Practitioner," is all business, all the time. I've never asked, but I wouldn't be surprised if that were her middle name. Jessica All-Business Chu.

"It's really a shame," I say. "A lot of people could really benefit from having nanobots in their blood—"

"Don't say that word."

"I'm not going to say it in the field."

"You're in the field right now," Jessica says. "Start practicing so it comes naturally. We don't know what our schedule will be like up there. You might be tired, you might be exhausted. Make this normal so you don't accidentally say something you're not supposed to." She picks up another instrument. "This is a noninvasive temporal probe."

"It detects time?"

She places it against the side of my head. "It goes here, against the temporal bone in your thick skull. Activate by pushing the button, then wait for the scan to complete." I feel her push the button, and a trilling electronic sound emanates from the instrument. She pulls it away from my head and taps at the screen of the tablet I'm holding. "You'll see three different diagnostic visualizations."

"Groovy," I say, trying to make sense of the mess of symbols and colors that fill the tablet display. Jessica actually likes looking at raw data, because her brain works differently than most human beings. "What am I looking at here?"

She points at the first chart, then moves her fingers on the tablet to enlarge one part of the display. "Read that number, in the green area."

"Forty-seven."

"Normal range is between thirty and forty," she says. "Higher numbers indicate more brain activity."

I can't stop myself from grinning. "So I'm smarter than the average bear?"

Jessica frowns at me. "Brain activity does not necessarily imply cognition."

"But you just said—"

"Your brain is unusual," she says. "This isn't news. Your weird brain is why you can use the pocket. We don't know the root cause of that weirdness. We can only measure its effects."

"So what exactly does this probe detect?"

"Electrochemical activity. If a brain is working more or less than expected, we want to know what it's doing or not doing. Given the age of most of the patients we'll be examining, I expect a few of them will read low, and we'll want to schedule them for more in-depth brain imaging."

"Okay, time out. Why have we literally never talked about my brain weirdness before?"

"Why would we need to talk about it?"

"Because it's my *brain*!"

Jessica frowns. "You're not a medical professional. You don't have the background to discuss these issues—"

"*My* brain!" I point at my head. "I'm the patient here. I have rights!"

Jessica folds her arms. "You are a clandestine operative for the United States government. You're in the military chain of command. You don't have the same rights as a civilian."

"I want to see that paperwork." I was a minor when I joined the agency, but lots of Earth teenagers enlisted to fight the Independence War against Mars. Nobody cared too much about the fine print at the time.

"Oh, so you're both a lawyer and a doctor now?"

I don't have a good comeback for that. We scowl at each other for a moment. I hear footsteps in the hallway outside. Then Paul walks in through the open doorway of the Surgical area, holding a large envelope. Perfect timing. I hope he wasn't eavesdropping on us.

"Your infil transpo," he says, dropping the envelope on the instrument tray next to the exam bed and turning right around to walk out again. The front is printed with a colorful photograph of a happy mixed-race family standing in front of what looks like a large missile. "Bon voyage."

Jessica picks up the envelope and frowns. "What is this?"

Paul stops, halfway to the door, and turns around. "Two tickets for tomorrow morning's rocket to the Moon, plus train passes from here to Florida. Pack light."

"No," she says, raising a finger for emphasis. "We are not taking a Saturn 5000. We are not going on a ridiculous tourist trap ascent."

"You are a VIP," Paul says. "This is one of the hottest tickets in the Solar System. Stanford University's Medical Group insists on treating you to this once-in-a-lifetime, historic opportunity."

"Stanford should be spending their money on other things," Jessica snaps. "We can take a regular shuttle. Hell, we can take a US-OSS personnel flight." She pronounces the acronym *you-sauce*. "It'll be faster and won't have any screaming children aboard."

"You are a civilian," Paul says, calmly and evenly. "There is no plausible reason you would be traveling on a military transport."

"I'm a reservist. Maybe I'm involved in a research project with US-OSS," Jessica says. "Something to do with low gravity and body adaptation."

Paul shakes his head. "Please tell me how much longer you would like to complain about this before I can leave and get back to work."

Jessica purses her lips and balls both hands into fists. She must know that she's never going to win an argument against Paul.

"I will just point out one more thing," she says, stealing a glance at me.

I raise my eyebrows innocently. "If Kangaroo and I are traveling in and amongst a civilian population, especially one with a high percentage of tourists and vacationers, we will be expected to make small talk about our personal lives."

"Is there a problem with your legends?" Paul asks. We've already received our cover story identities, including detailed personal backstories supported by agency-generated fake documentation, planted online in all the right places.

"Are you concerned about your ability to stay in character as a gruff and impatient practicing physician who, underneath her poor bedside manner, has a heart of gold?" I ask.

Jessica turns to me and extends a finger. "Not helping." She turns back to Paul. "The less exposure we have to random civilians, the better. Get us on a private spacecraft. Charter a flight. I'm sure we can find a service—"

"Stanford is generous," Paul says, "not extravagant. They're not going to pay for a private spacecraft for just two people. I'm sorry, Surgical, but you will have to suffer the indignity of traveling aboard a replica of one of the most famous spacecraft in history."

Jessica grumbles as Paul turns and walks out of the room.

"It won't be so bad," I say. "Remember that cruise I was on last year?"

She squints at me. "The cruise that was hijacked and nearly crashed into Mars?"

"Well, yeah. But aside from that. They had a great seafood buffet."

"I'm pretty sure we're not getting haute cuisine aboard an antique rocket."

"Come on, look on the bright side." I point at the clearly fake photo on the front of the ticket envelope. "You can pretend you're one of the first humans in space. Didn't you want to be an astronaut when you were a kid?"

"No," Jessica says. "I wanted to be a hospital administrator."

"That's a weird aspiration for a kid."

"I was a weird kid."

I hold up the tablet, which still shows my brain scan. "Speaking of weird—"

"Forget it," Jessica says, taking the tablet away from me. "You need to go pack."

There are lots of different ways to get to the Moon these days. But Jessica and I are in a bit of a hurry, so no weeklong space elevator ride for us; and we're posing as civilians, so no speedy military transport options. Fortunately, there is a booming tourism industry on the Moon, and it spikes in the last year of every decade for literally historic reasons.

The first manned Moon landing happened in July of 1969, so any year with a number ending in "9" is the something-and-tenth anniversary of that event. Once humanity established permanent Lunar colonies, there was a regular influx of lookie-loos—somewhat pejoratively called "niners," since they don't tend to visit at any other time—who want to gawk at the piles of peculiar debris, which our brave ancestors left behind on their first tentative forays into outer space, and take part in the various celebrations of that first giant leap for Mankind.

All of the Apollo landing sites were preserved as historical areas long ago, the Lunar Museum of Human Spaceflight was one of the most successful crowdfunding efforts in history, and there's an entire United Nations working group dedicated to Lunar tourism. People care a lot about the Moon. Maybe because you can look up and see it on just about any night, sometimes during the day, and it's a big, bright reminder that there are people living off the Earth.

Being able to actually see some of the structures on the Moon with a telescope or a decent pair of binoculars is an awe-inspiring thing, especially when you're a young boy living in an orphanage and your prospects of getting out of the building—much less off the planet—are vanishingly slim. Just knowing that some people were able to escape the world of their birth means that it's possible. It's something to strive for. It's not just ancient history or science fiction; it's real, and it's attainable.

At least, that's what all the commercials say.

The "Saturn 5000" that Jessica and I will be riding up into space is not an exact replica of the original Saturn V spacecraft from the Apollo era. If it were, the tour company wouldn't be able to fit more than three people aboard, and that's hardly cost-efficient. They've reproduced the exterior look of the original—a tall, pointed, hundred-meter-tall cylinder, painted in black and white with small protruding fins and the letters "USA" emblazoned in bright red next to a twentieth-century vintage American flag. The engine bells at the business end of the rocket are different than the originals, since this new spacecraft is using a mini-ionwell for thrust—much more efficient than the old chemical propellants, and also frees up more interior space for passengers.

This rocket isn't going to fire in stages like the original Saturn V, so it won't shed large pieces of itself on the way up until the only bit actually going to the Moon is the tiny crew capsule at the top. It's a little mind-boggling to realize that every one of those Apollo missions involved a huge expenditure of resources just to send a little tin can to the actual destination, but I guess we had to start somewhere.

The crew capsule at the top of our Saturn 5000 is supposed to be a mostly accurate historical re-creation, but each one of the three available seats cost a small fortune. There was no chance that Jessica or I would be able to secure those accommodations, even if they hadn't been reserved months ahead of time. Stanford was only willing to spring for two basic, economy-class seats for its VIPs, but as the travel agent pointed out, these were already very scarce and expensive.

So it's a little surprising how many children are on this rocket.

The rocket's interior is divided into doughnut-shaped levels, with a transparent elevator tube running through the center and rings of seats around that. The seats face outward, and the entire interior wall is actually a display surface. Right now it's playing various historical footage from the Apollo missions, which appear as squares—that was how vid screens looked back then—floating on top of the view outside the rocket. According to the promotional materials, all these walls will become fully "transparent" during launch, thanks to hidden holo-cameras built into the exterior, so every passenger will have a clear view of the Earth dropping away below us.

I really hope none of these kids throws up.

Because honestly, how many of them actually wanted to come on this trip in the first place? It seems unlikely that the wailing infant three levels above us, or the crying toddler partway around the circle to my left, or the preschooler farther down to my right—I'd guess she's five years old and singing what she believes is the old American national anthem— would have been able to persuade their parents or guardians to shell out the small fortune this flight must be costing their family. Perhaps the parents think it'll be an educational opportunity. I really hope they get their money's worth. I can turn down the volume in my ears, but everyone else is suffering in order to give their kids this once-in-a-lifetime experience.

Jessica has broken out a pair of wireless earbuds and is preparing to put them in. I elbow her arm to interrupt. I don't want to be stuck on this voyage to the Moon with nobody to talk to, and more importantly, nothing to distract me from these noisy children.

"We didn't get to finish our earlier conversation," I say. "You know. About my B-R-A-I-N?"

She frowns at me. "You know we can't talk about that here."

"We can discuss the general scientific—"

"We can't talk about that here," she repeats.

I take a second to judge her mood and my own desire to argue this out right here and now. "Fine. How about the rest of my medical briefing? We were interrupted before you could train me on the new equipment. Can we talk about that?"

"Doctor," she says.

"Can we talk about that, Doctor?"

"Good. That's all you need to know."

Now I'm confused. "I don't know anything."

"'I don't know anything, *Doctor*,'" she says.

Now she's just messing with me. "Seriously?"

"We are not friends," Jessica says. "We're not even colleagues. You work for me. You only need to know two things. One, always address me as *Doctor*. Two, always do whatever I say, no hesitation, no questions."

"And what if I don't know *how* to do what you want, Doctor?"

"I'm not going to ask you to scrub in for surgery. You'll mostly be recording data. You know how to do that." She leans toward me and lowers her voice. "And if you don't, just pretend. We're only interfacing with the hospital personnel so we can get to Clementine."

"You know, Oliver actually wants to teach me things," I say. It's not a lie. He would prefer for me to learn more sci-tech stuff on my own, but my lack of enthusiasm for self-directed study usually results in him spitting impromptu physics lessons at me. "Don't you think more medical knowledge would benefit me in the field?"

"No," Jessica says, "you'd just want to show off the last interesting thing you learned and would quickly get in over your head."

"That's not true," I say. "I always have at least two or three things I want to show off."

Jessica points at herself. "Doctor." She points at me. "Do what I say."

I do my best to stare daggers at her, but my eye-daggers can't beat her eye-daggers. After a few seconds, I grumble, "Understood. Doctor."

"I'm taking a nap." She puts her earbuds in. "I suggest you try to do the same."

Several baby-shriek-filled minutes and one long safety briefing later, the countdown finally begins.

CHAPTER SEVEN

The Moon—nearside—Armstrong Spaceport
2 hours after I learned the words to all four verses of
"America the Beautiful"

When we get to the Moon, the capsule at the top of the rocket separates, and the rest of us orbit while those extra-super-special first-class folks get the full historical experience of landing on the Moon in a replica of the original Apollo Lunar lander. They're really getting their money's worth, and the rest of us get to watch their flimsy little module spiral down to the surface, with the descent explained on our seat-back screens with diagrams and historical NASA footage in surreal grayscale vid images.

The rest of our Saturn 5000 rocket orbits once, passing over farside and highlighting landmarks below us, before touching down on nearside. Jessica and I ride our rocket's central elevator directly into the underground hub of Armstrong Spaceport, where we join multifarious crowds disembarking from other arriving flights. Talking signs and service robots direct us toward the intake areas for each nation's citizens.

One quirk of the Moon Treaty—created way back in the twentieth century and later amended to allow commercial and military uses—is that each national sector operates as its own little island. The U.S., Russia, and China have most of the historic sites, but other nations have found different ways to attract tourists. The Moon itself isn't much to look at—the scenery's mostly a bunch of gray craters and gray rocks, and if you've seen one Moon rock, you've kind of seen them all. But there's also plenty of open space for low-gravity shenanigans, including a variety of stadiums and arenas for sporting events that emphasize leaping.

All those national sectors are joined together by a network of underground public transit tubes—originally a UN colonial project, now maintained by robots and supported by advertising. Being an unregulated commercial district makes every Lunar tube trip vibrant and somewhat unpredictable in terms of what you can't unsee, but we'll have to get used to it. Surface transport options are limited due to the rough terrain and radiation exposure hazard of staying topside for too long. The tube is the safest and most efficient way to get around the Moon.

Jessica and I are met just outside the spaceport's U.S. arrivals area by a tall blond woman holding up an electronic sign with DR. J.S. CHU in big letters underneath a red-and-white Stanford University logo. Subtle.

The blonde introduces herself as Breyella Wilgus and shakes our hands enthusiastically in turn. "Welcome to the Moon, Dr. Chu, Mr. McDrona! I hope your flight was enjoyable?"

"More or less," Jessica says. "And you can call him Edwin."

"Of course, Doctor. Edwin. If you'll take a seat?" Breyella gestures behind her toward a small, four-person go-cart. "Your checked bags are being delivered to your hotel rooms right now. I'll get you through customs."

Jessica and I follow Breyella onto the go-cart. She selects our destination on the control panel, and the vehicle chirps and starts moving through the spaceport. The auto-drive does an impressive job of gently weaving us through the multitudes of flying cam-bots and luggage-toting service robots streaming everywhere.

"We're so happy to see you both!" Breyella swivels her driver's seat backward to face us. "Dr. Chu, I know our hospital staff are very excited to show you around the facilities and get your opinions of how we're set up here."

"Just out of curiosity," Jessica says, "are you going to be escorting us the whole time?"

"Oh, yes," Breyella says with a broad grin, either not picking up on Jessica's lack of enthusiasm at this prospect or simply choosing to ignore it. "As you might imagine, with the big anniversary celebrations all over Luna, there's increased security everywhere. We'll get both of you badged at customs, but I've been here long enough to warrant higher clearance levels, and it'll just be so much easier for you to get around if I'm with you to present my credentials."

"Great," Jessica says, unconvincingly.

I can guess what she's thinking: it's going to be harder to sneak around if Breyella's tagging along the whole time. But at least she'll be more cheerful company than Jessica promises to be. And who knows? Maybe we'll learn some fun new Moon facts.

As promised, Breyella breezes us through customs, then delivers us to our hotel and gives Jessica and me a few minutes to freshen up. We have adjoining rooms, and barely two minutes after Breyella leaves us—just enough time for me to slip out of my shoes and start massaging my feet, which always swell up something fierce after going through variable gravity—Jessica knocks insistently on the door between our rooms.

I sigh and walk over to open the door. My aching feet will have to wait. I'm surprised to see Jessica wearing completely different clothes than she had on during the flight. How is it humanly possible for her to have changed from a souvenir coverall into a business suit in less than two minutes?

"Let's pick up our dead drop," she says, walking into my room. She pulls the chair out from the work desk opposite the bed and sits down.

"Yeah." I open the pocket and pull out the insulated valise containing our mission computer. We stored any mission-critical supplies in the pocket so we wouldn't need to worry about getting them through customs. I unzip the valise, pull out the laptop, and hand it to her.

Jessica sets the computer down on the table and opens it. The camera above the screen glows red until she leans in and lets it scan her biometrics— face, retina, palmprint, subdermal transponder, and so forth—and then the screen lights up with a progress bar.

Oliver didn't have time to finish compiling reconnaissance data before we left, so he uploaded a briefing packet to an agency access point on the Moon. Our mission documents finish downloading in just a few seconds, and Jessica starts paging through them faster than I can follow.

"Are we going to push to see Clementine right away?" I ask. "Or do we let Breyella give us the dime tour first?"

"We don't want to be too obvious," Jessica says. "We let Miss Wilgus run her program, do whatever soft sell she's supposed to do. You don't need to pay much attention. They don't care about you; they're only trying to impress me."

"Sure."

"You're going to scope out the place." Jessica opens a map of the hospital. "Look for patient records, network access points, anything that might help us get to Clementine later without being detected."

"Got it." I verify that all the mission data has uploaded to my eye. Lunar General is new enough that we don't have detailed maps of its interior—especially anything that was added or changed after the official construction blueprints went into the public record. "Too bad Intel couldn't do all this legwork for us."

"Civilian medical facilities aren't generally hotbeds of espionage. Intel has other things to worry about."

"And robot spiders from the Moon sabotaging an agency shuttle wasn't serious enough to merit their attention?"

"Intel's working leads on farside. Clementine's a long shot, but she's *our* long shot."

"So Lasher just doesn't want to share."

Jessica turns around and glares at me. "Office gossip later. Did you review the file on this neurologist?"

"No," I say, and I'm not sure why she seems unhappy about that. "That's your deal, isn't it? I'm just the assistant. Why would I need to—"

"*Because* you're my assistant," Jessica says, closing the laptop. "You get to do all the work that I don't want to do."

"You don't want to talk to this neurologist? Dr. Raoul Helman?" I blink up his file in my eye and start reviewing it.

"I don't think talking will be the problem." There's a knock at her door.

"What does that mean?" She ignores me and walks toward the door. I see something interesting and stop scrolling through Helman's file "Wait. Sealed lawsuit? Is this what you're talking about?"

"Hello, Breyella," Jessica says loudly from the other room. "Yes, of course we're ready to go. Edwin!"

I put the laptop back in the pocket. "Be right there, Doctor."

"Shake a leg! We don't have all day!"

She might be enjoying her legend a little too much.

"Nice to meet you, Mr. Madrona," Raoul Helman says, smiling as he shakes my hand. He towers over both of us and Breyella. I wonder if living on the Moon for however long he's been here has increased his height significantly.

"*Mc*Drona," I say, correcting his pronunciation of my fake name.

Helman raises a thick eyebrow. "You don't look very . . . Scottish?"

"I'm adopted." One of these days I'm going to figure out how Paul chooses all these ridiculous aliases for me. And why they're always so ridiculous.

Helman moves on to Jessica and doesn't so much shake her hand as fondle it, ignoring her deepening frown. After he releases her, she makes no effort to disguise the motion of wiping her palm against the side of her suit jacket.

Breyella begins reciting our tour schedule in great detail, but Helman ignores her and continues talking to Jessica. I bring up a biomedical scan in my left eye. Helman's pulse, respiration, and body temperature indicate some kind of excitement, and the warm spot around his groin tells me exactly what he's getting excited about.

Well, this'll be interesting.

I think I might have an inkling of the reason for that lawsuit in Helman's file. On the bright side, I'm sure Jessica can fend off one horny neurologist, and with him distracted, I'll be free to scan as much as I want. I turn to say good-bye to Breyella, but her face doesn't look like she has any intention of leaving.

"I thought it would make sense for you to see the radiology section first, Dr. Chu," she says. "And then I'll walk you and Edwin through the intensive care unit and introduce you to some of our attending physicians."

"Oh, I can take it from here, Bree," Helman says, waving his hand in a downward, dismissive motion. "I'm sure you've got better things to do with your time."

The medical overlay is still in my eye, and I see Breyella's vital signs spike when Helman calls her "Bree." She obviously doesn't like that nickname.

"Dr. Chu is my responsibility, Dr. Helman," Breyella says, and I don't need any tech to hear the edge in her voice. "I'm afraid I just wouldn't feel comfortable leaving her for someone else to escort."

Time to run the numbers: if I agree with Helman, it might make my job easier for the next few minutes. But if I take Breyella's side, it'll probably make my job easier for the next few days. I think I'd rather take the latter odds.

Also, I don't like arrogant physicians very much.

"Actually, Doctors," I say, "if you don't mind, I suspect the two of you will be talking neurology the whole time, and I would appreciate the opportunity to pick Miss Wilgus's brain about other aspects of the hospital's operation." I turn to Breyella. "If you don't mind, that is. I do have to stay with Dr. Chu, of course, just in case she needs me for something."

"Of course," Breyella says. "I don't mind at all. Dr. Helman?"

If Helman doesn't like the idea of being chaperoned while he tries to work himself into Jessica's good graces—and, I'm sure he's hoping, eventually her pants—he hides it pretty well. I suppose that's a valuable skill for a medical practitioner too. I note with some relief that the hot spot in his own pants has cooled down a little.

"Fine," he says. "We'll start in the neuro lab."

Jessica nods. "Great."

Breyella leads us toward the elevator bank on the other side of the reception desk. I notice Jessica's hand flapping at her waist as I follow her and Helman and Breyella into an elevator, and after a second I realize she's telling me to close formation—one of the few X-4 hand signals I actually recognize. I position myself just behind and between her and Helman, ready to jump in and separate them if necessary.

While the elevator ascends, I use my implanted controls to open a secure radio channel back to the office. The Moon is close enough to Earth that I can get real-time comms with Oliver, with less than a second of transmission delay. The catch is, though he can talk to me through my cochlear implants, I have to send him silent text messages. I hope nobody thinks it's weird that I'm fidgeting so much.

Equipment, Kangaroo, I text to Oliver. **We're at the hospital. How's my signal?**

"Five by five," Oliver replies in my ear. "Remember to look around as much as you can. Keep your head on a swivel, as the saying goes. I'll prompt you if I want you to give anything a second glance."

Wilco, I send back.

I see the faint wireframe of my map data outlining the edges of the floor, walls, and ceiling. My eye is streaming some basic sensor readings back to the office—so Oliver can monitor my progress—and also recording a lot more for later analysis.

I'm doing my best to sweep my eye over everything, so I'm only half listening as Helman walks us around the neurology lab. Right now we're in some kind of control room, with a large window above a bank of computer consoles looking into a scanning chamber, where a transparent plexi chair is mounted inside a spherical metal lattice.

"How many beams?" Jessica asks Helman.

"Six, naturally," he says. I have no idea what they're talking about. I do notice that Helman's putting his hands on Jessica's shoulders a lot—guiding her around the room and also just groping her. I hope she can resist the urge to break some of his fingers. At least until I finish my scans.

I keep looking around—at the floor, at the ceiling—to make sure I give Oliver a good overview of the space. There's probably some shielding in here, but the location and composition of the shielding will give an indication of what it's supposed to protect.

"Bored?" Breyella asks. She's joined me at the back of the room, where I'm turning slowly in a circle. I suddenly realize how that must look to someone who doesn't know what I'm doing.

"Just getting a look around," I say.

"Most people are interested in the shiny expensive machines." Breyella points at what I can only assume is some kind of body-scanning setup.

"Sure," I say, "but the sideshow tells you more about what kind of circus it is."

Breyella smiles and scrunches her nose. "That's an odd analogy."

I shrug. "Credit Dr. Chu." Jessica has very strong opinions about hospitals.

We move on to another area with a similar setup—control room overlooking a second chamber—but these two rooms are much smaller, and the machine in here is a large apparatus that looks like a dentist's chair with a salon-style hair dryer bubble on top. A wedge-shaped bank of equipment sits behind and below the chair. I look closer and see that the bubble is a plexi dome shot through with wires and electrodes, mounted on a moveable arm.

"This calls for a demonstration," Dr. Helman says. "Breyella? Would you mind?"

I don't even need to see the panicked expression on Breyella's face to know that this is a shady request. "I'll do it," I say before she can respond.

"No," Jessica says quickly. "Not you, Edwin."

Helman frowns at her. "It's perfectly safe."

"Not for him," she says. "That's some kind of neural stimulator?"

"*That* is the latest in multifocal transcranial induction technology," Helman says, his chest puffing up. "The dome rests over the top of the patient's head. It's made of a programmable plexi material. We can sequence a patient-specific treatment, combining both magnetic and direct current stimulation in the most effective pattern to address the medical complaint."

Jessica nods. "Edwin's got a metal plate in his head. He'll have to stick to pharmaceuticals. And I don't need a demonstration, I've seen finger puppets before. What's next?"

She walks out of the room. Breyella follows her.

Helman frowns at me. "It's hard to impress your boss, huh?"

I stare at him. "She has standards."

He looks at me for a moment, then shakes his head and walks out. I finish scanning the room and follow.

CHAPTER EIGHT

The Moon—nearside—Hotel Tranquility
4 hours after the most mansplainy hospital tour in history

"Handsy bastard," Jessica says, pouring herself a drink from the mini-bar in my hotel room. "Thanks for running interference today."

"Just doing my job," I say, sitting at the work desk and waiting for my mission recorder logs to sync down to the laptop. My left eye collected a lot of data in the hospital. "I'm curious, though, why didn't you want me to stick my head in the brain machine?"

She looks at me like I'm an idiot. "Your brain is what you use for the pocket."

"But he was just going to make me move my fingers, right?" I've seen this demonstration before: a transcranial inducer can be used to suppress or amplify signals in the brain, and if you know which areas to stimulate, you can cause specific muscle movements. "That's not a big deal."

"We don't know how your brain works," Jessica says.

I frown at her. "I'm pretty sure we do, a little bit."

"I mean we don't know exactly how you open the pocket or control its characteristics," she says, rubbing the back of her neck with one hand. It's not like Jessica to be imprecise with language. Or to drink a straight double vodka. "I didn't want to accidentally reveal your superpower to a civilian douchebag."

"Come on. He wasn't that bad, was he?" I'm doing my best to lighten the mood. "I mean, he's a doctor, he went to Stanford, he works on the Moon . . ."

Jessica glares at me. "I'm not in the market for a relationship right now."

She gulps down the rest of her drink and walks back to the mini-bar. I hope she's going for something solid, but she pulls out another tiny bottle of vodka and starts opening it.

"Anything you want to talk about?" I ask.

She refills her glass. I try to stay optimistic: at least she's not drinking directly from the bottle. "No. How's that data transfer going?"

I look at the laptop. "Seems fine."

"Oliver didn't call back?"

"Not yet." I sent a status update when we left the hospital, but Oliver hasn't acknowledged it yet. I'm not too concerned, but it is unusual for him to wait to tell me what I did wrong, no matter how minor the consequence. "Are you sure there's nothing on your mind?"

"I appreciate your concern," Jessica says, not looking at me, "but this really isn't something you and I need to discuss."

"Fine." I am concerned about her long-term emotional stability, but right now I'm more interested in making sure she's not going to lose it in the middle of our mission. "You don't have to tell me about it. But will you promise that you'll talk to someone about it? Soon?"

Jessica chuckles, staring down at her glass. "Yes. I promise, I will."

The laptop beeps, indicating that the download from my eye to the laptop has finished. I start configuring the upload back to the office—we're on a public connection to the internet here, and anything else would look suspicious, so I have to use a special program to break up our massive data files into smaller packets that get sent over different routes at different times, to avoid interception. Everything's encrypted, but the agency is nothing if not paranoid. We always tear up the treasure map before putting the pieces through the mail.

"So," I say while typing away on the laptop, "what are you thinking for dinner?"

"I'll be fine on my own."

I stop typing and look at Jessica. "I'm not sure that's a good—"

"Don't push your luck," she snaps. "I promise I will talk to a medical professional about working through my grief. I promise I will not drink my dinner." She sets her empty glass on the desk. "But I would really rather be alone tonight. I'm asking you to understand that and respect my boundaries."

Her expression is uncharacteristically soft, and I hope that's due more to grief than alcohol. I nod. "Can I just say one thing?"

I can tell it's taking her a monumental effort to avoid rolling her eyes. "Go ahead."

"I know it's not nearly the same situation," I say, "but I know what it's like to lose a parent. If you change your mind and ever want someone to just listen."

She blinks, and I can tell she wants to frown, but she doesn't. "Thanks."

"And remember, our doctor-patient confidentiality goes both ways."

There's the frown. "Get some sleep. We've got a long day tomorrow."

"You know, gambling is legal over in the French sector—"

"Go to sleep," she says. "You never get enough sleep. Doctor's orders."

"Aye, aye, Doc." I give her a mock salute.

"That's insulting. Good night." She walks back to her room and pulls the adjoining door shut.

I am not an idiot, so after I secure the laptop and set up the sensor-film alarm on the inside of my hotel room door, I follow Jessica down to the lobby bar.

Jessica and I are both wearing external personal transponders for this mission. We always have agency-standard subdermal ID implants, which we use to unlock special equipment, but those don't transmit more than a few centimeters. Her necklace and my wristwatch broadcast secure beacons so we can locate each other if we get separated.

I bring up a map of the hotel and find Jessica's transponder blip blinking green on the ground floor. I add a basic infrared display so I can see where all the civilians are. I'm surprised so many people are still up and about this late at night. The crowd in the bar appears to be spilling out into the lobby, and they're not just standing around; there's a lot of activity.

I walk quickly away from my room, toward an exit stairwell. Not that I'm paranoid or anything, but even though it's highly unlikely that any hostile governments or terrorist groups know that Jessica and I are here and plan to abduct one or both of us, lots of random people in one place means a lot more collisions between them, and some of those interactions might turn unpleasant if one of the people in question is already tense because of the crowds and the recent death of her mother.

Sometimes it's not the nature of the threat we need to watch out for, it's the consequence if something goes sideways. A fistfight breaking out between two civilians is one thing. If someone happens to injure Jessica, that adversely affects our mission. I have to at least keep an eye on her, and make sure the crowd doesn't turn into a mob for some reason—or if it does, do my best to get us both the hell out of there before the trampling begins. It's not that I'm cynical and pessimistic about human nature. I've just seen too many things go wrong when you get a lot of people together in the same place and then scare the living daylights out of them.

Besides, I haven't tried the cocktails at this place yet. I recently developed a taste for vodka martinis.

I bound out of the stairwell on the ground floor, hanging in midair longer than expected because of the one-sixth gravity I'm still not accustomed to, and nearly crash into a very tall figure wearing what appears to be silver thermal blanket material that has been sewn into a notional spacesuit. I can't see the face behind the mirrored bubble helmet—which also has two silver antennae sticking out of the top—but I wave at the front of the person, which I can tell is the front because of the large nameplate reading ARMSTRONG across the chest.

"Sorry," I say, moving to one side and looking for a path through the crowd.

The bubble helmet nods, and a male voice crackles through a hidden loudspeaker somewhere inside the costume: "You ought to try taking small steps, friend, instead of giant leaps."

A few people around the silver astronaut laugh. Easy room. I flash a fake smile and move toward the bar.

There are a lot of people in costume here. Several other astronauts, wearing different variations on antique spacesuits, most of which are not accurate as far as I can tell—what the hell are all those hoses doing sticking out of the side there?—but one does have to admire their enthusiasm. Some of the other costumes include robots, one of which I recognize from an old twentieth-century entertainment vid, and various types of imagined fantastical alien creatures. There's a bunch of mice carrying chunks of green cheese. There's a pile of gray Moon rocks on the ground that rises to become an articulated humanoid form—a rock creature with small formations that separate to mimic a mouth and mitten-like hands.

"Sir! Excuse me, sir!" A young man wearing at least four different lanyards with holo badges around his neck plus display goggles bounces up to me. "If you're not part of the costume contest, I'll have to ask you to please stand to one side." I see some kind of display flickering in the lenses of his goggles. Probably not showing him information as critical as my own eye implant.

"Sorry," I say, following his gestures to move toward one wall—farther from the bar, but I can circle around. Jessica's transponder signal is still very close. "Seems like an odd time for a costume contest, though."

The kid literally rolls his eyes at me. "Midnight events are very popular. And we have programming at all hours right now. This week is the anniversary of the first Moon landing, as you may know."

"Yeah, kind of hard to miss that," I say.

Something flashes in his goggles, and his head whips around. "Sir! No, please, excuse me, sir, you can't do that here! Sir!"

I leave the enforcer to his duties and track down Jessica at the bar. She's chatting up a very pale redheaded man with freckles. Didn't know she was into freckles. I keep myself behind her back, using the transponder signal from her necklace as a guide, so she doesn't spot me. I'm not sure she would care, but I don't want to ruin her evening. It's too noisy in here for me to make out the conversation, even with my super-hearing implants, and I can't see her face to try out my eye's lip-reading software.

Might as well enjoy a beverage while you're waiting, Kangaroo.

The bar's crowded, though there are fewer costumes in here. It takes a good five minutes for one of the bartenders to notice me, and by the time he does, Jessica has apparently made plans to leave with the redhead. I see him negotiating with another bartender to pay his bill while Jessica downs the rest of her drink.

"What can I get you?" my bartender asks.

"Vodka martini," I say. "Dirty, with a pickle."

He stares at me for a moment. "Did you say pickle?"

"Yeah. Kosher dill, if you have one. Is that a problem?"

"Not at all." The bartender pulls a tablet out of his apron and scribbles something on it. "Are you staying with us here at Hotel Tranquility?"

"Yeah." I hold out my thumb so he can press it against his tablet's scanpad to charge the drink to my room.

"Thank you, sir. Your drink's coming right up."

He disappears around the curve of the bar. It'll take him some time to run back to the kitchen and scare up the ingredients for my pickle martini. I fight my way through the crowd to the other end of the bar and see Jessica and her redheaded boy toy stop in front of an elevator.

I duck back behind the wall as she turns her head in my direction and nearly crash into a woman wearing a sleeveless white leotard with black stripes and thigh-high matching boots, and carrying a complicated bulbous prop that looks just like—

"Barbarella?" I blurt out, surprised to see a character from a cheesy mid-twentieth-century B movie. The only reason I recognize it is because I had a huge crush on the actress when I was younger. Honestly, I don't remember much about the film besides her outfits. Or lack thereof, in certain scenes.

"Edwin?" the woman says, and it's only then that I recognize her. She's done her hair and makeup to match the movie character, and she looks stunningly different. "It's me. Breyella Wilgus."

"Right. I'm sorry. I didn't recognize you in that—" I gesture at her outfit, which I now notice is distractingly skintight. "That's quite a costume."

"I'm surprised you recognized it," she says. "I mean, I picked it because I was amused that the character's name was so similar to mine, but apparently it's from a very obscure old vid show."

I don't bother correcting her reference. "Please tell me you're in the costume contest, because otherwise this is a little weird."

She smiles. "Hey, what I do with my personal time is my own business. But yes, I am entered in the contest." She looks at the large round time-piece on her wrist. "My category isn't up for a few more minutes, so I was just going to grab a drink. What are you up to?"

"Couldn't sleep," I say. "Jet lag, I suppose." I look over her shoulder just in time to see Jessica and the redhead walking into an elevator. *Dammit.*

The bartender appears next to us at the end of the bar and sets down a glass of cloudy liquid. "Here you are, sir. Vodka martini, dirty, with kosher dill pickle juice."

"Thanks." I take a gulp of my drink.

"I don't think that's going to help you sleep," Breyella says, nudging my shoulder with her prop ray-gun.

Speaking of flirting. I blink my left eye to show Jessica's transponder location. It looks like her elevator's gone upstairs. That's fine. I'll be able to pick up her signal anywhere in the hotel. And I don't really need to see what I imagine she'll be doing with the redhead for the next little while, so I might as well wait here with Barbarella. I mean Breyella. Wow, that martini is strong.

"Something for you, miss?" the bartender asks Breyella.

I set my shoulder-phone to log Jessica's position at all times while Breyella orders a cocktail. "Put it on my tab," I say before the bartender leaves.

"Oh, that's not necessary," Breyella says.

"I insist," I say, and wave the bartender away. "I have an expense account."

"Well, thank you, Edwin." I hear something buzzing, and Breyella's smile goes away. "I'm sorry. I need to take this call."

"No problem." I turn away as she produces a mobile phone from some hidden compartment sewn into her costume, then use the opportunity to start a face-reco search on Jessica's redheaded friend. I blink my eye display off when I hear Breyella sniffling.

"Is everything okay?" I ask.

"I'm fine," she says, dabbing at her wet eyes with a tissue. That's some remarkably resilient makeup she's wearing. "Just going through some stuff with my girlfriend."

Now I'm confused by the flirting. "Does she also work at Lunar General?"

"No," Breyella says, wiping her nose and putting the crumpled tissue on the bar. "She's back on Earth."

Okay, less confused now. "Sorry to hear that. Long distance relationships are tough."

Breyella nods. "You too?"

She must have heard it in my voice. I really need to keep my guard up. "Sort of."

"So where's your partner?"

"She's—she travels a lot," I say, recovering. "Spaceship engineer. Interplanetary."

"Have you been together long?"

"Just since last summer. But I'm not sure we were ever really 'together,'" I add. "It's complicated."

"I hear that."

A lot of bad stuff happened last summer, when the agency's former D.Int went AWOL. But at least one good thing happened too: I met

Eleanor Gavilán—Ellie—the chief engineer aboard the spaceliner that we saved from crashing into Mars. And she didn't hate me.

The problem is, she doesn't know me. Not really. And I'm not sure how far our relationship can go if I can't tell her the truth about myself—who I am, what my job is, how likely it is I'm going to die or be captured on any given day.

I don't know how long I can keep lying to someone I want to love.

The bartender delivers Breyella's drink, a large ice cube in brown liquid garnished with a curl of lemon peel, before she can pry any further. She raises her glass toward me.

"To simpler things," she says.

I raise my glass and clink it against hers. "Simpler things."

My eye lights up with the results of the face-reco search, and I read them over as I take a sip of my drink.

The redhead is Jeremiah Burgess, a maintenance supervisor at the municipal power utility company. He's also flagged as an agency asset. Makes sense. Jessica wouldn't risk having a one-night stand with just any random person; she picked someone the government had already vetted for at least minimal security clearance.

I blink my eye over to check where Jessica is now and nearly do a spit take when I see the message TRANSPONDER OUT OF RANGE. I carefully set down my drink and rack my brains for a reason to excuse myself from Breyella's company.

"Pardon me for one second," I say. "I'm just going to find out what vodka he put in here."

"Not your brand?"

"I'll be right back."

I turn around so Breyella won't see me staring off into space while I bring up Jessica's transponder logs in my eye. I walk to the other end of the bar and pretend to wait for the bartender. Fortunately, he seems to be mixing a series of very complicated drinks, so I have some time to find out where Jessica disappeared to.

The log indicates that she went back up to her hotel room, stayed for just a few minutes, and then left again—but she rode a freight elevator downstairs and went out a service entrance. Probably went back to the room for some gear to crack hotel security. Possibly also contraceptives. Or cash to pay for gigolo services. I'm not going to speculate.

The problem is, Jessica didn't leave through the tube station, where the agency has data taps, and where I would be able to pick up her transponder signal. Her date apparently had his own vehicle, and her necklace transmitter isn't strong enough to reach our monitoring satellites. Especially if she's riding around in a radiation-shielded surface rover.

Goddammit, Surge, where are you going?

Something heavy taps my shoulder. I turn around and see the bright orange muzzle of Breyella's ray-gun resting next to my collar.

"Everything good here, citizen?" she asks in a gruff voice.

"Yeah. Sorry." I wave at the bartender, who ignores me. "He's just a little busy."

Breyella raises her other hand, and the bartender comes over immediately. I tell myself not to feel too offended. Maybe he'd pay more attention to me if I were wearing a saucy skintight outfit.

"Same again," Breyella says, pushing her empty glass forward. "And my friend would like a new vodka martini. From the top shelf this time, please."

"Of course, Miss Wilgus," the bartender says, bowing his head. "Right away."

"They know you here?" I ask as the bartender slinks away.

Breyella winks. "I come here often, Edwin."

Something occurs to me. "So you know this hotel pretty well."

"This is actually the most well-stocked bar in the sector," she says.

"Isn't there another bar upstairs?" I ask.

She makes a buzzing sounds with her lips. "Sure. For tourists who like watered-down drinks."

"Hey, I'm a tourist," I say. "And I haven't gotten a good view of the surface yet." Certainly not from a high vantage point where I might pick up a transponder signal.

"Oh, really," Breyella says. I'm not sure what to make of the twinkle in her eye. How many drinks did she have before this last one?

My eye doesn't have very sophisticated chemical or biological sensors; the implants wired to my optic nerve are mostly good for seeing electromagnetic radiation. But the medical scanning mode does tell me that Breyella's skin temperature is elevated, and it's not because she's wearing too many layers in this thoroughly air-conditioned hotel. Maybe asking her to take me to the roof wasn't the best idea in the world.

The bartender reappears with our drinks, and Breyella clinks her glass against mine. "Here's to getting high."

"You mean that literally, right? As in we're going to the bar upstairs?" I ask. She's finished her whole drink before I take my first sip.

"Come on," she says, tugging at my sleeve.

"Can I finish my drink first?" I ask.

She grabs my martini and downs it in one gulp. "There. You're finished."

"Thanks." I stand up and gesture for her to lead the way.

Breyella stands and stumbles, and I catch her elbow to keep her from doing a faceplant. Just her elbow. I don't want to give her the wrong impression here.

"Thanks," she slurs, bracing herself against the nearest wall. "Heels and Lunar gravity don't really mix well."

Neither do whiskey and vodka, Babs.

The throngs waiting outside the ballroom have thinned, so I don't have to maneuver Breyella around too many obstacles on our way to the elevator. She punches the button for the top floor of the hotel and turns to me with a crooked grin.

"I think the bar's on a different floor," I say as the elevator starts moving.

"You said you wanted to see the surface," she says. "Best view's on the roof."

"Are we actually going outside?" I ask. "Isn't there a lot of, uh, radiation out there?"

Breyella makes a face. "We're inside the dome, Edwin. *Inside* the dome. An entire fucking *dome* of transductile crystal. You know what that is?"

"Sure. I know about TDC." Large windows weren't popular on the Moon for a long time because of the constant and prolonged radiation hazards, but now we have transductile display crystal. With just a small application of voltage, TDC provides adequate radiation shielding for human life. Plus you can vary the voltage to turn those windows into translucent displays. "That's how they display all those announcements and advertisements, right?"

"Correct!" I wish she would stop gesturing with her ray-gun prop. I know it's not real, but the sight of a weapon being pointed at me still makes me nervous. "But more importantly, TDC is a"—she pauses and enunciates very carefully—"negative-index metamaterial that refracts harmful radiation away." She mimes something flying toward the wall and bouncing off. "Did I just blow your mind? Be honest."

I'm not sure what the right answer is here. "Um," I say.

The elevator dings, and the doors open. "We're here!" Breyella leaps out into the hallway, then steps back and grabs my arm. "Come on!"

She drags me to a stairwell, waits for a cleaning robot to pass us, then pushes the door open and shoves me inside first. I wait while she yanks open the gate with a NO GUEST ACCESS sign on it and bounds up the steps to the next landing.

"Slowpoke!" she shouts down to me as she covers the next flight of stairs in a single leap.

I walk up behind her. She holds the door to the roof open, and I step into one of the most amazing views I've ever seen.

Don't get me wrong. I've witnessed lots of incredible things. My uncomfortably long and monotonous outer space travels do get me into visual range of some of the most vivid astronomical wonders in the Solar System: Saturn's rings, the Great Red Spot on Jupiter, any number of comets shedding their icy mass in huge glowing tails. But nothing compares to seeing Planet Earth from space.

"Wow," I say, staring up at the blue-and-white marble in the black sky.

"You like what you see?"

I turn back to look at Breyella. She's put down her ray-gun and taken off her jacket. The climate inside the dome is controlled, so it's not too cold out here. But the way she sways her hips while walking toward me indicates she's reached the unwanted-sexual-advances stage of drunkenness. I quickly blink my eye to search for Jessica's transponder. Nothing. Either she's out of range already, or the dome is blocking the signal.

"I'm actually feeling a little chilly out here," I say. "Maybe we should—"

"You don't think this is romantic?" She points over my shoulder. "That's Earth up there, Edwin. Fucking *Earth*. The cradle of fucking civilization." She stumbles forward and nearly falls.

"Okay." I put out both hands to grab her bare shoulders and hold her upright. "This was a great tour, thank you very much, but let's go back inside now, okay?"

Still nothing from Jessica's transponder. I try turning up the gain on my receiver. Breyella glares at me for a moment while I blink to work my eye controls. Then her lower lip quivers. Then she starts bawling like a baby.

Aaand here are the sudden mood swings. I really hope she doesn't throw up on me.

I hold Breyella steady while she cries. After a moment, the blubbering turns into words I can understand.

"She refused," Breyella says. "She refused to come up and see the Earth."

"Who's that, then?"

"Mack." Breyella sniffles. "My girlfriend."

"Oh." I probably could have guessed that. "She visited you here?"

"She just wanted to see all the stupid tourist stuff." Breyella takes off a glove and wipes some tears from her face. "I wanted to sit on the roof with her. Just the two of us, no pressure suits, enjoying the view through the dome. She refused."

"Well," I say, "maybe next time—"

"She said she didn't want to risk damaging her reproductive system," Breyella says. "Her genes and shit. Because of the radiation. I *told* her about the TDC, but *she* said she didn't want to take any chances."

"That seems sensible. Listen, how about we—"

"It's ridiculous!" Breyella sputters. "We've only been dating for like a year! She's already talking about making babies? Who the fuck wants to get pregnant before thirty? I want to start my own life before I take responsibility for someone else's!"

"Also sensible," I say. "Look, I don't—"

"You get it, right?" Breyella looks at me with bloodshot eyes and grips my arms with both hands. She's got a really strong grip. And long fingernails. "Do *you* think I'm wrong? Is there something wrong with me? Do *you* want a baby, Edwin?"

"Not at the moment," I say. "And you're not wrong. This is just a difference of opinion."

"I should call her back." Breyella releases my arms and pulls her phone out. "Shit. Three missed calls."

Well, at least someone's comms are working up here. "You and Mack clearly have some stuff to talk about."

"I'm just going to sit down for a second."

"Okay."

I rub my arms to get the circulation going again, follow Breyella back toward the exit door from the stairwell, and watch as she sits down and rests her head against the wall.

"Just gonna rest real quick," she says, closing her eyes. "Then call."

"Sure."

Within a minute, Breyella's snoring. I walk to the edge of the roof, toward Jessica's last known location, and scan for her transponder again. Still nothing.

I adjust my eye's scan parameters to verify that I'm receiving radio signals through the dome. That means Jessica's out of range. There's no way to tell where she might have gone, and I'm not going to go on a wild goose chase across the Moon after her.

Hope you're having a better night than I am, Surge.

CHAPTER NINE

The Moon—nearside—Hotel Tranquility
Probably not long enough after our first cup of coffee

"So how was your evening?" I ask Jessica at breakfast the next day. We're dining very early in the hotel restaurant, which is still fairly empty. Our server left us a large carafe of coffee at Jessica's request. I suspect he was also happy that he wouldn't need to keep checking on us so often to maintain the hotel-mandated attentive service.

"Fine," Jessica says.

"Meet anyone interesting at dinner?"

She glares at me over her cup of coffee. "I don't see how that's any of your business."

"Just making small talk," I say. "Nice weather we're having, yeah?"

She grunts and sips her coffee.

I don't want to be too obvious about this, but it's killing me that I wasn't able to snoop on her date last night, and I really want to know what happened.

I could, of course, tell when she got back to her hotel room, since she's staying right next to me. The agency's standard "away from home" kit includes all kinds of nifty miniature sensor packages designed to be hidden around a living space to detect unusual motion, noise, electronic activity, or radio signals. I set up an additional sensor to watch for humanoid heat signatures entering Jessica's room, and the background job I left running in my eye after going to sleep reported that she got back to her room around four o'clock and stayed there. Her transponder showed up in the Hadley-Apennine tube station before then, and her signal trail led from there straight to the hotel. Guess she parted ways with her date after whatever carousing they did out there in the mountains.

I'm sure it wasn't anything sinister—this is Jessica we're talking about, after all. She probably just wanted to be let off the leash for a while. Especially since she's dealing with the emotional aftermath of losing her mother recently. And we've established that she doesn't want to talk about that.

"At least the coffee's good," I say. "You think it's expensive for them to ship it all the way up here? I mean, it's not like they can grow coffee beans on the Moon, right? We can barely grow them on Earth."

"They grow in specific equatorial temperate zones on Earth," Jessica says. "Here on the Moon, every habitat is climate-controlled anyway. It's not that difficult to adjust the settings to meet specific botanical requirements."

My phone chimes to tell me there's an incoming text message. I blink it into my eye. It's from Breyella Wilgus. "Hold on. Message from our liaison."

Sorry about last night, the message says. **Hope I didn't do anything too embarrassing. Thanks for not telling the hospital.**

You were fine, I reply. **How's the hangover?**

I'll live, she says. **See you & Dr. Chu at 0800.**

kk, I send. I hope that's still an accepted quick-messaging abbreviation for "okay" and I didn't just deliver a nasty insult.

"Everything okay?" Jessica asks the second I blink my eye into standby mode. I don't know how she does that. The heads-up display implant is supposed to be invisible to other people, even when I'm using it, but Jessica always seems to know when it's on or off.

"Fine," I say. "Breyella was just confirming our appointment. She's meeting us here in about half an hour to escort us over to Silver Circle. Do you want to talk about how we're going to do this?"

"Same as the hospital," Jessica says. "But we'll be under less scrutiny at the hospice."

"Isn't the preferred term 'retirement community'?"

"This institution is attached to an inpatient medical facility. Every person at Silver Circle has some kind of chronic illness or other medical condition which could be ameliorated by living in a low-gravity environment. It's a hospice."

"I thought you were a doctor," I say, "not a barber."

She frowns. "What?"

"You're kind of splitting hairs, aren't you?"

Before she can respond, the server brings our breakfast, and I switch the conversation to asking about how they get fresh eggs up to the Moon. Turns out you can actually raise chickens in Lunar gravity and they don't freak out. Who knew?

I have to hand it to Breyella: she doesn't look hung over at all, and if she's wearing more makeup than she was yesterday to conceal her fatigue, I can't tell. And her PR spiel is not noticeably less energetic than before.

Our tour of the Silver Circle retirement community takes a bit longer than the hospital tour, largely because the residents are more mobile and talkative than most patients at Lunar General. I suppose they're not getting a lot of visitors. I wonder how many of the residents' families sent their aged ancestors away to be enshrined here.

Gladys Löwenthal's room is on the fourth floor of H-wing, at the other end of the facility from the main lobby. Just like Hotel Tranquility, Silver Circle is circumscribed by a round dome that keeps a breathable atmosphere inside. The grounds here also feature aboveground planters, decorative shade trees, and a community vegetable garden. The greenery is easily the fanciest amenity of all: nothing grows on the Moon without incredible effort.

Our tour ends with a private subsurface tunnel connecting Silver Circle to Lunar General. Breyella explains that the tunnel is used for discreet movement between the hospital and the nursing home—if there's some kind of medical emergency, for example, and paramedics need to transfer a resident to the hospital without causing a scene.

"Positive pressure in the entryways?" Jessica asks as we approach the end of the tunnel that leads into Silver Circle.

"Oh, absolutely." Breyella places her palm flat on the scanpad next to the entry doors. The pad flashes green and beeps, and the doors slide open with an exhale of atmosphere blowing back any stray particles from the unsanitary tunnel. "There are airlocks at all dome exits, and they're biometrically secured to only let specific staff personnel through."

We follow Breyella out of the airlock into the lobby of the nursing home. Two figures in dark blue uniforms are standing at the reception desk, and they turn around as we approach.

"Dr. Jessica Chu?" says the one on our left.

Those aren't hospital uniforms. They're wearing badges and patches that say UNITED STATES MARSHAL SERVICE—the service that handles law enforcement in all American sectors on the Moon. The marshal on our right—her name tag says GURLEY—takes a step forward and out, flanking us.

That's arrest formation. That's not good. The marshal who spoke, WECKS, is holding out his identification holo card, and both marshals have their hands resting on the stunners on their equipment belts, holsters unbuckled, ready to draw.

This is really not good.

"I'm Dr. Chu's personal assistant," I say, stepping forward to meet Wecks and scanning his ID with my eye. It's legit—the agency database in my implanted computer core contains information on all law enforcement outfits in the Solar System, and that's a real United States Marshal Service badge, encrypted hologram verified. "May I help you, officers?"

"We need to ask Dr. Chu some questions," says Gurley. Wecks puts his badge away.

"What kind of questions?" I ask.

"We should probably do this in private," Wecks says. He leans over to project his voice over my shoulder. "Don't you agree, Doctor?"

His tone implies he thinks she should know what he's talking about. Worse, the expression on Jessica's face tells me that she actually does.

What the hell did you do, Surge?

Breyella leads us down the hall into an empty and rather sad-looking space with a few round tables and chairs. Most of the tables and chairs are stacked up against one wall, along with bins and boxes of other supplies, most of which appear to be for arts and crafts. Breyella closes the door once we're all inside and stands in front of it, as if to guard against any intrusions.

Marshal Wecks sits down at one of the few tables that's actually set up in the center of the room. His partner, Gurley, stands to one side. Wecks pulls another chair up beside himself and gestures for Jessica to sit down.

"I'll stand, if you don't mind," she says. "What's going on?"

Wecks pulls a small tablet out of his vest pocket. "Dr. Chu, are you a guest at the Hotel Tranquility?"

"We both are," I say. "We just had breakfast there. You can call and ask—"

"That's fine," Wecks says. "Dr. Chu, did you sleep in your hotel room last night?"

"Yes," I say quickly. "She was snoring like a wildebeest—"

"It's okay, Edwin." Jessica raises one hand. "I was out for most of last night. With a friend."

Goddammit, Surgical.

Wecks nods. "Do you know about what time you got back to your room?"

I could tell him exactly when she got back. But we're not in the business of volunteering information here at the agency. We collect information, and we control it. We don't talk unless we know why we're talking.

Jessica shrugs. "It was still dark out."

Wecks gives her a funny look. "Sun only rises once a month up here."

"Oh?" Jessica bats her eyelashes. "I'm sorry. It's my first time on the Moon. And we're mostly underground, it seems."

"What's your friend's name?" Gurley asks with a challenging tone. Bad cop, I guess.

"Jeremiah Burgess," Jessica says. "He works for municipal power."

Wecks holds up his tablet. The display shows a photo of the redhead from the bar last night. "Is this your friend?"

Jessica nods. "Yes."

Wecks stands up and puts the tablet away. "Dr. Chu, we'd like you to come back to the outpost and answer a few more questions, if you don't mind."

"What's going on here?" I say, stepping forward decisively but not suddenly. I want the marshals to notice me, but I don't want to make them nervous by thinking I'm going to attack them in any way. "We're in the middle of some very important business."

"More important than homicide?" Gurley asks.

"Excuse me?" I say.

"We're still working on determining cause of death," Wecks says. "But it does appear that you, Dr. Chu, were the last person to see Jeremiah Burgess alive."

"Some tour company workers at the Apollo 15 site found his body in Hadley Rille last night," Gurley says. "He wasn't wearing a pressure suit."

"Right near the Fallen Astronaut memorial," Wecks adds. "Somebody's got a sick sense of humor."

Jessica turns to Breyella. "Sorry, Miss Wilgus. We'll have to finish our tour later."

CHAPTER TEN

The Moon—nearside—Tycho Crater
1 hour after our nursing home tour was interrupted by murder

The United States Marshal Service outpost looks like a lot of the older buildings on the Moon: a somewhat haphazard mishmash of prefab habitat modules with generic docking collars and airlock tunnels. Some parts were clearly imported, and others look like they were manufactured on site from Lunar regolith. There are just a few newer facades of transparent panels. Transductile display crystal, I'm guessing.

I wonder what this place used to be, before USMS got a hold of it. The center of the building is actually an open area, a courtyard between four different hab modules, that's been partitioned with honeycombed walls to make holding cells, but only covered on top with a thin sheet of ceramic to keep radiation out and atmosphere in. I suspect that's to discourage the prisoners from getting too rowdy in their cells, or attempting to escape.

Wecks and Gurley won't allow me in the interview room while they interrogate Jessica. Wecks goes inside to talk to her while Gurley stays outside with me.

"I'm her personal assistant," I say again as the door closes behind Wecks. "I'm with her pretty much all the time. I could help answer any questions—"

"Oh, we're going to talk to you later," Gurley says. "Just sit tight."

Of course they're going to interview us separately. Just in case I'm an accomplice.

I still can't believe Jessica would kill someone. I mean, I can believe she would, but not under these circumstances. And why this guy?

A familiar sound chimes in my ear, and an alert lights up in my eye. I surreptitiously texted Oliver an urgent update as soon as we came out of the tube and I had satellite reception again, and now he wants to talk. I hope it's good news.

"Could I use your restroom?" I ask Gurley.

She leads me down the hallway and pushes open the restroom door for me. "I'll be right outside if you need any help with anything."

"Thanks."

I check the bathroom to make sure nobody else is in here and there are no unexpected recording devices, then duck into a toilet stall and pull the door closed before dialing my shoulder-phone to the secure line back to the office. It takes several agonizing seconds before Oliver answers.

"What have you got?" I ask.

"Not much," Oliver says. "Jeremiah Burgess was a maintenance supervisor for the municipal power utility, as you said. No criminal record, either on Earth or on Luna. He's been up there for just under a year."

"Any connection to Surgical? He's on the agency's asset list."

"None that I've uncovered," Oliver says. "Burgess was a low-level source for Intel—he had connections to Lunar gray market data brokers. No direct contact with anyone in OUTBACK." That's the code tag for our department, because Paul has a weird sense of humor. "This could just be a coincidence."

"Right," I say. "Surgical ditches me on the first night after we arrive here, and the guy she picks up at the hotel bar—an agency asset—just happens to die shortly after she takes a trip with him out and about on the Lunar surface. Must be a coincidence. Not suspicious at all."

"I don't appreciate the sarcasm," Oliver says. "My point is, in the absence of any other information, I am inclined to believe that Surgical is innocent of any wrongdoing. Perhaps she's being set up. Have you noticed any signs that you're being surveilled?"

"No," I say. "And I've been running my mission recorder on full-spectrum scans the whole time. We uploaded the raw data to you last night. Anything there?"

"I haven't done any manual analysis yet, but no red flags on the automated processing. I could look into some of the people you've interacted with up there. You said there were several doctors, and some kind of tour guide?"

"I'll send you their names," I say. "But I doubt it's any of them. That would be too obvious. We've seen their faces. We would have noticed if they were acting weaselly."

"It won't hurt to check."

"Okay, I need to get out of here." I flush the toilet and go to the sink to wash my hands. "I'll call again when we're back at the hotel."

"Right." Oliver ends the call.

Gurley eyes me suspiciously when I walk out of the bathroom. "You talk to yourself a lot, Mr. McDrona?"

"Only when I'm nervous, Marshal," I reply.

She gives me a very fake smile. "No need to be nervous, Mr. McDrona. We just want to get to the bottom of this unfortunate situation."

"I'm sorry, are you the good cop now?"

The smile disappears. "Let's go back to the waiting area."

Gurley walks me into a different interview room before Wecks brings Jessica out of hers. Then Wecks comes in to talk to me, and Gurley leaves—maybe going to follow up with Jessica, see if she tells the same story twice.

"So how's the Hotel Tranquility?" Wecks asks, sitting down across the table from me.

"It's nice enough," I say. "Crowded, though. Lots of tourists."

"Yeah," Wecks grumbles. "It's going to get worse before the end of the summer."

"Bet you folks are going to have your hands full with crowd control."

"Most of the tour companies are hiring private security to help with that," Wecks says. "But yeah, we're all going to be on call for the main event."

That would be the actual, precise anniversary of the very first manned Moon landing. I'm not sure how accurately the Lunar authorities are going to re-create the original timeline—from what I understand, it was several hours between the time the capsule landed and when Neil Armstrong first set foot on the surface. It was our first time putting humans on another world, and nobody knew what it was going to be like, so caution was the order of the day.

It's going to be crazy out there on the surface. Huge crowds. Lots of people from all over the Solar System. A perfect place for someone to hide who doesn't want to be found.

Still, killing a municipal employee days before your big escape—or your big act of terror—isn't exactly smart. The authorities are already on guard, anticipating people wanting to cause trouble around the occasion of this big celebration. Wouldn't you want to lie low until the time comes for you to strike?

Unless you actually wanted to frame someone else for the crime. But I'm never going to convince the police of that without evidence.

"Well," I say, "I'm sure you've got better things to do than investigate the wrong suspect for a murder. I can tell you, without a doubt, that Dr. Chu is not responsible for this crime."

"Can you, now."

"Yes. Absolutely."

Wecks looks at his tablet. "So you were with her all night, last night?"

I focus on not shifting in my chair or otherwise making fidgety movements. That's the first thing interrogators look for when questioning someone: physical signs of discomfort often indicate psychic unease. "Well, not all night. But pretty late. We were both in the bar up until around midnight. There was a big event there, lots of people in costume. You can ask the bartender. I'm sure he remembers her."

"He did," Wecks says. "He also remembered who she was talking to." He holds up the tablet, showing a picture of the redhead. "Did you see this man at the bar?"

I make a show of squinting at the image. "Yes. Well, it looks like him. It was dark, and I wasn't exactly invited to the conversation."

Wecks raises an eyebrow. "So you weren't at the bar with your employer?"

"No," I say. "She doesn't really like to socialize when we're not on the clock. You know doctors."

"If you say so."

"But it's not like there were many other bars nearby," I say. "Hotels, am I right?"

"I wouldn't know," Wecks says. "I don't travel much. Did you see your boss leaving the bar with this man?"

"I didn't see exactly the moment they walked out," I say. "But I did notice they were gone at some point after midnight."

"So you weren't watching her."

I give him my best puzzled frown. "Officer, I'm not sure what you're implying about my relationship with Dr. Chu—"

"How long have you been her assistant?"

"A few years."

"A few years," Wecks repeats, nodding. "And you've been doing pretty much the same job that whole time?"

"My responsibilities have expanded over time," I say. "I wouldn't say it's the exact same job—"

"But you've been her personal assistant for the last several years," Wecks says. "Same job title. No promotion. Is that right?"

"It's a good job," I say, doing my best not to sound too defensive. Or should I? No, I think that would be suspicious. Does that matter? Crap. We weren't prepped for this contingency. "And our relationship is purely professional."

"Still," Wecks says. "You happen to be in the same bar, you see that she's there, and you're not keeping an eye on her?"

"I respect her privacy."

"Is Dr. Chu married?"

"No."

"Divorced?" Wecks asks. "Widowed? Is she in a relationship? Does she go on a lot of dates?"

"These are all very personal questions," I say. "I think you should ask Dr. Chu instead of me. I'm not really comfortable discussing her personal life in this setting."

This is not good. I don't believe Jessica killed anyone, but if someone's trying to frame her, that means another player knows we're here, and they're targeting us. We need to figure this out ourselves and keep the marshals out of it.

Wecks spreads his hands on the table, palms up, and hunches his shoulders in a shrug. "Hey, I understand. I'm not looking for gossip. I'm not asking you to divulge anything more than what someone meeting her for the first time might learn. Just basic information."

"I think I would like to talk to a lawyer at this point," I say.

"Whoa there, slow down, Eddie—"

"Edwin." I've decided that's part of my character. He doesn't like nicknames.

"Mr. McDrona," Wecks says. "You're not under arrest."

"Then I can leave any time I want." I push my chair back from the table and stand.

"That is true," Wecks says, closing his tablet cover and standing up slowly. "But we would very much appreciate your cooperation in this matter. I understand you're going to be on the Moon for a few more days, is that correct?"

"Yes."

"It's going to get very busy around here," Wecks says. "And I don't know if you're aware, but there can be jurisdictional issues depending on where you are on the Moon. If you're visiting an Apollo landing site, that was an American space mission, so you're protected by the U.S. Marshal Service. But any of the Russian or Chinese sites, or the international museums?" He shrugs. "It could take a long time to extradite you from the care of another nation, if anything untoward were to happen in those areas."

"Are you threatening us, Marshal?" *Please don't threaten us.* We've already got enough to untangle without getting local law enforcement into the mix. Cops always get too excited when they sense the opportunity to make a bigger arrest. An off-world murder is basically a white whale if you're any kind of police. And we all know how obsessed people can get about white whales.

Wecks shrugs and gives me a hard stare. "I'm just stating some basic facts, Edwin."

"Thank you for the information, Deputy U.S. Marshal Wecks, badge number 6712," I say. "I hope we won't be seeing you again."

CHAPTER ELEVEN

The Moon—nearside—Hotel Tranquility
1 hour after I discovered I don't like U.S. marshals very much

I really hope Jessica wasn't as antagonistic as I was during my interview. If the marshals like her better than they like me, they'll be more inclined to scrutinize my behavior rather than hers. And I didn't go off the grid for several hours last night while a man was being killed.

We don't say anything to each other until we get back to the hotel and into our rooms. I follow Jessica into hers and wait for her to set up one of Oliver's "pesticide" devices on the wall—a noisemaker to defeat any nearby eavesdropping bugs. The horrible irritating sound actually seems rather soothing now. It means we can talk in private.

"Did you kill that guy?" I ask.

Jessica gives me a look that would probably stop a lesser man's heart. "No."

"Are you telling the truth?"

Now the look could probably melt steel. "Just who the hell do you think I am?"

"I don't know who the dead guy was," I say. "I don't know what happened between you and him last night. I do know that you would be willing to do just about anything for the right reasons. What I don't know is why you wouldn't tell me. I'm not judging you, Surge, I just need to know. What happened?"

"I'm a doctor," Jessica says. "I save lives. I don't kill people."

"Okay, fine. Do you know why your date last night ended up dead?"

She frowns. "You followed me?"

"Not out of the hotel, which is why I'm asking all these stupid questions. I saw you at the bar with what's-his-name."

"Jeremiah." She doesn't say the name like it means much to her. That's a relief. Probably not a crime of passion, then.

"Right. I saw the two of you at the bar, and then I saw you leave with him. I didn't follow because I respect your privacy." She doesn't need to know the truth about that. "If I had known he would end up dead in the morning—"

"He was alive when I left him," Jessica says, sliding open the door to her closet and pulling out her suitcase.

"What are you doing?"

"Packing," she says, yanking open drawers and pulling out clothes and tossing them into her suitcase. "I suggest you do the same. We need to leave."

I step into her path before she can put anything else in her suitcase. "If you didn't kill that guy, we have nothing to worry about. Right?"

"The marshals are going to be watching us day and night now," she says. "They'll probably even get the hospital and nursing home to cooperate. They can pull security camera vid from anywhere on the Moon. We're compromised. We can't complete our mission."

"They won't have cameras inside patient rooms at the nursing home," I say. "All we need to do is talk to Clementine. It won't take more than a few minutes. We're here already."

Jessica glares at me. "It's not safe."

"You understand what's at stake, right? That data could help us catch Terman Sakraida."

"*Could*," she says. "It's still a long shot. And there are other things at stake here."

I study her expression, but she's very good at hiding all her thoughts and feelings. Years of practice, I suppose. "What are you not telling me?"

"I've told you everything you need to know," she says. "I'm the primary on this mission, and I say we abort."

"You're not a field agent," I say. "And during an active operation, the senior field operative has the ultimate authority over mission continuance."

She squints at me. "Since when do you care about regulations?"

"Since they started helping me win arguments like this."

"Fine." She walks around me and continues packing. "You stay here if you want. I'm going home."

"Um, pretty sure I can get you court-martialed for that," I say.

"Wouldn't be the first time," she mutters. I step in front of her again, and she glares up at me. "Get out of my way, Kangaroo."

"Let's call Lasher," I say, "and see what he thinks."

There's that look again. "Your behavior has become very erratic."

I take a step back. "What?"

She reaches into her suitcase and pulls out a medkit. "You want to play rules lawyer? Fine. I am your Surgical officer, and I can decide whether you're physically and mentally fit to be on duty. If I determine that you are not, I'm authorized to provide whatever treatment I deem necessary to protect your health. Including sedation for transport back to an appropriate medical facility."

"Well," I say. "It seems we have a stalemate situation."

"Not really," she says, "since I'm pretty sure I can sneak a tranq dart into you more effectively than you can stop me from doing anything."

I ponder the situation for a moment. She's not joking. Jessica never jokes. Well, I've seen her joke exactly, let's see, maybe three times since I've known her. And it's really scary every time, because you're not sure whether she's joking, and if she's not, it's a really horrible thing she's suggesting. And then one time it was just the worst pun in the universe.

I'm not going to win this argument on any level. Worst case, she does exactly what she's threatening to do, and I wake up back on Earth not having completed our mission. Best case . . . what is the best case here?

"Okay," I say. "How about this. It's going to take you a couple of hours to pack up and book us on a flight out of here, right? The transport situation is going to be a little complex, to say the least."

Jessica lowers the medkit and turns down the intensity of her stare just a little. "Probably. What's your point?"

"You're the one who's a person of interest in a homicide," I say. "I have an alibi. You stay here and make our exfil arrangements. I'll go to the nursing home, meet Clementine, make the buy. Then we don't go home empty-handed. Win-win."

"She doesn't know you," Jessica says. "She wants to talk to me."

"And why is that, exactly?" I ask. "Are you old war buddies or something?"

"Not quite."

"Just tell me what to say. There must be some kind of shibboleth you can give me, right?" I'm sure she knows the Bible well enough to know what I mean by that: some kind of passphrase that will identify me as a friend.

Jessica puts down the medkit and taps the side of her suitcase thoughtfully. "Fine. Tell her you came to the Moon with me. Tell her about the police investigation; don't leave anything out."

"Except whatever it is you haven't told me."

She ignores that comment. "Explain that I can't be there myself because I'm being watched by the authorities, just in case I try something else."

"Like fleeing the jurisdiction?"

"I'm not under arrest yet," she snaps. "They can't stop me without some actual evidence. Tell Gladys that you're my colleague. Tell her there's no orange juice in his shoe."

"No orange juice in his shoe," I repeat. "Got it. Anything else I should know? Is she going to ask follow-up questions?"

"She can't know about the pocket," Jessica says. "So you'll have to go into the bathroom or behind a privacy screen or something when you pull the cargo. Can you handle it if she asks how you smuggled the precious metals up here?"

"Yeah," I say. "I've had lots of practice making up stories about what the pocket isn't."

Jessica sits down on the bed. "We can set up the laptop for full comms. I'll be able to see and hear everything from your eye, and transmit instructions by audio to your ear."

"Just like old times," I say.

Breyella is very concerned when I show up at Silver Circle's front desk by myself. I called ahead to let her know I was coming, but didn't want to say too much over the phone.

"Is Dr. Chu all right?" she asks.

I nod. "We probably shouldn't talk about this out here."

"Of course." Breyella leads me into a privacy booth toward the back of the lobby. She slides the door closed behind us, and the transparent plexi turns cloudy. "What happened? Is everything all right?"

"We're fine," I say. "The marshals just wanted to ask Dr. Chu some questions."

"About the man they found—outside? Her friend?"

"Not a friend," I say, hoping it's not too much of a lie—or at least that it won't blow back on me later. "Just some guy she met at the bar."

"But that's great. There were tons of witnesses at the hotel," Breyella says. "They can tell the marshals where Dr. Chu was."

"Unfortunately, not between midnight and seven A.M.," I say. "When she was asleep. That's apparently when the man died. And Dr. Chu was alone then." Boy, if any of this turns out to be untrue, I'm going to look like a real tool.

"Oh my God," Breyella repeats. "So what now? Is Dr. Chu still with the marshals?"

"No. They didn't have enough evidence to hold her," I say. "But I don't think she's going to want to go through with her presentation tomorrow."

"I understand," Breyella says.

"Have the marshals been back here? To talk to anyone else?"

"No. I haven't seen any more marshals. And nobody else has mentioned them showing up. I would have heard about it."

"Okay." I make a big show of taking a deep breath and letting it out. "I have a favor to ask."

"Anything I can do to help."

"I need to see one of your residents."

Breyella frowns again. "Why?"

"Dr. Chu reviewed the files you gave us access to earlier," I say. "She wasn't feeling up to coming here herself—you understand—but she wanted me to interview one particular person. For her research."

"Of course." Breyella nods. "Are you sure you don't want to wait? Until Dr. Chu is feeling more settled and can come back herself?"

I can't tell her we're planning to leave. That would require a whole new level of deception. It's not that I feel bad about lying to Breyella—it is unfortunate that she's done nothing wrong and is still being subjected to this deceit, but it's just part of the job. I just don't like going off book this much in so short a time, without any consultation.

But we are on the clock.

"To be honest," I say, "sooner would better. I think having something to distract her from this situation with the marshals will be good. I tried to talk her into coming herself, but she's still pretty shaken by the whole encounter here earlier."

"I understand," Breyella says. "I should be able to arrange something. Who's the patient?"

Gladys Löwenthal's room is toward the end of the one of the hallways on the second floor. Breyella gestures for me to hang back while she walks up and knocks on the door. I get a glimpse inside when she steps inside to introduce me: the walls are covered with what appear to be vintage, possibly original, posters from a variety of music concerts. I don't recognize any of the band names.

I've already started my comms link to Jessica. I can't see her, but I can hear her, and she can see and hear everything from where I am.

"Remember the passphrase?" she says in my ear.

"Shibboleth," I say under my breath.

"Pedant."

Breyella steps back into the hallway. "Go on in. Call me if you need anything."

"Thanks," I say. "This won't take too long."

I enter the room, and Breyella closes the door behind me. I take a moment to give Gladys Löwenthal a once-over with my eye's bio-scanners. Tufts of white hair ring her round face, which has the tanned and wrinkled texture of a longtime deep-space laborer. My scans confirm that her bones are brittle from living in microgravity for so long.

She moves a hand over the controls in the arm of her wheelchair, and the motorized seat glides up to me. "So. Breyella says you're here to service me?"

I blink at her. "No. What? I don't—that's not—"

"Oh, relax." Gladys laughs and backs up a little. "I'm just messing with you, son." She looks me up and down. "Though I wouldn't mind if you wanted to fool around a little."

"Just ignore her," Jessica says. "Introduce yourself."

"My name's Edwin McDrona," I say. "I work with Dr. Jessica Chu. She said I should tell you that there's no orange juice in his shoe."

Gladys stares at me—my face this time, thankfully. "You like music, Edwin?"

Masking noise. Old tradecraft dies hard. "Sure. Whatever you like."

Gladys taps at her wheelchair's control panel some more, and a very loud, rhythmic, and atonal barrage of sound explodes from the wall above the bed. I wince as she cranks the volume up even higher, until I wonder how bad her hearing actually is.

"Custom sound system," she says, grinning. "Had them install it special."

"Nice," I say. "What are we listening to?"

"Charley Horse Manipulation Strategy."

"Is that the song or the band?"

She shakes her head. "You kids these days. No education in the classics."

I don't feel it's worth debating this point. "We were told you have information to share."

"Can I offer you a drink?"

"No, thank you," I say. "I can't really stay long."

"You mind if I do?" She turns and rolls over to the kitchenette in the corner of her room, where there's a small sink and refrigerator and pantry.

"Go ahead."

"So where is Jess, anyhow?" she asks, pouring a glass of cranberry juice from the refrigerator. "I was hoping to see her. Catch up a little before getting down to business."

"She couldn't be here. She does send her regrets, though."

"Agency got you two doubling up on objectives this trip?" she asks, then sips her drink.

"It's a little complicated."

"How long are you going to be around?"

"We actually can't stay," I say. "There's been a . . . variation. We have to head back tonight, actually. Sorry."

Gladys squints. "That's disappointing."

"I hope this won't affect the arrangement you made with the agency. The exchange of information for goods?"

"No, no, I'm a woman of my word," she sighs. "I was just hoping for one last indulgence." She finishes her drink, puts the empty glass down on the counter, and looks up at me.

"I can talk to her," Jessica says in my ear. "We need her to cooperate. You can relay messages between us."

I'm not sure this is a good idea, but the very loud music is making it difficult to think clearly. And I'd rather not argue with both Jessica and Gladys. "If I may, Mrs. Löwenthal. I'm actually on comms with Dr. Chu right now."

She perks up at this and studies my face carefully. "No kidding. They really make those implants invisible, don't they?"

"Yeah," I say. "I'm transmitting back to her right now. She can see and hear everything. I can't broadcast her voice to you, unfortunately, but I'll be happy to relay whatever she says."

Gladys rolls forward and leans toward me. "Why aren't you here, Jess? Didn't want to see me in the flesh? What's the deal?"

I hear Jessica sigh. "Tell her I was unavoidably detained. Tell her about the police situation. Don't leave anything out."

I give a quick summary of our little dance with the U.S. marshals. Gladys chuckles as I finish.

"Jess motherfucking Chu," she says, grinning toothily. "Can't take your ass anywhere, can we?"

"Okay, now she's just being a jerk," Jessica says.

"She ever tell you how we met?" Gladys asks me. "It's quite a story."

"I like stories," I say.

"We don't have time for this," Jessica says. I ignore her and gesture for Gladys to continue.

"It was in the belt. Before the war." She doesn't have to specify; there's only been one interplanetary disagreement that escalated to open warfare. "I was working a private excavation on a previously uncharted asteroid. Big rock, metallic. We dug through some lead deposits and straight into a vein of transuranic ores. You know what that is?"

"Radioactive elements," I say. Oliver would be so proud right now. "You were exposed?"

"Yeah, that was the bad news. We weren't prepared for that kind of radhaz; our pressure suits weren't adequately shielded. Lucky for us, the OSS hospital ship *Virginia Apgar* was in range and heard our distress call before we started losing hair and coughing up blood."

"This all seems pretty straightforward so far."

"Oh, it gets weird," Gladys chuckles. "See, transuranic ores are extremely rare in nature. This was a major find, both scientifically and commercially. The captain of the *Apgar* got it into his head that he could seize the rock under eminent domain or some shit like that, deliver it to Outer Space Command, and score himself a medal or a promotion or both. When we protested our claim, he decided to cut off our medical care."

"That's . . . illegal?"

Gladys shrugs. "Hey, you're patrolling the outback, all alone for months at a time, you have wide discretion to prosecute the mission at hand. Treating radiation sickness is pretty standard. But with transuranics, it's heavy metal poisoning that'll get you—they're all a little different, and you never know if it's going to be brain bleeds or liver failure or some other life-threatening problem. The continuing care can be a real drain on resources."

"The captain ordered us to be discharged from sickbay as soon as basic radiation treatment was done—the minimum care he was legally required to provide—and then put off the ship at the nearest space station. He was betting that by then we'd all be too sick to file the official claim documents on the asteroid we'd been mining. Then he could circle back and annex the rock before our company could put together another crew with proper radhaz gear."

"And the other officers didn't have anything to say about this?"

"One of them did."

I nod. "Jessica Sunshine Chu."

"That's not my middle name," Jessica says in my ear. I turn down the volume.

"Of course, she wasn't dumb enough to confront the captain directly," Gladys says. "She knew the score. Her priority was treating her patients. She found a way to remove the obstacle that was preventing her from providing care."

"How did she do that?"

"This is the genius part," Gladys says. "You know how OSS makes all personnel requalify on unassisted spacewalks every so often?"

"I'm familiar with the regulation," I say. I'm not technically in the military, but the agency borrows a lot of procedures from the Outer Space Service. It's always a laugh and a half when I have to flail around in a spacesuit for the review board.

"Well, the captain was already overdue for his requal, and I think he also just wanted to see with his own eyes what treasure he was stealing," Gladys says. "Jess supervised his spacewalk. Including prepping his suit."

I nod. "I see where this is going."

"Wait for it." Gladys raises a bony finger. "Crafty ol' Jess reprogrammed the interlocks in the captain's life support backpack. So instead of separating all the input liquid into new breathing gases, the catalyzer evaporated just enough of the original compound to dose him with nitrous oxide."

"Laughing gas?" That, I wasn't expecting. I had a vague notion from Oliver's many lectures that modern life support systems stored oxygen and nitrogen in a compact liquid form that could easily be turned into breathable atmosphere—two parts nitrogen to one part oxygen—but I didn't realize they could also be sabotaged in this way. "She got the captain high?"

"Lowered his inhibitions," Gladys says. "So he was, shall we say, easily persuaded when she met him after the spacewalk and escorted him back to duty."

"And what did she persuade him to do?"

"Authorize additional medical treatment for us. He wasn't going to check on us before we got to the station anyway—plausible deniability and all that—but Jess got his thumbprint on an order to take any and all medical action to treat our symptoms, at her discretion. You can imagine his surprise when we were all alive and well and notarizing our claim before the *Apgar* even docked."

"But he didn't find out what Dr. Chu had done?" I've blinked up Jessica's military service record in my eye, and the dates indicate she continued in US-OSS for quite a while after that particular incident.

Gladys shrugs. "People who make bad decisions while drugged up don't typically like to admit it. Besides, the captain got a commendation for going above and beyond to save our irradiated asses. Not a bad consolation prize for such a jerkwad."

"And how do you know all this?"

"I was awake when Jess brought the captain back to sickbay after his spaced-out spacewalk. When she got him to sign the authorization, I saw it go down, and I wanted to know what the hell had just happened before she injected me with anything else." Gladys grins. "Jess figured I had just as much reason as she did to keep this secret. We parted ways at the station, but I kept an eye on her from then on. She had demonstrated a willingness to bend the rules for a higher purpose, and that's the kind of friend the agency likes to make."

"You recruited her?" I always wondered how Paul had lured Jessica into his web.

"Oh, no. That's above my pay grade." Gladys shakes her head. "Lasher simply asked me for some background later, and I was happy to give my recommendation. Jess Chu's a good egg. She'll get the job done, come hell or high water."

I can't argue with that. The question is, what job is Jessica doing now?

"Well, thank you for the backstory," I say, turning my radio volume back up, "but we are on the clock here. Let's talk about the intelligence data you agreed to share with the agency."

"Thank you," Jessica says, with only a mild tang of bitterness.

"Fine." Gladys nods. "Where's the payment?"

"I'll produce it once you provide the data."

She frowns at me. "I asked for twenty bars of gold bullion. You want me to believe you're carrying it on your person right now? Let's go to wherever you stashed it."

"Give her one of the bars," Jessica says. "Go into the bathroom and pull it from the pocket. Tell her we hid the rest nearby, and you can go recover them once she shows you the goods."

I tell Gladys I can give her a sample and excuse myself to go to the bathroom. Once inside, I close the door, then think of a golden statuette in the shape of a hippopotamus and open the pocket. I push my hand through the barrier and pull out a therm-pack containing one of the gold bars. It clanks onto the floor, and I hope the music outside is loud enough to mask the noise from Gladys's neighbors.

I open the door again, bring the therm-pack over to Gladys's wheelchair, and open it to reveal the gold. She extends one hand and waggles her fingers in the international sign language for "gimme." I pick up the bar and hand it to her.

"It's cold," she says. "You had this hidden in a crawlspace or something?"

"It wasn't easy," I say, not answering the question. "But we managed to get all twenty bars up here. I'll retrieve the rest after you show me the data."

She fondles the gold and nods. "Looks good to me. Okay, wait here." She rolls her wheelchair over to the desk and taps at the computer there.

"If you don't mind my asking, what in the world are you going to do with gold up here?" I ask.

Gladys turns and smiles at me over her shoulder. "It's a precious metal. Even more precious here on the Moon. You can't mine it out of the ground, and it's so heavy it's ridiculously expensive to lift out of Earth's gravity well in any significant quantity."

"Tell me about it," I say. "But what are you going to do with it? It's not like you can trade whole bars for anything. And I doubt this nursing home gives you access to a smelting furnace."

"You let me worry about that," she says, turning back to the computer. I see a collection of file icons on the screen, which she manipulates to copy them onto some kind of removable storage media. "Plenty of things people love doing with gold. Jewelry, obviously. But it's also an excellent conductor. And there's lots of people who want reliable electronics around here. You can get free solar power all the time—no clouds, no weather—but if you can't pipe the juice to the right place, it's worthless."

The files finish copying, and she locks the computer again and pulls a memory card out of one of the slots in the desktop. She hands me the small translucent rectangle.

"There you go," Gladys says. "Everything you ever wanted to know about the SKR-9500 series but were afraid to ask. And you didn't get this from me, understand?"

I tuck the card into my shirt pocket, wishing I could open a portal and store it safely in the actual pocket instead. But I can't do that in front of Gladys. "We understand."

"So what do you spooks plan to do with all that info, anyway? Is the agency branching out into industrial espionage now?"

"I'm just the courier," I say with a shrug. "I assume these files are encrypted?"

"I'm not an idiot," she says. "You get the passkey after I get paid."

"Sure. I'll be back in a few—"

"Oh, I think I'd like to see where you wily coyotes managed to squirrel away all these gold bars." She gives me that toothy grin again. "I'm very curious."

Well, that's no good. "Like I said, Mrs. Löwenthal, we are on the clock. And this will go much faster if I do it alone."

"If you think I'm letting you out of my sight before I get paid," she says, the smile disappearing, "you're crazier than a fox. We stick together until I'm cashed out."

"Isn't it going to look a little suspicious for you to be rolling around this place with a bunch of gold bars stacked on your lap?" I ask.

Gladys pats the side of her wheelchair, and a door swings open between her legs, revealing a hidden compartment. "That won't be a problem."

"Do you know how heavy gold is?"

"One-sixth gravity, son," she says. "Now we can stand around here talking and wasting time, or you can start our little treasure hunt any time you're ready."

I've been waiting for Jessica to suggest some alternative to this, but she's been silent for a while. I decide I need to prompt her. I turn away from Gladys slightly. "Any thoughts here?"

"Just do it," Jessica says. "Pretend to use her as a lookout. Sneak into some storage closets, bathrooms, other private spaces around the home. And hurry up. I've booked us on the next flight out of here, and it leaves in two hours."

I turn back to tell Gladys we're ready to go when I hear a knock on the door.

"What was that?" I ask her.

"What was what?"

"Turn off the music."

She does, and I listen to the audio feed from Jessica's hotel room. More knocking.

"I'll be right back," Jessica says. "Go."

I walk toward Gladys's door. In my ear, I hear Jessica talking to some people, but I can't quite make out what they're saying.

Then I hear Jessica shouting. "The suitable wallet is in my alternate trousers!"

I freeze with my hand on Gladys's door handle. That's an emergency code phrase. Jessica's in trouble. I turn up the gain on my audio feed and wish I had a video link back to her.

"We'll get it for you," I hear a male voice say. "Where are they?"

"Over there," Jessica says. "On the bed."

Gladys rolls up next to me. "What's going on? You listening to something?"

"Shh," I say, waving a hand at her and muting my comms in the same motion. "Wait one."

"Got the wallet," says a female voice. A very familiar female voice. Who is it?

"All right," says the male voice. I hear something click. Metal? "Dr. Jessica Chu, you are under arrest for the murder of Jeremiah Burgess."

"Shit!" I say out loud.

"You have the right to remain silent," continues the male voice, which I now recognize as Deputy U.S. Marshal Wecks. "Anything you say can and will be used against you in a court of law. You have the right to an attorney . . ."

"Sorry, Gladys," I say, yanking open the door, "I need to go. There's a situation."

"I'm coming with you," she says, following me into the hallway and keeping up even when I start jogging toward the central wing.

"I'm going back to my hotel," I say, "and possibly elsewhere."

"I'm not a prisoner here," she says. "I'm not letting you out of my sight with that data. Not until I get paid, son."

Goddammit.

CHAPTER TWELVE

The Moon—nearside—Tycho Crater
1 hour after I acquired a new best friend

The USMS outpost looks the same as before, except I feel like more of the marshals and clerks are staring at me now. Maybe it's because I brought an old lady in a wheelchair with me this time. Or maybe they all know what's going on with Jessica.

The deputy at the front desk tells us to wait for a supervisor. I sit down in one of the uncomfortable plastic chairs in the lobby, and Gladys parks her wheelchair next to me.

"So," she says, "you want to catch me up on what's been going on with my old friend Jess?"

"I told you," I say. "I heard the marshals come into her hotel room and arrest her. That's all."

"They had to charge her with something," Gladys says. "What crime is she accused of?"

I hesitate before answering.

"Murder in the first degree," says a voice to my other side.

I stand and see a new marshal wearing plainclothes with a badge clipped to his belt. He's tall, with skin maybe half a shade darker than mine, short black hair, and a thin mustache. His thoughtful eyes look over Gladys and me.

"I'm Supervisory Deputy United States Marshal Sundar Punjabi," he says, not offering his hand in greeting. "Is one of you Dr. Chu's lawyer?"

I step forward. "I'm Dr. Chu's personal assistant. This is Gladys Löwenthal, an old friend of hers."

Punjabi pulls out his phone and looks at it. "You're Edwin McDrona?"

"That's me."

He gives me an amused half-smile. "Married into the name?"

"Adopted. We'd like to see Dr. Chu, please."

Punjabi shakes his head. "Sorry. We don't allow visitors to any felony suspects until they've consulted with defense counsel."

"That's at discretion," Gladys says, rolling her wheelchair forward. "Isn't it, Marshal? You're not legally required to sequester her. You can let us in to see her if you think it's appropriate."

"I can," Punjabi says, "but I don't think it is. I'm sorry, Mrs. Löwenthal, what did you say your relationship to Dr. Chu was?"

"Oh, we're old friends," Gladys says. "Met in the asteroid belt. She came here to the Moon on business, and she knew I was here and wanted to pay me a visit. Unfortunately, she wasn't able to do that before you fellows collared her for—what was it again?"

I can tell Gladys has dealt with law enforcement before. She might actually be an asset in this situation. Spies and criminals: we're not that different. We use a lot of the same tricks. We just don't have the same eventual goals.

"I'd rather discuss that with Dr. Chu's attorney," Punjabi says. He looks back at me. "Does she have someone she can call here? Or should we go ahead and assign one of our public defenders to her case?"

The Moon isn't a normal community. Everyone here is a transient; nobody actually lives here. You can only be invested in a place for as long as you know you're going to be tied to it. And I don't trust any of the local public defenders as far as I can throw them. Even in Lunar gravity.

This is a bad idea. But I know who I trust, and I'm pretty sure he can pull this off.

"I'm a lawyer," I say.

"Excuse me?" Punjabi says, raising both eyebrows.

"Yeah, me too," Gladys says, turning to stare up at me.

"I was hoping to track down someone more experienced," I say, "but those efforts have been unsuccessful. Therefore I am officially presenting myself as Dr. Chu's legal counsel in this matter."

"Are. You. In. Sane?" Jessica hisses at me as soon as the interview room door closes, giving us some measure of privacy. Gladys had to stay outside, and I'm pretty sure USMS isn't legally allowed to record our conversation, since attorney-client privilege still applies.

"I think you already know the answer to that," I say. "But calm down. I've got Oliver on comms. He's getting my eye feed, so he can see and hear everything, just like you were doing earlier."

"And how is that supposed to help you be a lawyer?" Jessica asks.

"Is that a rhetorical question? He's in the office. He has access to the complete criminal justice codes for every jurisdiction in the Solar System. You know how good he is at doing research, and how fast he is."

"I appreciate the vote of confidence," Oliver says in my ear.

"All he has to do is tell me what to say, and when," I continue. "Easiest thing in the world."

"I can't tell if you're hopelessly optimistic or just blithely ignorant," Jessica says. "Being a lawyer is not just about database lookups. You need to have a nuanced understanding of the law, how different statutes interact, how to interpret—"

"Do you have a better idea?" I ask. "You want to go with a public defender who's definitely a short-timer here and almost certainly underpaid for what she does? Do you know a good attorney on the Moon we can trust with the details of your case?"

Jessica glares at me. "You're wasting time here. Go pay Gladys. The sooner you get that data back to the office, the sooner we might find our friends in the belt. That's what you wanted, right? To finish the mission?"

She's right about that, but it'll take weeks to analyze all the robot data and even longer to develop our hack. I'm not leaving my Surgical officer in jail. After what happened in Kazakhstan last year—when I ran, and another agent died—I'm not abandoning my partner. Never again.

"I'm not leaving you behind," I say.

"I'm not in any danger here."

"You've been accused of murder. Aren't you even a little concerned about that?"

"I'll be fine."

"*Mur-der,*" I repeat, emphasizing both syllables as much as I can.

"The case will take months to try," Jessica says. "Lasher will get me out of it."

"So you're just going to sit around here, on the Moon, and wait for that?" I ask. "Am I supposed to get a new Surgical officer in the mean-time? And what if Lasher can't get you out of it?"

"He'll get me out of it."

"Just tell me what's going on," I say. "Tell me what happened last night."

Jessica stares at me for a second, then stands up. "Get out of here and do your job, Kangaroo."

Before I can stop her, she's at the door and knocking on it, asking for the marshals to take her back to her cell.

"I want to see the evidence," I say to Marshal Punjabi when he meets me in the hallway. Gladys sits in her wheelchair beside him.

Punjabi indicates Gladys. "You want her to see it, too?"

I think about this for a moment. Oliver says in my ear, "Probably not a good idea, Kangaroo."

I know it's not a good idea. But if Gladys knows more about Jess's past—if she can shed any light at all on what's going on with her—I have to take the risk of trusting her.

After all, what's the worst that could happen? We need to pay her more hush money? The agency has deep pockets.

"Yeah, she's good," I say. "Mrs. Löwenthal is here to help Dr. Chu."

"Absolutely," Gladys says.

"Fine. This way." Punjabi leads us down the corridor to a different con-ference room. "How did you know we had physical evidence, anyway? I didn't say anything about it."

"You arrested Dr. Chu," I say. "Which means you had to charge her with something. And you couldn't charge her unless you had something solid. I thought it was just going to be surveillance footage or something, but now you've told us it's physical evidence, and I want to see it. So you can show us now or wait for me to file a discovery motion."

"Well played," Punjabi says with a smile. "But just so you know, McDrona, it's not all going to be this easy. We run a pretty tight ship up here."

"Sure."

"I'm serious," he says. "We know there's all kinds of petty crime on farside. That's unavoidable. But this is the first death on the Moon that even looks like a homicide, and once people start killing each other up here . . ." He shakes his head. "It's not going to be pretty."

"I promise you this is a mistake," I say. "Dr. Chu's not a murderer."

"I hope you're right." Punjabi opens the conference room door. "But we have to follow due process."

"Of course."

Gladys and I wait in the conference room while Punjabi goes to get the evidence. I sit down and try not to stare at Gladys.

"Just so you know," she says, "I'm not entirely unsympathetic to Jess's situation. But I'm here for my own interest. Don't expect me to help too much."

"Really don't think this is a good idea, Kay," Oliver says in my ear. "We don't know if we can trust her."

"Fine," I say to Gladys. "But just remember, you don't get paid until I feel like I have some spare time to go retrieve those caches."

"Maybe I'll just go a-huntin' on my own."

"The Moon's a big place. And you're not going to fit that wheelchair into a spacesuit."

Gladys chuckles. "I got nothing but time, Edwin."

"The sooner we get Dr. Chu out of this mess, the sooner you get paid," I say. "So feel free to help out if you can."

"I'll consider it."

Punjabi returns, carrying a small plastic bag with something inside. He closes the door and places the bag on the table between us. It's clear plastic with a red-and-white EVIDENCE label. Inside is a silver necklace with a crucifix pendant. The crucifix is very detailed, with a tiny Jesus Christ nailed there, a crown of thorns on his head. I can even see little trails of blood sculpted down his face.

I blink my eye into scan mode and run a quick battery of forensic tests—as much as I can without actually touching the object. Oliver's seeing all this too, and I hear him verifying my scan results.

"Silver," he says. "It's solid, die-cast metal. Nothing inside. Just jewelry."

That's somewhat disappointing. I had hoped to be able to scan something unusual here, but it's not always the case that seeing more gives useful information.

"We found that on Jeremiah Burgess's body," Punjabi says. "Your client's fingerprints were all over it. We also got some skin cells; we're testing those now."

"Any other prints on it?" I ask.

"Sure. Burgess touched it too. But he was Muslim." Punjabi sits down across from me. "Wouldn't be caught dead with a Christian religious icon like that. So to speak."

"Funny," Gladys says.

"And there was a third set of prints," Punjabi says, "but we haven't been able to identify those. No match in Lunar records. We're checking with other jurisdictions now."

That's unexpected. Jessica took her one-night stand to meet someone else? Maybe I don't want to know exactly what she was up to, recreationally.

"So she didn't tell you about the third party, either," Punjabi says. "That's interesting."

I really need to work on my poker face. "You found the necklace on Burgess?"

"Yeah. We tracked his whereabouts last night back to an all-hours café in the Apennine Terraces. Witnesses say he met with your client and another woman."

"Have you located this other woman?" I'm very proud of myself for sounding so calm when inside, I'm screaming with frustration.

"Unfortunately, no," Punjabi says. "Surveillance footage from that time appears to have been lost. Which is very unusual, since we back up that data all the time."

"I will check on that," Oliver says in my ear. "And the fingerprints."

"Well," I say, "accidents happen. I presume you're already canvassing the area? Circulating a composite sketch or something like that?"

"Human witnesses are unreliable," Punjabi says. "That's why we prefer to get vid if we can. We would also prefer it if your client was more willing to talk about her other friend."

I return his hard stare. "I can't discuss that at the moment."

"Suit yourself." Punjabi sweeps the evidence bag away and stands. I stand so I don't have to look up at him. "Any other questions for me?"

"Not at this time, Marshal," I say. "I'll be in touch."

"Can't wait." He opens the door and walks out into the hallway, then waits for Gladys and me to leave.

"This is very odd," Oliver says in my ear as Gladys and I head for the lobby. "I'm seeing an agency order to scrub Lunar surveillance in the Apennines from last night. And the name on the order is Jessica Chu. I'm still trying to track down who authorized it at the higher level."

"Shit," I mutter as we leave the outpost.

"News from the office?" Gladys asks.

"Surveillance footage is gone," I say.

"How do you know that?"

"I can't tell you."

"Suit yourself." She turns her wheelchair and heads away from the transit tube entrance.

"Hey, where are you going? Our train's over here."

"Not if we want to go to the Terraces," Gladys says, coming to rest at another platform.

I frown at her. "How come you're suddenly interested in playing sleuth? I thought you didn't care about this."

"I didn't know the dead man was Jeremiah Burgess."

"You know him?"

Gladys shrugs. "We've crossed paths."

I'm starting to get a very different picture of this little old lady than my initial impression. "You didn't move here to retire, did you, Gladys?"

"Oh, I'm retired," she says. "I just have a lot of hobbies."

CHAPTER THIRTEEN

The Moon—nearside—Apennine Mountains
20 minutes after I became 50 percent more suspicious of Clementine

Gladys knows exactly where she's going as she leads me into the Terraces. We exit the lift from the tube station and she turns and rolls along the "street"—actually a wide ledge between a belowground cliff face and an empty chasm.

The Apennine Terraces are a shopping district bordering the Apennine Mountains in the northern part of nearside. Most Lunar guidebooks tell visitors to avoid it. It's one of the older established districts on the Moon, and as such, isn't as glitzy as some of the newer tourist spots. The eponymous terraces are actually below ground level, carved out of the sides of a chasm. It is literally a hole in the ground, covered with a thick transparent plexi sheet that offers a mediocre view of the mountains. If you actually want to see the Apennines, any number of tour companies in the Terraces will sell you a ticket on a vehicle that rises above the Lunar surface.

I wouldn't exactly call it a ghetto, but it's not the suburbs, either—as much as either place has an analog on the Moon, where nobody resides for more than a year and a half at a time. I wonder what's going to happen if we discover that the elderly in Silver Circle start living much longer because of low-gravity effects. Will all of Luna turn into an old folks' home?

Gladys seems to be leading me toward a dead end. "The café's back that way," I say, pointing to where the map showed Jessica met Burgess and the mystery woman.

"We're not going to the café," Gladys says.

I follow her to the dead end and see the crack of a small alley in the side of the cliff. There's a young man leaning against the wall at the corner, his face in shadow.

"Ay, Nans!" he calls as Gladys approaches, and steps out of the shadow. He can't be much older than a teenager. His clothes are colorful and shiny. As soon as I get a clear image of his face, I fire up my agency data link to do a lookup. "Not seen you here in an age, what."

"Been relaxing," Gladys says. "You catch the game this week?"

"Indeed," the teen says. "Righteous goal at the end, wannit? Seconds to spare!" He mimes throwing some kind of object. A ball, I suspect. They're probably talking about sports. I've never been big on athletics, since those are the guys who liked to administer regular beatings to me when I was younger.

"As you say," Gladys says.

The young man waves at me. "So. You the man, then?"

It's been a while since I heard that street slang. I refrain from responding in an uncharacteristic way. "I suppose I am."

Gladys nods. "This here's my friend, Edwin."

"Oi." The teen makes a high-sign with one hand. I wave back at him in the most boring way I can. Everything about this kid reminds me too much of my own early teenage years.

"Edwin, this is Yodey. He can hook us up with what we need."

"Yodey?" I repeat.

"Right on," Yodey says. "Nice repeat. Most people can't nearly get the pro-no right."

"Okay," I say. My face-reco search results come back from the warehouse: Dayton Hughes, small-time criminal offspring of tour-company executive parents. Probably glad to get away from the family business right now, during the height of the niner invasion.

His record indicates he's pretty well connected. I'm a little surprised that street kids are still using the same kinds of nicknames I remember— "Yodey" is a contraction of "Yo, Dayton." Confusing to old fogies, but easy enough to decipher if you know the lingo.

"So what you need?" Yodey asks, ducking back into the alley and motioning us forward. "Some get you up, some get you down?"

"Not today," Gladys says, rolling her wheelchair forward. I follow them into the shade—and, presumably, out of view of the vid cams mounted on the cliff wall. "We need information."

Yodey nods. "See what I can do. Specs?"

"Last night, at the Cup and Saucer Café down the street," Gladys says.

"I know the place."

"Edwin?" Gladys looks at me.

"A friend of ours was out here last night," I say. "She met with two other people, a man and a woman. The man turned up dead this morning. We're looking for the woman."

"Toughs," Yodey says. "Might be we get the vids from street cams. I'll ask."

"We've already talked to the U.S. marshals," I say.

Yodey takes a step back. "What you say?"

"It's cool," Gladys says. "He's a lawyer. Defense attorney, representing his friend in the case. The marshals said their vid footage was deleted."

Yodey looks us both over and folds his arms. "Curious. Security cams airtight in the zone. Copies, yeah, but po-po don't lose data. You sure?"

"They wouldn't lie to us," I say. "They're looking for the woman too."

"So let them do their job," Yodey says. "Why I got to get involved?"

"I don't trust the police," Gladys says.

Yodey laughs. "Tell me more news, Nans."

"I think they're covering something up," Gladys says. "Isn't that right, Edwin?"

Well, this day just got very interesting. "You said it yourself, Yodey. Law enforcement normally protect their data very well. So if something got deleted, what's more likely? That someone hacked into their system from the outside, or that someone on the inside did it to hide something they don't want a criminal defense lawyer to know about?"

Yodey considers this for a moment. "Don't you fear getting disbarred or what? Legal misconduct and such? Whatever I get you, not going to be admissible in court or how you say."

"The defendant is a personal friend," I say. "I'm her friend first and a lawyer second. I just want to get to the bottom of this and help her however I can."

"A friend in need," Yodey says, nodding. "All right, Nans and Eddie."

"Edwin," I say.

Yodey inclines his head. "Apology. Edwin. Give me some time, see what I dig up."

"How do I get in touch with you?" I ask.

"You don't. I call you. Got digits?"

I give him the burner contact that Oliver set up for me. It'll ring through a secure agency relay to my shoulder-phone, and Yodey will never know.

"Be seeing you," Yodey says, then disappears down the alley.

"Well," I say to Gladys, "better get you back in time for your afternoon nap, 'Nans.'"

"Not until I get paid, son."

The Moon's tube transit system is shockingly efficient. I guess that's one of the advantages of having a limited number of places that you know people will want to go, and being able to plan for that as you build out your colony. The underground high-speed rail cars travel at five hundred kilometers per hour, so it doesn't take more than a day to get across the entire nearside of the Moon, even though it's as far across as the North American continent back on Earth.

It's a very quick trip from the Apennine Terraces, which are on the east side of the mountain range, to the nearest Barclays branch. The agency maintains a safe deposit box in at least one big bank in every major city in the Solar System—it's an easy way to store something private. And it's a perfect place for me to go when I need to pretend to retrieve something that I'm actually taking out of the pocket.

I pull the rest of the gold bars, put them into a carrying case, and also pull our mission computer so I can verify Gladys's data after she gives me the password. After leaving the private room the bank maintains for safe deposit clients, I meet Gladys in a handicapped restroom down the hall.

"Well, that is pretty," she says when I open the case of gold for her to inspect.

"Password?" I ask, shutting the case when she reaches for it.

She gives me a dirty look, then rattles off a string of letters, numbers, and punctuation symbols. I open the computer, insert the memory card, and type in the password. After a few seconds, a whole mess of files appears on screen. I open up a few documents, do a quick search to verify that the customer database contains three specific records we know should be in there, then close the computer and slide the case over to Gladys.

"Pleasure doing business with you," I say, standing to walk out of the restroom.

"Don't be a stranger."

I find a different restroom, hide inside a stall with the computer, decrypt all of Gladys's data, and transmit it to Oliver. Then I dig into it myself.

I was an analyst before Paul put me in the field. I know how to go through records looking for signal. But I'm not prepared for the scale of the SKR database. It's arranged in some proprietary structure that doesn't immediately make sense; I find the serial number of the spider that killed my shuttle pretty quickly, but it takes a lot longer to link that manufacturing information to the sales invoice.

I don't recognize the company name—Niemann/Abadia—but I find it in the agency data warehouse using my shoulder-phone. "N/A" is a shell company that our Intel division uses to purchase equipment. SKR sold this particular robot to N/A a few years ago, while Sakraida was still D.Int. Agency records indicate the bot went missing from inventory last April, four whole months before Sakraida and his inner circle escaped. I suspect they stole a lot of office supplies during that time.

I put away the computer and shut down my eye. This is good. It's unlikely that our bad actors would have taken just one robot, and if they're still using the others in the belt, that will make it even easier to pinpoint their location. Now it's just up to Oliver and the other techies back at the office. They'll be able to make full use of all this data.

And speaking of data, since I'm waiting for Yodey to get back to me, there is one other batch of information that I can go collect. To satisfy my own curiosity.

The Apollo 15 landing site on Mount Hadley is ringed by a series of transparent tunnels. I fight through crowds of tourists to argue with the uniformed security guard standing at the entrance to the Fallen Astronauts Memorial section.

"I don't care who you are," the guard says. "Nobody goes out there until after the marshals say they're finished with it."

"And when will that be, exactly?" I ask.

"You may have noticed we're a little busy around here." The guard points at the tourists shuffling past behind me. "I can't tell you what I don't know."

"I'd like to remind you that I am defense counsel for the accused in this matter," I say, "and I'm entitled to examine the crime scene." I don't actually know if that's true, but I'm guessing this guy doesn't either.

"Obstruction of justice," Oliver says in my ear. "Make a threat."

I repeat the phrase, and the guard grimaces at me. "I'm sorry, but I can't let you go out there."

"I don't need to go outside," I say. "I just want to see it for myself." I can use my eye to get a pretty good scan through the tunnel wall, as long as I have a clear line of sight and some time to calibrate the sensors. "Let me into the nearest maintenance tunnel. You can allow that, can't you?"

The guard sighs. "Wait just a minute."

After a brief radio conversation, a maintenance worker shows up, grumbles at the guard, then waves for me to follow him. He leads me into a narrow, empty section of tunnel, with brightly colored safety markings printed on the inside of the transparent panels. They're not electronic displays, so it can't be TDC. I ask him about the material, pretending to be concerned about radiation but actually needing to know how to calibrate my eye scanners.

"Thermocoated plexi," the worker replies. "Don't worry. Your little guys are safe." He points at my crotch. "Just don't walk around naked in here."

We get to the end of the tunnel, a small airlock module, and the worker stops and points out the side at a fissure in the ground. The dust at the near edge of the rille has been disturbed, showing lots of footprints and tracks. A black-and-yellow striped CRIME SCENE dome has been set up to cover the area where Burgess's body was found.

"Found the body right on the edge there, just outside the range of our security cameras," the worker says. "No spacesuit or nothing. Frozen solid, though, so whoever killed him must have done it in the dark."

I'm half listening to him and half paying attention to Oliver, who's giving me instructions for adjusting my eye scanners. I operate my implanted controls to look for more details than unaided human vision can see—zooming in, trying different scan modes, and so on.

"There it is," Oliver says. He's monitoring the live feed from my eye, and at first I don't see what he's talking about. I've zoomed in to the center of the crime scene and adjusted my eye scanners to see through the evidence dome. There's an irregular pool of frozen blood still there, mixed in with the Lunar regolith. I add radar to my eye overlay, and then I see it.

There's a hole punched into the ground right near the middle of the sheet of blood-ice, like someone perforated the Lunar surface with a tool. I look closer and see that the hole is triangular—a three-sided shaft, coming to a point at the bottom.

Just like the leg of an asteroid mining robot spider.

What does this mean? Was Jessica's mystery date mixed up with Sakraida in some way? And if that's the case, does that mean—was Jessica—could she have been involved? Could she have been compromised?

No. I can't believe that. Because if that's true—

One thing at a time, Kangaroo.

"Do you use robots at this site?" I ask the worker.

"What? No. It's all human labor. We don't have enough repetitive tasks we can automate." The worker squints out at the rille. "You think the killer used a bot to dump the body here?"

"I'm sorry," I say, blinking off my eye scanners. "I can't discuss an ongoing investigation."

The worker grunts. "You seen enough?"

"Yeah." Oliver now has all the raw footage to analyze, in any case.

"Okay. Let's get back before my boss starts looking for me."

I don't have anywhere better to go while waiting for Oliver to finish his analysis of my crime scene vid, and there are a lot of freaking tourists around here, so I get on the tube and head back to the hotel.

It's midday now, so the tube isn't very crowded. Like most urban transit systems, I imagine there are well-defined rush hours when the majority of their riding population are going to work or coming home, and that's when eighty to ninety percent of their traffic occurs. Right now it's just me, a woman who struggled aboard with seven different bulging shopping bags but refused my help when I offered, and a young man bundled up in what appear to be winter clothes, nodding his head to whatever music he's hearing through his shoulder-phone. They don't look like tourists, but I remind myself that there are plenty of people who are on the Moon for work, and since it's daytime for a month at a time, many of them work odd hours.

Like Jeremiah Burgess, the now-deceased power company supervisor who met with Jessica last night. Jessica and another woman. Who was she? What is Jessica hiding? Why didn't she tell me where she was going last night?

I shake my head to clear it. Regardless of what Jessica was doing with Burgess, it sure looks like he was killed by a robot. Which means that whatever Jessica's hiding, it's connected in some way to the attack on my shuttle. Are the bad guys trying to kill her, too? Is it possible that she made other enemies during her time in the belt? Or did she have other questionable "friends"—like Gladys—who are now blackmailing her to do—what?

Until I heard what had happened aboard the *Virginia Apgar,* I would never have doubted Jessica's integrity as a medical professional. But now I know she's willing to bend the rules, and risk doing some harm, if she feels there's a greater good. That's worrying, to say the least. If I can't trust my own doctor—I've been there before, and it's a bad place to be.

This is all making my head hurt very badly.

Suddenly, a loud ringing sound fills the train. All the wall screens that had been showing advertisements and public service messages go red, then blank out. A second later, the word EMERGENCY appears on every display surface, and I feel the train lurch momentarily. The words NEXT STATION: LAST STOP appear under the word EMERGENCY.

"Um, what's happening?" I say out loud. Both of the other passengers have also looked up at the screens. The man in the heavy coat taps his ear, presumably turning off the music from his implants, and the woman with the shopping is gathering up all her bags, I guess preparing to exit the car.

Oliver answers first. "I'm checking now. Wait one."

"This happens every now and then," the music man says. "Probably some kind of obstruction on the tracks. Or an older section of tube got warped or cracked or something. But hey, at least they can sense it before it becomes a real problem."

"Terrorists," the woman shopper says.

"I'm sure it's not that," the man says.

"Yeah," I add. "Probably just some kind of maintenance issue—"

"No," the woman says, holding up a small tablet showing a live news vid feed. I didn't see it earlier because she had it resting inside one of her shopping bags. I wondered why she had her head down this whole time. I just thought she was drowsy.

"It's all over the news," she continues. "Somebody blew up a solar plant."

"What the fuck?" the man says, crowding next to her to see the vid.

I stay where I am and blink my shoulder-phone into operation to receive a live news feed in my eye. Oliver comes back at the same time I see the first pictures, of a giant cloud of gray dust rising from the Lunar surface.

"Kangaroo?" Oliver says. "Ah. You're seeing the news. I can summarize. Someone—we don't know who yet—has detonated several explosive devices in the solar power generation ring located in the Lunar zone of eternal daylight. Still working on getting numbers and details."

"Approaching last stop," says a recorded voice over the public address loudspeakers. "Prepare to exit."

I turn away from the other passengers, who are glued to the tablet vid anyway, and speak under my breath to Oliver. "Is this related to the intel we recovered from Gladys?"

"Unknown," Oliver says. "Analysis is ongoing. But yes, it does seem like a pretty huge coincidence."

That's not the worst of it, I realize. Someone just blew up a power plant.

And Jeremiah Burgess was a municipal power maintenance supervisor. Someone who would know how to sneak an explosive device into a sensitive area. Someone who would know which parts of a solar-electric generator were the most vulnerable.

What the hell were you doing with him, Surge?

"Are you in a position to investigate?" Oliver asks. "Lasher will almost certainly re-task you—"

"Wait one," I say as the train slows to a stop. "I'll call you back."

CHAPTER FOURTEEN

The Moon—nearside—Taurus-Littrow valley
10 minutes after terrorists ruined everything

There's a uniformed transit police officer and several hovering cam-bots waiting on the platform when we get off the train. The uniform checks each of our IDs, making sure we stand still long enough for a cam-bot to get a clean image of our faces before letting us leave.

I bunny-hop out of the tube station—it's nearly impossible to run normally in Lunar gravity—and blink up a map of the local area in my eye. My train stopped below the Apollo 17 site, in the commerce district. There are lots of retail stores here, which means lots of tourists. Especially right now. Easy for me to hide in, but there's no chance local security is going to let anyone here wander around unescorted.

I find a restaurant that isn't too filled with screaming children and their long-suffering parents, insist that the hostess seat me at a booth, and order a stiff drink and an appetizer. Then I blink my comms back on and wait for Oliver to answer.

"Good news and bad news, Kangaroo," he says by way of greeting. "The good news is, spaceways are clear. Satellite images confirm these were explosions on the surface, not impacts from projectiles."

Everyone's afraid of getting rocks thrown at them from outer space these days. Even a small mass moving fast enough will devastate a large area. That's where all these craters on the Moon came from, after all. "What's the bad news?" I ask.

"There were actually three solar plants hit," he says. "Two at the north pole, one in the southern hemisphere. And they were the three dedicated plants supplying power to the tube transit system. Lunar authorities are working to rebalance the grid, but with all the extra population right now, they don't have a lot of power to spare."

My stomach does a flip. "You're telling me somebody doesn't want all these civilians to be able to move around the Moon." *Including Jessica and me.*

"There are other transportation options," Oliver says. "We're working something out for you now."

"Can't I ask the marshals to drive me around or something?"

"I think you overestimate the goodwill law enforcement personnel normally extend to criminal defense attorneys."

My ear buzzes with an alert, and I see the incoming call details in my eye. "Sorry, EQ, I have another call. I need to take this. I'll call you back."

"Very well," Oliver says, and signs off.

I answer the new call. I didn't recognize the number, but as I guessed, it's Yodey. "Ay, Edwin. You chill?"

"More or less," I say. "You've seen the news?"

"Pretty messed up," Yodey says. "Don't affect our business, though, do it?"

I sure as hell hope not. "No. Did you find the information I asked for?"

"Right as rain. Would suggest a meet, but that tough now. Unless you might pay extra."

It takes me a second to comprehend what he's saying. "You have access to a surface vehicle?"

"Nothing too flash, but I know a guy."

"Great. Can he come pick me up?" I give my location. I'm sure there's a public airlock near here. How else could folks get topside to see the historical sights?

"Ay, no probs," Yodey says. "I'm not too far. Let me find a good meet spot."

"I want to meet at the U.S. Marshal Service outpost," I say.

"You joking."

"I'm a criminal defense attorney. I have business with the marshals. And a client locked up in their jail right now that I need to speak to."

The line hisses for a second before Yodey speaks again. "I meet you near. Rover's coming, meet you topside at museum flagpole. Driver's name: Zoo. I call you in a few, tell you exact where to go."

"Thanks," I say. "By the way, how much *is* all this going to cost me?"

Yodey snorts. "We'll see."

Zoo's rover turns out to be a large six-wheeled vehicle that looks like it rolled straight out of an advanced concepts showroom: sleek and shiny on the outside, even though there's no need for aerodynamics in hard vacuum, with plenty of multicolored running lights. There's not a lot of surface traffic on the Moon, but you'll definitely see Zoo coming from kilometers away.

I send Oliver a surreptitious text message while we proceed to the marshals' outpost: **On my way back to see Surgical again. Need all data you have ASAP. Are her dead guy and power plant attack related?**

Oliver could text me back and have the message show up in my eye, but it's easier for him to just talk like normal, like I can't right now. "I'm working on it, Kangaroo. Keep this channel open and I'll be able to see when you reach Surgical. I'll download whatever I have at that point."

Thanks, I text back, and then relax as much as I can while riding in the back of a shady vehicle during what is shaping up to be a Moon-wide crisis.

It can't be just a coincidence that the guy Jessica picked up at the bar last night—who just happens to be a municipal power supervisor, with access to solar plants—turned up dead this morning, mere hours before a well-coordinated group of terrorists launched simultaneous attacks on three different utility stations on opposite sides of the Moon. There's just no way.

I text to Oliver: **Does Lasher have new orders for me?**

"Lasher's a little busy right now, as you might imagine," Oliver says. "No, he didn't tell me anything different as far as what you're to do."

That's a bit strange. Usually when there's a "variation" and I'm able to make contact with the office, Paul has something to say. Even if it's just a brusque and sternly worded reprimand for going off-script.

But maybe he really is too busy right now. This is, after all, the first major terrorist incident that's ever taken place on the Moon, and the biggest crisis involving a large civilian population since—well, since last year, when a certain former director of intelligence tried to crash an interplanetary cruise liner into Mars. Only this time it's several million people in immediate jeopardy, instead of just a few thousand.

I do a quick omnipedia lookup on the population of the Moon. Nine million people, give or take, depending on the time of year and whether there's a big tourist event happening. Like now. There are probably another million additional people here this week. And most of them are stuck in place until the tubes come back online.

I could sneak Jessica out of jail myself. Put her in the pocket, leave before she suffocates, pull her out again. We've got access to one of the best hospitals in the Solar System; I'm sure she'd survive the brief exposure. Would that help, though? If she's not going to tell me what she was up to last night, will she be forthcoming about anything else?

The pocket is handy, but it's not immediately useful in every situation. And it's not the only trick I've got up my sleeve.

Yodey hasn't called by the time we reach the USMS outpost. I tell Zoo I need to go in and conduct some business.

"Just keep the meter running," I say.

"What now?" He gives me a confused look.

"Stay here. I'll be right back. And then I might want to go somewhere else," I say. "By the way, how much to hire you indefinitely?" It might be useful to have a surface vehicle at my disposal, if the tube is going to be offline for a while. The agency might not be able to spare any resources for me now that I'm technically done with my mission. Especially if Paul is too busy to yell at people on my behalf.

Zoo chuckles. "You can't afford me."

I fish my wallet out of my jacket, find the largest bill in there, and hand it to him. "Just don't leave until I get back."

"Okay. I'll stay." He gives me a firm stare. "But we talk pricing later."

"Fine."

Jessica doesn't look happy to see me when the clerk brings her into the meeting room. She glares at me from across the table until the clerk closes the door, giving us some privacy.

"What the hell are you still doing here?" she asks. "You need to get out of here."

"Borders are closed," I say. The news announced it just before we arrived at the outpost. "We're all stuck here until the authorities sort out this terrorist attack."

She frowns at me. "What terrorist attack?"

I give her a quick run-down.

"You should have left when you had the chance," Jessica grumbles.

"Well, that's water under the bridge now." I turn on the biomedical scanners in my left eye. "Who were you and Jeremiah Burgess meeting with last night?"

Jessica glares at me. "That's not your concern."

"You're accused of murder," I say, scrutinizing the heat map of her face. "If this other woman can exonerate you—"

"Who said it was a woman?"

"There were witnesses." I give her a hard stare. "You may have been able to get the security footage erased, but people still talk."

Jessica shakes her head. "Leave it, Kangaroo."

She didn't deny erasing the vid. Interesting. "Tell me what happened."

"No."

"Is there any possibility that it's connected to these terror attacks?"

Jessica scowls. "No."

"Are you sure about that? Jeremiah Burgess worked for municipal power. The terrorists hit three solar power plants—the exact locations that would disable the tube transit system. How did they know which facilities to target? And why do they want to prevent people from traveling across nearside?"

"Those are all excellent questions," Jessica says, "and you should be out there tracking down the answers instead of in here wasting time with me."

"What are you not telling me?"

"Whatever it is," she says, "we can't discuss it here. You have a job to do. I'll be fine. The marshals can only hold me for forty-eight hours, and this isn't a military prison with enhanced interrogation. I can do a couple of nights in a cell. You and Oliver are going to make sure the marshals don't come up with any actual evidence that can—are you even listening?"

I'm not. She said *military prison*. That's ringing a bell in my head. "The marshals can't hold you."

"Not for more than forty-eight hours. It's called habeas corpus. I thought you had Oliver feeding you legal information—"

"No," I say, slapping the table. "They can't hold you at all, *Lieutenant Commander.*"

CHAPTER FIFTEEN

The Moon—nearside—Tycho Crater
5 minutes after my brilliant epiphany

I can't get Paul on the phone after the marshals take Jessica back to her cell, so I have to spend precious minutes in the restroom explaining to Oliver what needs to happen next.

"Judge advocate general," I repeat. I can't believe he doesn't know what JAG stands for. "There should be an office at Copernicus Base. I need you to call them."

"And say what?" Oliver asks.

"I don't know what the precise language is," I say, "but Jessica's in the OSS reserves, isn't she? That's what she said before we left Earth."

"Retired Reserve, I believe," Oliver says.

"Whatever. She's still, what do you call it, service connected?"

"Sure."

"So the UCMJ applies to her."

"What's that, then?"

I really can't believe this. "Uniform Code of Military Justice. Do we have a bad connection here? This is all basic military stuff."

"I was never in the military," Oliver says.

"Just go look it up, okay?" I lower my voice as another person walks into the restroom. "Then get Copernicus to send someone here to the marshals outpost and get her out. And pick me up too."

"That might be a bit tricky," Oliver says. "What with the terrorism and all."

"I'm sure you'll figure it out, EQ. Call me back." I hang up just as the new person, a burly middle-aged man in a business suit, gives me a dirty look while walking up to a urinal.

"You got phone service?" he asks.

"In and out," I say.

Burlyman grunts and shakes his head. "Fuckin' terrorists ruin everything."

"No argument there. Excuse me."

I leave just as he spits into the urinal, and my shoulder-phone rings again. I bounce out into the lobby, which is filled with muttering people waiting for the police to talk to them, before answering.

"Edwin?" It's Breyella Wilgus. "Where are you? Are you and Gladys okay?"

"I'm at the U.S. marshals outpost," I say. "I'm fine. I don't know where Gladys is."

"She's not with you?"

"She didn't go back to Silver Circle?"

"No," Breyella says. "And she's not answering her phone. I know service is spotty right now, but we're a little concerned. You're the last person we know she was with, so—"

"I left her at Barclays," I say, and give the address for the bank. "Maybe she's still there. I don't know."

"She wasn't behaving strangely, was she?"

"Does she do that?" I wasn't feeling bad about ditching a black market information dealer, but abandoning a senile elder during a terror crisis would make me feel much worse.

"No, I just—" Breyella sighs. "Sometimes I worry about our residents."

"Gladys seemed fine," I say. "Does her wheelchair have any sort of tracking device in it?"

"Why would it have a tracking device?"

"I don't know." Too bad I didn't think to plant one earlier. I didn't expect we would need to keep tabs on her.

"Okay. I'll call the bank," Breyella says. "If you hear from Gladys, would you please let me know?"

"Of course."

She thanks me and hangs up. I take a moment to breathe and look around the lobby. I don't know what all these people are doing here, but nobody looks very happy. That's not surprising; people generally don't go to a U.S. Marshal Service outpost for happy reasons.

Sometimes I wish I could do more to help. But that's not my job.

My shoulder-phone rings again, and I recognize the number this time.

"Yodey," I say after the call connects. "Are you here?"

"Near," he says. "Tell Zoo, deliver you to Planned Parenthood in Sabine Crater."

Sabine Crater is near the Apollo 11 landing site—where the big anniversary party will happen—and it takes me a little longer to fight through the crowds underground, after I get through the topside airlock.

The Planned Parenthood free clinic is one of the less popular venues here. It's dark inside, and a large electronic sign on the front window reads CLOSED FOR THE HOLIDAY—OPEN AGAIN AT 0700 UTC ON JULY 22ND. Smaller displays surrounding the sign advertise different services the organization provides: health exams, contraception, medical testing, and information.

One of the displays mentions radiation hazards, and I think of Breyella. Maybe I can bring back a brochure for her to share with—

The front door buzzes and clicks, then swings open. Yodey pokes his head out.

"In here." He waves me inside.

I follow him into the clinic, noticing that the front windows appear transparent from this side. Probably some kind of tunable plexi, so the clinic workers inside can see trouble coming and the clients inside have some privacy from gawkers. "Nice place."

Yodey turns and gestures us into the back of the clinic. "I got connections."

"How is your mother, by the way?" Mrs. Hughes is on the board of directors for Lunar Planned Parenthood.

Yodey stops in the middle of opening up one of the exam rooms and turning on the lights. "So you did some checking up on me. Respect. I looked you up too, Edwin. You pretty young to be a big-shot crime lawyer."

"Who says I'm a big shot?" I'm flattered, but also nervous that I'll actually have to live up to this reputation.

"Double docs don't pony up retainer fees for less than the best," Yodey says. "So you must be pretty slick, seeing what mi madre says good about your amazing client, Jessica Chu."

Hope you're ready to make me look good, I text to Oliver. "I don't like to brag." I also don't like talking about something I haven't made up yet. "So. What do you have for me?"

"Let's talk pricing first," Yodey says. "Guessing you'll pay cash?"

"Yeah. I don't need a receipt."

Yodey chuckles. "I won't tell. So, two thousand for the data—"

"Two *thousand*?" Oliver shouts in my ear. I wince, and Yodey notices.

"Wasn't easy to get," Yodey says. "Plus I made it a rush order, since your doc's in jail."

"No, no, that's fine," I say, turning down the volume for my comms. "What about for the transportation?"

Yodey shrugs. "Say five hundred for the pickup. Beyond that, I'm not the boss of Zoo. You want shuttle service, negotiate with him."

"Fine." I should probably be haggling more. "I might not have access to quite that much cash right now. How about twenty-one hundred for everything?"

"Twenty-four," Yodey says without blinking.

"Twenty-two."

His expression is unreadable. In my ear, Oliver says, "Don't say anything more until he does." I twitch my fingers and text back: **I'm not an idiot.**

After a few seconds, Yodey says, "Twenty-three-five, low as I can go. Expenses and such."

I pretend to think about it for a moment. I've actually got several thousand in cash stowed in the pocket for emergencies, but I don't want this kid to think I'll roll over so easily all the time. Especially if I need to buy something else from him later.

"I can live with that," I say. "May I use the restroom?"

Yodey points me toward the hallway. I go inside, open the pocket to retrieve the cash—plus a few more hundred-dollar-bills for Zoo—and then return to where Yodey is sitting in front of a desktop computer.

"Here." I hand him a folded stack of bills.

He flips through the cash. "This only half."

"I want to see the data first."

"Fair enough."

Yodey turns to the computer, wakes it up, and inserts a small memory card. The screen lights up with a file listing, reminding me of the data I bought from Gladys. I hope our analysts can make sense of that soon, and find something actionable in there.

Some of these file listings resolve into thumbnail images, and some of those look like different "street" levels in the Terraces. "You were able to recover the security footage?" I ask.

"Official cams not the only eyes on the street," Yodey says. "I asked around. Found some phone vids and stray selfies with your mystery woman in the bee-gee. Might be some noise in there—my supplier didn't check for anything beyond location coordinates. Might be some cams pointed the wrong way, showing irrelevant scenes. Trust you to keep all this on the down-low, yeah?"

"Yeah," I say. "Seeing as how I'd probably get disbarred for even accepting this information. Thanks."

"Why you do this, anyway?" Yodey asks. "You trying to get Doc Chu off the hook, this no way to do it."

"My client isn't cooperating," I say. "But I'm legally required to do whatever I can to mount a compelling defense."

"You the man," Yodey says, shrugging. He leans back and holds out one hand, palm up. "We good?"

I pull the rest of the cash from my jacket and hand it to him. "Yeah, we're good."

He pockets the cash without counting it—I suppose that's a sign of respect—and stands. "I give you a few minutes to scan, then we gotta bounce. You can check deets later. Just make sure you got all you need."

"Thanks."

I wait until Yodey walks out to the waiting room and starts talking on his phone, then lean forward so Oliver can get a better look at the computer files through my eye.

EQ, what am I seeing here? I text to him.

Oliver gives me instructions for unpacking and sorting through the vid files. The first few are not useful—some kids recording vid journals of themselves, talking into the camera from inside closed rooms. No views of the street outside, even if they're facing the right way. Another vid appears to be one side of a phone call between a man and his girlfriend. He's trying to talk her into sending him some naked pictures of herself. I wonder how Yodey got access to a private phone call and whether he and his associates do this all the time. I'm really glad all my comms are end-to-end encrypted with the agency's strongest algorithms.

The next vid shows me what I'm looking for. But it's not what I want to see.

"Son of a bitch," I say out loud. "What the *fuck*! Are you fucking *kidding* me!"

Oliver says in my ear, "That looks like—"

"It sure as fuck does!" I stand up, toppling the chair. "Mother*fucker*!"

I yank the memory card out of the computer and leave the clinic before Yodey can stop me. I don't actually care about anything right now except calling Paul and having a one-on-one with him.

Zoo takes me back to the Hotel Tranquility and agrees to wait for another five hundred dollars. I go up to my room, slam the door closed, and pace around for I don't know how long in a vain effort to calm down. Then I pull one of Oliver's pesticide disks out of the pocket and stick it on a wall. I've already turned off my comms feed back to him. Now I open a new channel, direct to Paul's office.

He answers in a few seconds, full vid and audio. "Kangaroo."

"Alisa Garro is on the Moon," I say. "Did you know about this?"

He hesitates, and it's not because of the transmission delay or because he doesn't remember who she is. Paul was the one who wanted her convicted on five counts of treason. I see his upper lip twitch before he answers. "No. I did not know about this."

I smack my palm against the wall. It hurts, but that means I'm not dreaming. *Goddammit.* "Don't lie to me. Why is she on the Moon?"

"I promise you, I do not know," Paul says. "How is this relevant to your current assignment?"

"What the fuck *is* my current assignment, Lasher?" I say. "You send me to the Moon, but apparently Surgical has other orders, because she wanders off without me, meets with Alisa fucking Garro and some other guy, and this morning the other guy winds up dead, and I find out all surveillance vids from the meeting were erased, and I need to go to the fucking black market to get a picture of—"

"Slow down," Paul says, frowning and leaning forward. "Who gave Surgical other orders?"

I gape at him. "You didn't give her a secondary objective?"

"No, I didn't," Paul says. "And what is this about erasing data?"

"Don't you bullshit me," I say. "This is a secure channel. You tell me the goddamn truth here."

"I promise you, Kangaroo, I am currently as confused as you are."

This is worse than I thought. "EQ looked into the hack. There was an agency authorization order. Jessica requested it, but somebody at C-level or above had to sign off."

"Tell me the details," Paul says.

I give him the relevant names, dates, and times. "EQ saw the data through my comms link. He can verify it. But if this was faked, then someone knows way too much about us. And if it wasn't—"

"I'll get to the bottom of it," Paul says. I'm sure he will. But I want more than just information.

"I want to talk to Alisa Garro," I say.

Paul hesitates for the briefest of moments, barely long enough for me to notice. "I don't think that's a good idea, Kangaroo. Let me handle this."

"I have transport that can get me to Copernicus Base," I say. "I have an operational responsibility to investigate and resolve anything that may interfere with successful completion of my mission objectives. And given the fact that there's just been a multi-site, highly coordinated terrorist attack, I'm pretty sure the Lunar authorities will agree, once I identify myself as an OSS officer, that I have a blank check to call out some goddamn spacemen and start digging!"

I give Paul a moment to think about it. Neither of us blinks.

"I'll get you a contact," he says finally. "Give me thirty minutes."

"You have fifteen."

"Thirty minutes," Paul repeats.

He disconnects the call before I can say anything even dumber. In hindsight, it probably wasn't a great move to give my boss an ultimatum. Especially since I do not have the slightest idea of what's going on anymore. Why did Jessica meet with Alisa Garro? And how is Alisa Garro on the Moon and not rotting away in prison?

CHAPTER SIXTEEN

Earth—United States—Washington, D.C.
Here's what happened 9 years ago

The last time I saw Alisa Garro, she almost killed me. On purpose.

When I first joined the agency, my medical care was an immediate priority. Science Division wanted to establish a baseline for studying me, and Paul wanted to make sure my ability wasn't just a temporary aberration, or some weird phenomenon caused by a brain tumor or something else that was going to kill me. He wanted the best physician he could find to take care of me and tell him how long he could expect to use me. He's all heart.

That physician was not Jessica Chu. No, she was a replacement for my original Surgical officer: Alisa Garro. Because she turned out to be an evil witch.

Okay, that might be a slight exaggeration. But only a slight one.

Alisa Garro was—and still is, judging by the vids Yodey found—a very attractive woman. Natural blond hair, sparkling green eyes, daily-workout body. I'll admit, when I met her for the first time, my teenage body got a little excited. Her voice made it even worse—distinctly feminine, with the barest edge of huskiness that she could turn up when she wanted to work you over. She knew what she had going on, and she knew how to use it. Brains and beauty are a powerful combination in this business.

She was good at her job. She presented a friendly, caring, almost maternally nurturing front. She asked all the right questions. With those brilliant emerald eyes, it felt like she was staring into my soul. At first, I found it comforting—she knew exactly how I was feeling, she knew how to fix whatever the problem was, I could trust her when she touched me.

Later, though, once I realized it was all an act, it became deeply disturbing. Because then it felt like I couldn't hide anything from her. I felt naked whenever I was in a room with her, and not in a good way.

Paul Tarkington may be a shameless manipulator, but he doesn't pretend to be nice about it. Alisa Garro, on the other hand, wheedled and cajoled and seduced to get what she wanted. She could convince you that you wanted to *give* her what she wanted. It was insidious. And once I saw through her act and became impervious to her charms, it turned my stomach to see how she continued to use it on other people, especially men, and how they kept falling for it.

It's sad but true: you can lead a male pretty much anywhere by his penis.

The day she betrayed me and shattered my trust irrevocably, I call "Surprise Day." First, Science Division surprised me by doing unexpected things in all their tests that morning—they figured that they'd never get the opportunity to do it again, so they packed all their pranks into a single session.

This was before the war with Mars, before the agency officially put me in the field, but they were talking about it. I think they were stringing Paul along, but I wasn't privy to the conversations they were having at that level. What I do know is that the agency insisted that Science Division run battery after battery of tests on me, making me push the pocket to its limits, to see exactly how useful it could be—how big I could make the portal, how long I could hold it open, what happened if I were knocked unconscious while the portal was open, all kinds of fun stuff like that.

Anyway, after the third unexpected projectile flying at my head while I tried to open a portal, I called bullshit on their shenanigans and left the lab ahead of schedule. Then I got an even bigger surprise when I returned to the office.

Alisa wasn't in the exam room when I returned, sporting some nasty bruises and wanting something to help relieve the pain. She must have been gone for only a minute. Her workstation was unlocked, and I couldn't resist peeking at my file. After all, don't I have a right to my own medical records?

I learned that she was dosing me before sending me off to each of my sessions at Science Division. According to her notes, she wanted to see how various brain-altering chemicals might affect my ability to use the pocket, and she'd been slipping me progressively stronger neurotoxins the whole time.

After overcoming my initial shock, I copied all the files and sent them to Paul. When Alisa returned, I confronted her. She denied it, of course, and tried to talk me down. When that didn't work, she tried to seduce me. That was insulting. Yeah, sure, I was a horny teenager and she was a stone cold fox, but did she really think I'd fall for that after an entire day of increasingly unpleasant surprises?

Also, I was starting to feel kind of sick.

I stormed out of the office before she could try anything else. Then I collapsed in a Metrorail station on my way home and wound up unconscious in a civilian hospital. It was hours before Paul retrieved me, and nobody was happy at that point.

I know Alisa Garro didn't actually want to kill me. But I don't think she would have cared much if she had. I was just another curiosity to her. Dead Kangaroo? Oops, my bad, let's find another unsuspecting subject to experiment on.

I couldn't believe it when she wasn't court-martialed, or even officially reprimanded. I mean, I know we do a lot of bad stuff in secret here at the agency, but we still have some measure of government supervision. The secretary of state still jumps down Paul's throat every time I introduce some "variation" into one of my missions. Alisa Garro must have had powerful friends—or influential people she could blackmail—in very high places to get away as clean as she did.

They wouldn't tell me where she had been reassigned. I suspected that Paul knew, but he wasn't at liberty to say. He always deflected whenever I asked about her. He told me that she had been exiled from the United States, and that he would make sure she never bothered me again.

I trusted him. I still trust him to keep her the hell away from me. But now I want to see her. I want to know why Jessica wanted to see her. I want to know what the fuck she's doing on the Moon.

Paul calls back forty seconds before the half-hour deadline. No free pizza for me. But I do have plenty of time while waiting to review all the vid that Yodey's sources recovered from Jessica's meeting with Alisa Garro.

I can't hear their conversation on any of the vids, and the resolution is low enough that there's no chance of reading anyone's lips. What I do see, after reconstructing all the footage, is Alisa arriving at the café first and sitting by herself for a while. Then Jeremiah Burgess shows up and greets her. While they're talking, Jessica walks up to the table.

Alisa stands up as soon as she sees Jessica. They argue for a while, and Burgess works pretty hard to get them to calm down and sit. The conversation remains relatively calm until Jessica pulls out a necklace—the one now sitting in the U.S. marshals' evidence room—and pushes it across the table to Alisa, who picks it up and immediately throws it on the ground.

Then it's more standing, gesturing angrily at each other, and finally walking away from the table in opposite directions. Jeremiah Burgess doesn't seem overly concerned at this point. He doesn't try to follow either Jessica or Alisa; he just picks up the necklace and sits and finishes his drink. Maybe he thought he could pawn the necklace later.

Based on the timestamps in these vids and when Jessica's transponder came back into range at the hotel, she had to come straight back by tube after leaving the café. Jeremiah Burgess stayed in the Terraces for a while, got drunk, and left about half an hour before he was killed by a robot. Whoever paid him for his power plant insider information must have wanted to make sure he wouldn't be around to talk about that transaction.

I can't tell where Alisa Garro went after she left the café. But Paul's going to help me with that.

"I hope you appreciate this, Kangaroo," he says. "I just cashed in a big favor at the White House."

"And?"

"I was able to confirm that Alisa Garro is on the Moon. Special assignment for State."

"What's the assignment?"

"I wasn't able to find out."

"You're director of operations for Outback." There can't be more than a dozen people in the whole State Department who rank higher than Paul. "What do you mean, you couldn't find out?"

"Perhaps I wasn't clear. When I say 'State,'" Paul says, "I mean the *secretary* of state."

I blink. "What?"

"Garro is on special assignment, personally allocated, reporting directly to the secretary of state." Paul doesn't look happy about this. "I wasn't in the loop."

"But that—" I can't wrap my head around this. Paul reports directly to the secretary. There are only eight directors at his level in the agency. "Is that even allowed?" There can't be more than a handful of people in the entire Solar System who have higher security clearances than Paul. If he's not authorized to know about this . . . "State's not supposed to run operations. That's why the agency exists, right? So the secretary's hands don't get dirty."

"State has broad authority to act in Non-Territorial matters," Paul says with a sneer. "I'm not going to speculate about motives yet. I was able to isolate the code-tag. It's a project named GENESIS."

"That doesn't tell me anything."

"It tells you what to look for," Paul snaps. "And it's leverage you can offer when you tell Gryphon that State went behind her back to home a full-black secret project at Science Division's Facility One."

I'm learning all sorts of interesting things today. "Garro's in *the crater*?"

"That's what my sources tell me."

"And you want me to take this over the fence? To D.Int?"

"You said Gryphon wants to be friends," Paul says. "What's more friendly than a common enemy?"

I'm not sure I like where this conversation is headed. "Just to be clear, do you think—"

"No. This is politics, not security." He gives me a sour look. "But I'd very much like to know what State felt it was necessary to hide from literally everyone else in the agency."

"Yeah," I say. "Me too."

"I want you to go to SDF1 and find out exactly what Alisa Garro is doing with Project Genesis," Paul says. "I understand Oliver's already arranged military transport for you."

It's a good thing I'm not drinking anything, otherwise I would totally have done a spit take just now. "He told you?"

"Oliver works for me," Paul says. "Good idea, by the way, asking JAG Corps to retrieve Surgical. Make sure you take her with you when you visit SDF1."

"Is there some reason I wouldn't?"

"She may be reluctant to go."

"Why would that be?" I'd like to know why Jessica and Alisa seemed to be at each other's throats last night.

Paul hesitates. "It's not my secret to tell."

Sometimes I hate this job.

CHAPTER SEVENTEEN

The Moon—nearside—Hotel Tranquility
30 minutes before I check out

The Moon is a pretty big place. It takes a few days to drive a typical rover across the entire surface of one hemisphere, either nearside or farside. So it was easy for the first colonists and companies establishing bases here to find open spaces far enough apart from each other to allow for plenty of potential future expansion. The tube transit system came later.

The thing about the surface of nearside is, anyone on Earth can see you out there on most any given day. A kid with a decent telescope can go out at night, point his lens skyward, and count the number of vehicles or people moving around in any outside area.

The agency prefers to start its digs on farside, where in theory fewer prying eyes are watching at any given time, and that's why there's a huge network of poorly maintained construction tunnels under the Lunar surface that are occasionally used to hollow out a new secret underground facility. Of course, no one wants to have to go very far in a dark underground tunnel every time they want to get in or out of one of these bases. So the agency looks for places where it can create out-of-the-way access points. They don't have to be totally secret and completely hidden, but they do need to be not obvious to the casual observer.

Hence the Crater of Eternal Darkness.

Because the Moon is tidally locked, with one hemisphere always facing Earth, there is a "twilight zone" around its circumference where, depending on the exact geography, there can be areas of "eternal light" or "eternal darkness." The former tend to be high mountain peaks, and the latter

149

tend to be crater floors. All of these are at either the north or south pole. In the north, the rim of Peary Crater is home to an entire range of solar power plants; same for the Malapert Mountain region in the south. And right at the south pole, there's Shackleton Crater, whose rim is not ideal for power generation, but whose floor is perfect for spacecraft to approach from farside and land in secret.

Underneath Shackleton Crater is Science Division's Facility One, the agency's first off-world base for research and development. The agency has since established newer and fancier bases on the Moon and elsewhere, but even though it has older equipment and somewhat outdated infrastructure, there is still a certain mystique associated with SDF1. Most of the actual research and experiments have moved to sites with better containment or quarantine failsafes. SDF1 is now only used for administrative purposes.

And, apparently, for hiding secret projects with exiled personnel like Alisa Garro.

The phone in my hotel room rings while I'm packing up Jessica's and my things and putting them into the pocket.

"Mr. McDrona," the hotel front desk clerk says, "there's a Lieutenant Hong in the lobby to meet you. He says he's from Copernicus Base?"

"Great. Thank you. I'll be right down," I reply.

I finish packing, then run upstairs to the topside garage, pay Zoo the rest of what I owe, and tell him to go home. Then I head to the lobby, where a clean-cut OSS officer is standing with his hands folded in front of him.

"Lieutenant Hong?" I say. "I'm Edwin McDrona."

We shake hands, and I blink my left eye into verification mode. The scanners check the ID chips embedded in his dog tags and subdermal transponder in his wrist. Clean match.

"Are you ready to go, Commander?" Hong asks. Sometimes it's very useful to have a high-ranking military cover identity. "I have transportation waiting. And your colleague is with us."

"Yes, thank you, Lieutenant. Lead the way."

The tubes still aren't running, but Hong walks me out to the transit hub next to the hotel and through a door marked AUTHORIZED PERSON-

NEL ONLY. We ride an elevator up to a hangar where a small spacecraft is parked.

"How long will it take us to get to the south pole?" I ask as Hong leads me toward the shuttle.

"Just a couple of hours," he says.

"And how's Dr.—I mean, Lieutenant Commander Chu—doing?"

Hong gives me a look. "I think she's been better."

"This is a bad idea," Jessica says when I sit down next to her in the shuttle.

"Liftoff in thirty seconds," Hong says, going forward into the cockpit.

"You know what else is a bad idea?" I say to Jessica while buckling myself in. "Not telling me that you were meeting with Alisa Garro."

Jessica's eyes widen for the briefest of moments, then settle back into her normal scowl. "We can't talk about this here."

"Oh. So you know that she's working on some ultra-top-secret project called Genesis?"

"What the hell are you talking about?"

Now I'm really confused. "That's not why you were meeting with her?"

Jessica shakes her head. "It was a personal matter."

"I don't believe you." I fold my arms. "You don't have a personal life."

The scowl intensifies. "You don't know my life."

"Lifting off now," Hong says over the intercom.

"Thank you, Lieutenant," I call into the cockpit.

Jessica and I continue our staring contest as the shuttle leaves the hangar and rises into the black sky. Gray landscape blurs past as we speed toward the south pole.

"Tell me why you met Alisa Garro," I say.

"No," Jessica says.

"Tell me who killed Jeremiah Burgess."

"I don't know that."

"Why did you try to give a crucifix to Alisa Garro?"

Her scowl deepens. "It's a personal matter."

"This trip is going to take a couple of hours," I say. "So we can talk about this, or—"

"Did we get what we needed from Clementine?" she asks.

And we're back. All-Business. "I sent the data to Oliver for analysis."

"It will be more useful for us to talk about our mission," Jessica says, enunciating the last two words, "instead of my personal life."

"Fine. I'll call EQ and we can have a nice little conference here. Is that what you want?"

"For a start."

I blink up my shoulder-phone and call Oliver. He doesn't answer. I try Paul. No answer. "They're not picking up. But I'm not seeing any internal alerts." I'd be able to tell if something were wrong with the agency's secure communications network. "You don't think—"

"Somebody just blew up the Moon," Jessica says. "I'm sure it's all hands on deck working that crisis. Show me the data we got from Clementine."

While I set up a link from my shoulder-phone to one of the shuttle's display screens, I tell her what I've already found in the database. "This is a huge breakthrough, right? If we can trace some of these other robots directly to Sakraida—"

"He was director of intelligence," Jessica says while manipulating the display on the seat back in front of her. "He's not an idiot. He won't tap the same resource twice. But he and his pals were planning their breakaway stunt for months. They knew they'd need robots to survive in the belt. We should look for purchases by other Intel shell companies, and private corporations which might have been controlled by Sakraida or his associates."

"Um, what do you mean 'we,' kemo sabe?" I point at the screen, which she's turned into a dense jumble of alphanumeric strings. "Can you actually read that mess?"

Jessica gives me an irritated look. "This 'mess' is the database. I thought you looked at this already."

I realize she's displaying the actual database code instead of filtering it through a user interface. I forgot that Jessica actually prefers looking at raw data feeds. She says it's easier for her to see patterns and spot anomalies that way. "I looked at it in a human-readable format. You know, because I'm a human?"

"I find this more efficient."

"Okay, well, you have fun with that. I'm going to get a snack. You want a snack?"

"No."

I go to the back of the shuttle and dig through supply lockers looking for rations that appear halfway edible. At some point, I hear gentle snoring and look over to see that Jessica has dozed off in her seat. Apparently robot data isn't actually that interesting.

I sit down across the aisle from Jessica, chew on a so-called candy bar, and watch the Moon slide past beneath us. Just for laughs, I try scanning through her raw database view myself. I fall asleep before I finish eating the candy bar.

CHAPTER EIGHTEEN

The Moon—South Pole—Shackleton Crater
10 minutes before landing

Jessica wakes up after I do, just as the shuttle descends below the rim of Shackleton Crater.

"Copernicus sure looks different in the dark," she mutters, rubbing her eyes.

Right. She thinks we're at the OSS base, because JAG took custody of her from the U.S. marshals. I never told her that we were actually going to SDF1, and she never asked.

I decide not to tell her yet. It'll be more fun to surprise her when we get inside.

"Last chance," I say. "You want to tell me about Alisa Garro now? While we still have some privacy? Or do you want to wait until I find someone who can order you to talk?"

"I'm already under arrest," Jessica says. "I'll wait for my lawyer. My *actual* lawyer."

"Suit yourself."

The shuttle touches down on the pitch-black floor of the crater, then dims its own running lights and rolls forward into a hidden hangar bay. An airlock tunnel extends toward us and mates with the side of the shuttle. Air hisses into the tunnel, and Hong cycles open the door and leads us into the base.

The person who greets us on the other side of the airlock is a tall woman with skin the color of wet sand and eyes like obsidian. She's not wearing a uniform, but the way she carries herself implies that she's had military training.

"Kangaroo, I presume," she says, staring at me.

"That's me."

She turns to Jessica. "And Dr. Chu?"

Jessica nods. "Happy to be here."

"Welcome to Science Division, Facility One. I'm Director Khan."

"Wait," Jessica says. "What?" She looks at me. "I thought we were going to Copernicus!"

"Surprise," I say, smiling.

Jessica looks like she wants to murder me. "I'm not going in there."

"You don't want to say hello to your old friend Alisa Garro?" I ask. "You can continue the conversation you were having last night."

"I'm sorry," Khan says. "Is there a problem here?"

"More than one," Jessica says. "I'm staying in the shuttle."

"You can't stay in the shuttle, Doctor," Khan sighs. "This is a full-black secure facility. We can't have heat signatures lingering on the hangar deck." It's pretty unlikely that anybody would be able to sense one single human's body heat through the crater doors, but agency regulations are very clear about taking no unnecessary risks when it comes to hiding personnel.

"Fine," Jessica says. She turns to Hong. "Then we're leaving."

Hong points at me. "Sorry, ma'am. I was ordered not to leave the commander's side."

Jessica glares at him. "You can call me *sir*. And who gave you that order?"

Hong gives her a sheepish look. "My orders came directly from Lasher, sir."

Jessica actually growls. "I should have stayed with the marshals."

"We can discuss this inside, people," Khan says. "Kangaroo. Lasher said you want to meet with Dr. Jill."

I frown at her. "I'm here to see Alisa Garro."

"My apologies," Khan says. "Same person. 'Dr. Jill' is her code name. If you'll follow me, please." She turns and leads us into the facility.

"Why is her code name 'Dr. Jill'?" I ask.

"No idea."

"Why does she even need a code name?"

"Look," Khan says, "I just work here."

At Jessica's request, Khan points her toward the cafeteria. I don't know exactly how big this facility is, nor are there helpful floor plans or emergency escape route diagrams posted around SDF1. One of the issues with secret bases: you don't get many inspectors coming through looking for building safety code violations.

Khan walks Hong and me down a curved corridor to an intersection and then in toward what I'm pretty sure is the center of the place—given the way things are shaped and placed, it appears that SDF1 is a circular setup, with the main corridors dividing it into four quadrants and then curving across each of those four wedges to make concentric circles. I blink my eye to do an omnipedia lookup and find a basic floor plan for SDF1—either it's not that classified, or I have high enough security clearance to see the layout of the place. Nothing is labeled, but I can at least tell where we are and where we're going.

"You're in luck. She's out of the cave right now," Khan says.

"The cave?" I ask.

"Her project labs are restricted access," Khan says. "But one of our maintenance crew had an accident, and Doc's the only surgeon within a hundred kilometers. We managed to coax her out to perform an emergency procedure."

She leads me into the third concentric-circle corridor out from the round command center at the middle of the facility, past a variety of service robots and scientists, then about halfway down the arc until we get to a door labeled EXAM FOUR. The door slides open as Khan approaches, and Hong waits outside while I follow Khan inside.

We're in a medium-sized room with a medical examination bed in the center, surrounded by counters and cabinets along the walls. A burly man in a jumpsuit is sitting on the bed, staring at one hand while he flexes the index finger. There's a bulbous bandage wrapped around the second knuckle.

A woman stands against the far wall opposite us, working at a computer console. Her shoulder-length blond hair is pinned back against her skull. She's wearing a white lab coat. She mutters to herself as she works, apparently oblivious to Khan and me entering the room, and the motions of her arms against the console are short, sharp, and precise.

Just seeing her makes me angry.

"I can move it, but it still feels numb," the man says, squeezing together the tips of his thumb and index finger. "Is that the anesthetic?"

"Don't put too much strain on it. The nerves will take a couple of months to grow back," says the woman with her back to us, in a familiar voice that makes my blood boil. "The bio-wrap will augment the healing process. It's waterproof, but don't submerge it. And use your other hand as much as you can."

"When should I come back for a checkup?" the man asks.

"You don't," the woman says. She points to the nurse-bot in a charging slot in the corner of the room. "Any nurse-bot in the crater can do a follow-up."

The man gives the nurse-bot a wary glance. "I didn't know they were programmed to do surgeries."

The woman sighs. "You just need it to change the bandage and make sure your finger's not getting infected. That's it. Simple. Any other questions?"

"I guess not." The man looks over at Khan and me. "You need the room, Director?"

The woman stiffens, then turns to glare at us.

It's definitely Alisa Garro. She looks older now, but not much. Has she been on the Moon this whole time, since Paul got her kicked off Team Kangaroo? The low gravity might have contributed to her current youthful appearance.

"Yes, thank you, Mr. Amendolara," Khan says. "Best wishes for a quick recovery."

"Thanks, Director. Thanks, Doc."

The man hops off the bed and leaves the room, still fascinated with flexing his finger. Khan closes the door behind him.

Alisa Garro has picked up a tablet and is making some notes on it. She's half turned toward us, mostly looking at the computer. "Who's this, now?"

Of course. She doesn't recognize me. She hasn't seen me in nearly a decade, and I've had three—no, *four* cosmetic surgeries since the last time we were in the same room.

I could just tell her who I am. But it'll be more fun to show her.

I gauge the distance to the other side of the room and open the pocket right next to her tablet, without the barrier. She's not expecting it, of course, and the tablet slips out of her hands and into the black disk floating in midair. I close the portal, and she looks up at me with an astonished and horrified expression on her face. *Mission accomplished.*

Her mouth remains pressed into a thin horizontal line. Her eyes return to their normal appearance, narrowed slits that make it look like she's always a little bit suspicious of you, and she folds her arms across her chest.

"Kangaroo," she says. "It's been a while."

I don't feel like making small talk. "What's Project Genesis?"

Alisa blinks before answering, and I see the barest hint of uncertainty flicker across her face. "I can't tell you that. I'm sorry—"

"That's unlikely," I can't resist saying.

"My hands are tied," she snaps, her eyes flashing. That's new.

Nine years ago, even when I was screaming my head off at her, even when Paul got her exiled from Earth, she was always calm and controlled. I hated how she always made it feel like she knew exactly what she was doing, and it was the rest of us who were floundering in uncertainty. This is the first time I've seen even a hint of uncontrolled emotion from her.

"This is above your pay grade," Alisa continues.

"Yeah, I know," I say. "You report directly to the secretary of state."

"We cannot talk about this," Alisa says through clenched teeth. "I have nothing more to say."

"Okay, Kangaroo," Khan says, stepping between us. "I need you to brief me on your situation. You can continue your conversation with Dr. Jill later."

"This conversation is over," Alisa says. She looks at her computer, then glares at me. "I need my tablet back."

I shrug. "What's the magic word?"

Her glare turns into a scowl. *"Antidote."*

That's a low blow. I'm almost tempted to not return the tablet.

"Kangaroo," Khan says. "If you're going to keep that tablet, I'm going to need you to submit some paperwork." She certainly knows how to wield the power of bureaucracy.

"Fine." I open the pocket again, but closer to myself this time, rotated and with the barrier. The tablet falls out through the glowing white disk, and I catch it and close the portal.

I make a show of looking over the medical charts before tossing the tablet forward onto the exam bed with a careless flip of my wrist. I have no idea what the display says. I just wanted to annoy Alisa Garro.

Khan turns to face Alisa. "Kangaroo is our guest, Doc. Let's do our best to make him feel welcome."

"He's *not* welcome." I can't see Khan's face, but Alisa's is priceless. "And I'm going to be busy for a while."

"I'll be here for a while," I say. "Borders are closed. Nobody's going anywhere."

"Okay," Khan says, waving me toward the door. "Let's allow the doctor to finish up in here, Kangaroo."

I take a deep breath and give Alisa one final glare. I point a finger at her before I turn around. "We're not finished."

I only have a vague recollection of being guided to Khan's office, in another quadrant and a different concentric circle of the facility. I wonder if there are nine concentric circles here. Like the nine circles of Hell in Dante's Inferno. I didn't count the lines on the diagram I found earlier in the agency omnipedia. But it sure feels like I'm being punished for something.

As soon as Khan closes the door to her office behind us—leaving Hong outside again—I ask: "What do you know about Project Genesis?"

Khan sits down behind her desk before answering. "Not much more than you do."

"Aren't you the commanding officer around here?"

"I am the administrative director of an outdated research facility," Khan says. "All I know is, State turned an entire wing over to Garro for her project. She's got two assistants on the access control list, but no one else is allowed into that area. They receive supply shipments from Earth in shielded containers. I don't even see the cargo manifests. Whatever Genesis is, they've got it locked up tight. Would you care to sit down?"

I stop pacing and drop into the chair in front of her desk. The chair is surprisingly comfortable. It looked like just a molded plastic shape, but what looked like a hard surface is actually some kind of padded upholstery. The feel of it under my fingers distracts me for a moment, and I run my hand over the material for a moment before remembering how angry I am. Maybe these chairs are here for a reason.

"How long has she been here?" I ask.

"Nine years."

"But not continuously, right? She has to rotate to higher gravity locations every other year. Where does she go then?"

"I've only been in the command rotation here for five years," Khan says. "And Garro hasn't left the Moon in that time. Records indicate she started on a nine-month rotation, just like her assistants, but the year before I started here, she stopped rotating off. She's been living here for almost six years straight."

"That can't be right." I sit up in my chair. "That means she can never go back to Earth."

"From what I understand, she's persona non grata there anyway."

Every question I ask seems to raise a dozen more. Or maybe I'm just asking the wrong person.

"I need to use your radio room," I say.

CHAPTER NINETEEN

Every off-world agency facility is required to have a dedicated, heavy-encryption communications link back to Washington, D.C. Khan takes me to a private booth connected to the main radio room and shows me how to operate the communications terminal. Then she leaves me alone.

I think of a bright red bird with bushy black eyebrows and open the pocket to retrieve the red key Admiral Morris gave me. I plug the data card into the terminal and wait for the call to connect.

After a few seconds of a spinning globe, the vid blinks and shows Morris's office on the Eyrie. She's standing behind her desk, leaning down over it, and the bags under her eyes imply that she hasn't been sleeping well—or at all. She frowns into the camera.

"I need to know everything you can tell me about Project Genesis," I say.

"Kangaroo?" she says. "You're in the crater?"

"Project Genesis," I repeat.

"Nice to see you, too."

"I thought you preferred to skip the small talk."

Morris sits down. "I assume you've already spoken with Director Khan?"

"Yes." I give a quick recap of what I know. "So what's important enough to convince Alisa Garro to live here on the Moon, with no hope of ever returning to Earth?"

"Yeah, well, maybe you can just go and ask her."

"She's not being very cooperative."

"Welcome to my life," Morris says, spreading her hands over her desk.

"Look, I ran into that brick wall when I first took this job. I couldn't get anywhere either. And I was able to get meetings with the secretary of state."

"You don't—" I can't believe this. "How does the *director* of *intelligence* not know about this?"

"I know *about* it," Morris says. "I just don't know what it is."

"How does this organization even function?" I say. "Lasher isn't talking to you, we lost pretty much all of Intel last year, and State's keeping secrets from everyone—"

"This is a spy agency," Morris says. "We're basically state-sponsored professional liars."

I frown. "It sounds pretty unsavory when you put it like that."

"It's the truth. We do secret things every day of the week and twice on Sundays, and we can't talk about most of those things. You either learn to live with it, or you find a new job."

"Right." *Not really an option for me, lady.*

"I'm sure there are plenty of things that State doesn't tell us," Morris says. "National security, planetary security, I don't need to know. I have enough on my plate. And so do you."

"Aren't you the least bit curious? I mean, the name implies—"

"Do you know how many different code-tags show up on my screens every day that I don't recognize?" Morris snaps. "I have a lot of keys. I don't have *all* the keys. And right now, I'm just trying to keep my head above water, Kangaroo. We have a full-blown international crisis on the Moon. And I mean *all* the nations. Every sector is affected by this power outage. Ten million civilians from fifty different countries are losing their minds. The governor wants to declare martial law."

She pauses to take a breath. "That seems like a bad idea," I offer.

"It's a terrible idea!" Morris looks as outraged as she sounds. "And now I have to go through the U.N. Security Council to talk him down. Do you know how much I enjoy working with the United Nations?"

"Is that a rhetorical question?" I detected a bit of a snarl when she said *working.*

"This is *not* what I signed up for when I took this job. But I'm here now, and I'm dealing with it." Morris points a finger at me. "Do *your* job, Kangaroo. Don't go looking for trouble."

She disconnects before I can protest that I *am* doing my job, and also, trouble seems to find me regardless.

Paul wanted me to get to the bottom of Project Genesis. Nobody around here has been very forthcoming so far, but who knows how long Jessica and I are going to be stuck here until the Lunar lockdown is lifted. I might as well start looking for the weakest link among SDF1's personnel.

I step out of the communications booth to find Alisa Garro waiting in the corridor, standing next to Hong and tapping away at her tablet. I suppose it's technically not an ambush, since she's not hiding, but I am very surprised.

"Are you ready to talk about Genesis now?" I ask her.

"Kangaroo," she says, lowering her tablet and putting on a fake smile. "You know I can't talk about that."

"I don't know anything," I say. She wants to treat me like an idiot? Fine. "Why don't you explain it to me like I'm five years old?"

A strange expression flickers across her face. Then she recovers, clears her throat, and says, "It's been a long time. How about we start slow and catch up over some coffee?"

I can't stand this good-witch act. "With all due respect, I'd rather drink hemlock with a rabid weasel."

"Oh, for fuck's sake!" She smacks the tablet with her palm. "I was helping you, don't you understand?"

"You were *poisoning* me!"

"They were nowhere near lethal doses!" she shouts.

"Nonlethal doesn't mean nonharmful! I was in the hospital for—"

"We needed to know how toxins in your system might affect your ability! It wasn't just for operational efficiency; it was to protect you, to keep you safe!"

"Then why didn't you tell anyone?" I ask. "Why did you do it in secret? You were my doctor. I trusted you!"

"Would you have agreed to it?"

"Of course not!"

"And that's why!" she jabs a finger at me. "You never understood, Kangaroo. We need to do things for the greater good. We all need to make sacrifices."

"And what the hell have you sacrificed? You're sitting pretty in your own secret lab—"

"I'm living on the Moon!" She clutches her tablet so hard I'm afraid she might break it in half. "I haven't left this crater in six years!"

"You're lying," I say. "You left the crater last night."

She blinks. "You don't know that."

"I have an eyewitness and multiple vids showing your face in the Apennine Terraces."

"That's not possible."

"Jessica already told me she met with you," I say. It's not a lie—Jessica didn't deny it when I confronted her earlier—and I find it deeply satisfying to watch Alisa Garro squirm. "And State might have been able to wipe the street-cam footage, but I've got resourceful friends too."

"I misspoke," Alisa says in a tight voice. "I haven't left *the Moon* for six years. Khan told you that, right? I've been here longer than she has. And I can never go back to Earth now. *That's* my fucking sacrifice, Kangaroo."

Before I can summon an appropriate retort, a loud buzzing noise fills the corridor. It takes me a moment to recognize it as an alert sound. Red light floods the corridor, and I hear voices shouting and running footsteps all around us.

"That seems bad," Hong says.

Alisa turns away and taps at her tablet. "Control, this is Garro. What's going on?"

"We've got incoming," says Khan's voice from the tablet.

"On my way," Alisa says, walking down the corridor.

"Hey!" I shout, jogging after her. Hong follows me. "Where do you think you're going?"

She stops and whirls around. "Are you kidding me? We've got a red alert and you want to keep arguing about ancient history?"

When she puts it like that, it does sound a little ridiculous. "Fine. We deal with the red alert first. But you and I are not even close to being finished."

"Whatever." She shakes her head and walks away. I follow. Hong doesn't say anything. I can't decide whether he's being politely discreet or annoyingly neutral.

CHAPTER TWENTY

The control center at the middle of the circular facility is divided into two hemispheres—or rather, two halves of a squat, hollow cylinder. Alisa and Hong and I enter through a door at the back, nearly running into Jessica as we all head for the center of the room.

"*You're* here?" Alisa says, stopping in her tracks when she sees Jessica. "What the hell!"

"It's a long story," Jessica says. "You should have just taken the necklace."

"I didn't want the stupid necklace," Alisa says.

"Excuse me, sir, and Doctor," Hong says, "but can we go deal with the emergency first?"

Alisa grumbles and walks away. I point at the back of her lab coat.

"So how long have *you* known about all this?" I ask Jessica.

"I hate you," she says, and follows Alisa. Hong's right behind them, and I follow him.

We pass by banks of computers and walk up onto an elevated circular pedestal in the middle of the room, where Khan is standing, surrounded by personnel seated at wedge-shaped control stations. Both her hands grip the railing around that central area. More control stations line the front of the room, between the pedestal and the wall of vid screens that make a huge grid before us.

The main display is currently showing some kind of orbital diagram, with the Earth and the Moon and a whole lot of other lines in multiple colors spiraling around those two bodies. One particular red line is pulsing,

167

and I see that one end of it goes off the edge of the screen, and the other end touches the disk of the Moon.

Khan turns to look as the four of us join her on the pedestal. She points to Alisa and Jessica. "So *this* has happened already?"

"Just now," Alisa says.

"Sorry I missed it," Khan says.

"Am I the only one who cares about the red alert?" Hong says. "What's going on, Director?"

"There's a rock headed for us," Khan says, pointing at the orbital diagram. "US-OSS projections give us about two hours before impact."

"Do we know where it came from?" I ask.

"We know it's fancy," Khan says. That's what the military calls any flying object that can maneuver under its own power and isn't just being pulled around by gravity. "OSS sent a deflector drone to intercept, but lost contact before it could get close enough to blast the bogey."

"Someone's shooting at us?" Hong says.

"Not just anyone," Khan says, pointing at the screens. "Someone who knows exactly where all our defenses are. This object's trajectory bypasses all our standard asteroid interception measures, and if it maintains course and acceleration, it will collide with Shackleton Crater dead center. That's not an accident."

"They're targeting SDF1," Hong says.

"Yes," Khan says. "But they knew we'd see it coming. Maybe we can't stop it, but they know we have to evacuate. That's probably their objective."

"But the tubes are offline," I say. "So we have to use surface vehicles or spacecraft, both of which are in limited supply."

"SDF1 has enough shuttles to evacuate all our personnel," Khan says. "But I think we should also use the pocket."

Alisa blinks. "What?"

"We don't have time to stagger our shuttle launches," Khan says. "There are close to ten million civilians on the Moon who will notice a whole bunch of ships leaving the south pole all at once, and that is a huge security breach. I'd rather make it one ship, with Kangaroo aboard, and the rest of us in the pocket."

"No," Alisa says. "That's a bad idea. What if he loses track of us? What if he—"

"He's not an idiot," Jessica says.

"Thank you," I say. "How big are these shuttles?"

"No more than five meters across," Khan says. "You can open the portal that wide, correct?"

"I can do up to fifteen," I say, "but only if I have to."

"The shuttles will fit in five," Khan says. "This is our best option, Doc. We've got a lot of people and equipment to move."

"Will you need any help getting everything out of the Genesis cave and into a shuttle?" I ask. If nobody's going to tell me what this secret project is, maybe I can sneak a peek with my own eyes.

"What's Genesis?" Jessica asks.

Alisa glares at both of us. "My assistant and I can handle it." She turns to Khan. "We'll need a path cleared between B-wing and the hangar bay. No spectators."

"Fine," Khan says. "You've got thirty minutes."

"Alisa. Seriously. Do you want any help?" Jessica asks as Alisa steps off the pedestal.

"Don't talk to me," Alisa says, and walks out.

I wait until Alisa has left the control center to ask, "Can't OSS send any other spacecraft to intercept the incoming object? Or at least get some telescopes on it to see what it is?"

Khan speaks to one of the officers seated next to her, who works his controls. One of the wall screens changes to a series of blurry still images of an irregular grayish rock.

"That's our bogey," Khan says. "Looks like your basic stray asteroid, right? Except when you look at it in infrared."

The screen changes to a very colorful shape, with a bluish fuzz off one side of the rock, separated by a stripe of solid black like the empty space around it.

"Wait," I say. "That looks like heat back there. And why is the rock itself so warm?"

"Because it's not a rock," Khan says. "Not entirely, anyway. Looks like someone hollowed out a small asteroid and hid some drone controls and a mini-ionwell inside. That heat flare back there is a plasma exhaust."

"But there's no engine trail."

Khan gestures to her officer, who changes the display again. Now the background becomes gray, with tiny pinpoints of light—distant stars, invisible until the brightness gain was turned up—but the stripe to the left of the rock is still solid black.

"Stealth cone," Khan says. "Energy-absorbing material around the engine bells. Unless you're directly behind the rock's direction of travel, meaning way out in the outer solar system, you won't see any heat. But it's accelerating at ten gees."

"Son of a bitch," Hong says.

"OSS is scrambling some X-4 interceptors," Khan says. "But we won't know for at least another hour whether they were successful. I'd like us to prepare for the worst. Kangaroo, do you need any special preparation to open the pocket with a five-meter barrier'd portal?"

"No," I say. "Not really. I'll be dehydrated afterward. And probably have a headache. Maybe just have some vitamin water and painkillers on hand for that."

"We can do that." Khan makes a note on her tablet. "Mr. Hong, why don't you show Kangaroo to the hangar deck so he can get a look at the shuttlecraft."

"Just one more question," I say. "Do we have any idea who's attacking us?"

Khan frowns. "Knowing who threw this rock isn't really going to help us stop it."

"Not the rock," I say. "But if they do have people on the Moon, just waiting for you to evacuate so they can expose you, knowing who it is might tell us something about their methods or help us identify who their operatives or accomplices might be."

"Jeremiah Burgess," Jessica says.

"Who's that?" Khan asks.

"Municipal power employee. He was on the agency payroll. But he was—flexible."

"A loose asset?" I ask. The agency deals with a lot of people who are "loosely affiliated"—meaning we just pay them to fill a specific need, whether it's information, hardware, or services. These assets are usually mercenaries or career criminals, but in some cases, all you need is a lowly maintenance worker to copy some data or open a back door.

Jessica nods. "He had contacts here at SDF1. Burgess arranged my meeting with Alisa, without telling her it was me."

"And if you could pay him to do that on the sly," I say, "someone else might have bribed him to find out which specific power plants to bomb in order to shut down the tube transit system."

"Thereby forcing SDF1 to evacuate into space instead of underground," Hong says. "That's fairly devious."

Khan shakes her head. "I see your point, Kangaroo, but this is all we have to go on right now." She waves at the pictures on the screens. "And anyone in the Solar System could have made that rock."

"But how would they know exactly where and how and *when* to hit us?" I ask. "Not many people have access to all that information."

"Maybe not last year," Khan says, her mouth turned down at the corners, "but our former D.Int has been selling a lot of secrets on the black market."

Something clicks in my mind. "You think this attack is happening because Sakraida sold information about this facility?"

"Yeah."

Holy shit. "He knew about Project Genesis!" What one D.Int—Morris—can find out, another D.Int—Sakraida—probably discovered a while ago. "He didn't know *exactly* what 'Dr. Jill' was doing here, but he knew it was beyond top secret, and he knew the secretary of state was directly involved."

"Which is why he wants to destroy it," Khan says.

"No," I say. "If he wanted to destroy it, he could have gotten somebody into this facility with a suitcase nuke and turned it into an actual crater. He knows your security procedures. He knows exactly where this base is. Think about it. Why would he get someone to attack in a way that gave us two hours' warning? Enough time to evacuate the entire facility?"

"He doesn't want to destroy it," Jessica says. "He wants to steal it."

"Dollars to doughnuts," I say.

"What?" Hong says.

"You know what a doughnut is, right?"

"They cost more than a dollar."

"Forget it," I say. "The point is, Sakraida knows you're running high-value research up here—including whatever the hell 'Genesis' is, and whatever it is, it's clearly super important to State. So it's definitely worth a ransom, if nothing else."

"That's all very interesting," Khan says, "and I look forward to reading the analyst reports once we're safely repositioned."

"I can find out," I say. "I can talk to them."

"Excuse me?" Jessica says at the same time that Hong asks "How?" and Khan says "I hope you're not proposing what I think you're proposing."

"Hear me out." I hold up a hand to request silence while I explain. "If we're right about this, whoever threw that rock will be watching, waiting for us to evacuate so they can intercept us. Right? Well, when they see only one ship leaving, they're going to be extra curious. And I can make it very easy for them to catch me—"

"No," Jessica and Khan say at the same time. Hong raises his eyebrows and shrugs. *Some support would be nice, fella.*

"You're a triple-A Diamond asset," Jessica says. "We are not risking your safety."

"Or the safety of everyone in this facility," Khan says. "I need to ensure the security of all personnel and agency material from SDF1. We can worry about unmasking the villains later."

"We may never have another chance to make direct contact!" I say. "This is primary source intel. Agents have *died* for less reliable data." Both Jessica's and Khan's eyes widen at that remark. In hindsight, that probably wasn't the best argument. "Come on, am I really the only one who sees the value of this? Lieutenant?" I turn to look at Hong.

He raises both hands, palms up. "I'm just a pilot, sir."

"No one is disputing the potential value of that information," Khan says. "But it's not worth the risk, Kangaroo. We don't know what these people might do once they capture you. They could knock you out and take you back to the asteroid belt or somewhere else without enough empty space for you to pull our vehicles and personnel out of the pocket. If their other ships are also equipped with stealth canopies, the agency won't be able to track them."

"I'll have two whole days before your air runs out," I say. Agency shuttles are overengineered to provide life support for pretty long flights, just in case there's a "variation" that requires them to stay out in space longer than expected. "I can find a way to get a message back to the office. I'll figure something out."

"Not that I don't trust your operational prowess, Kangaroo," Khan says, "but there are too many unknowns. We're not taking the risk. We need to evacuate. We put you in our fastest ship, we put everyone else inside the pocket, and then you outrun these bastards when they try to catch you on the way out. *That's* the plan."

"Your plan doesn't get us any more information about who's behind this," I say. Doesn't anyone else around here actually want to *catch* the bad guys?

"That's not my priority," Khan says.

"Maybe it's not your decision."

She frowns at me. "Are you going to disobey a direct order from a superior?"

"I'm Operations," I say. "You're Science. I'm not in your chain of command—"

"Okay," Jessica says, putting a hand on my shoulder. "You can stop playing lawyer now, Kangaroo."

I continue staring down Khan. "I'm not *playing* anything—"

"I apologize, Director," Jessica says, yanking me backward. "He gets like this sometimes. Low blood sugar." She turns me to face her. "When's the last time you ate something?"

As if on cue, my stomach rumbles. "I'm fine."

"You'll be fine after you eat something." Jessica glares at me. "Doctor's orders."

"I think that's a good idea," Khan says. "We can finish this discussion after you've had breakfast."

"Breakfast?" I look around, confused. "Wait, what time is it?"

CHAPTER TWENTY-ONE

I hate it when Jessica's right and I'm wrong. Which means I hate large portions of my professional life. Maybe I should look into that.

She marches me out of the control center, down to the cafeteria, and makes sure I'm seated at a table with a large plate of food before leaving me to dig in. Hong sits next to me and sips a cup of coffee while I eat. It's a surprisingly palatable breakfast, for a government facility: the scrambled eggs actually have the proper consistency, and the texture of the bacon is almost entirely unlike cardboard.

"Excuse me," says a voice from the other side of the table.

I look up and see a man with big eyes and curly hair. The name tag on his lab coat says JOHNSON. He's carrying a cage with a chicken inside.

"Is that a chicken?" I ask.

"Oh. Yeah. Are you—" He darts his eyes left and right, then leans down and lowers his voice. "Are you Kangaroo?"

That's not a question I hear very often. Usually, people either know exactly who I am, or they think I'm someone else entirely. "Yes. Who are you and why do you have a chicken?"

"Oh, I'm—may I sit?"

"Feel free."

He sits across from me, puts his tablet down, and extends a hand. "Richard Johnson. It's a real pleasure to meet you, Mr. Kangaroo."

I shake his hand. "It's just Kangaroo."

He nods. "Cool. Uh, you can call me Rich."

175

"I suppose that's better than the other thing." *Dick Johnson? Your parents had some sense of humor.*

"What other thing?"

Ignorance is bliss. "Never mind. But seriously, what's with the chicken?"

"Oh, we have a few different animal species housed here for experimental purposes," Rich says. "Rats and mice, mostly. We're studying how they develop in the lower gravity environment."

"Do you keep snakes here?"

He frowns. "No. Why would we have snakes?"

"Forget it. Not important." His staring is making me really uncomfortable. "So how do you know who I am, Rich?"

"Oh, yeah. Sorry if I ambushed you a little. It's just—" He waves a hand. "Let me start over. I work with Dr. Jill. Alisa Garro. You know her, right?"

I nearly choke on the food in my mouth, but manage to wash it down with some orange juice. "Yeah. I know her."

"Well, Science Division—the agency—had to give me a very high security clearance in order to work on her project—that vetting process was not a lot of fun, let me tell you—but it did turn out to be worth it, you know, because one of the perks is I was authorized at a high enough level to also know all about you, Kangaroo." He waves an open palm at me. "And, wow, your ability—the pocket—is just amazing."

"Yeah, it's something." I study Rich's face. "So what *is* Project Genesis?"

Rich frowns. "You know I can't talk about that. I'm sorry."

I shrug. "Worth a try." *And now I'm going to see just how much you're willing to trade for some pocket chitchat, Rich.* "So let me guess. You want to talk about the pocket."

"Oh, I would love that. If it's not too inconvenient? I know you're probably busy, planning the evacuation and all that."

"I'm not busy right now," I say, doing my best to not sound bitter. "What do you want to know?"

Rich leans forward again, conspiratorially. He seems to be studying my tray of food. "Have you thought about lungs?"

"Not for breakfast, no."

He chuckles. "Sorry. I mean—" He waves his hands, like he's trying to grasp an invisible ball. "When you open the pocket, you manifest a portal, but the event horizon of that portal can't interact with solid matter. Right?"

"Yeah. I can only open a portal in empty space."

"But you can do it in atmosphere," Rich says. "I mean, you have to. So there's some threshold for how much stuff can be in the empty space before it interferes with portal formation."

"That's what they tell me," I say. "Science Division tests that every so often. Apparently the threshold hasn't changed since they started tracking the numbers. Solid matter, no; liquid, no; gas, yes up to a certain pressure. I don't remember the number, but supposedly it's high enough that I'd be crushed to death in that environment anyway."

Rich nods enthusiastically. "And you can vary the size of the portal, right?"

"Yeah. And put a barrier over it, if I don't want to suck all the air out of the room."

"That's what I want to talk about," Rich says, waggling a finger. "Because there's air—empty space that would allow portal formation—*inside* someone's lungs, right?"

I frown at him. "I'm not sure what you're getting at."

"You could—in theory—open a tiny, microscopic portal inside someone's lungs." Rich makes a circle with his thumb and forefinger. "You don't need to see the portal to open the pocket, right? You've done it from the other side of a wall before."

I've suddenly lost my appetite. "You're talking about suffocating a person from the inside."

"Yes!" He's way too excited about this prospect. "It's theoretically possible, right? And it would be a completely undetectable method of assassination—"

"I'm going to stop you right there, Rich," I say, holding up a hand. "It wouldn't work."

He frowns. "Why not?"

Because I'd have to stay there and watch someone die. "Like you said. Solid matter interferes with the portal. I'd have to stay in the same position for however long it would take to kill a person that way."

"But the portal moves with your body," Rich says. "Once you open it, it's locked to your position in space. Right? That's why you yourself can't go inside. You can only reach in to store or retrieve items."

"Right. But also, like you said, solid matter interferes with the portal."

"That just means if the portal gets moved, you move along with it," Rich says. "Right?"

"Not exactly." I always have trouble explaining the pocket to people. There's no easy point of reference, no other well-known bodily function I can compare it to. I make a fist with my left hand and hold it up. "Think about this."

"Whoa!" Rich leans back, holding up both palms in a gesture of surrender. "I'm sorry, I didn't mean to offend you."

"No, I'm not—I'm just making an analogy," I say.

"Oh."

"Using the pocket is just something I can do. Like making my hand into a fist. I think about it, and it happens." I flex my fingers open, then closed again for emphasis. "I don't think about moving individual muscles or how far each finger has to go or anything like that. It just happens by instinct, by feel. You understand?"

"Okay. Yes."

"So once you've made a fist," I say, "you have to *hold* it closed, right? If you relax your fingers"—I let my left hand uncurl—"they don't stay together. And if someone stronger than you pries your fingers apart"—I use my right hand to pull my left thumb away from the other fingers on that hand—"they can undo your fist."

Rich nods. "Yeah, still with you."

"Same thing with the pocket," I say. "I have to concentrate to open it and keep the portal open. If I lose consciousness, the portal disappears. If something solid pushes on the event horizon hard enough, the portal disappears. You see?"

I finish prying apart all the fingers of my left hand, then put both hands back down on the table. Rich continues nodding his head.

"So you're saying the action of someone moving their lungs to breathe could compress the micro-portal enough to dissipate it," he says.

"That's what I'm saying."

He looks directly at me. "But you've never actually tried it."

I really want to stop talking about this now. "You know, there's a procedure for suggesting new experiments to Science Division. Why don't I give you my case number—"

"I know the procedure," Rich says, his nostrils flaring for a split second before returning to their normal, nonthreatening appearance. "I've submitted several proposals over the last few years. They've all been rejected."

And you thought you could short-circuit the process by going straight to the Kangaroo. "Well, like I said, it's up to them to decide what wacky experiments they want to run. I'm not in charge of that. They've got a whole process, they don't like to deviate from it."

Rich leans forward again. "Maybe we could do something unofficial here. Just you and me."

I glance over at Hong, who's been pretending not to listen to any of this. "I'm not sure we have time for that."

"You said you weren't busy. This will just take a few minutes." Rich grabs his tablet and starts tapping at it. "We have some animals earmarked for experimentation. I can't bring you into the Genesis labs, but I can bring the specimens out—"

"No," I say quickly. *I'm not going to kill a rat, you sick fuck.* "Actually—sorry, Rich, I just noticed the time. We're supposed to check in with Director Khan, aren't we, Lieutenant Hong?"

Hong stands up with flawless military posture. "Yes, sir. I didn't want to interrupt, but we really should go now."

I stand and shrug at Rich. "Sorry. Maybe we can talk more later. Nice to meet you."

"Yeah, okay," Rich waves at me. "We'll talk later!"

I've never been so glad to leave a cafeteria in my whole life. And that includes the year I attended an inner-city public high school.

"Thanks for the save," I tell Hong as I follow him down the corridor away from the cafeteria. "It's not just me, right? That was a little unsettling back there."

"I suppose you get a lot of questions about the pocket," Hong says.

"All the time."

"Speaking of which," he says. "I wanted to ask you something about that."

I frown at him. "Really?"

He stares at me, then laughs. "No, not really. I'm just messing with you."

"Hilarious."

"Seriously, though," Hong says, "what do you think they're doing in there for Project Genesis? Something with animals, I guess?"

"Nothing good, I'm sure." The word "genesis" implies the creation of life, which means they're breeding things and probably attempting some kind of unorthodox genetic manipulation. *Awesome, he said sarcastically.*

We walk into an elevator that takes us to the hangar bay at the top of SDF1. There's a lot of activity here. I count eleven shuttles being prepared for flight and dozens of people and service robots moving equipment around and loading up the vehicles. Everyone seems to know what they're doing.

It's easy to find Khan in the crowd—she towers over everyone else by a good fifteen centimeters. She sees Hong and me walking over and comes to meet us.

"X-4s were not able to intercept the incoming rock," Khan says by way of greeting. "The attacker appears to have a full complement of countermeasures—anti-missile flash-lasers, radio jammers, who knows what else. The fighters are still tracking it, but they won't be able to keep up for long."

"Wait," I say. "The rock has been *responding* to the attempts to shoot it out of the sky?"

"Yes."

"That means there's a pilot on board," I say. "A human pilot. Don't you want to know who's crazy enough to sacrifice a trained astronaut in order to kill this base?"

"We'll find out later," Khan says. "Suicide bombers are nothing new. Besides, it could be a remote-operated drone, being driven by someone in another spacecraft within a few light-seconds. They wouldn't need immediate reaction time."

"What if—"

"We're done talking about this, Kangaroo," Khan says. "Let's focus on the evacuation. Go check in with your Surgical officer."

She points to one shuttle that is not surrounded by busy clusters of people and robots. The name painted on the side is *Calypso*. I walk up the ramp into the open doorway and poke my head inside. It looks very similar to the military shuttle Hong brought us here in, but with more seats and a door leading to a cargo section. Jessica is sitting in an aisle seat in one of the middle rows, working on a tablet.

"Permission to come aboard?" I call out.

"Granted," she says without looking up.

I walk into the shuttle. Hong follows me in and looks around. "Am I flying this thing?" he asks.

"That's the plan, Lieutenant," Jessica says.

"I'll start the preflight checklist," Hong says, and goes into the cockpit.

"Kangaroo, sit." Jessica waves at the seat across the aisle from her. "I'm just finalizing the evacuation manifest."

"Cool." I sit down. "Tell me about the necklace."

She doesn't look up. "No."

"Why not?"

"Because I don't want to."

"Not good enough," I say. "We are on mission. We are required to do all sorts of things we don't want to do. I need to know what is going on between you and Alisa Garro and whether it's going to adversely affect your operational performance."

Jessica stops tapping her fingers on the tablet. I'm sure she recognizes that last phrase, and this whole lecture—it's the same one she's given me countless times to get me back on track, when I'm starting to go off-script too much. I hope she recognizes that I'm only trying to help her.

"I'm fine," she says, looking straight at me. "It's you we need to worry about."

I narrow my eyes at her. "What's wrong with me?" Jessica can see my medical status at all times, but she doesn't always tell me when strange things are happening inside my own body.

"Nothing yet," she says. "But you're going to be opening ten different five-meter portals, one right after the other, all in the space of about half an hour. That's an enormous physical strain."

"And you're going to give me something to help me with that, right? Some kind of stimulant, or run a special nanobot program to counteract the pocket stress?" Using the pocket dehydrates me and suppresses certain neurotransmitters, similar to what a night of heavy drinking would do—basically, it gives me a hangover.

"We're still working on that," Jessica deadpans. "I'll let you know as soon as I patent a hangover cure and become a billionaire." It's true: if she developed that, she'd never have to work another day in her life. Of course, I don't know why she chose to work for the agency in the first place. Maybe she just likes doing espionage.

"I'm not hearing an actual solution here," I say.

"Sixty seconds to get each shuttle into the pocket," Jessica says. "One hundred and twenty seconds between each portal opening. We've got plenty of vitamin water on hand for hydration, but I don't want to risk dosing you with too many painkillers. So there will be some discomfort."

I can tell when she's underselling bad news. "Now, when you say 'discomfort'—"

"I don't know exactly how bad it will get," she says. "I'll start you on some acetaminophen before the first portal, then move on to naproxen and start the anti-nausea meds only when you start feeling it. I want to save the opiates as a last resort. If you're too sedated, you won't be able to use the pocket."

"I also won't be able to use the pocket if I'm in too much pain," I say. We've run into both situations before, on different missions, and it wasn't pretty either time. "What are we talking about here? Scale of one to ten?"

"I don't know," Jessica repeats, overenunciating the words. "You've never done anything like this before."

"I've opened bigger portals," I say. "What was the biggest? Fifteen meters?"

"This is different. You know this is different." She's getting impatient with me. I can tell. "Maybe you can bench-press a hundred kilograms once because you're on an adrenaline rush. That doesn't mean you can do ten reps with half the mass. It's a different type of exertion."

"Once again," I say, "I'm not hearing any solutions here."

Jessica glares at me. "You keep telling us you can't describe what it feels like to use the pocket. We can't work without information. So it's really up to you, Kangaroo. Describe the symptoms and maybe I can diagnose and treat them."

I glare back at her. "I can't work without information, either. Tell me about the necklace."

"*Relevant* information."

"Hey, raise your hand if you actually received agency training to be an intelligence analyst?" I put up my hand while Jessica scowls at me. "Oh, it is just me? Then how about you let me be the judge of what's relevant and what's not."

"It's a personal matter," she says.

"You don't *have* a personal life."

"I don't *tell* you about my personal life because it's not relevant to our work."

I can't believe she's saying this with a straight face. "You got arrested and nearly blew our entire mission. That's pretty *relevant* from where I'm sitting."

"You worked around it," she says. "It's no longer an issue."

I feel like punching something. "So you would have told me if I had asked *earlier*?"

She shrugs. "Let's not dwell on the past."

"Excuse me," I say. "I'm just going to punch this seat for a minute."

I turn and hammer my fists into the upholstery until I'm out of breath.

"Feel better?" Jessica asks when I turn back to face her.

I raise my right hand and extend my middle finger. "How's that manifest coming along?"

She hands me the tablet. "All done."

I look over the data. The evacuation manifest lists the name of each shuttle, who's piloting the vessel, all the passengers' names, and what reference object I should use to place each one in the pocket.

The first shuttle, the *Mapalé,* is carrying just three passengers: Alisa Garro, Rich Johnson, and "Project Genesis." The pilot is listed as AUTO. That seems unusual, and I scroll through the rest of the manifest to verify: only the *Mapalé* is going into the pocket on autopilot. And all the experimental animals—chickens, rats, mice, et cetera—are going into other shuttles. Whatever Genesis is, it's the only thing on that first shuttle.

I look up at Jessica. "The ultra-important secret science cargo doesn't get a human pilot?"

She shrugs. "Their choice. For security reasons, I'm told."

"What if something goes wrong?"

"It will take at most thirty seconds to remote-pilot the shuttle into the pocket," Jessica says, "and another thirty seconds to pull it out again later. You're going to rotate the portal for the extraction anyway, and inertia will carry them back out. They only actually need to have control for that first half-minute. I imagine they'll be fine."

I hear footsteps coming up the ramp, and then Khan enters the shuttle. "How are we doing in here?"

"Fine," Jessica says.

"Any issues with the manifest?" Khan asks.

"Nope," I say. "Are you sure you don't want to ride with someone else?" This final shuttle, *Calypso*, only has four passengers: Khan, Lieutenant Hong, Jessica, and myself.

"You're a VIP, Kangaroo," Khan says. "I wouldn't trust anyone else with your care."

"Thanks." I transfer the manifest data to my eye and check the time: fifty-two minutes until impact. "Let's get started."

CHAPTER TWENTY-TWO

I'm standing in a spacesuit in the hangar bay, whose atmosphere has been pumped out, like a giant airlock. I can now open the pocket in here without the barrier and not have to worry about the pressure differential.

Time to get this show on the road.

I walk over to the *Mapalé* and position myself next to its nose. Hong, also in a spacesuit, follows and stands next to me. He wasn't kidding about not leaving my side. Everyone else is loaded into their respective shuttles.

"Opening the pocket now," I say over the radio. "Shuttle *Mapalé* into location one."

I think of a blank prescription pad and open the pocket. A pitch black circle ringed by a white glow pops into being in front of me, five meters tall, the event horizon just touching the floor of the hangar bay.

"Wow," Hong says. I forgot: this is the first time he's actually seen me use the pocket.

"Save your questions until the end, please," I say.

"That's . . ." He shakes his head. "Wow."

"Whenever you're ready," I say. "I can't hold this open forever."

"Right. Sorry." He taps the control pad on his spacesuit's forearm. "Shuttle *Mapalé* into location one, moving now."

I feel the deck vibrate as the shuttle rises upward on its thrusters, then glides forward into the pocket. Once I'm sure the tail of shuttle has passed the edge of the portal, I close the pocket again, and there's one less shuttle in the hangar bay.

"Wow," Hong says again.

"Kangaroo, Surgical. How are you feeling?" Jessica asks over the radio.

"You tell me," I say. I know she's monitoring all my vital signs remotely.

"Drink some water," she says. "I'm dosing you with naproxen now."

"Thanks." My medical implants include a number of sealed drug capsules I can release into my bloodstream as needed, and that can also be operated remotely. I sip vitamin water through the drinking tube inside my space-suit helmet and try not to think too much about what might happen to those drug capsules if they got punched too hard.

We continue down the line of shuttles, putting two more into the pocket before Hong needs to replace the empty water bottle in my life support backpack. I'm only a little lightheaded after the fifth shuttle.

"Fifty percent done," Jessica announces. "We're doing good on time."

"Great," I say, walking across the hangar to the other line of five shut-tles. I don't mention that those extra steps make the lightheadedness worse. Just need to get this over with.

Two more water bottles and three more painkiller doses later, there are just two shuttles—*Calypso* and *Seungmu*—left in the hangar bay. I follow Hong up to the boarding ramp but have to stop and brace one arm against the hull until the dizziness passes.

Just one more portal, Kangaroo. Then you can rest.

"Are you okay, sir?" he asks.

"Just a second," I say, gulping some more water and hoping these spots I'm seeing will go away soon. "How much time?"

"Fifteen minutes," Khan reports. "Opening hangar bay doors now. As soon as you get *Seungmu* into the pocket, we're dusting off."

The hangar bay doors slide open in complete silence, revealing empty black space above us. Looking through that circular opening is almost like looking into the pocket.

I turn back to *Seungmu* and try to open the last portal. No dice. The good news is, I manage to keep my breakfast down. Barely.

"Sit down, Kangaroo," Jessica says.

"I'm okay," I say.

"No, you're not," she says. "And I can't dose you with any more stimu-lants right now. Sit down and keep drinking water until your blood pres-sure evens out."

I sit down next to *Calypso* and wait for my stomach to settle. Hong hovers over me.

"You can go inside, Lieutenant."

"Thank you, sir, but my orders are—"

"Never leave my side. Right." I breathe deeply and slowly. "Just one more second here."

I hear a loud, repetitive beeping noise. I hope it's not my audio implants malfunctioning again. Or my brain failing.

"Does anybody else hear that?" I ask.

"External transmission," Khan says. When we loaded everyone on the base into separate shuttles, we also tied all our radios into a common channel to make communications easier. "I'll answer." The beeping ends with a rising trill. "This is Shackleton Crater, go ahead."

"Shackleton, this is Dieker, X-4 pilot tracking your incoming bogey." The fighter pilot's voice crackles with static. "We have eliminated the threat, repeat, threat eliminated."

"Dieker, Shackleton, thank you!" I can hear the excitement in Khan's voice. "Lieutenant Hong, can you confirm on radar? Sorry, Dieker, it's not that I don't trust you."

"No offense, ma'am," Dieker says. "And Lieutenant, you're going to see a lot of fast-moving debris, but now that we've killed the engines, deflector drones should be able to clean up the junk before it reaches you."

"Confirmed!" Hong says, working his wrist controls. I see glowing radar displays dancing across the visor of his spacesuit helmet. "Fancy bogey incoming is destroyed, repeat, destroyed!"

"Thank you, Dieker," Khan says. "We're all much relieved down here."

"Happy to help, ma'am. We'll keep an eye on these drones and let you know if anything unusual happens during cleanup."

The pilot signs off, and Hong lets out a whoop of joy.

"Okay, secure that, Lieutenant," Khan says. "Let's start bringing our people back."

Oh, boy. "Can we wait just a few minutes? I'm not quite fully recovered here," I say. I am not looking forward to pulling all nine of those five-meter portals again.

"I concur," Jessica says. "Kangaroo needs more time to recover."

"No worries," Khan says. "We've got nothing but—"

A new, louder beeping noises fills my helmet, and I see red lights flashing all around the hangar bay. A synthesized computer voice says: "*Intruder alert. Intruder alert . . .*"

"What the hell is that?" I swing my head around, looking for any signs of movement. I blink my eye into scanning mode, but all the doors into the hangar bay are still sealed. "I don't see anything. Is this a sensor malfunction?"

"Get in the shuttle!" Hong shouts.

"What? Why?"

He jumps off the ramp, grabs my arm, and swings me up into the open shuttle airlock. I keep forgetting that we're in one-sixth gravity. I poke my head out of the airlock and look up at the open hangar bay roof.

I see dozens of flat gray spiders, made to resemble Moon rocks, scuttling down into the unprotected hangar.

My left eye has sensed a threat and automatically come out of standby mode. The overlay paints each spider with a yellow outline, indicating an unknown status—green would be friendly, and red would be hostile. But these spiders aren't transmitting anything that positively identifies them as either one.

"Get inside!" Hong bounds up the ramp.

"Wait one," I say, and tell myself that it's okay to throw up. "*Seungmu,* do you read?"

"Affirmative," says *Seungmu*'s pilot over the radio. "If you're going to give us an exit, sir, you'd better do it fast."

I see the other shuttle rising from the floor of the hangar bay, outlined in green in my eye, and the wriggling mass of yellow spiders closing in on us.

Now or never, Kangaroo.

I think of a colorfully painted sideways drum and open the pocket on the other side of *Seungmu.* My head pounds, my vision blurs, and I can barely make out the shuttle turning and thrusting into the portal. At least I think that's what I'm seeing.

"Hong," I say, "are they in?"

"They're in!"

I close the pocket and let him push me into our shuttle. I don't even try to stop myself from doing a faceplant. At least it's my spacesuit helmet and not my actual face hitting the deck.

"Good to go! We are good to go!" Hong says, climbing in after me.

"Affirmative," Khan replies. "Deploying countermeasures."

Hong smacks the control to cycle *Calypso*'s airlock. Before the outer door fully closes, I catch a blurry glimpse of storage booths opening around the hangar bay and service robots rolling out of their charging slots and toward the invading spiders. I kind of want to stay and watch the imminent robot battle. But mostly I want to get the hell out of here before one of those spiders latches on to our shuttle.

The inner door cycles open, and Hong bursts into the cabin, throwing off his helmet and diving into the cockpit. "Everybody strap in!"

Khan and Jessica drag me out of the airlock. "We don't have time to get him out of this suit," Khan says.

"Then we lock down the suit with him inside," Jessica says.

"Very well."

They carry me back to the spacesuit storage locker—hooray for one-sixth gravity—and ease me backward into a holding slot. The magnetic latches click into place around the waist of my spacesuit. Both women grab handholds on the wall.

"Good to go!" Khan calls forward.

"Lifting off!" Hong calls back through the open cockpit door.

Jessica pulls off my helmet. "Just breathe, Kangaroo." She locks my helmet into a holding slot. I do my best to follow her instructions.

She presses an injector slug against my neck. "What's that?" I ask as it hisses and pinches my skin for a moment.

"Something to help with the nausea."

It feels like my stomach is being pushed into my feet when the shuttle ascends. *Don't throw up. Don't throw up. Goddammit don't throw up Kangaroo.*

Something bumps the shuttle sideways. "Please tell me that's not a spider," Jessica says.

"I can't see it," Hong says. "How high can these things jump?"

"They jump?" I say, my voice sounding squeakier than I intended.

Another bump rattles the shuttle. "They're jumping," Khan says.

"We can get into orbit," Hong says. I feel two more bumps. "I just need to maneuver—"

The entire shuttle judders, and an alarm starts sounding. I look forward into the cockpit and see lots of flashing red lights. "That seems bad."

"Main engine is out!" Hong struggles with the control yoke. "We've still got thrusters. I'm going to get us as far away from here as I—"

Something actually explodes. I feel it through the hull.

"That's definitely bad," Khan says.

"That was a thruster," Hong says. "I need to set us down. Everybody brace for impact."

Lieutenant Hong is an excellent pilot. Our landing is a bit tooth-rattling, but nobody suffers any injuries, and the shuttle stays right side up.

I'm starting to feel better now that we're on solid ground again. Whatever Jessica injected me with is probably also helping. Then I hear thumping noises all around us.

"Is anyone else hearing that?" I ask.

"Sounds like more jumping spiders," Khan says.

"Please tell me we can electrify the outside hull or something," I yell forward while struggling to unlatch my spacesuit from the wall.

"No effect," Hong calls back. Jessica helps me get the spacesuit free. I stagger forward into the cabin.

"Can you see how many of those things are out there?" Khan asks.

"Well," Hong says, "there's a lot of them."

"I mean how many are physically attached to the shuttle," Khan says.

"Yeah," Hong says. "There's a lot of them."

"Ballpark?" Jessica asks. "Ten? Twenty?"

"There's a lot of them," Khan says, staring out the window.

"For crying out loud," Jessica mutters and walks forward. She looks out a window in the aisle behind Khan's, and her eyes widen. "Shit."

I stumble forward in my spacesuit and look out the next window. It takes me a moment to understand what I'm seeing.

Hong landed the shuttle just outside the rim of Shackleton Crater, so there's sunlight touching the ground around us. And the Lunar surface, which is normally perfectly still in the vacuum of outer space, is *moving*.

It's not actually the Lunar surface, of course. It's hundreds of spider-bots, their carapaces painted and textured to resemble gray Moon rocks, skittering toward and into the crater. I hope those hangar bay doors are closed by now.

I also hope SDF1's service robots are tougher than these spiders. They don't appear to have any weapons, other than their needle-sharp climbing legs.

Which are strong enough to stab a man to death.

And pierce the hull of a spacecraft.

Goddammit.

"Please tell me SDF1 has a self-destruct and you activated it before we left," I say to Khan.

"Every serv-bot in the base has a self-destruct," she says. "I'm not worried about protecting that location. I'm more worried about us."

"They seem to be ignoring us," I say. The spiders are continuing to stream toward the crater.

"For now," Khan says. "But whoever was watching and waiting for our evacuation definitely saw this shuttle lift off, blow an engine, and then put down again. They're going to come after us as soon as the spiders tell them there's nobody left in the crater."

"How are you feeling, Kangaroo?" Jessica asks.

I look over at her. "Um, fine, I guess? Better? Why do you ask?"

"Because I'm thinking we could use some of those anti-mech weapons Equipment loaded out."

"Right." I step back from the window and turn to face an empty spot in the aisle. Hong is standing in the doorway of the cockpit. "Stand back, Lieutenant."

He nods, his eyes wide with what I can only assume is awe. *That's right, everyone, Kangaroo to the rescue!*

I concentrate on opening the pocket.

Nothing happens.

"Just give me a second," I say, holding up a hand. I close my eyes and try again.

Still nothing.

"Your acetylcholine's reading low," Jessica says. I open my eyes and see her working a computer tablet. "Sit down and drink some more water. I'll find the first aid kit."

"This rarely happens," I say to Hong and Khan as Jessica moves forward into the galley area. "It's just, you know, I'm under a lot of pressure to perform right now, and I just pulled all those portals for the shuttles—"

"We understand," Khan says.

I feel my ears growing hot. "It'll just be a few minutes."

"Meanwhile, let's work on plan B," Khan says. "We have spacesuits for everyone?"

"That's affirmative," Hong says, going to the storage lockers and checking the gear. "Looks like four hours of air in each suit."

"Good," Khan says. "Let's start suiting up. Anything we can use for weapons?"

"Not looking great on that front," Hong says, rummaging through lockers. "This was a Science Division vehicle. It's mostly repair tools and spare parts back here."

"Well, look for blunt instruments," Khan says. "At least it'll be satisfying to whack the legs off one of those spider-bots, if it comes to that."

I finish the water bottle in my suit and swap it out for a new one while Hong and Khan put on their spacesuits. Jessica returns from the galley with a handful of pills.

"And what are those?" I ask as she moves to stuff them into my mouth.

"Stimulants." I give her a dubious look. She sighs and says, "Caffeine, glucose, vitamins, and amino acids. Nothing dangerous."

"That's a lot of pills."

"I'm a doctor. Do no harm, remember?"

"Fine." I hold out my gloved hand, and she transfers the pills. I gulp them down with some more water. "How long should I wait before trying the pocket again?"

"Save it," she says. "You might only get one use in the next hour. Wait until we're out of other options."

"Right."

I put my helmet back on while Hong helps Jessica into a spacesuit. When we finish, Khan is standing by the airlock door, holding what looks like a large wrench in both hands.

"Ready to go?" she asks.

"So what's the plan?" I ask. "Step outside and tell the spiders to take us to their leader?"

"Whoever's controlling those bots must be close," Khan says. "I'm guessing they'll come to us. They are looking for about two hundred evacuated base personnel, after all."

"You're not worried they'll just stab us to death?"

Khan frowns at me. "This is *your* theory, Kangaroo."

"How is this my—"

"You supposed that whoever threw that rock at us was trying to expose Project Genesis so they could steal it. They don't know what it is any more than we do. They're not going to kill any of us until they know for sure they have Genesis and not some other cargo." Khan looks around at all three of us. "Are we all on the same page?"

Hong, Jessica, and I all nod and mutter our agreement.

"Let's just hope these bad guys think the same way we do," Hong says.

"All right." Khan motions to the pile of tools by the storage lockers. "Everybody grab a weapon and let's go."

CHAPTER TWENTY-THREE

The Moon—South Pole—badlands
3 minutes since I swallowed a whole bunch of pills and I feel
fantastic, just great, why do you ask

There's a small cluster of spider-bots gathered at the bottom of the ramp when we open the airlock. Khan leads the way out. The spiders back away as she steps onto the Lunar surface. They don't have any visible sensors. It's kind of creepy. I turn on my eye and confirm that they're communicating with one another by radio. One big creepy wireless network.

"Well," I say, "the good news is, they don't seem to be that interested in attacking us."

"They're keeping their distance," Jessica says. "Like they've been programmed to herd us, but not engage."

"Let's see if we can find their master," Khan says.

"Copy that," Hong replies. "Scanning."

I turn my attention to the sky above us. Hong's using a handheld active radar unit, so I use my passive EM sensors. If there is a spacecraft above us, it should see Hong's radar unit pinging it, and will hopefully use that to zero in on our position. Not like they don't already know where we are. *Hey, bad guys, come and get your prisoners!*

Some of the stars look brighter, or different, when I switch to EM sensing. Some of them are brighter when you look at radio waves or other parts of the spectrum. And then there are pulsars, like those over there, flickering as if I were looking through atmosphere—

Wait a minute. Those stars aren't just changing brightness. They're also changing position.

And they're getting bigger.

"There!" I point at the center of the mass of not-stars. There are five or six points of light, flickering and rotating around an invisible central point and getting larger. "Incoming!"

I feel it before I can see it: thrusters that looked like stars, pushing out propellant to slow the spacecraft's descent. It must be coated in some kind of energy-absorbing stealth material, except for those thruster jet ports and possibly the main engines. Just like the fancy rock, but this vehicle isn't on a collision course—it's headed for a soft landing right next to us.

I move closer to where Jessica and Khan and Hong are standing—is it my imagination, or are these spider-bots closing in around us?—and keep watching the spot where the reverse thrust seems to be centered. I'm still amazed at how efficient modern stealth materials have gotten. You can tell where a stealthed vessel is by the absence of stars and even cosmic background radiation, if your sensors are that sensitive. But usually they can sneak right up on you and get off a shot before you even know they're there.

Spiders move away until there's a clear circular area in front of us. The ground shudders when the ship touches down, and then a bright horizontal line of light appears in midair. The light expands downward until it's a rectangle, with a humanoid silhouette in the center.

The spacesuited figure takes a few steps down the ramp, and by then it's obvious he or she is holding some kind of assault rifle on us with one arm. With the other arm, the figure points at our tools, then at the ground.

"People are so untrusting," I say as we all drop our blunt objects to the ground. Four spiders immediately scuttle forward, grab the tools, and drag them away.

The figure on the ramp braces the assault rifle with one arm and waves us forward with the other hand. The spiders clear a path from the small circle where we are to the stealth ship.

"Here we go," Hong says.

"Stay frosty," Khan says, stepping forward.

"One use," Jessica mutters. "Make it count."

No pressure, Kangaroo.

I don't know how many gees the stealth ship pulls while leaving the Moon, but it feels like at least five elephants' worth on my chest. Our captor doesn't even have to tie us up or restrain us in any way; the gravity keeps all four of us down on the floor of the spacecraft.

Our mystery host keeps the assault rifle trained on us while sitting in a jump seat at the front of the compartment. Whoever this is, he or she has definitely had some astronaut training.

After a few minutes, three multiarmed robots emerge from a storage niche and grab Hong, Khan, Jessica, and me by the arms and legs, holding us down and removing our spacesuit helmets. Only then does gravity abate to what feels like roughly Earth normal.

Our captor steps forward and taps the side of his or her helmet, which is mirrored so we can't see the face inside. The chestplate of the armored spacesuit sports a stylized image of a blood-red scorpion.

"Where are the rest of your base personnel?" The voice coming out of the helmet's external speakers is modulated and disguised. I can't tell whether it's male or female. As a bonus, it also sounds really creepy.

"Wouldn't you like to know," Hong says.

The assault rifle flips up, then smashes stock first into Hong's face. To his credit, Hong only emits a grunt. I see blood leaking from his nose.

Our captor steps over to stand in front of Khan and uses one boot to tap the robot holding her down. The robot lifts Khan upright.

"You," our captor says. "Where are the rest of your personnel?"

"I'm not in charge," Khan says, then jerks her head in my direction. "He is."

Our captor considers this for a moment, then taps the robot again. The bot pushes Khan to the ground. Our captor moves to the robot holding me down and taps it with a boot.

Good. Whoever this is doesn't know that Khan was the base commander. That means there's a lot of other stuff this person doesn't know.

Like who I am and what I can do.

Once the robot has raised me to a standing position, our captor raises the assault rifle and points it at my chest. "Where—"

I don't wait for the rest of the sentence. I open the pocket right behind him or her, two meters tall, without the barrier. The figure barely has time to squeeze off one burst from the assault rifle, which goes wild as he or she gets sucked into the vacuum of the other universe. Then I close the pocket.

"That trick never gets old," I say, and collapse to the ground. *Don't throw up.*

Hong has managed to dismantle his robot's arms despite having what is probably a very painful broken nose, and now he's working on Khan's bot. The two of them apparently hid some extra tools inside their space-suits earlier.

I watch the forward door for any sign of our captor's accomplices. It seems likely that whoever's flying the ship will come back here to check on us sooner or later.

Nobody does before Hong and Khan get free of their robots and then bang on the ones holding Jessica and me until enough pieces break off to free us. Hong and Khan use their tools to remove all the robots' power sup-plies while Jessica kneels down next to me and helps me out of my space-suit.

"Kangaroo," she says. "I don't have my tablet. You need to blink up your vitals and read them off."

I nod, taking slow, deep breaths, and bring up the medical display in my left eye. I recite numbers to Jessica until she seems satisfied. She pulls the water bottle from my spacesuit and wraps both my hands around it. I don't know why I'm trembling so much.

"Drink," she says.

I chuckle. "Worst drinking game ever."

"Stay here and rest." She stands up and joins Khan and Hong, who are inspecting the compartment.

"Hong? Weapons?" Khan asks.

Hong is prying open hatches and cabinets. "Nothing yet. Probably up in the cockpit to keep prisoners from getting to them."

Jessica is trying the control panel leading to the cockpit. "Total lock-out." She looks at the cockpit door. "Kangaroo? Can you see through this?"

I switch my eye to scanning mode and check the door to see its compo-sition, and also to check for booby traps. Can't be too careful when you're riding in someone else's spacecraft. Especially when that someone tried to shoot you just a minute ago.

"Looks clean," I say, standing up.

Jessica steps back toward me. "You need to rest."

"I'm okay." I don't know what was in that bunch of pills Jessica fed me, but they seem to be kicking in now. "Stand back, please."

I open the pocket—just a small portal—and pull a plasma cutter and safety mask. Jessica grabs them out of my hand as soon as the portal closes.

"Read me your vitals," she says.

I give her the numbers. "It's cool. Your magic pills are working."

She grunts. "All the same. I'm not letting you operate this." She puts on the safety mask.

"Do you know how to—" I start to say, then stop as she fires up the cutter.

We all stand back as she moves forward and uses the plasma cutter to draw a bright line around the lockpad next to the cockpit door. After she gets it open and sets the cutter and mask aside, Hong takes her place at the lockpad, fiddling with the electronics inside.

"Looks pretty standard," he mutters. "Think that'll do it."

The cockpit door slides open partway. Khan leaps forward, grabs the edge, and wrenches it all the way open. Hong charges through, followed by Jessica, then Khan. I feel a tingle of excitement. I'm sure it's not just the pills.

After a moment, Hong calls the all-clear. I stagger through the doorway, being careful not to touch the still-red-hot lockpad, and see Hong and Khan sitting in the pilot's and co-pilot's seats, respectively. Jessica is standing behind Khan, looking over the navigation console.

"What the hell?" I say.

"Ship's on autopilot," Hong says.

"Looks like our friend was flying solo," Khan says.

"That's—" I shake my head. "You're telling me one person rigged up that rock to hit the crater? And was planning to kidnap an entire facility alone, with no help?"

"There might be other ships out there," Jessica says.

"Agreed," Hong says. "I'm leaving the autopilot on for now."

"Are there any clues to who these people are?" I ask. "Where's the autopilot taking us?"

"There's no destination programmed," Hong says. "Just a simple ascent to get us off the Moon."

"Kangaroo. Did you set a timer?" Jessica asks.

"Set a timer for what?"

"For the prisoner," Jessica says. "That spacesuit probably doesn't have more than a few hours of air. We need to pull him out before he suffocates and interrogate him."

"Right." I blink a timer into my eye. "Four hours on the clock. We can decide what to do with him then."

"We should expect our would-be captor's accomplices to contact him," Khan says. "Or be waiting for him to report in about us."

"We probably have a few more minutes," Hong says. "He was clearly going to interrogate us and get whatever information he could. Then the robots would have to secure us for long-range transport before he could get back to the cockpit and change course."

"We'll have to shut down the autopilot then," Khan says. "If the other ships in this pirate fleet are also stealthed, we won't be able to contact or locate them by conventional means. Hong, check the flight computer for a rendezvous plan."

"On it." Since stealth vessels can't see each other, they need to coordinate their movements so they don't run into each other. It's similar to how underwater submarines operated back in the twentieth century, except they could at least detect each other by underwater sonar. Fully stealthed spacecraft can't radiate anything or risk being detected by the enemy. More than one warship has gone missing, but never been confirmed destroyed, because we simply don't know where to look. Space is really big.

A light starts blinking on one of the control panels between Hong and Khan. I point at it and ask, "What is that?"

They both look at the light, then at each other. "Communications?" Khan asks.

"Yes," Hong says, reaching over to work the controls. "That makes sense. These mercs can't direct their comms at each other—too much risk of detection—so they're just broadcasting encrypted bursts. When a burst comes in addressed to a specific ship, the computer auto-decodes it." The screen above the indicator lights up with some kind of status display. "Looks like a video message. Playing back now."

The display changes to show a woman's face in front of a flat gray wall. The face is Gladys Löwenthal's.

"What the fuck?" I say.

"Scorpion, this is Clementine," Gladys says, speaking directly into the camera. That is definitely her voice. And her code name.

"What the fuck!" I repeat.

"Friend of yours?" Hong asks.

"I'm at the rendezvous point," Gladys continues. "Since the news hasn't reported any major asteroid impacts near the south pole, I'm guessing you were able to infiltrate the objective. I'll give you two hours to meet me here, then I need to move on." She pauses and exhales. "But I hope we can do this in person. I hope you'll grant me the courtesy of doing this in person." She looks into the camera, and I can't tell whether she seems angry or sad. "Out."

The screen goes dark and the cockpit is silent for a moment. Then I hear someone chuckling next to me. I look over and see Jessica starting to laugh out loud.

"You picked a fine time to have a nervous breakdown," I say.

Jessica wipes tears from her eyes and shakes her head. "Oh, she's good. That is one crafty old bitch right there."

"Um, what's going on?" Hong asks.

"She played us," Jessica says. "Gladys and her merc buddy. They knew we'd have to investigate an attack on an agency shuttle—"

"An attack on *me*," I say.

"Nobody wants to kill you, Kangaroo," Jessica snaps. "You have far more value as a hostage. Or a live test subject."

I'm not sure how to feel about that.

"They used a robot—an SKR spider—to attack that shuttle because they knew the agency would come to Clementine for information," Jessica continues. "I'm guessing the database she sold us is missing some crucial records that would have revealed a few hundred rogue spiders roaming the Lunar surface."

"Excuse me, sirs," Hong says, pointing at the screen. "You *know* the accomplice?"

I give a quick recap of our original mission parameters. "We didn't know Clementine was working with anyone. We didn't know what she was really up to."

"They've been planning this for a while," Jessica says. "All this stealth material must have taken months to procure on the black market. We need to find out who sold them the information on where Project Genesis was located."

"I've got a guess," I grumble. "It starts with 'Sak' and ends with 'raida.'"

"Well, I suppose this is our chance to find out," Hong says.

"Except we don't know *where* 'Clementine' is," Khan says. "And I'm guessing our friend 'Scorpion' didn't leave any unencrypted data just lying around his ship's computer."

"I've been looking," Hong says, "but so far, nothing."

"So much for shedding light on the situation," Khan mutters.

Shedding light.

"I can find out where Gladys is," I say.

There's a lot of information embedded in a high-res vid stream, if you know where to look for it. And I don't just mean the metadata encoded within the stream, telling you how it was captured and what compression algorithm it's using. The visuals can actually tell you a lot about exactly where the vid was recorded.

Sunlight contains known frequencies of EM radiation, and the angle of sunlight and lengths of shadows can tell you exactly where on Earth a particular image was captured. The same goes for the Moon. We know exactly which way the Moon will be facing at all times with respect to the Sun. Measuring the intensity of the sunlight and looking at the angles at which shadows fall can tell us exactly where on the Moon this particular vid was captured, assuming it happened just now when the transmission was received.

Oliver loaded up my computer implant with the relevant software a while ago. It's a straightforward matter to start up the program, tell it what to look for, and run the vid through its processing algorithms. The results come back after just a few seconds.

Looks like we got lucky: Gladys was transmitting from a place with external sunlight coming in through a window, and that flat gray background made it easy for the software to analyze the light intensity. And I had reference images of her face from my earlier mission recordings, which were perfect for calibrating shadow lengths. I overlay the coordinates returned by the software onto a map of the Moon's surface and look for buildings.

Bingo.

"Mister Hong," I say, "set a course for farside."

CHAPTER TWENTY-FOUR

The Moon—farside
75 minutes before I give Gladys a piece of my mind

It's going to take over an hour to get from where we are, hovering above the remains of SDF1, to the location my eye software extrapolated from the vid image. Our destination appears to be an industrial helium-3 processing plant, abandoned for several years according to Lunar building authority records. It's in an old special economic zone, which nobody cares much about now that the United Nations has standardized intra-Lunar trade across national sectors.

I suggest putting on some music over our commandeered ship's audio system but am outvoted by everyone else. Hong prefers to fly in silence. Khan and Jessica want to conduct a thorough inspection of the vehicle's interior and storage compartments without distraction.

After half an hour of unproductive ransacking—well, I'm ransacking, anyway, doing my best to turn over every access panel and equipment hatch I can, while Khan and Jessica are being more methodical and neat with their searches. Hong, probably wisely, limits his search of the cockpit to the computer systems. We don't really want to damage our flight controls.

Khan's wrist controls beep out an alarm. "Kangaroo," she says, pausing her search and motioning for me to stop tearing apart the side of the cargo bay. "Time to do a radio check."

"Right." I put aside the hatch I just pried off from above one of the benches and blink my eye to bring up the list of reference pointers to the ships in the pocket right now.

The inside of the pocket looks and acts like deep space, but it's in a whole other universe, as far as we can tell. And every pocket location is farther apart than we've been able to measure, so each shuttle inside the pocket right now is totally isolated. Once I closed the portal, there was no way to communicate with anything inside the pocket. But because these ships are basically in deep space—and if anything goes wrong, they're looking at a disaster in space, which is always bad—we need to check in regularly to make sure they're all still doing okay.

"Start with one," Jessica says, unnecessarily.

"Starting with one," I say.

I open a pinhole to the first ship. I'm not actually retrieving the item from the pocket, so we just need a small opening to the other side. Technically it could be a microscopic hole, invisible to the naked eye, but it helps to have visual confirmation that I've actually established the portal. So I pop open a small portal, just about a centimeter in diameter, with the barrier in place. It glows in midair, roughly level with my throat, about a meter in front of me. I turn so Khan can see that it's there. Once a portal is opened, it's locked to my position in space, so when I turn, it turns, always facing toward me.

It still bothers Oliver that this "pinhole radio" trick works at all, since he can't figure out the physics of it. Science Division knows that once I put an object into the pocket, associated with a particular reference image, the reference is tied to the *object*, not the location in the pocket universe—which is why the "back door" trick works at all, and why even though each of these shuttles is moving farther away from the pinhole while we talk, I can still close the portal and reopen it later to let them out. I can't explain it. The pocket just works like that.

Khan works her wrist controls. "*Mapale*, this is Khan. Radio check, over."

The radio crackles, then blasts out a cacophony of sound. It takes me a few seconds to make out two voices shouting at each other: Rich Johnson and Alisa Garro.

"Is it closed?" Alisa asks.

"I think it's closed!" Rich replies.

"You need to make sure!" A clattering noise erupts from the speaker. Then, in a louder voice, as if Alisa's moved closer to the microphone: "*Calypso*, are we clear of the crater? Are we being pursued?"

"Yes, we're clear," Khan says. "Out of danger. But—"

"Good," Alisa says. "We need an emergency exit, right now."

She's asking me to pull them out of the pocket.

"Request denied," Khan says before I can weigh in with my opinion. "We are not in a good position to land your ship."

"This is not a request!" Alisa says. "Emergency exit! We are bleeding oxygen and we need to land! Now!"

"What happened?"

"Small electrical fire. It's out now, but life support was damaged."

"What started the fire?"

Alisa hesitates, then says, "I can't tell you."

"Doc, if we don't know what the problem is—"

"You don't need to know," Alisa snaps. "Your orders are to safeguard my project and give me whatever support I require, right? Well, right now we require a portal out of this pocket!"

I see the sides of Khan's jaw bulging. She must be clenching her teeth. "Wait one." She mutes her radio and turns toward the cockpit.

"We're on a pretty tight schedule here," I say, following her.

She ignores me. "Hong, what's our ETA to the destination?"

"Forty minutes and change," Hong replies. "Is there a problem?"

"I need you to find a crater to put down in," Khan says.

"Is that really a good idea?" I ask, poking my head into the cockpit over Khan's shoulder. She's standing in the doorway, probably hoping I would be reluctant to invade her personal space. So wrong.

"They're losing atmosphere," Khan says, not looking at me.

"Is there a problem with their shuttle?" Jessica asks.

"Or with Project Genesis?" I ask.

Khan glares at me. "We're done talking about this. I'm still the ranking officer here, and I'm giving you an order, Kangaroo."

"Hello?" Alisa's voice burbles out of Khan's wrist controls. "We've got a situation here!"

"Hong, put us down in the nearest crater with a rim elevation of at least ten meters." Khan backs out of the cockpit doorway. "Kangaroo, sit." She points at the co-pilot's seat.

I look at the chair, then at her. "I haven't actually flown in a long time."

Khan glares at me. "I'm not asking you to take the stick. I just need some privacy." She waves at Jessica. "Doctor. Jump seat, please."

Jessica moves forward and sits down behind my chair.

"Thank you," Khan says. "Now the three of you, stay in here while I go sort out Garro."

"I heard that," Alisa says over the radio.

"I know," Khan says into her wrist. She moves out of the doorway, and Hong closes the door behind her.

"Do you want a refresher on piloting, sir?" Hong asks. "This bird's actually pretty interesting—"

"No, thank you," I say. "And quiet, please. I'm listening."

Hong frowns at me. "How can you hear through that door?"

"Implants," Jessica says.

Hong shakes his head and smiles. "Right." He puts a finger to his lips and turns back to his controls.

I turn up the gain on my audio sensors and tilt my head toward the cockpit door.

Khan: "Did I understand you correctly? You are venting atmosphere?"

Alisa: "If you get us out of the pocket and on the ground quickly enough, we'll be okay."

Khan: "Is this equipment failure? A malfunction? I can ask Kangaroo if he's got any repair items in the pocket."

Alisa: "No, it's not equipment. I can't say any more. Just get us out of the pocket and on the ground."

Khan: "We're looking for a crater to set down in. Shouldn't be more than a few minutes."

Alisa: "Good. I also need you to ask Kangaroo if he's got any food stored in the pocket. Specifically, anything sugary."

Khan: "You mean like glucose pills?"

Alisa: "No, I mean like candy."

Khan: "Candy."

Alisa: "Yeah. Candy. Chocolate. Anything like that."

Khan: "What the hell is going on, Doc?"

Alisa: "I can't tell you anything else."

Khan: "I can't help if I don't know what the problem is."

Alisa: "I don't need help. I need some goddamn candy. Just ask him, okay? I'll bet he's got some hidden away. Tell him it's an emergency."

Khan: "A candy emergency."

Alisa: "This is *my* project and *I* decide what constitutes an emergency! Do I need to remind you that I report directly to the secretary of state? If anything goes wrong here, it's your neck on the line, Khan!"

Khan: "Terrorists are attacking the Moon, Doc. I'm sure State has more important things to worry about than whatever lab animal you've got caged up in there that needs to have its sweet tooth satisfied."

Alisa: "Just get us out of here and get me some damn candy."

As soon as I hear Khan moving toward the cockpit again, I strike up a conversation with Hong.

"She's coming back," I say. "Pretend you've been teaching me about the controls here."

To his credit, he doesn't miss a beat, and starts speaking a split second before the cockpit door slides open. "Normally the stealth coating will absorb all incoming energy, including visible light and radio waves, but the override pops open a hatch to do passive sensing for four hundred milliseconds. That's long enough to confirm the ship's position from stars and navigation beacons." He turns to look at Khan. "All done?"

Khan looks at me. "You were listening, weren't you?"

There's really no point lying to her. "Yes. But it's not like she told you anything I couldn't hear anyway."

"No," Khan agrees. "But I had to pretend to play her game to get her talking."

"I notice you didn't tell her we're out of immediate danger," I say.

"She doesn't need to know that." Khan turns to Jessica. "You have any idea what her project might be?"

"You seem to already know that it involves live animal test subjects," Jessica says.

"They can't hide all their supplies," Khan says.

"They wouldn't need to hide it so badly if it wasn't highly sensitive," Jessica says. "I'm guessing it's either nanotech with biological components—"

"Swarms?" Hong says, with more than a hint of terror in his voice. Ever since the Fruitless Year, the public has been understandably skittish about hybrid biotech. Robots, cool. Cyborgs, not so much.

"—or some kind of noninvasive gene therapy delivery system," Jessica continues. "Her Ph.D. thesis dealt with artificial airborne viral vectors."

"Wait," I say. "You went to school with Alisa Garro?"

Jessica sighs. "We've known each other for a long time."

"How long?"

"Save the backstory deep dive for later," Khan says. "Kangaroo. Do you have any candy?"

"Yeah, I can spare a couple of—"

"Good. Hong, status?"

"Found us a crater to land in," Hong says. "ETA four minutes."

Khan turns back to me. "Let's finish those radio checks, Kangaroo."

Five minutes later, we've confirmed that all the other ships in the pocket are doing just fine, and Hong has set us down in a crater half lit by sunlight. Khan and Jessica and I move back into the cargo bay and start putting on spacesuits.

"How concerned are we that someone's going to spot us out there?" I ask while stepping into the bottom half of my suit.

"Minimally," Khan says, climbing into the top half of her suit. Why is she so much faster at this than I am? "I'm more worried about someone noticing when you pull an entire shuttlecraft out of the pocket."

"Fair point." I pick up my helmet. "Anything we can do about that?"

"This ship was only designed to hide itself," Khan says. "No detachable camouflage devices." Some military spacecraft carry their own stealth canopies to hide certain maneuvers or deployments from external view. I definitely prefer to use the pocket out of public view.

"Maybe there's survival gear here," I say, waving around the cargo bay. "We just need some sort of opaque covering, to hide us from potential orbital observers."

"You have emergency structures in the pocket," Jessica says. "Survival shelters, triage tents—"

"Oh! Yeah." I blink my eye to bring up Oliver's list of supplies. I can't remember all the stuff he makes me pack into the pocket for every active mission, so we always make a list and check it twice. "Here we go. Three work shelters. Each one stands three meters tall, with a hexagonal canopy three meters across. We can fit them together to hide the shuttle."

"We'll also need to raise them higher than three meters," Khan says. "You can't open the pocket into solid matter, right?"

"Right," I say. "Solid objects will stop the event horizon from expanding any farther." That can be useful sometimes, when I want to pop open a portal that fills an entire hallway, for example. Don't even have to think about controlling the dimensions; just open it until it stops on its own.

"Pull all three canopies," Jessica says. "We'll take the support struts from one and add them to the other two. That'll get us six meters of height, which should be enough to bring the shuttle through."

"Should we get Hong to help us?" I ask.

"Negative," Khan says. "He needs to be ready to fly us the hell out of here if anyone does notice us."

The work shelters are packed into pretty compact cases, so I open the pocket inside the ship's cargo bay—we've already opened it to vacuum, so I can open portals without the barrier—and pull all three items. Khan and Jessica help me drag out each one—the cases are weightless inside the pocket, but once they cross the portal threshold the Moon's gravity takes over and pulls them to the deck.

We quickly assemble the canopies just outside the open cargo bay doors, planning to open the portal perpendicular to this ship's ramp so *Mapalé* has plenty of runway for a dead-stick landing.

"Good to go," Khan says after testing the last strut she lashes into place. "Six meters by three."

"Okay," I say. "Let's hope nobody's looking in our direction."

I stand at the edge of the canopy that ends next to the cargo ramp and visualize my reference object—a blank prescription pad—and open the portal on the other side of the next canopy, six meters away. I push the portal open, without the barrier, all the way up to the canopy and down to the Lunar surface.

The shuttle comes sailing out of the portal, headed straight for me. It's not moving fast, but it's big, and it gets bigger by the second. I can't close the portal until it's all the way through, or bad things will happen.

"Slowing down?" I say over the radio. "Slowing down would be good now, *Mapalé*!"

I see Khan working the wrist controls on her suit at the same time that the thrusters in the nose of the shuttle fire, sending Lunar dust flying everywhere and obstructing my view of the approaching spacecraft.

"Got it," Khan says over my suit radio. "Just hold tight."

I bite my tongue and will myself not to throw up my arms in a reflexive but futile gesture of defense. The Lunar dust doesn't hang in the air—no atmosphere, so nothing to hold it up—and I get glimpses of the shuttle, looming ever larger, as the thrusters pulse to slow its forward motion. Then gravity drags it down to the surface of the Moon, and the ground shudders as the hull of the shuttlecraft slides along the rocky ground, kicking up even more dust and rattling me in my space boots. Literally.

A moment later, the shuttle grinds to a halt, and I open my eyes again. When did I close my eyes? At least I didn't throw my hands up. That would have been really embarrassing.

The nose of the shuttle rests about half a meter from where I'm standing. Behind it, I can see the outline of the portal still shimmering, a white ring glowing against the blackness of space. I can also feel a familiar dull ache in the back of my skull—the beginnings of a pocket hangover. I close the portal and turn my head, nudging the helmet controls to extend a drinking tube, and suck down some water.

"Any landing you can walk away from, right?" Khan walks around the side of the shuttlecraft and waves at me. "Okay, give me the candy and I'll take it inside."

I bump my head against the in-helmet controls and put away the drinking tube. There's a reason I didn't pull the sweets before we did this little stunt.

"Negative," I say to Khan. "We go in together."

"I'm coming, too," Jessica says.

Khan sighs. "She's not going to like this."

"She can join the club," I say.

CHAPTER TWENTY-FIVE

The Moon—farside—shuttle *Mapalé*
Let's say 3 minutes before shit gets real

Alisa Garro is waiting for us when the shuttle's airlock cycles open. She's standing just inside the inner door, arms folded, the fingers on one hand tapping her elbow. The tapping stops when she sees all three of us—Khan, Jessica, and me—standing in the airlock with our helmets off. Rich Johnson, standing behind her, looks very nervous.

"He can't be here!" Alisa points at me, then shakes her finger. "*They* can't be here!"

"Hello," I say, waving. "We're here for the petting zoo tour. I'm going to feed the animals!" I smell smoke. I hope Project Genesis doesn't involve airborne psychotropic compounds.

Alisa walks up to Khan. "Get them out of here."

Khan shrugs. "Your problem, Doc. By the way, we've got ten minutes before we need to leave." They've silenced the audible alarms, but red alert lights are still flashing all around the cabin. A warning message on one screen says they've got less than fifteen minutes of life support remaining.

Alisa fumes and turns to me with a fiery glare. "You are not authorized—"

"Let me explain the situation," I say. "It's real simple, *Doc*. I have something you want. You have something I want. We make the exchange, and everyone's happy."

"I can't do that," Alisa says.

"Well, then, I guess we'll be leaving," I say, moving to put my helmet back on.

Jessica steps forward. "Ali." She pronounces it like "alley." *Why are you on a nickname basis with this person?*

"I'm not talking to you," Alisa says.

"Then you're going to listen," Jessica says. "I know you've got some kind of live animal specimen back there." She points to a sealed compartment behind Alisa. "And if this shuttle really is losing oxygen, you're risking that life to keep a secret that isn't even yours."

"You don't know what you're talking about," Alisa says.

"What's more important?" Jessica says. "Keeping your animal alive? Or keeping your job with State?"

"You have no idea what you're asking."

"Stop being so dramatic," Jessica snaps. "Just tell me. Tell me what's so important you can't attend your own mother's funeral."

"Wait," I say. "Wait, what?"

"Six years!" Alisa says, her hands balled into fists. "I have been on this rock for six years straight! I couldn't tell anyone. That was the deal. I had to give up everything so I could—"

She slaps a hand over her mouth and screams into it. Jessica waits for her to finish before speaking again.

"Why?" Jessica asks, in a softer tone. "Why didn't you rotate back to Earth?"

"I chose to stay. There was a window, but then—" Alisa shakes her head. "We had a breakthrough, and I had to choose. I couldn't just hand off the project to someone else and go away for more than a year. I couldn't leave—" She squeezes her eyes shut. "I chose to stay. So now I can't go back. That's why I couldn't be there."

"You could have said something," Jessica says. "Anything. We would have understood—"

"Like you're understanding now?" Alisa snaps.

"I'm working on it," Jessica says. "I'm here, aren't I?"

They stare at each other for a while.

"Okay," I say. "What the hell is going on?"

"Let them talk," Khan says to me. "Haven't you ever seen sisters arguing? Just give them a minute."

I feel lightheaded for a second. Then I step closer to Jessica and say in a very loud voice: "SISTERS?" No wonder her personnel file was so light on personal information.

"Half sisters," she says without looking at me. "We had the same mother."

"I'm sorry," Alisa says. "I know it's not worth much, but I am."

Jessica puts a hand on her shoulder. "It's a start."

I turn to Alisa. "ARE YOU FUCKING KIDDING ME?"

Khan grabs the collar of my spacesuit and pulls me back. "You're not helping, Kangaroo. Doctors, we need to leave in less than nine minutes."

"Understood," Jessica says. She's still looking at Alisa. "What's the candy for?"

Alisa shakes her head. "I'll show you." She points at me. "But not him."

"No deal," I say.

"Dr. Garro," Rich says quietly, "Kangaroo might be able to offer some insight into our issue—"

"No," Alisa says. "This is not happening."

"We never anticipated this particular situation," Rich says. "You know that term you're so fond of? A 'failure of imagination'? Well, I would really argue that's what we've run into here."

Alisa puts her face in both hands and mumbles something that might be severely profane.

"We're in trouble," Rich says, "and the two people who might know how to help are standing right in front of you." He glances up at me. Still creepy.

Alisa drops her hands and shakes her head. "This is not happening."

"Remember that other saying you like? 'No secret keeps forever'?" Rich shrugs. "Maybe you've kept this one long enough."

"State will not like this," Alisa says.

"Which do you think State will like less?" Rich asks. "Sharing the secret? Or letting it die?"

"Fucking Sophie's choice," Alisa groans.

"Hey!" I didn't think anyone else knew that antiquated reference. "I know what that is!"

I look at Jessica. She's not nearly as excited about this as I am.

"You know what?" Alisa throws up her hands. "Fuck it. I'm losing my job anyway at this point. I might as well go out in a blaze of glory." She glares at me. "It'll be better than the last time I got fired, anyway."

"To be fair," I say, "I was just the whistleblower."

Alisa jabs a finger at me. "Fuck you." She turns the finger on Jessica. "Fuck you." Then Khan. "Fuck you." Finally Rich. "Fuck all you mother-fuckers."

I lean toward Jessica. "Are you sure you're related?"

"Quiet," she replies.

"All right!" Alisa twirls around and walks to a locked hatch. "Come one, come all! Step right up and see the show!"

"It's going to be fine," Rich says, walking backward to the hatch. "It's going to be okay. Just—" He gives me a hard stare. "Don't freak out."

"Why would I freak out?" I ask.

"It's going to be okay," he repeats, as if he's trying to convince himself.

Bright, raucous music fills the shuttle as soon as Alisa opens the hatch. Not just music, though—I also hear a cacophony of overlapping human voices. Recordings? Why do they sound familiar?

We enter the compartment on the other side of the locked hatch, which appears to be an entire separate cargo bay. But there's no cargo here. The whole space appears to have been converted into a habitat for someone very messy. There are clothes piled in various places on the floor, computer tablets and other electronic gadgets strewn about, and at least three different vid screens playing entertainment programs.

That explains the music and voices. I recognize all the vids, too—they're old twentieth-century animations. Some of my favorites when I was kid, in fact. There's that yellow sea sponge in the pineapple, there's the duck and rabbit arguing about hunting season, there's the moose and squirrel—

Who the hell is living in here?

I follow a trail of short-sleeved shirts around a stack of boxes. There's a small human figure sitting in a chair—some kind of medical treatment setup, like the scanning chambers back at Lunar General, with instruments on flexible arms and a control panel on the side. A black medical-signal collar is closed around the person's neck, and the display surface is lit up with numbers and colors indicating his physiological state.

I look closer and freeze in my tracks.

The person in the chair is a child. A boy. His eyes are closed. Looks like he's asleep. Brown-skinned, messy mop of black hair, a face that shows its angles even through the baby fat that still clings to it. Lights in the transparent dome over his head flicker over that face. A face that I'm intimately familiar with.

It's my face. The face I was born with, before all this cosmetic surgery—

I'm not freaking out. I'm not freaking out. I'm not—FUCK!

It feels like all the moisture has been sucked out of my mouth. This can't be happening. This can't be what I think it is.

And yet, some part of me is aware that this was probably inevitable.

"Who's that?" I hear myself asking.

"His name's Joey," Alisa says.

I stare at the boy for a moment, then turn to give her an incredulous look. "Really?"

She shrugs. "Not my decision."

"Really?" I seem to be shaking both fists in the air. *"Joey? Really?"*

"Explains why she's 'Dr. Jill,'" Jessica mutters.

"I don't get it," Khan says.

"They're terms for kangaroos," Rich says. "The animals, I mean. An adult male is a 'jack,' a female is a 'jill,' and a baby is a 'joey.'"

I can't fucking believe this.

"How old is he?" Jessica asks.

"Six years old next month," Rich says.

This is ridiculous. This is completely insane.

"What does this have to do with the shuttle venting atmosphere?" Khan asks. That's good. It's good that one person here is still on task.

"He's never been in a spaceship before," Rich says. "He's just a little—excitable."

"We didn't have time to childproof this shuttle," Alisa says. "He pried open a maintenance hatch and crossed some wires."

"Where?" Jessica asks.

"I can show you," Rich says.

They move back toward the hatch. Khan starts to follow them, then stops. "No," she says, observing the staring contest I'm having with Alisa. "I'd better stay here." She turns back and folds her arms as Jessica and Rich exit.

"Thank you," Alisa says.

I point at Joey. "What's wrong with him?"

"I don't have time to explain right now." Alisa walks over to the control panel of the chair. "The treatment cycle's almost done. Depending on how long it takes to repair life support—"

"We don't have time for that," Khan says. "There's room for all of us in the other ship. Start packing up whatever you need."

Alisa's eyes widen. I'm not sure I've ever actually seen her frightened before. "No. That's not going to work."

"I'm not asking, Doc," Khan says. "We're on the clock here."

"Whatever your issue is," Alisa says, "it can't possibly be as important as saving his life." She points at Joey.

I feel a lump in my throat. "He's dying?"

"Not exactly," Rich says behind me. He and Jessica rejoin the circle. "But he does need regular treatments in the MTI rig."

"How bad is the damage to this ship?" Khan asks Jessica.

"He did more than cross some wires," Jessica says. "It looks like someone let a five-year-old child play with a plasma cutter."

Khan looks at Alisa. "Is that right?"

"We didn't *let* him do anything," Alisa says. "He's been very difficult to control since we left the crater. Overstimulated."

"And we can't sedate him," Rich says, "because the risk of—"

"The point is," Alisa says, "moving him into another new environment is just going to wind him up again."

"We're four adults here, Doc," Khan says. "I think we can handle one kid."

"*Five* adults," I say. "Six, if you include Lieutenant Hong. But hey, who's counting?" I'm sure she didn't *intend* to insult me.

"I'm only counting the people who are free to babysit Joey. Hong's flying the ship. And *you* are going to stay as far away from the kid as possible." Khan points at me. "This situation is already complicated enough."

"No," I say, starting to feel angry. "No, that's not how this is going to work."

"Kangaroo, we've got six minutes—"

"I'll talk fast." I point to Joey. "That appears to be a real live human being, cloned from my illegally obtained genetic material."

"It wasn't illegal," Alisa says.

"We can debate that later," Jessica says. She turns to Rich. "Is he having seizures?"

"They're more like episodes," Rich replies. "But MTI is the only effective treatment we've found so far. Medication doesn't work, and we can't predict when he's going to have an episode. We also haven't been able to identify any specific triggers or warning symptoms—"

"We need the machine," Alisa says. "And as you can see, it's not exactly portable."

"That's not true," Jessica says. "The chair's just a chair. All you need is the armature—"

"Oh, and did your Ph.D. in nuclear medicine teach you how to manually calibrate Tay-Mar Effect coils?" Alisa snaps. I don't know exactly what those coils are, but I know the Tay-Mar Effect is used for magnetic containment in ionwell propulsion systems, so the components in question must need to be configured very precisely. "Or does it just come naturally because you're a fucking robot?"

"I need a third vote!" Khan says. She points at Rich. "What do you think?"

"Me?" Rich seems surprised. "I'm just here to assist."

"You're a nurse practitioner, and you've been working on this project for as long as she has," Khan says, jerking a thumb at Alisa Garro. "What is your medical opinion?"

Rich glances over at Alisa. She glares back at him. Rich opens his mouth slowly.

"Who are all these people?" asks a childish voice behind me.

I look over at the chair. Joey's eyes are open. They're dark, just like mine. He's looking around. He can't move because of the chair restraints.

"Can I get up now?" he asks.

I move to undo his restraints. He shrinks back from me.

"I'll do it," Alisa says, stepping out from behind the control panel.

"Ali?" Joey says. He pronounces it "ah-LEE," like the Muslim name. Like the famous twentieth-century boxing champion. Greatest of All Time. But Joey's looking up at Alisa Garro.

That's funny. That is fucking hilarious.

"It's okay, Joey," she says, opening the med-sig collar and pulling away the restraining straps around his arms, legs, and torso. "These people are our friends. How are you feeling?"

"Fine." Joey climbs out of the chair and walks right up to me. "Who are you? You're brown like me."

Of course he doesn't recognize me. Even if he would have recognized his own face, aged forward two decades, I no longer have the face I was born with. The agency likes to invest in cosmetic surgery for its field operatives, to minimize the chances that they'll be recognized by people or computers. There are ways to shape facial features that will confuse a large percentage of automated scanners, and look forgettably average to most humans.

"What's your name?" Joey asks.

"Kangaroo," I say without thinking. I swear I can hear Jessica grinding her teeth.

"That's a weird name. What kind of name is that?"

"It's a long story."

"I like stories! Tell me the story!"

This cannot be happening.

"Hold that thought," I say. Joey's bouncing up and down now and chanting, "Story, story," over and over again. I turn to Rich. "Medical opinion, please?"

"We can disassemble the MTI rig," he says. "It's modular. Is there enough space to set it up in the other ship?"

"Yes," Jessica says.

"Okay, time's up," Khan says. "We need to go. Doc, you got a spacesuit for Joey?"

"I got it," Rich say. He opens a locker and starts pulling out a tiny space-suit.

"Whoa! Rick! Are we going outside?" Joey asks.

"Yes, we are."

"Yay!" He starts making noises that could generously be interpreted as singing.

Alisa walks over to me and puts her face centimeters from mine. "I hope you're happy."

I gape at her. "You're kidding, right?"

A loud screeching noise fills the room. I look over and see Rich struggling with Joey.

"We're not finished," Alisa says, then goes to help Joey into his space-suit.

CHAPTER TWENTY-SIX

The Moon—farside—anonymous crater
10 minutes after the universe blew my mind

Once everyone's in spacesuits, Alisa Garro walks Joey from the *Mapalé* over to Scorpion's stealth ship. Jessica and Rich Johnson take apart the medical machine that Joey was sitting in and move it out, one piece at a time, while Khan and I box up other equipment and supplies from Joey's room and stow them in the pocket. I hope there's nothing in there that won't survive a few hours in hard vacuum.

Joey. I still can't believe it.

After we get everything into the stealth ship's cargo bay, I stand on the open ramp and look at the abandoned shuttle sitting on the Lunar surface.

"I'm not sure I can put that shuttle back in the pocket," I say. Opening tiny pinholes for radio checks doesn't take too much out of me. But making a five-meter hole in the universe is more of an effort.

"Forget it," Khan says, walking down next to me. "We'll blow it after we dust off."

"We're going to destroy an entire shuttlecraft?"

"This is farside. No one's looking. And we're low on time," Khan says. "Our priority is keeping you and Joey safe."

"Right."

"And making that rendezvous with Clementine."

I turn to look at her. "Is that still on the agenda?" I feel like our priorities might have shifted in the last few minutes. Of course, Jessica and I have already wandered pretty far from our original mission: what should have been a simple info buy has turned into the craziest road trip of all time, with a side of dysfunctional family reunion.

"Look," Khan says, "I understand this"—she waves back up the ramp, toward the passenger compartment of the ship—"is a frankly earth-shattering revelation, especially for you. But I still have a job to do. I need to keep my people safe, and that means making sure 'Scorpion' and 'Clementine' aren't planning any more terror attacks. I want to know they're contained before you pull anyone else out of the pocket."

I nod. "Right."

The dust on the Lunar surface is so still. No atmosphere. No wind. Nothing changes here without external intervention. It's so peaceful—

Khan nudges my shoulder. "Are you listening to me, Kangaroo?"

"I'm listening," I say. "Take down the bad old lady. Make sure she won't hurt anyone else. Eighty-five percent chance of punching."

"Let's get inside."

I follow Khan up the ramp and through the airlock into the crew cabin. Alisa and Rich are sitting on either side of Joey, on a metal bench along one wall. Jessica is securing the disassembled pieces of the MTI rig against the opposite wall. I see Hong through the open cockpit door, sitting in the pilot's seat.

A loud, high-pitched noise fills the compartment when I remove my spacesuit helmet. It takes me a second to recognize it as Joey screaming at the top of his lungs. Did I ever sound like that when I was a kid? I sure hope not.

"What happened?" I ask.

"He's fine," Alisa says.

"He didn't want to come inside," Rich says.

"Seriously?" This is another reason I don't work with kids.

"Wanna Moonwalk!" Joey screeches.

Rich gives me a shrug. "He likes jumping really high." Well, at least that implies they do let him out of the lab every once in a while.

Alisa holds up a small plastic toy. "Hey, Joey, you want your dinosaur?"

"No!" He slaps it out of her hand and continues screaming.

"A little help here?" Alisa says, glaring at me.

"Hey, Joey," I say, "you want to blow up a spaceship?"

The screaming stops, and Joey gives me his full attention. "For reals?"

"Wait, what?" Rich says.

"Khan?" I say, turning to the tall woman scowling behind me. I seem to deal with a lot of scowling women. Weird.

"You sure about this?" she asks.

"Yeah. You're doing a remote detonation?" She nods. "Have Hong turn the ship so Joey can see it. Then let him push the button."

"Hell, no!" Khan says. "He's a five-year-old kid!"

"I'm almost six and I wanna push the button!" Joey starts bouncing up and down on the bench. Alisa and Rich do their best to restrain him. "Push the button! Push the button!" he starts chanting.

I lean in close to Khan. "You remember being five years old?"

"A little," she mutters.

"Can you think of a better way to distract him?"

She glowers at me. "*You* get to write up the after-action report on this."

"Sure."

Khan steps forward and waves toward the cockpit. "Okay, Joey. Let's go."

Alisa stands up. "Are you sure this is a good—"

"Talk to Kangaroo," Khan says, ushering Joey into the cockpit.

"Thanks, Kangaroo!" Joey calls back before the door closes on him, Khan, and Hong. Now it's just Alisa, Rich, Jessica, and me in the cabin.

"We need to talk," I say to no one and everyone.

"Agreed," Jessica says.

"Yeah, you first." I point an accusatory finger at her. "SISTERS?"

"Half sisters," she says.

I turn my finger toward Alisa. "A FUCKING CLONE?"

"It wasn't my idea," she says, as if that makes a difference.

"And YOU!" I point at Rich.

He holds up both hands. "What did I do?"

That's fair. I don't have a specific complaint about him. But I'm still mad as hell.

I unleash a torrent of obscenities at the world in general. It takes at least a solid minute before I'm out of interesting swear words.

"Finished?" Alisa asks, her arms folded.

"*You're* finished," I say. I've decided I'm angriest at her. "You are *so* fucking finished!"

"I have to agree." Jessica sounds remarkably calm. "You're all going to prison."

"Whoa!" Rich says. "Who said anything about prison?"

"That," Jessica says, pointing at the closed cockpit door, "appears to be a whole clone of a living human being."

"Well, yeah," Rich says. "It's a medical breakthrough—"

"It's a felony is what it is," Jessica snaps, looking at Alisa now. "This is a violation of at least seven different interplanetary statutes, not to mention basic medical ethics. What the hell were you thinking?"

"I was thinking my career was over and I didn't have a whole lot of options," Alisa says.

"What could possibly have possessed you to come up with such a ridiculous idea?"

"*My* idea?" Alisa's hands ball into fists. "You think *I* could have talked State into supporting something like this? Especially after how thoroughly Lasher burned me?"

Jessica frowns. "You mean—"

"Genesis has been running since the day after State found out about *him*." Alisa points at me. "The name's a joke. A double entendre. It's about creating life, but the project itself was only brought to life because of Kangaroo."

"More like a *meta* entendre, actually," Rich says.

"Should have called it Project Frankenstein," I mutter.

"Joey doesn't have the ability yet," Alisa says. "We don't know if he ever will. Hell, we don't know if he'll live to be ten years old. It's a miracle that we brought him to term at all."

"Wait." I can't believe it took me this long to do the math. "He's almost six years old?"

"That's right."

I point at Alisa. "He's the reason you stayed on the Moon. Why you didn't leave. You've been here ever since he was born."

She glares at me. "I wasn't going to abandon an infant."

"Or you didn't trust anyone else to look after him."

"I don't have to explain myself to you," Alisa snaps. "I told you. I chose to stay."

I'm not sure how to read the expression on her face. Is it possible that dealing with a baby awakened some maternal instinct inside the evil witch? Could her heart actually have grown three sizes over the course of those first few months? Or did she just want to maintain control over her experiment, to micromanage what Joey ate, what he read, what vids he watched—

"No." I suddenly realize something. "Oh, no, you didn't. You did not!"

"I'm guessing she did," Jessica says.

I can't come up with a gesture intense enough to convey what I'm feeling. "You *also* stole my *parents'* vid library?"

I didn't think it was possible to feel more violated than being cloned, but here it is. As an orphan, that archive of ancient movies and television series was the only connection I had to my dead parents. I watched those shows over and over again while I was growing up. I can quote entire episodes from memory in some cases.

"I didn't *steal* anything," Alisa says. "You consented to medical procedures which gave us blood and tissue samples. And you asked Equipment to load your vid library into your eye."

She's right. Years ago, I asked Oliver to copy all those vids into my implanted computer memory so I could rewatch my favorites during long space voyages. I didn't think about who else might have access to them.

"That put the vids in the agency warehouse," Alisa continues. "Just like your blood and tissue samples. They're property of the agency now. And come on, that data's not private anyway."

"So you just wanted to rub it in?" I say. "It wasn't enough to steal my DNA for your crazy illegal experiment, you had to steal my entertainment, too?"

"Kangaroo," Jessica says, "that's not why she did it."

I frown at Jessica. "Are you actually defending her?"

"No," Jessica says. "They were trying to condition Joey's brain."

I gape for a moment. "You think *watching television* is why I can use the pocket?"

"We don't *know* why you can use the pocket!" Alisa says. "We needed to reproduce the stimuli you had as a child as closely as we could."

"So you're also going to bring in some bigger kids to knock out his front teeth in a couple years?" I can't believe any of this. "Jesus Christ, don't you think *raising him on the Moon* has already skewed the results?"

"Low gravity doesn't significantly affect brain development," she says. "Science Division has been doing animal studies here for decades. We've established that. But we know exposing infants to vid screens can influence mood, behavior, learning—"

"And you did it anyway?"

"We had to take a calculated risk."

"And now Joey's sick."

Alisa scowls at me. "That's not because of the vids."

"I want to see your records," Jessica says. "I want to see all the research—"

"Wow, real classy, sis," Alisa says. "You're just going to *assume* we did something wrong? The only possible answer is that we missed something because nobody could possibly be as perfect as the golden girl, Jessica fucking Chu?"

"This isn't personal," Jessica snaps. "This is *science*. This is about independent verification of experimental results."

"You've seen the result." Alisa points at the cockpit door. "We made a life."

"You made a sick child," Jessica says. "What's wrong with him?"

"We don't know," Rich says.

"You had him in an MTI rig. You were treating him."

"What the hell is MTI, anyway?" I ask.

"Multifocal transcranial inducer," Jessica recites, still staring at Alisa. "State of the art for diagnosis and treatment of chronic mental illness. I'm guessing it's something congenital?"

Alisa's arms are folded tight across her chest. "Have you ever tried to clone a human being? It's not as easy as it looks."

"He's five years old," I say. "State's been running this project for over a decade. That means—"

"Yeah," Alisa says. "You don't want to know what we went through before we succeeded."

"You haven't succeeded," Jessica snaps. "What's wrong with his brain?"

"We're closing in on a diagnosis—"

"You don't even know?"

"They appear to be psychogenic nonepileptic seizures," Rich says. "We haven't been able to pinpoint the cause, but we're able to treat the symptoms using noninvasive stimulation."

"How bad?" Jessica asks.

Alisa raises a finger. "You don't know this patient's full history. If you're going to do a proper consult—"

"Hold on," I say. Something just clicked in my head. "He was born on the Moon. Joey's never left the Moon."

Alisa's mouth curls up on one side. "He's the first Lunar native. Too bad we can't tell anyone."

"Why here?" I ask. "Why not an asteroid, or a Jovian satellite? Why hide on the Moon? There are millions of other people here, civilians—"

"There's infrastructure. State didn't want us too far away, just in case something did go wrong. The Moon's only a few hours from Earth orbit, in case there was some kind of medical emergency, or some other critical situation we couldn't resolve independently. We could mitigate his exposure to higher gravity if we needed to."

"Nine years," I say, feeling lightheaded again. "Jesus fucking Christ."

"It's not personal, Kangaroo," Alisa says.

"It's a little hard *not* to take it personally when someone *clones* you."

"I mean they would have done it with anyone," she says. "Anyone who showed up on the agency's doorstep with a superpower. State isn't in the business of being nice to people. State is in the business of protecting our national interests. And learning more about the pocket has always been the priority."

"You mean the second priority," I say.

"What are you talking about?"

"The first priority was training me to use the pocket for field missions, right?"

Alisa gives me a look that breaks my heart.

"*You* wanted that, Kangaroo," she says softly. "You and Lasher. State never wanted to risk you in the field. That's why you weren't in the war."

My head starts spinning. I knew Paul was trying to protect me, but—

"They wanted a fucking *backup copy* of me?" I say.

"I'm sorry, Kangaroo," Alisa says, and for the first time, I believe her. "But we're all on the same side here. We're all working toward the same goal."

"And what the hell is that *goal*?" I'm not going to cry. I'm not going to fucking cry in front of her.

"The more we understand about the pocket," she says, "the better we can help you figure out how to live without it."

I frown. "What the fuck does that mean?"

She opens her mouth at the same time my eye starts flashing an alarm. I hold up my hand before she can speak.

"Shit," I say, remembering why I set that alarm.

"What's wrong?" she asks.

"That's the timer."

"Timer for what?"

"Time to let the prisoner out," Jessica says.

Alisa frowns. "What prisoner?"

We check in with Khan and come up with a plan for dealing with Scorpion. Joey seems pretty happy to stay in the cockpit with Hong and Alisa, but I pull a toffee-and-chocolate candy bar out of the pocket and give it to Alisa, just in case she needs to bribe the kid at some point. If a sweet tooth is hereditary, I'm pretty sure he'll like it.

Khan joins the rest of us in the cargo area. A few minutes later, we're ready to receive 'Scorpion.'

Rich, Khan, and I are holding spare bulkhead panels in front of us like shields. They're designed to be welded onto the spacecraft in case of hull breaches, and should be thick enough to stop any bullets. We've arranged ourselves up against one wall of the cabin, with me facing the wall, Khan on my left, and Rich on my right, making a rectangular opening between us and the wall.

I'm going to open the portal in that gap, and as soon as our mystery guest pops out we're all going to rush him and hold him in place there. Then, once we've got him pinned down, Rich is going to step back and Jessica is going to step in and smash Scorpion's helmet visor and spray a suppression compound in his face. Hopefully before he can shoot her. But hey, she volunteered for that spot. We're counting on the element of surprise to be on our side anyway.

"Ready?" I ask my partners in crime.

They reply in the affirmative. I count down from five and then open the pocket.

I can't see through my shield—even with my eye sensors, this material is designed for spacecraft, so it's radiation-opaque—so the only way I know Scorpion has come out is when his weight thumps against me. I close the pocket and shout when that happens, and we all rush forward, clanging our shields against his spacesuit. Sounds like the suit is armored. I hope the helmet visor isn't too tough for Jessica to shatter with the tactical baton I pulled.

Rich calls out just before he steps back, and Jessica moves into the gap between his shield and mine immediately. Scorpion is facing away, and Jessica gets behind him before he turns and starts firing his rifle into the cabin. She cracks his helmet and sprays him before he can get off a second burst. I hear a hideous screech as he drops the rifle and claws at his face, which must now be both lacerated from the broken helmet visor shards and burning from the suppression compound.

Rich drops his shield and picks up the assault rifle from the floor. Khan and I also toss our shields aside, and Jessica steps out of the way as we move in to grab Scorpion's arms and pull him to the deck. It's like we're doing a little dance. A very poorly choreographed, very violent dance, with dangerous chemicals and bullets as props.

My heart is still pounding after we wrestle Scorpion to the ground and he stops convulsing. Jessica leans over him and sprays a negating compound in his face to stop the burning sensation he must be feeling. I look closer and realize—

"This is a woman," I say out loud.

The woman opens her eyes and blinks at us. "Yeah, no shit," she says, her voice still modulated to a growl. "Are you single, asshole? Looking for a date?"

"I'm not sure how to respond to that," I say.

"She's probably not your type," Khan says.

"Let's get this helmet off and clean her up," Jessica says.

Rich holds the assault rifle muzzle less than a meter from the woman's face while we strip off her spacesuit and restrain her to a bench against the wall. She doesn't struggle while Jessica brushes the bits of shattered visor from her face and sprays some ointment over the small cuts. Her undershirt is sleeveless, and there are scorpions tattooed on both shoulders— one red, one green. She really committed to her merc handle.

On general principle, I blink my eye into scan mode and check her for any hidden weapons. She's got some communications implants— shoulder-phone, satellite antenna, subdermal microphone and earpiece— but nothing that looks dangerous.

"Thanks," Scorpion says when Jessica's done treating her. Her voice is still a modulated growl. I exchange a surprised look with Khan.

"That's your real voice?" I ask.

Scorpion scowls at me. "Throat cancer. Figured if I was going to get a synthetic voicebox, I might as well sound like a badass. What's your fucking excuse?"

"Okay," Khan says, stepping between us. "We need to ask you some questions."

"Fuck off," Scorpion says. "That's my answer."

"No," Khan says, "that's not how this is going to work."

She grabs Scorpion's left thumb and twists it. The woman howls in pain and tries to head-butt Khan. Khan dodges and grabs Scorpion's right wrist and presses into it with her own thumb. The howls of pain get louder, then subside to whimpering.

"This is how it's going to work," Khan says. "I'm going to ask you some questions, and you're going to answer as truthfully as you're able to. Got it?"

"Fuck . . . you . . ."

"What's your name?"

"Fuck—"

Khan does something that must hurt even more. Scorpion goes silent, and her entire body is trembling now.

"Khan," Jessica says before I can chime in. "Maybe there's a better way."

Khan releases the woman and steps back. "We don't have much time."

Rich is still holding the weapon on Scorpion. Jessica pulls up a cargo box and sits down facing the woman.

"Hi," Jessica says. "I'm Dr. Chu. Are you feeling okay? I want to make sure Khan didn't do any permanent damage."

Scorpion glowers at Jessica. "Oh, are you the good cop, then? Am I supposed to get all doe-eyed 'cause you're a fucking hottie? Maybe lift your skirt and show me the goods, maybe then I'll be interested, you cunt."

Jessica, to her credit, doesn't even blink at this. "Okay. We do it the hard way."

She moves faster than I expected, slapping an injector slug onto the side of the woman's neck. Scorpion struggles, but with her arms tied down, she can't get the slug off. A moment later, she shudders and slumps back against the wall of the cabin.

"That's better," Jessica says. "Now, tell me your name."

"Jane Doe," the woman says, "you fucking bitch."

"Truth serum?" Khan asks.

"Yeah," Jessica replies. "Sometimes it works better than others."

"Maybe give it a minute to sink in?" I ask. I've used this stuff before. It usually works better if the target's self-control has already been softened up by alcohol or other controlled substances.

"I know what I'm doing," Jessica snaps. "Let's try this again, friend. Tell me your name."

The woman looks at Jessica with heavy-lidded eyes. "My name is Jane Doe."

Jessica sighs. "Or maybe it's not working at all."

"No, it's working," I say. I've turned on my eye's medical scanners, and I can tell the woman—Jane—has calmed down, and she's not showing any of the physiological signs of deception. "Jane, what's your merc handle?"

"Scorpion," Jane replies.

"One big happy mercenary family," I say, and nod at Jessica. "Go ahead."

"Who hired you to do this job?" she asks Jane.

"Belter," Jane says, using the slang term for a permanent resident of the asteroid belt between Mars and Jupiter. "Charlie Angel. Middleman. Connects buyers and vendors."

"Boy, you mercs sure have fun with your handles," I say.

Khan turns to me. "You think that's an alias?"

"'Charlie Angel'? Uh, yeah."

"Why?"

"Come on. *Charlie's Angels*?" Everyone gives me blank stares. "Really? Private detective show, hugely popular for years? Jaclyn Smith, Cheryl Ladd, Kate Jackson? Come on, nobody else has heard of this?" Clearly I'm the only one who took advantage of a huge digital library of twentieth-century entertainment vids during puberty.

Khan turns to Jessica. "Does he do this a lot?"

"Just log the name, Kangaroo," Jessica says.

"Fine." I blink up my agency data link and queue up a search for when we get back into radio coverage. Maybe it is a real name. Maybe it'll lead us to some other terrorists. If nothing else, the agency can roll the middleman for more information.

"Who else are you working with, Jane?" Jessica asks.

"My mother."

That's odd. I would have expected "yo momma" instead.

"What's your mother's name?" Jessica asks.

Jane's neck muscles tighten before she answers through clenched teeth, like she's trying to keep the information from escaping. "Gladys Löwenthal."

"WHAT," I say, "IN THE ACTUAL FUCK."

Jessica holds up a hand. "Do you mind?"

"ACTUAL FUCK," I repeat. "I AM DONE." I can't take any more of these surprises. I start pacing the cabin to distract myself.

"What was the plan?" Jessica asks Jane Doe.

"Mod a rock and . . . throw it at Shackleton," Jane says, still glassy-eyed. "Wait for you to evacuate base. Send in the spiders. Capture . . . base personnel."

"So you were just supposed to intercept our evacuation?" Khan asks. "Nothing more?"

"Buyer wanted a specific retrieval," Jane says. "Wanted to find . . . Dr. . . . Alisa Garro and her secret project. Didn't tell us what it was. But it was worth a lot of money to him."

"Shit," Jessica says. She's right. Not even Paul knew Alisa Garro was on the Moon. If Sakraida's behind this, that means he cracked some heavy-duty encryption on the files he stole from Intel. How many other secrets does he also have access to now?

"What were your orders after completing the retrieval?" Khan asks.

"Rendezvous with Charlie to deliver the doctor and her project. Get paid," Jane says. "Guess that's not gonna happen now."

"Okay," Khan says, nodding to Jessica, "we're done here."

Jessica slaps another slug onto the side of Jane's neck, and her eyelids close and her body slumps to one side. She starts snoring almost immediately.

"That's going to be pleasant to listen to for the next few hours," I grumble.

The cockpit door slides open, bringing us the sound of Joey wailing like a banshee.

"Rich," Alisa says, "we need to set up the MTI."

CHAPTER TWENTY-SEVEN

The Moon—farside
5 minutes is a long time to listen to a screaming
kid in a small enclosed space

Not even the offer of a second candy bar can stop Joey's wailing. It takes Rich and Jessica way too long to set up the MTI rig—it's bulky and takes up most of the width of the compartment—and endless minutes for Alisa to power up the machine and start the treatment program. Joey finally quiets down when the plexi dome over his head starts flexing and rippling, pressing electrodes against different parts of his head in sequence.

"How often does he have pain during the seizures?" Jessica asks.

"Never," Alisa says. "It only started after we put him in the pocket."

"It's fascinating, isn't it?" Rich says, sounding more excited than I feel he should. "Your brain controls portal formation, but maybe something in the pocket universe also affects your brain. Or his brain, because it's the same! You know?"

"Let's talk about this later," I say. I'm really not looking forward to all the new tests Science Division is sure to want to perform on me in the very near future.

"The basic anodyne program seems to be working for now," Alisa says.

"For now?" Jessica repeats.

"He's five years old," Alisa says. "His brain's still developing. We have to adjust his treatment every few days to remap neuronal hotspots."

"How much time is he spending in the chair?"

"He's fine."

"You can't do this with just two people," Jessica says. "The research alone—"

"Hey, it's not my call, okay?" Alisa says. "You think you can talk some sense into State, be my guest."

"Well, it does look like things will change now," Rich says. "I mean, we'll have to relocate, at the very least. Dr. Chu, maybe you'd consider joining our team? Or consulting every once in a while?"

"Rich," Alisa snaps. "Let's focus on keeping Joey alive right now."

Rich nods. "Sure. Absolutely. Sorry if I overstepped."

"Wait," I say. "What do you mean, 'keeping Joey alive'? His condition isn't life-threatening, is it?" I look at Alisa. "You didn't say it was life-threatening!"

"It wasn't before," she says. "I don't know what it is now."

I look around at all three of the stooges. "Are you fucking kidding me?"

"His episodes are becoming more frequent," Alisa says. "The most common symptom is loss of consciousness due to autonomic irregularity. Stimulants just make it worse. The only reliable treatment we've found is using MTI to stabilize his brain function."

The cockpit door opens, and Khan comes back into the crew cabin. She looks around and points at Jane Doe. "How much longer is she going to be out?"

"Probably another hour," Jessica says. "We could wake her up. Why?"

"We're almost at the rendezvous point," Khan says. "How do we want to play this?"

"What rendezvous?" Alisa asks.

Khan gives a quick summary.

"This is a bad idea," Alisa says. "Our priority is keeping Joey safe."

"He's safe," Khan says. "We need to contain Clementine. And it's my call."

"Waking up Jane Doe isn't going to help," I say. "Why would she cooperate with us?"

"We need some other way to get close to Clementine," Jessica says. "She's going to be expecting Scorpion. That armor pattern's very distinctive."

Khan rubs her chin with one hand. "How tall are you, Kangaroo?"

Jane Doe's spacesuit is snug on me, but I'm pretty much the only option for getting into it. Khan's too tall, Hong's flying the ship, and Jessica and Alisa and Rich have their hands full with the medical mystery that is Joey.

So I sort of de facto draw the short straw and have to put on the suit.

Joey wakes up while I'm in the middle of suiting up, so Alisa and Rich squeeze into the cockpit with him and Hong. Jessica and Khan finish helping me get ready. We leave Jane Doe snoring in the corner.

"I've disabled the radio transmitter and helmet microphone," Jessica says as she hands me Scorpion's backup helmet, after I've stepped into the lower half and squirmed into the torso section and closed the seals between those two parts. "You'll still be able to receive and hear, but just remember to respond nonverbally."

"Right," I say, taking the helmet. "Because I can't do a reasonable impression of Scorpion's voice."

"Just let Clementine do the talking," Khan says. "Follow her lead, look for cues—"

"I have done this before, you know," I say, lowering the helmet onto the collar of the spacesuit and locking it into place. "This isn't my first silent rodeo."

"And now we can't hear you anymore," Khan says. She moves behind me and tugs on my life support backpack. "Seals look good. How's your air?"

I look at the status indicators on the suit's wristpad and give Khan a thumbs-up. This spacesuit is similar to the armored numbers I've worn sometimes, borrowed from either military or law enforcement inventories, but feels a little different. I suspect Jane Doe has made some of her own special modifications to better suit her mercenary lifestyle.

"Five minutes out," Hong says over the intercom.

"Have you found the helmet visor controls yet?" Jessica asks.

I nod at her, then work the wristpad to darken the visor on the helmet, making it reflective on the other side. This feature is usually turned on to reduce glare from the naked sunlight astronauts encounter in outer space, but can also be used to hide the wearer's face from other people, like I'm doing now.

"Sixty seconds out," Hong announces. "Got a visual on the landing site. Putting it on your screen."

One of the cargo bay's wall displays lights up with a view from one of the forward cameras—Hong must have opened a sensor slot to get some bearings as we approach. We're descending toward an industrial facility, one of the old helium-3 processing plants with large pipes going everywhere in what seem to be random paths but that are actually very specific configurations. I remember Oliver explaining to me once how the lack of atmosphere and low gravity on the Moon mean that energy companies can build structures that are less sturdy but more efficient. The Sun is shining at a low angle, casting long, dark shadows across the entire facility, making it look like some of the pipes disappear in the middle and then reemerge later from pure blackness.

"Any sign of a vehicle?" Khan asks.

"Not yet," Hong replies. "I'm going to set us down facing away from the building, and hopefully he'll see you from wherever he is inside when you open the ramp and step out."

"Copy that." Khan turns back to me. "Now remember, Kangaroo, you're going out there alone."

"Yes, I know. I'm not an idiot," I say before remembering that she can't hear or see me. I raise one hand with my thumb and index finger touching in the OK sign.

"Doctor Chu and I will be watching from just behind this partition," Khan says, patting the slot in the wall from which a safety baffle will extend, hiding them from anyone who might be looking up the open cargo ramp. "We'll be able to monitor you over the security vid feed. You remember the signal if you want us to intervene?"

I nod and make the hand signal we agreed on: left arm down at my side, palm facing backward, and then I make a fist and extend all my fingers three times in rapid succession. There should be no other reason for me to make that particular motion, and it should be obvious to the ship cameras watching me from behind and less noticeable to Gladys and whoever else might be watching me from the front.

"I've got the vid feed from your eye here," Jessica says, holding up her tablet. "We'll be able to see if anything goes wrong."

Khan hands me Jane Doe's assault rifle and helps me clip it into place on the chestplate of the spacesuit. I practice holding one hand on the grip, hoping I won't actually have to use it. I hate putting bullets into people if there's any other option.

Unfortunately, if Gladys meets me out in the open, I won't be able to use the pocket-right-behind-you trick to suck her in; we'll both be in vacuum already. And it's going to be tricky, talking her into doing anything specific when I can't actually talk.

The ship touches down, and Khan retreats behind the safety line at the end of the ramp. "All right, everyone get into position."

I stay standing at the edge of the ramp while Jessica joins Khan behind the baffle. They're both wearing spacesuits, and now they close their helmets, ready to come after me if anything goes wrong. Alisa and Rich are still in the pressurized crew cabin with Joey.

"Clear," Hong says. "You can open the ramp when you're ready."

"Okay, Kangaroo," Khan says. "Here we go."

I give her a thumbs-up, then wait as the door slides shut behind her and Jessica and air hisses out of our section. The ramp descends, thumping gently against the Lunar surface, and I walk out into the sideways sunlight.

The abandoned factory looks more imposing from down here, at human height, than when we were flying over it. I walk forward slowly, one hand on the assault rifle clipped to my chest, the other swinging as casually as I can manage. I don't want Gladys and whoever else might be watching to think I'm off my guard, but I don't want them to think I'm trigger-happy, either.

I blink my eye into passive scanning mode and look around. No signs of heat or movement. I hope we're in the right place.

Two alerts pop up in my eye: now that I'm out of the stealth ship and back in radio coverage, my name search on Charlie Angel has been transmitted to the warehouse, and I've received a message from Oliver asking for a status update.

"It's been a while, Janey," comes Gladys's voice over the suit radio.

I dismiss the alerts—I'll deal with Oliver later—and look around, but still see nothing. I raise my left and wave hesitantly, then hold up my palm in a *What now?* gesture.

"Inside," Gladys says.

An airlock door pops open around the corner from where I'm standing. It's a good thing I've switched my eye sensors on, otherwise I wouldn't have seen that—I'm now seeing the glowing outline of the heat from inside the airlock, where atmosphere was until just a second ago, and the mist of rapidly dissipating air molecules escaping from the opened door. I hope this building's structure won't interfere with my eye transmission back to Jessica.

I walk over to the airlock, not too fast, not too slow, still keeping a lookout for any snipers or other confederates that Gladys might have brought. I enter the airlock, pull the door closed behind me, and look for controls to start cycling it. Before I find them, the pressurization cycle starts, as indicated by blinking lights above me. Gladys must have started the cycle from inside.

The inner door of the airlock pops open, and I step through. Gladys is standing alone in a large, bare, empty area.

I blink. Gladys is *standing*.

There's no sign of her wheelchair, but as I walk forward, I notice metal bands around her torso and legs. A power-assist exoskeleton. I wonder how many gold bars she traded for this new toy.

"Long time no see," she says.

I do my best to hide the motion of my head as I look around the room, using my eye to scan for other radio sources or heat signatures, but Gladys notices.

"Don't worry, we're alone," she says. "This is a private family reunion."

Gladys takes a step forward, her exoskeleton flexing as she walks. I take a step back.

"Really?" Gladys says, stopping her motion and putting her hands on her hips. "Is that how it's going to be?"

I do my best to shrug through the armored spacesuit.

"Oh, for pity's sake. Aren't you even going to talk to me? Say something."

I shake my head.

"Take that damn helmet off."

I shake my head again.

"Fine," Gladys says. "You don't want to talk, you can listen."

She snaps her fingers, and I see motion to either side of me. Before I can react, two industrial assembly robots clamber up to me on their six legs and clamp multiple manipulator arms onto my spacesuit's armpieces, shoulderpads, and helmet. They lift me up until I'm dangling a full meter off the ground.

"I was worried that you might bring some of your little robot friends along," Gladys says. "I saw what you did out at Hadley Rille, dumping that body. I would say it was sloppy, but maybe you wanted me to see it. Maybe it was a subconscious cry for help."

My suit radio crackles. "Kangaroo, Khan. We're right outside the airlock. No other tangos in sight. We're going to breach as soon as Clementine turns her back. That should give you a little extra time to drop her in the pocket."

I can't acknowledge, of course. All I can do is wait for the earth-shattering kaboom.

"Did I do something to drive you away?" Gladys says, now pacing back and forth below me. I keep my eye on her—literally, so Jessica can pick the best time for her and Khan to breach the building. "I lie awake some nights asking myself that. Did I do something wrong? Could I have done something more? Did I fail you, Janey? I ask myself that a lot.

"But then, after I've thought about it for a while, I always reach the same conclusion." Gladys stops pacing and looks up at me. "No. I did everything I could for you, as a parent, as a mother, as a mentor. But for some reason, it just wasn't enough. I could never get through to you."

"Just breach," I mutter. "Breach now, goddammit. This monologue is going to go on for hours."

"And what are you getting mixed up in now, Janey?" Gladys shakes her head. "All this crazy spy stuff? Murdering people with robots? Do you even know who you're dealing with? I didn't want to take this job at first, because I could smell Sakraida's stink all over it. He's a mean old sonuvabitch. He can hold a grudge like nobody's business, and he's still got the resources to make it hurt.

"You have no idea how bad these situations can get, Janey. And if you get too deep into it, you'll never be able to get out. These people will dig in their claws and never let you go."

Gladys sighs. "I'm sorry, Janey. I can't let you do this to yourself. I know we made a deal, but I'm your mother. No matter how far you run or how much you do to make yourself unlike me, we're still family. I still care about you.

"So I talked to your pal Charlie," she says, waving one hand in a way that makes me think the gesture has some significance between her and Jane Doe. "We negotiated a price for the secondary objective. It'll be enough to buy you some breathing room with your creditors." She turns her hand to face me, palm out. "Don't even start. I know this'll burn you off the Moon, and I know it's a cliché, but I really mean this: it's going to hurt me more than it hurts you."

She turns away from me. "I'm sorry."

"There is it," I say. "Come on!"

I hear an explosion behind me. Gladys's head snaps up.

I open the pocket right behind her and suck her into vacuum. The look on her face is priceless.

I blink a countdown timer into my eye. I don't actually want Gladys to suffocate or freeze to death in the pocket; I just needed her out of the way briefly. She'll be fine for at least twenty seconds. Maybe push it to thirty. She's not that old or frail.

Khan and Jessica each run up to one of the robots holding me in midair and smash at the manipulator arms with their weapons. Fortunately, Gladys didn't program these bots with defensive programs, and she didn't bring any others for fighting.

The clamps release me, and I fall gently to the floor. Hooray for one-sixth gravity. I pull off my helmet so I can talk to Khan and Jessica.

"Took you long enough," I say.

"Let's get Gladys out of the pocket," Jessica says.

"Oh, come on." I check my timer. "It hasn't even been fifteen seconds yet."

Jessica glares at me. "Kangaroo."

"I'll catch her," Khan says, standing next to me and putting one leg back to brace herself.

I count down from three and open the pocket, rotated so Gladys will fall toward us. The older woman tumbles out of the portal toward me, right into Khan's waiting arms. She gasps and shivers. The moisture on her clothes and all over her face and hair has frozen into tiny little ice crystals.

"What—what—" she blurts, choking down mouthfuls of air. "What was that?"

"Surprise," I say as Khan turns her around. Her eyes widen when she sees me.

"Wh-where's Jane?" she asks.

"Wouldn't you like to know," I say.

Jessica presses an injector slug to the side of Gladys's neck, and she closes her eyes and slumps against Khan's spacesuit. She lowers Gladys to the floor.

"She's got to have a pressure suit somewhere in here," Khan says.

All of our radios buzz at once. "Khan! This is Hong! We've got a situation out here!"

"Hong, Khan, what—"

"Joey's locked us out of the cockpit!" Hong shouts. "I think he's trying to fly the ship!"

CHAPTER TWENTY-EIGHT

The Moon—farside
1 minute into Joey's first solo flight

The nearest airlock is useless, since Khan and Jessica blew out the inner doors just now. I blink my eye into scanning mode to look for another exit.

"There!" I point to the back of the building. "Vehicle entrance. We can seal the inner door, then blow the other side to get out."

"We don't have time to get Clementine into a suit," Khan says. "Someone needs to stay and guard her."

"Are you volunteering?" Jessica asks.

Khan shrugs. "I guess I am."

"He's figured out how to work the maneuvering thrusters!" Hong calls over the radio. It sounds like things are rattling in the background. "He's not responding to the intercom. We're still on the ground, but I don't know how long it'll be before he gets to the main engines."

"Copy that," Khan says into her radio. Then, to Jessica and me: "I'll call Copernicus and ask for a pickup. *Go.*"

I start bounding toward the other airlock. Jessica follows. We must look pretty ridiculous, but bunny-hopping is actually the most efficient way to travel long distances on the Moon by foot. If an Earth-born human tries to run here, her legs will push off the surface with too much force and propel her into the air anyway. I notice that we're getting out of sync as we approach the airlock.

"It might be tricky getting both of us onto the ship," I say.

"No," Jessica says. "You're going to put me in the pocket, and then you're going to run for the ship."

"Oh. Right. Good idea."

We reach the airlock and put our helmets on. I pull the inner door shut. Jessica fixes a small explosive charge to the far edge of the outer door, then comes back to my corner and detonates it. The door flies away, taking the atmosphere in the airlock with it. In the distance, I see the black mass of the stealth ship shuddering off the ground in a cloud of Moon dust.

"Reference object," Jessica says over the radio. "Cluster of crocus."

"Got it." I think of a bunch of five purple flowers, and open the pocket.

"Get us on that ship," Jessica says. She steps through the portal.

I close the pocket and run for it.

Hong's status reports over the radio are helpful, yet not helpful. Helpful, in that he provides important information that is directly relevant to my current objective; not helpful in that he's basically screaming in my ear the whole time. I don't blame him for freaking out a little. I am starting to get annoyed, though.

"The prisoner is still secured!" Hong says as I round the corner of the building and see the stealth ship hovering maybe half a meter above ground. "But I think she's starting to wake up!"

"Great," I mutter, knowing no one else can hear me. "Another person to contribute to the scintillating conversation."

One of my boots slips on a loose rock, and I tumble head over heels for a few meters before catching a toe on a small crater and stopping myself. I spring up again and launch myself into the air. I keep forgetting I can't run in this low gravity. Have to bounce. Just bunny-hop along, like in all those tourism promo vids. *Kids love it!*

What else do kids love? Hijacking small spacecraft, apparently.

I don't know if I would have done something this audacious, myself. I never had the chance. The most sophisticated vehicle I ever saw as a child was a police hovercar, and I was always in the backseat, behind a bullet-proof plexi barrier and usually shackled for transport. No chance of me getting loose and going for a joyride.

Before I can get within ten meters of the stealth ship, I see its black bulk tip forward, lifting the open cargo ramp into the air. The nose digs into the Lunar dust, stopping the ship's forward rotation with a shudder.

"He's figured out how to turn up the thrusters!" Hong shouts over the radio. "If he figures out how to sync the controls, he won't need the main engines to get off the ground. Is anyone receiving me? Hello?"

"I'm on my way! Keep your pants on!" I shout, before realizing that my radio isn't transmitting. "Goddammit!"

"Kangaroo is on his way," Khan says over the radio. "Just hang tight, Hong."

"That's a funny choice of words," Hong says.

I do my best to ignore the radio chatter as I bound toward the ship. The thrusters are still firing, mostly pushing the nose into the ground but also sliding the ship forward very slowly. I blink my eye into range-painting mode, so the built-in distance-measuring lasers can tell me exactly how far it is to the ship and just how high up that open cargo bay is.

Oliver, in his wisdom—or possibly just boredom and surplus of free time at the office—has programmed my range finder with a helpful estimation software module, which will tell me how fast I have to run to get somewhere or whether I can jump high enough to reach a platform that might be rising up and away from me. The software knows how much I weigh and how strong my legs are, and will do the math to draw glowing lines in my field of view so I know whether I have any chance of making a given jump.

I don't have a lot of time to use the implanted motion-sensing controls in my eye and fingertips to enter the precise parameters for the software to show me exactly what my chances are here, so I just turn it on with its gross estimation features. The target lines are wide and blurry, but it looks like I can jump into the open cargo bay.

I'm now about five meters from the ship, which is still scraping along slowly away from me. I look up at the open cargo bay again. It's about seven meters above me in the air, and five—no, make that six meters in front of me. Oliver's software gives me a wide ribbon of probability that I can make it inside from a standing jump. I bend my knees and prepare to leap.

Then the cargo ramp door starts closing.

I let loose with a string of expletives as the range-finder ribbon changes from green to yellow and then starts flashing red. I blink to change the parameters—how fast do I need to run, dammit?—and watch as a new set of arrows and numbers lights up in my eye.

"He's closing the ramp!" Hong shouts. "If you're trying to jump in here, you better do it soon! Once that door closes—"

I tap my suit's wrist controls to mute the radio. It's going to be hard enough to concentrate without all that noise right in my ear.

I turn, bound backward, then skid to a halt in the Lunar dust. I swivel around again on one heel, check my distance, and run toward the stealth ship.

When my suit's speedometer flashes green, I plant both feet on the next step, bend my knees as deep as I can in the armored suit—I really hope the estimation software isn't too far off—and push off the ground with all my might.

I can tell I'm going to fall short when I reach the top of my parabolic arc and start descending again. My jump didn't take me high enough above the ship's off-kilter back section. I stretch out both arms in a vain attempt to grab the lip of the rapidly closing cargo ramp, but the fingertips of my gloves just slide off the edge.

Time to take one giant leap, Kangaroo.

I bend at the waist, pushing my boots as far forward and up as I can, and work my wrist controls to activate the magnets in the soles. I see the touch indicator light up in my helmet, and I feel the slight vibration as the electromagnets power up.

My boots clank against the outside of the cargo ramp, and I exhale in relief.

Then I continue sliding downward.

"What the hell?" I cry, to absolutely no one except myself. I check the mag-boots again, but they're working just fine—

Fuck me. This is a stealth ship. Of course it's going to be nonferrous—not magnetic—to avoid any possible detection by electrical induction sensors. *Goddammit.*

And now my upper body is tilting backward, because there's nothing to stop it from falling faster than my legs, which are scraping against the hull and thus being slowed down by friction. That's great. I'm going to fall ass-over-teakettle and—

Wait. Wait a minute. Scraping. Clawing. *Claw!*

I think of an angry crow, open the pocket right in front of my chest, and reach in to pull out a grappling claw gun. I charge the firing bolt, aim the gun at the edge of the cargo ramp, and pull the trigger.

The recoil from the grapple-gun spins me backward, so I can't even see if it's hit the mark. I hope that my backward spin doesn't yank the tether back so much that the claw is stopped short of connecting with the stealth-ship's hull.

My anxiety evaporates when my arms are nearly yanked out of their sockets by the claw tether pulling me forward and up. I probably didn't need to worry at all. Given the fact that momentum is the product of an object's mass times velocity, my larger mass would have sent me backward at a much lower speed than the smaller claw was shot forward, which means that it would have hit the ship faster than I could spin it away, as long as I was close enough—

Hey, it looks like I'm actually learning some science stuff. Too bad Oliver isn't here to witness this. Or to tell me what to do next.

I work the controls on the side of the grapple-gun to reel in the tether cable. Halfway to the ship, I feel a shudder as the cargo ramp closes.

Well, *that's* another problem.

I unmute the radio, but Hong has stopped shouting for the moment. When the cable is fully reeled in, and I'm right up against the hull of the stealth ship, I pull my legs up and brace them against the hull. Then I open the pocket again, to another location, and use my free hand to pull out a pair of modified icepicks and matching crampons, specially designed for use with standard spacesuits—which, thankfully, this armored number appears to be.

Thank you, Oliver, for thinking I might have to go mountain climbing on the Moon for some reason.

The climbing gear is designed for quick attachments, and I snap the crampons onto my boots in a matter of seconds. I've got the first icepick attached to my right forearm—the one holding on to the grapple-gun for dear life—when the ship shudders, and I feel myself falling backward again.

"Thrust reversed!" Hong calls over the radio. "Kangaroo, I can see you on camera. Get the hell out of there before you're crushed!"

"Working on it!" I shout back, no longer caring whether anyone can actually hear me.

I switch the grapple-gun to my other hand. This second icepick really doesn't want to attach to the left wrist cuff of my spacesuit.

A red proximity warning flashes on the visor of my suit helmet. I'm out of time. I drop the second icepick, slap the grapple-gun onto my belt, push off the hull with my boots, and reach up as far as I can with my right arm and swing forward.

The icepick snags the hull of the ship, and my kick-off from the ship swings my lower body back behind me. I grab at the hull with my left glove. It's too smooth for me to get a purchase. My hand just slides off.

I feel the ship pulling down on me. I need to move fast to avoid being smashed between this very large vehicle and the rocky Lunar surface.

The thrusters are still firing. I can see their faint pale blue lines coming out of the hull above me and feel the slight vibration of the ship back here, right between the rear jets. I push myself back, pulling the pick out of the hull and shoving myself away with my left hand. The ship falls away from me. But I know where it's going—it's going to stop when it hits the ground again. I just need to grab it again before it leaves. And hopefully little Joey isn't that good at flying yet.

I pull the grapple-gun off my belt and work to reset the firing mechanism. Below and in front of me, the stealth ship smacks into the ground, sending Lunar dust up momentarily. It's weird how nothing hangs in the air here, but of course it doesn't; there's no air to suspend any loose particles and counteract the force of gravity. Things fall differently on the Moon.

Hong is yelling at me again, or possibly still yelling. Doesn't matter. I know what I need to do.

The maneuvering thrusters shut down just as I get the grapple-gun reset. I aim it at the top of the ship and fire a split second before I see the main engine covers irising open, revealing the large rockets that propel the ship forward.

"Don't leave yet," I mutter through clenched teeth as the grappling claw sails through vacuum toward the ship. How did I drift so far away in such a short time? "Not just yet—"

The claw hits the ship and sinks into place. I have barely enough time to breathe a sigh of relief before the main engines fire, and I'm yanked forward with not quite enough force to dislocate my shoulder, but more than enough to make it very painful.

CHAPTER TWENTY-NINE

The Moon—farside
11 minutes after the slapstick hijinks began

I'll say this about Hong: he's persistent.

"I don't know if you can hear me, Kangaroo," he says over the radio, "but it looks like you're still out there. At least, I hope you're hanging on. Something's attached to the ship, anyway, judging from the way that tether cable is stretched taut back there."

"I'm here!" I yell. Fun fact: yelling a lot does help reduce frustration. Even if no one can hear you. Something to do with the physical act of producing sound. I don't know. I'll ask Jessica when we have some free time.

The motor on the grapple-gun is having a lot of trouble right now. Probably because young Joey has pushed the throttle wide open on this souped-up stealth ship and is flying us across the Moon at what seems like a very dangerous speed, considering that nobody can see us.

The grapple-gun reels me in with agonizing slowness. I really hope the motor doesn't burn out before I get close enough to stick my climbing pick into the hull again. The ship's main engines are accelerating continuously, but not staying on course. Joey must be flying the ship manually, judging from how we're weaving all over the place. All the jerking around is starting to get really annoying.

We're in this situation because of one stupid kid who has no idea what he's doing and doesn't understand just how much trouble he's making for everyone else around him. I hate this kid. This kid is *not* me. He's not me at all. He hasn't had the same upbringing, the same environment, or the same terrible circumstances that led me to Paul Tarkington and my current life of interplanetary intrigue.

Joey may have my DNA, but he's a totally different person. He's just like my identical twin. Time-shifted by a couple of decades.

Boy, Science Division is going to have a field day with the whole "nature vs. nurture" argument on this one.

I'm finally close enough to catch my boots on the back edge of the ship. I pull myself onto the top of the hull, crouch down to secure my right-wrist icepick into the hull, and release the grapple-gun. Then I reset the grapple, aim it over the left side of the ship, and fire into the engine pod there, hoping it doesn't cause any significant damage. I'm pretty sure it won't; this hull needs to withstand micrometeoroid impacts while it speeds through outer space. And the engines inside need to be shielded. I'm sure it's fine.

The claw digs into the engine pod, and I reel the line in until it's tight. Only then do I release my pick and start walking, slowly, carefully, one cramponed boot at a time, over the hull toward the port side airlock.

"Okay, I see you moving, Kangaroo," Hong says. "I'm coming to meet you at the airlock."

I am so glad for Lieutenant Hong right now. I plan to give him a glowing write-up in my after-action report.

The airlock's outer door pops open as I approach. Good thing Joey hasn't figured out all the ship's override controls yet. I pull myself inside the airlock, leaving the grapple-gun attached to the engine pod just in case, and pull the airlock door closed behind me.

The airlock cycles, and sixty seconds later I step through the inner door. Hong is waiting for me, and he starts shouting immediately. I can barely understand him through the suit helmet. Behind him, Jane Doe is awake but still restrained, giving me an angry glare. Alisa and Rich are huddled around the MTI rig.

"What happened to your radio?" Hong says. "I've been trying to reach you this whole—"

I hold up one hand, which turns out to be my icepick-equipped hand, but that's probably good as it causes Hong to shut up quickly. I remove the icepick and take off my helmet.

"Nice to see you, too, Lieutenant," I say. "I'll explain in just a minute.

Right now I need to do a thing." I point at Jane Doe. "Would you mind knocking her out again or blindfolding her or something?"

"I don't have any sedative slugs," Hong says.

"Touch me and you're dead," Jane growls at us. That voice is really effectively creepy. I can understand why she went for that particular personal modification.

"It's not like that," I say. "Secret stuff. We can't let you see what we're doing. You understand, right?"

"Apparently you let a child take control of my ship," she spits at me. "I'm not really interested in cooperating any further."

"Oh, for crying out loud." I point to a spot on the floor between Jane Doe and me. "Lieutenant Hong. Stand right here, please."

He nods and steps between us. I think of an antique hypodermic syringe, open the pocket between Hong's torso and my own, and pull out an emergency medkit. Hong's eyes go wide just for a moment.

"Here." I give him the medkit. "Sedate her, please?"

Jane struggles as Hong approaches her with an injector slug, but she's tied down pretty well. He slaps the slug onto the side of her neck, and a few seconds later she's snoring again.

I open the pocket and retrieve Jessica. Hong helps us remove our spacesuits.

"What happened?" I ask Alisa. "There were *three* of you here to keep an eye on *one* child."

"This ship isn't exactly childproofed," Alisa snaps.

"Joey always gets a little hyperactive after an inducer treatment," Rich says.

"He found some hydrazine fuel cells," Hong says. "Thought they looked like flying disks, started throwing them around."

"Oh," I say. Hydrazine is a highly toxic, highly flammable rocket fuel, and normally shouldn't be stored anywhere near human passengers. But I guess a freelance mercenary like Jane gets to make up her own safety rules, or ignore common sense if she sees fit.

"He ran into the cockpit while we were back here cleaning up," Rich says. "And figured out how to lock the door."

"Can we talk to the cockpit?" Jessica asks, pointing at the door leading forward.

"I believe so," Hong says, "but either Joey's muted us, or he's just not responding."

"Having too much fun, maybe," I say.

Alisa whirls to face me. "This is *your* fault."

I throw up my arms. "How is this my fault? He's your project. If we're talking learned behaviors, there's only one place he could have learned them."

"You're setting a bad example," Alisa says. "He feels a bond with you, for obvious reasons. And you're strutting around, being insubordinate, demonstrating—no, actually *taking pride* in how you can get away with outrageous breaches of security and discipline. You think you're special, and the rules don't apply to you. Well, guess what! You're not the only person in the world! Your decisions affect others!"

Jessica steps forward. "Calm down, Ali."

"I will not calm down!" Alisa says. "I had everything under control. Why couldn't everyone just leave us alone and let us do our work in peace?"

"Your work," Jessica says, "is illegal."

"His entire *job* is illegal!" Alisa points at me. "The point of this whole fucking *agency* is to circumvent international law!"

Jessica slaps her across the face, hard, with an open palm. That's a little surprising. But it does shut Alisa up, at least for a few seconds.

I notice that Rich and Hong have moved forward and are fiddling with the intercom. Maybe they'll be able to distract these two before we have a full-on catfight here.

"Are you done?" Jessica says. "Because we have actual problems to solve."

Alisa gives her a look that could melt steel. "If you weren't my sister, I would straight up murder you right now."

Hong turns toward us. "Dr. Garro. Can you come talk to Joey, please?"

"This is awesome!" Joey says, his voice high-pitched and excited. The intercom is audio only, but I can imagine the oblivious grin on his immature face.

"Joey," Alisa says, leaning close to the intercom panel, "are you okay?"

I wave my arms in frustration. Alisa hits the mute button on the intercom.

"What?" she asks through clenched teeth.

"Is that really the first question you needed to ask?" I say.

"She's showboating," Jessica says.

I turn to frown at her, too. "What?"

"She wants him to know that she cares. Present concern first, not anger. Parenting basics."

"What would you know about it?" Alisa says.

"Careful," Jessica says.

"Both of you, shut up and let me work," Alisa says. She unmutes the intercom. "Can you hear me, Joey? Are you okay up there?"

"Yeah! I'm fine!" Joey replies. "It's so cool out there! Just like the history vids!"

"Jesus Christ," Alisa mutters, muting the intercom again and turning to point at Rich. "You need to talk to him."

"I guess I'd better," Rich says, stepping forward. He trades places with Alisa at the intercom and unmutes the microphone. "Hey, Joey. It's Rich. Are you seeing some cool stuff out there?"

"It's the Moon!" Joey says. "And space! And I can see Earth, way out in the distance!"

"Wow," Rich says, much more convincingly than I would have. "That does sound pretty cool. Where is the Earth? Can you tell me where in the sky it is?"

Smart. You're trying to figure out our position. The stealth ship is still jamming all our external comms, so we can't even get a location fix to know where we are.

"It's just hanging there, up out in space," Joey says. "Hey, if I put up my arm, I can cover the whole planet with my thumb!"

"Yeah, that's right, Joey." Rich shakes his head at the rest of us. "We're very far away from the Earth. Hey, can you tell where we are above the surface of the Moon? Do you recognize any craters or other features from our lessons?"

"Lessons?" I hiss at Alisa.

"He's been learning about the Moon." Then, after she notices me glaring at her: "Give me a break. He knows where he is. He knows what year it is. We couldn't exactly not teach him about his homeworld."

"Does your facility have a suggestion box?" I ask. "Because I need to fill out a few thousand comment cards and shove them—"

"Stand down, Kangaroo," Jessica says. "You can vent later."

"Yeah, you're on the list too," I say to her.

She replies with her trademark steely gaze. I lose the staring contest, as usual.

I look back over to where Rich is chatting with Joey about the mineral composition of the Lunar surface.

"Very good, Joey," Rich says. "What else do you remember?"

"There are three common isotopes of oxygen," Joey says. "They can tell you which planet a rock came from!"

"That's great. You've really been paying attention to your lessons. Well done." Rich nods at Alisa. "So, Joey, can you see any craters? Are we still flying too fast?"

Too fast? Too fast for what? That seems bad. Where could we possibly be going? I hope the kid hasn't been running the engines at full throttle. It wouldn't take much for a small ship like this to reach escape velocity and spin out into open space.

"Oh, we're over the Sea of Crises now," Joey says, matter-of-factly, as if he weren't in huge trouble. "I started slowing down a minute ago. We're almost at the Sea of Tranquility."

"What?" I say out loud.

Rich hits the mute button. "That's really distracting."

"Did I hear that right?" I ask. "We're headed for the Apollo 11 landing site?"

"Unless I can talk him out of it," Rich says, "which I can't do if you're making noise back there."

"Okay, go," I say, nodding. "Hurry up."

He unmutes the intercom. "Hey, Joey, you know that place is going to be really crowded, right? Maybe we should head somewhere else. There are lots of other historical sites around the Moon. Do you remember some of the ones you learned about last week?"

"Oh, it's cool," Joey says. "The Sea of Tranquility has been cleared of people. Some kind of security alert or something. I heard it on the news."

We all exchange confused looks. Rich waves at us to stay quiet.

"That's very interesting, Joey," he says. "What else did you hear on the news? Are you listening to the news right now?"

"Nah," Joey says. "It was too distracting. I need to concentrate on flying the ship. That's what you always tell me, right? Don't try to 'moldy-task' when you have one really important thing to do?"

"That's right. That's very good, Joey," Rich says. "Are we going to be landing soon?"

"In about fifteen minutes," Joey says. "Oh, yeah! I need to figure out how to land. Bye!"

"Wait, Joey—"

The intercom beeps, and the screen goes dark, indicating the channel has been closed. Rich taps at the panel, but apparently Joey has control of everything at the moment.

"That's no good," Rich mutters, then starts rapping the cockpit door with his fist. "Joey? Joey!"

While that continues, I turn to Hong. "How the hell can he be receiving anything? I thought the stealth hull absorbed all incoming energy."

"It should," Hong says. "Maybe some kind of new transductile stealth material? Something that *redirects* incoming energy instead of just absorbing it?"

"That wouldn't work," says a gravelly voice behind us. We all turn, and I see Jane Doe watching us with a toothy grin.

"How long have you been awake?" I ask.

Jane Doe chuckles. With her voice, it sounds like a rockslide ending in a bottomless pit. "The forward shutters are open. The kid's looking out the window."

"And radio signals can get through the plexi," I say. "But then why aren't we getting signal back here?"

"Bulkhead's shielded," Jane Doe says, tilting her head toward the front of the cabin. "Can't smuggle very effectively unless you can hide your passengers and cargo from scanners."

"Great," I say. "So not only does he have control of the ship, he also has more information than we do." I still can't quite bring myself to call him "Joey" out loud. It's just too ridiculous.

"At least he told us *something*," Jessica says. "We need to stop this ship. If we get anywhere near the Apollo 11 site, whatever security forces are there will detect us and mostly likely shoot us down." She turns to Jane Doe. "How do we get into the cockpit?"

"We don't," Jane Doe says. "This is my ship. I made sure nobody back here could cause too much trouble. I'm afraid we're just along for the ride, Doc."

"This *ride* is likely to end with a surface-to-air missile blasting us out of the sky," Jessica says. "Are you going to help us, or are we going to sedate you again?"

"You could hire me," Jane Doe says.

"Excuse me?" Jessica says.

"Hello? I'm a mercenary," Jane Doe says. "I got nothing against the government. I mean, I got no particular love for you feds, but I'll take any job if the price is right. Especially if I'm saving folks instead of hurting them or stealing their stuff. That's like a bonus and shit."

Alisa moves up next to Jessica and speaks under her breath. "I don't trust her."

Jessica grimaces at Alisa. "I don't trust you. We're still talking."

"I'm the ranking officer here," Alisa says. "And I don't like this."

"Maybe we should sedate you, too," Jessica says.

Alisa scowls at her, and now I see the family resemblance. "Do you *like* being court-martialed? Because I can definitely arrange that, *sis*."

"Kangaroo," Jessica says, projecting her voice in my direction, "what's our ETA?"

Yeah, I'm predictable. I blinked a countdown clock into my eye as soon as Joey told us where we were going. "Twelve minutes, twenty seconds."

"You have two minutes to think of another plan, *Doctor*," Jessica says to Alisa. "Otherwise we're hiring a mercenary."

After conferring with Rich for ninety seconds, Alisa gives up and grudgingly tells Jessica to go ahead and waste her money. Hong has managed to stay neutral and quiet through all this.

"Are we really doing this?" I ask Jessica, turning away from Jane Doe and lowering my voice in an attempt to get us some minimal privacy.

"Do you have a better idea?" she asks.

"Do you always answer a question with another question?"

"Does that bother you?"

If I didn't know her better, I'd think she was making a joke. "Forget it. Do you need some cash? I have emergency funds in the—"

"Shut up," Jessica says. "We're not reading her in to any classified information. We just need her for tactical support. Understood?"

I nod. "So how are you going to pay her?"

"I have a discretionary fund for medical emergencies."

"I mean, are you going to use a credit card, or what? I don't think she's just going to accept a handshake deal here."

Jessica makes a noise that could be the most ladylike grunt I've ever heard. "Currency is nothing more than promissory notes, backed by the faith and force of the United States government. All she has to do is trust me."

"Right. And how is that going to work?"

Jessica glares at me. "Just let me handle this, Kangaroo."

I raise both palms in a gesture of surrender and step back. Jessica walks forward to where Jane Doe is still restrained to the bench against the side of the ship.

Jessica holds up the key for the restraints. "I'm going to release you now."

"You don't want to negotiate first?" Jane Doe asks. "Haggle for a lower price while you still have some leverage over me?"

"We're all in the same boat," Jessica says, kneeling and undoing Jane Doe's ankle clasps. "Consider this an olive branch."

"I don't know what any of that means," Jane Doe says, "but I appreciate the gesture."

After Jessica finishes, Jane Doe stands up and stretches. I hear joints cracking.

"Ah, that's better." She nods at Jessica. "You ready to do some business?"

"Fifty thousand dollars," Jessica says.

Jane Doe doesn't react, but I have to work to contain my surprise. "Length of contract?"

"One week, or until Joey—the child—is safely returned to a federal facility under our control. Whichever comes sooner," Jessica says.

"I can live with that," Jane Doe says. "Also. I want any damage to my ship repaired."

Jessica snorts. "Dream on. You'll be lucky if US-OSS doesn't impound this spacecraft."

Jane Doe raises her eyebrows. "That's not okay with me."

"How many illegal modifications have you made to this vehicle?" Jessica asks. "No, wait, don't answer that, let us figure it out for ourselves. It'll be more fun that way. Don't worry, we'll compensate you for the blue book value of the original spaceframe."

"You're just going to let the feds steal my personal property?" Jane Doe asks.

"You were going to kidnap a child," Jessica says.

"I didn't know," Jane Doe snaps. Apparently this is a sensitive subject for her. "The job spec just said to grab her"—she points at Alisa—"and her medical equipment and anybody traveling with her. They didn't tell me it was a kid."

Whoever hired Jane Doe couldn't possibly have known about Joey, but Jessica doesn't reveal that. Better to let Jane Doe stew in her own guilt for a bit and soften her up for the ongoing negotiations.

"You can ask for an independent appraisal of this ship if you prefer," Jessica says. "But I recommend you let my department's Equipment officer perform the inspection. He'll give you fair value for the parts, if nothing else."

"Serves me right for agreeing to work with a government," Jane Doe grumbles. "Anything else?"

"We'll compensate you for any reasonable expenses. That includes all consumables: food, water, ammunition, medical supplies."

"Right. I'll make sure to save my receipts."

"And you report to me," Jessica says. "No one else."

"What if you're called away? Or sleeping?" Jane Doe asks. "Who's your second in command?"

"Nobody," Jessica says. "If I'm out of commission, you follow the last standing order you got from me, or you keep your own counsel. I'm paying your bills for the next week. Do we have a deal?"

Jane Doe smiles and extends a hand. "Sounds good to me, Doc."

"The name's Chu." Jessica shakes Jane Doe's hand.

"Whatever. You got a preferred handle?"

"Call me Surgical." Jessica turns to include the rest of us. "Let's talk about getting into that cockpit."

CHAPTER THIRTY

The Moon—nearside
11 minutes before we start buzzing tourists

Jane Doe is awfully sanguine about discussing possible ways to take apart her own ship, but maybe the idea that the feds are going to take it away anyway has softened the blow already.

"What about the cockpit door?" Jessica asks. "That's our most direct point of entry."

"Heavily reinforced," Jane Doe says. "Sorry. I transport a lot of, shall we say, unusual cargo back here. It's in my best interest to make sure the door stays locked. And it appears you've already bypassed the lockpad"—she points at the panel we cut through earlier—"so we can't use that trick again."

"It's still just a door, though, right?" I ask. "Didn't you build in any kind of failsafe, just in case you got into a situation like this?"

"Where I'm trapped in my own cargo bay?" Jane Doe gives me a dirty look. "I figured if I ever ended up here, I'd already be dead."

"Pessimistic much?"

"It's the life I chose," she says. "I don't have a government or a guild to hide behind. But I also don't have to pay taxes or union dues. I call that an even trade."

"Freedom's just another word for nothing left to lose," I say.

"What are you, a socialist?"

"Let's stay on topic," Jessica says. "Are there any other ways into the cockpit? Through a service hatch? The avionics array?"

"Sorry to disappoint you," Jane Doe says, "but I've made a lot of special modifications to guard against intruders."

"Hey!" Rich shouts from the forward part of the compartment, next to the intercom. "Has anyone else noticed we're not descending yet?"

"I guess he hasn't figured out the landing sequence yet," I say. "That's good. It gives us more time to figure out how to get into the cockpit."

"No, he knows how to work the thrusters," Hong says. "Otherwise he wouldn't have been able to tilt the ship upright from dragging along the ground."

"He might be—" Alisa starts, then clears her throat. "Joey might be unconscious."

"Um, why?" I ask.

She glares at me. "You know about his medical condition."

"We should send somebody outside to look in the window," Hong says, looking at Jane Doe.

"Yeah, sure," Jane Doe says. "I've got a cable rig for my suit. We'll be able to talk to each other while I'm outside."

"Go ahead," Jessica says.

I step close to Jessica and lower my voice to speak to her while Hong and Rich help Jane Doe into her armored spacesuit.

"Should, uh, somebody go with her?" I ask Jessica.

"Do you have another armored pressure suit in the pocket?" she replies.

"You really want 'Scorpion' in the cockpit? By herself?" I ask. "What's to stop her flying the ship away after she regains control?"

"We made a deal," Jessica says.

"You shook hands," I say. "She's a mercenary. I don't think we can trust her to—"

"If she breaks the contract, we have every reason to go after her with all the resources at our disposal," Jessica says. "Besides, I'm sure she can't wait to get all these strangers out of her home. Our interests align, for however briefly."

"Let's hope you're right."

"Let's keep our eyes open."

Jane Doe goes out the side airlock with a spool of tether cable. We all stare at each other for a minute while waiting for her to connect the cable to the communication port she claimed was on the outside of the ship. I wonder if anyone else is having the same doubts I am about Jane's trustworthiness.

The intercom chirps, and Jane's voice comes through in a filtered buzz. "Comms check, repeat, comms check, over."

Jessica taps the intercom. "We receive you, five by five. Acknowledge, over."

"Sounds good," Jane says. "I'm moving forward now."

I don't hear her breathing or any other ambient noises. The suit microphone must automatically mute itself until it detects sound that resembles human speech.

"Fuck me, that's close," she says after a few seconds. "Moving faster."

"What's close?" Jessica asks.

"We're approaching the museum," Jane Doe says. "Still got time, though."

"Can you be more specific?" Jessica asks.

"Hey, I can whip out my range finder, or I can get into the cockpit and stop this bird. Which one do you want?" I'm impressed that Jane manages to say all this with a minimum of attitude in her tone.

"Get to the cockpit," Jessica says, then turns to me. "Kangaroo, what's our ETA?"

"Five minutes, twelve seconds," I read off the countdown timer in my left eye.

"Maybe we should all get strapped into safety harnesses," Hong says. "Just in case."

"Shit," Alisa mutters while sitting down.

Hong and I help her and Rich get belted in, then sit down and strap in ourselves. Jessica takes the seat nearest the intercom panel amidships and buckles her harness without looking at it. She's watching the intercom display very intently.

"Shutters are still open," Jane reports over muffled scraping sounds. "I'm going to take a look inside. Hopefully the kid hasn't heard me banging along the hull out here . . ."

She trails off. After a second, Jessica says, "Scorpion, are you still there? What do you see?"

"Kid appears to be asleep," Jane says. "At least, I hope he's asleep. His face looks a little blue."

"Tell her to get in there *right now*," Alisa says.

Jessica holds up a hand. "We're short on time, Scorpion."

"Copy, Surgical, I'm working on it," Jane says. I hear more noises I can't quite identify. "Going to use a small shaped charge to crack the starboard window. Shouldn't take me more than thirty seconds to get inside and seal it up again."

"You need to get an oxygen mask on Joey as soon as possible!" Alisa shouts.

Jessica nods. "Did you get that, Scorpion?"

"Oxygen mask on the kid, copy that." I hear soft beeping noises. "Fire in the hole."

A muffled *thump* vibrates the front part of the ship, and then I hear more scraping and banging noises through the cockpit door. Jane must be making a lot of noise for it to be getting through the shielded bulkhead.

"Sounds like she's in," I say.

"Twenty seconds," Alisa says, looking at her wristband. "Come on!"

The cockpit door slides open with a loud whoosh. Jane Doe walks through, her helmet off, and swings her head around the compartment. "Who's the doctor back here?"

"I am," Jessica and Alisa say at the same time. They both start unbuckling their safety belts, but Jessica wins the race and bounds forward into the cockpit after Jane. Alisa follows close behind, and I move forward to see if I can look out the window.

"Three minutes to target," I call out into the cockpit. "If anyone's going to see us, it's probably going to happen soon."

"Yeah, we've got another problem," Jane says. "The kid locked up the thruster controls. I shut down the main engines, but I can't change course."

"How the hell did he—"

"What can we do?" Jessica asks.

"I can set off another charge against the dorsal hull and push the ship into the ground."

"You want to *crash* us?" I ask.

"Hey, it's plow into the museum or plow into the ground," Jane says. "And there are fewer civilians outside the building, on the surface."

"How about up into space?" I ask. "There's *no* civilians out there—"

"There's a whole fleet of security and military spacecraft circling overhead," Jane says. "They can't see us to avoid a collision, and I'd rather not be arrested for attacking a law enforcement vehicle. The ground will stop us from hitting anyone else."

"Turn on your distress beacon," I say to Jane. "You still have one of those, don't you?"

"Kangaroo," Jessica says.

"We're done talking," Jane says, standing up. "I'm going outside."

I block the cockpit doorway. "They're going to see us anyway when we crash."

Jane glares at me. "This is my ship. And I say we go down."

I narrow my eyes at her. "Who's up there that you don't want to run into?"

"Get out of my way," she growls.

"Kangaroo!" Jessica says. "We don't have time. Let her go."

I give Jane one more glare, then move back out of her way. She grumbles something unintelligible as she moves past, bumping me with her shoulder.

Hong checks the controls while Jane Doe positions her charge on the outer hull. The rest of us all put on our spacesuits, except for Alisa, Rich, and Joey—they're going into a rescue bubble. Hong comes to the same conclusion Jane did.

"Thrusters are locked," he says. "We can't change course."

"How is that even possible?" I glance back through the open doorway at Joey, who's lying on the deck with Alisa and Rich kneeling over him with a medkit. "Are you seriously telling me a five-year-old kid broke the spaceship?"

"Too clever for his own good, apparently," Hong mutters.

"Sound familiar?" Jessica says.

I give her a dirty look.

"Look, I'm working on it. Just give me some time," Hong says.

"Ready to blast," Jane says. "Everybody brace yourselves!"

Jessica shouts back into the cabin. Alisa shouts something in return.

Jessica slaps the intercom. "Scorpion, you may fire when ready."

"Blasting in three, two, one, now!"

A sizable explosion makes the entire ship shudder, and the view out the cockpit window tilts down. The gray Lunar surface reflects sunlight back at us, filling the window with a bright grayish glow.

"See you on the ground," Jane says.

"Kangaroo!" Jessica says. "Pocket. Now!"

I step back into the cargo bay and open the pocket for Jessica to jump into, then close and open to another location for Hong. I walk farther back to where Alisa and Rich are carrying Joey inside the rescue bubble.

"Good to go," Alisa shouts through the transparent material when they're safely inside.

I try to think of something meaningful or at least amusing to say, but give up after a second and just open the pocket and push them inside.

Then I go back to the cockpit and strap myself into the pilot's seat. If I'm going to crash on the Moon, I want to at least have a front-row view of the experience.

CHAPTER THIRTY-ONE

The Moon—nearside—Sea of Tranquility
10 seconds to impact...9...8...7...

Crashing a moving vehicle is not pleasant under the best of circumstances. Every time I'm inside a hovercar when it jars against something—even if it's as gentle as gliding over a curb or speed bump—my mind has to imagine the wreck that killed both my parents.

I was only five years old at the time, and I wasn't in the car, so I don't actually know what it was like. But maybe that's why I can't stop imagining it. I have a morbid curiosity about what their last moments must have been like. And, even more morbid, I wonder if I'll die in a similar fashion. I wonder if that will bring me closer to them in some way.

It's true, I had a really messed-up childhood.

The stealth ship plows into the ground with a loud crunch followed by a long groan of metal bending around me. The impact rattles my brain inside my skull, but the pilot's seat absorbs a lot of the initial shock. The view out the cockpit window seems to be shaking a lot more than I am.

The ship continues plowing along the ground for several more seconds, digging up gray dust that may not have been disturbed for centuries or millennia and spreading it across the window, obscuring my view. Then I can't see anything and am just left with the rough vibrations as we scrape across the ground, accompanied by the noise of loose equipment banging against walls and alarm sounds blaring on all sides of me.

How many different alerts do you really need when you're crashing,

264 CURTIS C. CHEN

anyway? The nature of the emergency should be pretty obvious at this point.

The ship finally shudders to a halt, and the dust settles in front of me, sliding down to cover just the lower part of the window. Without an atmosphere, the particles drop much faster than I'm used to, and I see something glinting as the dust falls away and onto—

The crumpled remains of the Apollo lander.

We appear to have crash-landed right in the middle of the museum courtyard—in the original Apollo 11 landing site. Where the first human beings set foot on the Moon. An unspeakably important historical monument, lovingly preserved for more than two centuries.

And we just ran a huge spaceship into it.

Fuck fuck fuck.

But, okay, let's be totally honest here: that isn't the original Lunar lander out there. The top section, the crew vehicle, is a re-creation—the original vehicle was launched back into orbit when the astronauts left, to rendezvous with the capsule that had the big engine that would get them back to Earth. And the lower section with the spidery legs has also been cleaned up.

Even if there's no atmosphere out there to carry corrosive bacteria or other microorganisms, effectively preserving these artifacts indefinitely, there's been nearly constant sunlight bleaching the color out of these parts for a long time. The museum staff must have been touching up these pieces over the years, making sure they continued to look pristine, replacing any damage done by vandals or souvenir-seekers. Most of what's out there at this point is just a replica.

That doesn't mitigate the fact that I just rode an out-of-control spaceship into a major historical site, but it does make me feel a little better about not having destroyed too much of an irreplaceable artifact.

My brain is a little more settled inside my skull now, and the ringing in my ears has subsided to a dull background hum. I check my surroundings for debris and then unbuckle my safety harness. The low gravity minimizes the lurch as I fall out of the pilot's chair, but I still brace myself against the main control panel. The ship landed at an angle, tilted to port by maybe thirty degrees and canted forward at least fifteen or twenty degrees. I'll have to climb up to get out of the cockpit, then continue upward to the cargo ramp. The airlock's facing the ground now, so the ramp is my only way out of this wreck.

I wonder where Jane Doe went. Did she manage to stay on the outer hull during our little touchdown maneuver? Or did she jump off and clear the area on purpose? I thought I noticed some controls in her spacesuit, when I was wearing it before, which might have been maneuvering thrusters. It's possible she bugged out to avoid running into the authorities after we crashed.

Two massive spotlights illuminate in front of the ship, shining into the cockpit.

And speaking of the authorities . . .

These lights are supposed to do two things. One, illuminate the inside of a dark place so the good guys can see in. Two, blind whoever's inside that dark place so they can't see out.

I blink my left eye into blackout scanning mode, then cover my right eye with one hand so I can look around the area.

With my vision overlay blotting out the ultra-bright spots and the infrared and lidar sensor readings overlaid, I have a mixed-false-color image of the courtyard in front of me. The range finder says I'm about ten meters from the museum building, which rises three stories from the ground and has several decorative spires reaching into space above.

The two spotlights are positioned directly in front of me, and on the scans I can see more spotlights arrayed around the circumference of the circular courtyard. I wonder if law enforcement put them there, or if the museum had already set them up for the big anniversary celebration event.

There are a dozen spacesuited figures advancing toward the ship, all leveling various firearms at me. I tell my eye scanners to search for equipment profiles, bar codes if visible, and identify the weapons being used. That should give me some idea of who's walking up, and also how dead I am if they open fire.

The eye scan completes, and green outlines appear around all the advancing figures.

"What the hell?" I say out loud. Green means friendly. But how would my implants know—

The answer pops up a second later in the form of headshots, names, and ranks in a small square readout above each green helmet. These are military personnel—OSS spacemen. And I have access to all their records through the agency's data link.

I find the highest ranking spaceman on the field, a petty officer third class named Gorski who's also the closest to me on the starboard side of the ship. Everyone else is a spaceman first class, one rung down the OSS rank ladder.

Obviously Copernicus wasn't expecting much resistance here—if they really expected trouble, they'd have sent some X-4s instead—but they did want to cover their ass.

My eye also shows me the most likely radio channel that the spacemen would be using in this situation. I slowly move my right hand off my face and tap the wrist controls on my spacesuit's left forearm to activate the microphone in the collar.

"OSS spacemen, this is Commander Edwin McDrona," I say, doing my best to keep my voice even and to not shout in desperation. "If you can hear me on this frequency, please acknowledge."

All the spacemen stop advancing. A couple of them turn their helmets toward each other—can they actually see through those things right now? I don't hear anything, but they must have heard me. I keep talking.

"I say again, my name is Commander Edwin McDrona, on special assignment from—"

"Keep your hands where I can see them, sir," says a female voice. "We're verifying your identity now."

I notice that one of the spacemen on my far left has lowered his weapon and is holding up a scanning device. I turn toward him and hold up both arms, palms up, wrists facing out, hoping this isn't too far a distance for his scanner to read my subdermal identity chip. I also hope Oliver remembered to program the right security codes for this week.

The spaceman with the scanner lowers the device and nods to the next person on his left. They must be talking on a private channel in addition to monitoring the standard OSS frequency. I can't imagine that a simple head nod would communicate enough information in this circumstance.

On my right, Gorski lowers his own weapon and makes a hand signal. All the spacemen stand down, pointing their weapons at the ground. I breathe out as quietly as I can.

"Commander McDrona, I'm Petty Officer Third Class Gorski," comes a male voice. "We'd sure like to know what the hell you're doing here, sir."

"Happy to tell you all about it," I say, picking up my spacesuit helmet. "But first let's get inside to a private area."

"Anyone coming out after you?" Gorski asks, looking at the crashed ship.

"Not that I know of." I snap on my helmet and start climbing toward the back of the ship. "I'm coming out the cargo ramp. Meet me there?"

"Affirmative."

It takes me a minute to remember how Jane Doe operated the ramp controls. The metal slab creaks open and stops when one corner hits the ground. I climb out and find myself standing in the middle of quite a bit of historical wreckage. I try not to think about that. It could have been worse, right?

I move forward, toward the advancing spacemen, and my boot catches on something large and curved and half-buried in the ground. I kneel down to dislodge my boot and move the debris.

It's the plaque.

Well, most of it, anyway. The stealth ship must have landed right on top of it, and the centuries-old metal was no match for the armored stealth composite. I can barely read anything but the last line of the inscription stamped into the metal:

WE CAME IN PEACE FOR ALL MANKIND

"Well," I mutter, "that's one small crash for Kangaroo, one giant fuck-up for Outback."

"Say again, sir?" Gorski says, walking up to me.

"Nothing." I gingerly step over the plaque fragment. "Let's get inside."

"Kangaroo!" Oliver's voice shrills in my ear as I follow Gorski and the other spacemen. "Kangaroo, Equipment, please respond!"

"Kangaroo here," I reply. "I hope your day's going better than mine, EQ."

"Please tell me that wasn't you who just crashed a stealth spacecraft into the Sea of Tranquility," Oliver says.

"Well, technically no, since I wasn't operating the controls," I say. "Like you always say. Blame Sir Isaac Newton."

Oliver groans. "Let's back up. Were you able to evacuate SDF1 before the incursion?"

"Yes. Everyone's safe." I give him a quick rundown. "Somebody needs to go pick up Khan and Clementine. Does Copernicus have any spare transports?"

"Lasher will arrange something," Oliver says. "He's going to have a lot more questions for Clementine."

"Right. Hey, listen, can I call you back later?" I notice Gorski giving me a funny look. I muted my suit radio to talk to Oliver, so to Gorski, it must look like I'm talking to myself. "I'm actually a little busy right now."

"Turn on your active locator beacon," Oliver says. "We need to track you at all times."

"Fine." I turn on my shoulder-phone to broadcast my position and switch off the radio.

The temporary OSS command post is on the other side of the museum. It's probably better that I don't have to walk through the building proper, since everyone inside almost certainly saw me smash up the very thing they all came here to celebrate.

Once we're inside the temporary shelter, all the spacemen and I take off our spacesuit helmets. Now I can see the full range of suspicious gazes being directed my way by the entire detachment. There's nothing like pulling rank in the middle of a crisis to make people dislike you.

I use my agency data link to check the spacemen's security clearance ratings. I'm going to have to read them in before using the pocket in front of them. And it's probably going to have to be all of them, since they've been deployed together and trained not to split up too much. Well, this is what legends are for.

"Gorski," I say, then turn to address the rest of the detachment, "and everyone, I'm going to need to read you in to a higher security clearance."

"How do you know what our clearance is?" asks the woman who spoke first on the radio. Her name, according to my eye, is Varonfakis.

"You didn't notice him blinking up a storm this whole time?" says another woman, Nguyen, pointing at my eye. "I'll bet he's got like half a dozen implants, including a display in his eye. We got us a cyborg here."

Half of the spacemen take a step back, and those who don't stiffen up. I see at least one finger moving off a trigger guard before Gorski turns to his subordinates.

"Everybody stay frosty," he snaps, then turns back to me. "What do we need to know, Commander?"

"First of all, I'm not a cyborg," I say. "I do have some tech implants, but they're tech only. Electromotive interfaces. No biologics." It's not a lie. Even my nanobots are pure tech.

Everyone's skittish about mixing Man and machine ever since the Fruitless Year. The military continued to experiment with implants during the Martian Independence War, but civilians didn't really go for more than simple shoulder-phones and medically required, limited-function implants like cardiac pacemakers, insulin pumps, and vision correctors. Nobody wants actual cybernetics with organic components that could mutate out of control.

"Check my records if you want, Petty Officer Third Class," I continue. "You should have access."

"I will," Gorski says, staring at me with an impressively flat expression. I'm sure he's feeling some anxiety—my medical scanners are showing elevated heart rate and some heat flush around his collar—but he's doing a good job of keeping it contained in front of his people. "What's the security issue?"

"I'm carrying a device I need to use." I make a point of tapping the wrist controls on my spacesuit instead of using my implants. It'll be a bit slower, but I'd rather not make the armed soldiers more nervous than absolutely necessary. "I'm granting all of you a field-authorized security clearance right now."

"Cyborg spy," Nguyen whispers to Varonfakis. She doesn't know how good my hearing is.

"Not a cyborg," I say, glaring at her. She looks surprised for a moment, then her face settles back into a light scowl. Not too belligerent, just challenging enough to discourage casual conversation.

"But you are a spy," Nguyen says.

I stare back at her. "Your security clearances should go through in just a few seconds." *Come on, Oliver, help me out here.*

"Which agency?" she asks.

New status indicators light up above each of their heads. Security clearance granted. "You're not cleared for that information. What I can tell you is that I have a wormhole device, and I need to use it right now to retrieve some passengers."

"What the fuck?" says a thick-necked young man in the back of the group—the name label floating above his head reads HENDERSON. He doesn't look like he's out of his teens, even though the records say he's old enough to drink.

"I thought wormholes were only theoretical," Varonfakis says. "You've got a device?"

"I'm sorry. I don't have time to explain." I walk over to an open area of the shelter. "I need to clear a space about three meters square."

Gorski claps his hands. "You heard the commander. Let's go, people!"

The spacemen start moving, and it's clear that they've been working together for a while. They know who their partners are, and they clear the space with a minimum of chatter. What they do say is directed toward me, the stranger in their midst.

"How's this wormhole device work?" Nguyen asks.

"Can't tell you that," I say. I don't explain that it's because we don't actually know how my ability works. They're not cleared to know that anyway. "All I can tell you is what it does. I'm going to open a portal here and pull out a rescue bubble, then two other people in spacesuits."

"Whoa," Henderson says. "You're hiding *people* inside a wormhole?"

"Yes."

His eyes light up. "So if someone else has another wormhole device in a different location—"

"Doesn't work like that," I say. I look over the open area as the spacemen move aside. "Okay. Here we go."

I open the pocket, rotated around the rescue bubble, and the transparent sphere rolls out toward me. I stop it with both hands. Alisa and Rich fall to the bottom—there's no gravity in the pocket, and the Moon is reasserting its grip now—and do their best to cradle Joey against the impact. He's still unconscious.

"Holy shit!" one of the spacemen exclaims.

"Is that a kid?" Varonfakis says.

"Cut the chatter," Gorski says. "Let's get this bubble out of the way. You got two more coming out, Commander?"

"Yeah," I say.

"He's not breathing!" Alisa shouts through the bubble. "We need the inducer! Now!"

"Shit," I say. "Spacemen, uh, Varonfakis and Henderson, with me. We need to get some equipment out of that wreckage."

I put my helmet back on and run out of the tent, back toward the crash site. I'm very surprised to see the stealth ship rising slowly from the landing site.

The ship turns and rights itself, sending gray dust sliding off its hull, and I see an armored spacesuit through the smashed cockpit window.

It's Jane Doe.

"What the hell?" I turn my radio on. "Scorpion, Kangaroo, what the hell!"

Jane waves at me and replies over the radio. "Sorry, Kangaroo. It's in my nature."

"We need that machine!" I say. "There's a medical rig in the cargo bay—"

"Oh, I know." The ship is rising straight up into the air, blending into the black sky. "Multifocal transcranial inducer, right? I've got buyers lined up from here to Jupiter for that piece of tech. Maybe it'll even pay for the repairs to my damn ship."

I point up at the ship. "Spacemen, open fire—"

I don't even see the panels open up on the bottom of Scorpion's ship, but I sure as hell see the muzzle flashes and the gouts of dust kicked up by the artillery impacts. One of the spacemen tackles me to the side before the line of fire passes through me.

I roll over and see the other spaceman firing up into space. But it's nearly impossible to see the stealth ship now that it's against the black sky.

"I mean, seriously, man," Jane chuckles. "You think a five-year-old *kid* could fly my ship? You people got some weird notions."

"*You* were flying the ship?" I say, mentally kicking myself. "By remote? Shit!" Those comms implants did more than I thought. Also explains why she was twitching so much while she was unconscious.

"Y'all thought I was asleep that whole time," Jane laughs. "Guess my snoring was pretty convincing, huh? Sometimes I even impress myself. Oh, yeah, thank those spacemen for me too. They did a great job of distracting you while I snuck back in here."

"This *child* is going to *die* if you don't come back!" I shout.

"That is tragic," Jane says, "and it's not my problem. Good-bye."

The radio clicks off. I yell up into space for a few more seconds, but I really can't see the ship now.

"Shit," I say, and turn back to the OSS tent. Several spacemen are standing between me and the tent, waiting for my next order.

"Commander?" Gorski says.

I point up into the black. "I don't suppose you've got a ship up there that can intercept her?"

"Sorry, sir. We're a ground detachment. There might be a satellite in intercept range, but that stealth armor—"

"Forget it," I say. "We need to regroup."

CHAPTER THIRTY-TWO

The Moon—nearside—Apollo 11 Historical Site
2 minutes after Scorpion screwed us over

I go back into the tent and pull Jessica and Hong out of the pocket. I give them a quick rundown of the situation. We all go over to where Alisa and Rich are standing over Joey. They've put a respirator mask over his face and an IV cuff around his left upper arm. He looks very small and frail.

"Goddammit," Alisa says after I repeat my report. She glares at Jessica. "If he dies—"

"Let's debrief later," Jessica says.

"We need to get him to Lunar General," Rich says.

"That's too far," Jessica says. "There's another hospital—"

"Stanford has an MTI rig," Alisa says. "It's the only other unit on the Moon."

I remember our tour of the hospital and feel a surge of hope. I turn to Gorski. "Can you give us a ride?"

He frowns at us. "You said Lunar General?"

"Yeah."

"We can get you there, Commander," he says. "But there's a situation."

"What kind of situation?"

"Hostile mechs on site."

I don't quite comprehend what he's saying at first. *Robots?*

"Of course there are," Alisa grumbles.

"They just stormed the building and took over the radiology wing," Gorski says. "No human operators in sight, and comms jamming isn't shutting them down. They must be running independent programs. All the units appear to be armored against projectile firearms."

"Of course they are." Alisa laughs.

"Clementine's secondary objective," Jessica says. "She's stealing Stanford's MTI rig."

"With *killer robots*?" I can't believe I'm actually saying these words.

"There's another way to help Joey," Jessica says. "Kangaroo, a word."

She steps aside and motions for me to follow her. I walk over to one corner of the tent with her. We angle our bodies away from the others, and she says quietly, "I'm going to draw a sample of your blood."

I step back. "No. Are you fucking kidding me? No!"

Jessica glares at me. "We can deal with big robots or tiny robots. Take your pick."

She's talking about the nanobots in my bloodstream. We've used my nanobots to treat medical conditions before; Jessica was able to reprogram them to do something other than just convert blood sugars to energy to power my body-wide wireless mesh network. Radiation damage, specifically—but that was something she'd been researching for years before she actually wrote the software. And the nanobots are highly classified technology, even more so than my pocket. We shouldn't even be talking about it out here in the open.

"We don't know what's causing Joey's seizures," I say.

"Episodes."

"Whatever the right word is. The nanobots can't even deal with my earwax. And you and Science didn't do so well with the last software update. What makes you think you can program them correctly to fix Joey's brain?"

"I can try."

"You're not thinking clearly." I jab a finger in her direction. "You've been off ever since the funeral."

"Don't."

"Your mother didn't die of old age, did she?" I can tell by Jessica's expression that I guessed correctly. "Whatever unfinished business you had with her, going crazy trying to make the nanobots cure other people is not going to resolve it."

Jessica blinks and turns away. "You are not a licensed therapist."

"No. I'm just the guy who has more professional contact with you on a daily basis than any other human being in the world." I risk moving closer to her. "This isn't you, Surge."

"Stop calling me that."

"I trust you to call me on my bullshit," I say. "And now I'm returning the favor. You're going through some stuff right now. Don't try to deal with it by fixing anyone else. It's okay if the only person you save is yourself."

Jessica wipes a sleeve across her eyes. "You could have just said, 'Physician, heal thyself.'"

"My name's not Luke."

She laughs. I can always get her with a Bible joke.

"Are you two done trading barbs?" Alisa says, making me jump. She's standing right behind me. How much of our classified conversation did she overhear?

"Private conversation!" I say.

She folds her arms. "Were you talking about using your nanobots to treat Joey?"

My head. Exploding. Again. I grab Jessica by both shoulders.

"You *told her* about the *nanobots*?" I say through clenched teeth.

Jessica slaps away my arms. "She has the clearance. I wanted her to join the project. I knew Ali was on the Moon; State read me in because I was family. I didn't know what she had going on here."

"And I *so* appreciate you assuming that my life was a disaster and I needed you to rescue me," Alisa says. "That's sarcasm, by the way."

This whole thing is finally beginning to make some kind of twisted sense. "You thought because your mother—"

"I hoped," Jessica says. "I didn't know about Joey, obviously."

"*That's* why you snuck out of the hotel in the middle of the night?" I sputter. "To *recruit* her?"

"I didn't want her to be alone." Jessica looks at Alisa. "I wanted you to have our mother's holy cross."

Something that might be a human emotion flickers across Alisa's face. "Whatever. I'm vetoing your insane nanobot proposal. We need to get Joey to the hospital."

I shake my head. "You do remember the killer robots, right?"

"We've got all these spacemen here," Alisa says. "They can take back the building. Kill two birds with one stone."

She clearly hasn't ever tried to fight bad guys in confined spaces. I have, and it's not pleasant or easy. Going into the hospital, even with a superior force, is asking for trouble.

"We don't know anything about those robots," I say. "We can't attack without more information."

"Maybe we should let the professionals make that decision." Alisa turns and walks back to where the spacemen are gathered.

"*I'm* a professional," I say, holding out my arms in a gesture of incredulity.

Jessica nudges me. "Come on."

We walk over and join Alisa's conversation in progress with Gorski.

"You've been talking to people on the scene," Alisa says, pointing to the communications gear stacked on the table. "What do they say?"

"They're working the problem," Gorski says.

"What the hell does that mean?" Alisa snaps.

"*Doctor*," Jessica says, stepping forward, "maybe we should let the professionals do their job. OSS doesn't have jurisdiction over civilian facilities."

Alisa turns to stare at Jessica. "Joey's dying."

"His vitals are stable," Jessica says.

"He's unconscious," Alisa says. "His EEG will become more and more erratic if we don't treat it. His autonomic nervous system will go haywire. His heart will stop."

"I'm afraid I have to concur," Rich says. "It doesn't look good."

"We'll wire him with a pacemaker," Jessica says.

"He's five years old," Alisa says. "If he slips into a coma, we don't get him back. Do you understand that?"

"I understand that he's the product of an illegal medical experiment who shouldn't exist in the first place," Jessica says.

"Whoa," I say. That's a little harsh, even for her.

"Jesus Christ," Alisa says. "You *are* a fucking robot. He's just a little kid. How can you be so heartless?"

"Heartless?" Jessica points at me. "I'm sorry, which one of us *poisoned* this person?"

"I was helping him!" Alisa bangs a fist on the table, rattling the communications gear. Gorski puts one hand on the sidearm at his hip. I catch his eye and shake my head. I hope he trusts me to handle this if it escalates.

"You've always had a funny interpretation of medical ethics," Jessica says.

"And you've never been able to see your patients as people!" Alisa spits back.

"Okay, okay, let's take it down a notch!" I slice a hand through the air between them, to no effect. I step forward to physically place my body between the two women. They don't budge a centimeter. "And can we try to stay on topic here? What's our next move?"

"Get Joey to Lunar General," Alisa says.

"Stabilize Joey for medical exfil," Jessica says at the same time. "We'll find another MTI rig and get it into Earth orbit—"

"That will take too long," Alisa says. "And I am not soliciting suggestions. I have primary authority over this project. My mandate comes directly from the secretary of state. I'm pretty sure that supersedes any sort of paper you"—she jabs a finger at Jessica—"or you"—she points at me—"or you"—she indicates Gorski—"can summon. So let's suit the fuck up and take back that hospital."

"I don't work for you," Jessica says. "Neither does Kangaroo. And neither do these spacemen. Isn't that right, Petty Officer Third Class?"

Gorski looks uncomfortable. "She's right about my chain of command." He points at me. "Commander McDrona is actually the ranking officer here."

"Who's the man?" I raise both arms in triumph. "Who is the man!" Nobody responds appropriately. *If only Yodey were here.*

Alisa glares at me. "Are you going to let Joey die?"

Right. The good news is, I'm in charge. The bad news is: I'm in charge. I lower my arms but put my hands on my hips to still assert some authority.

"We have other options," Jessica says, also addressing me. "It's irresponsible to risk a dozen lives to save one."

"It's not just math," Alisa says. "The agency would risk any number of lives to protect *him*." She points at me. "Standing orders, remember?"

"This is different," Jessica says.

"Because Joey doesn't have the—"

"Careful." Jessica glances at the spacemen.

Alisa clenches her jaw. "He's just a child. A five-year-old child."

"Almost six," I say.

They both turn to look at me. I realize that I've already decided.

"Petty Officer Third Class," I say, turning to Gorski, "are your spacemen qualified on anti-mech armaments?"

His eyebrows rise. "No, sir."

"Well, you're going to get a crash course. No pun intended."

"Yes, sir."

"This is insane," Jessica says. "You are going to get a lot of people killed."

"My judgment is not impaired," I say quickly, remembering her previous threat to relieve me. "And there's another qualified medical professional here who will certify me fit for duty." I point at Alisa.

Jessica scowls at Alisa. "If I can't stop you, I'm coming with you." Then me. "Call Oliver and have him walk the spacemen through their new load-out."

"I can show them myself—"

"I recommend we have a subject matter expert supervise this particular training."

"You don't trust me to know how to use my own equipment?"

Jessica gives me a strange look. Gorski seems to be having a coughing fit.

"Let me rephrase that," I say.

"Call Oliver," Jessica says, and walks away.

CHAPTER THIRTY-THREE

The Moon—nearside—Lunar General
20 minutes before we face off against a horde of killer robots

I have been waiting to use Oliver's anti-mech weapons ever since he demonstrated them in his workshop and we loaded them into the pocket three days ago. The spacemen definitely appreciate what I pull during the ride to Lunar General: handheld EMP cannons, armor-piercing harpoons, heavy-duty freeze-foam grenades, and more. I patch my shoulder-phone into our rover's intercom so Oliver can narrate a quick rundown of how to operate the weapons.

"Sorry for razzing you earlier, Commander," Nguyen says while loading up a grenade launcher. "Apparently spies get all the best toys."

"Happy to share," I say. I don't say: *I'm also happy to share the risk.* I try not to dwell on the fact that I just took responsibility for an entire detachment of OSS spacemen, and if anything goes wrong during this little incursion, it's going to be my fault.

"We're entering the tube," the driver says over the intercom. The rover bumps over something and tilts downward. There are no windows back here, so I check our position in my eye. Yup, we're going into a transit tunnel.

Nobody else seems alarmed by this. I tap the intercom to talk to the driver. "So the trains aren't running yet?"

"We've secured clearance from the transit authority," the driver says. "They'll divert any trains in service out of our path. No worries, Commander. ETA twenty minutes."

"Thanks." I sit back and look around. Everyone seems to know what they're doing. Or at least they're pretending to. Guess I'd better join the club.

Our exit from the tube system deposits us in the subsurface tunnel connecting Silver Circle to Lunar General, and I see a familiar face as soon as I step out of the rover.

"Edwin?" Breyella Wilgus runs up to me and grabs my arm. She's wearing an overcoat and carrying a ruggedized tablet on a cross-body strap. "You're with the spacemen?"

Before I can answer, Gorski jogs past us toward a cluster of dark blue uniforms. "We'll meet you at the mobile command post, Commander!"

"Yeah. Thanks. See you there," I say.

Breyella frowns at me. "'Commander'?"

"Miss Wilgus," Jessica says, walking past my other shoulder, not even slowing down as she passes us. *Yeah, it's cool, Surge, just let me deal with this.*

"Dr. Chu." Breyella nods.

Jessica follows Gorski and the other spacemen. The last people out of the rover are Alisa and Rich, wheeling Joey's gurney between them.

"Is that a child?" Breyella asks, her eyes wide.

"I can explain—"

I freeze when I see Yodey and Zoo walking toward us. I probably shouldn't assume they're up to no good, but given my own dealings with them—

"Dayton!" Breyella says, waving at Yodey. "Excuse me for just a second, Edwin."

I'm so surprised, I don't have anything to say for a second.

"Edwin?" Yodey says. "What you doing here?"

"I'm with Dr. Chu," I manage to say, pointing over at Jessica.

Breyella looks from Yodey to me and back again. "You two know each other?"

"Indeed," Yodey says. "Edwin also boost Planned Parenthood. Had a smooth chat over in Sabine lately." He gives me a significant glare, and I get the message: *Let's not reveal our actual business arrangements in front of a third party.*

"Whatever." Breyella shakes her head and turns to Zoo. "Zubayr. Status?"

"Five by five," Zoo says, holding up a tablet. The display shows a list of names, mostly green text with some yellow. "All ICU patients out of the dome. We loading folks with breathing gear now."

"Good," Breyella says, making a notation on her tablet. "Call me when you get to the IPM cases." It's funny how I know that stands for "impaired physical mobility" because of the time Science Division "accidentally" broke both my legs.

"Wilco," Zoo says.

"We out," Yodey says. They both jog off toward Zoo's rover.

"Okay," I say, watching them go, "just to be clear, I'm asking this because I know Dayton personally—but are you sure you can trust those two with that job?" I've never been the best thief, but even I know the elderly and infirm are easy marks.

Breyella frowns. "Dayton and Zubayr have volunteered at Lunar General every summer for the last six years. I know I can trust them. You, on the other hand—"

"I can explain."

"Well, apparently you're in the OSS reserve," she says. "Just like Dr. Chu. Did you serve together?"

Thank you, Breyella, for jumping to conclusions. "Yes. I suppose you could say we're still serving together." It's not a lie.

"And you didn't identify yourself previously because . . . ?"

"Because this isn't a military matter. Wasn't, anyway." I spread my hands apologetically. "Dr. Chu doesn't like to advertise the fact that she was in the war. You understand." The Independence War is still a touchy subject for a lot of people.

Breyella blinks. "I didn't realize—wow."

"See? That's why." People always think differently of someone who's been in an armed conflict. Even if she never picked up a weapon. She still picked a side.

"Okay. Water under the bridge. We have bigger problems now." Breyella taps at her tablet. "We still haven't located Gladys Löwenthal. I don't suppose you—"

"We found her. She's fine." Again, not a lie. I'm sure Khan is taking very good care of our darling Clementine.

Breyella glances over her shoulder, but the OSS spacemen have disappeared into the crowd of people filling the tunnel. "Who's the child?"

"That," I say, "is a *very* long story."

"He's the reason you're here, isn't he?" Breyella says. "You need something in the hospital to treat him? What's his condition?"

"I'm not a doctor," I say. "All I know is, we need the MTI rig in radiology."

Breyella's face falls. "You know about the mechs, right?"

I nod. "That why we brought the spacemen." I hold up my EMP rifle. "And these goodies."

Breyella nods. "Guess I should introduce you to the marshals."

"I don't think that will be necessary," I say. I've already spotted a few more familiar faces. Apparently this crisis is the social event of the season.

Breyella leads me over to the mobile command post, where Jessica and the spacemen are gathered around a display table with a group of U.S. marshals—including Deputy United States Marshal Gurley, Deputy United States Marshal Wecks, and Supervisory Deputy United States Marshal Sundar Punjabi. These folks have even longer titles than the military.

"Mr. McDrona," Punjabi says, eyeing me as I join them. "Or should I say *Commander* McDrona?"

I shrug. "It's a long story, Marshal."

"I would love to hear it sometime," Punjabi says. "But right now, I am happy to let you and your spacemen deal with those mechs inside the hospital. We have other fish to fry."

"Thanks."

He motions for the other marshals to follow him, then leads them away, but stops next to me first and says quietly, "I don't like spies."

"And how many spies have you known?" I reply.

He frowns. "I have no idea. That's the point." He leaves before I can toss off another witty rejoinder. I hate it when other people have the last word. Leaves me without a sense of closure.

I turn my attention back to the group. Breyella has interfaced her tablet with the large table, and the display surface is lit up with a map of the hospital. She points out where the MTI rig is located, and where we are.

"Elevators are shut down?" Gorski asks.

"Absolutely," Breyella says. "Standard emergency protocol. And all patients and hospital personnel have been evacuated from the radiology wing."

"And the nearest stairwell is—"

"Here."

Henderson walks up next to Gorski carrying a large black bag.

"Merry Christmas," Henderson says. "Body armor and radio buttons for everyone." He opens the bag and starts laying out supplies.

"All right, people, suit up," Gorski says. "Commander, I recommend a two-element infil, one at ground level, one coming up through the basement. We split up the docs, breach at ground level first, then bring the kid up the stairs to radiology. Do you approve?"

He draws lines across the tabletop display as he talks, and I try to imagine this going well. I'm glad he's giving me a recommendation to approve and not just asking me an open-ended question. This is not my area of expertise. But I am technically in command, so I need to make a show of being commanding. I swear I can feel everybody watching me.

"Sounds good," I say. "Gorski, you lead the ground-level team. I'll take the basement. I want Mr. Johnson and Joey—the kid—with me."

"I want to stay with Joey," Alisa says. "I'm his primary care—"

"Like Gorski said," I say, "we split up the docs. That's you and Mr. Johnson. I want you to get to the MTI rig first and make sure it's ready for Joey."

"It's okay, Doctor," Rich says. "He'll be fine."

"I'm coming through the basement with you," Jessica says.

"Of course you are." I stare at the glowing red blips—hostile mechs—moving around the map. *Are we really doing this? We're really about to go shoot up a hospital?* "Gorski, you split up your spacemen however you want."

"Varonfakis, Henderson, you're with the kid. We'll keep the basement team small. The rest of us will do our best to draw fire upstairs so you can sneak in," Gorski says. "Looks like the robots are engaging anyone who gets close, so weapons free as soon as we breach. If it's not human, take it out."

"Are we worried about property damage?" Nguyen asks.

"Negative," Gorski says, glancing over at Breyella. She nods in agreement. "Security cameras show the robots are dismantling the MTI rig for transport. Our priority is securing that room and getting the child in there for treatment ASAP."

"Hope this kid's worth all the trouble," Varonfakis mutters.

"Every human life is precious," I say.

"Tell that to my mother-in-law."

The basement of the hospital is quite well appointed, as such things go. I was expecting some dark, narrow corridors with pipes everywhere spitting steam or dripping water, but this looks like pretty much any other part of the hospital: corridors wide enough for two gurneys to pass side by side, bright lighting everywhere. The only thing that's missing is people. There are no patient rooms down here.

According to the map, the morgue is at one end, and most of the rest is storage areas. Our current objective is the stairwell that will get us upstairs and closest to the radiology department. But we're not supposed to go up those stairs until we get the all-clear from Gorski's team.

My team reaches the stairwell without incident. I'm leading the way, followed by Jessica and Rich pushing Joey's gurney, then Henderson and Varonfakis covering our six.

I push open the stairwell door and am greeted by a spray of bullets.

"Jesus fuck!" I shout while pulling the door shut again and dropping to the ground.

"Report!" Gorski shouts over the radio.

"Tango in the stairwell!" Henderson replies.

"Just one?"

Henderson looks at me. "Sir?"

I blink my eye to rewind my mission recorder. I only see one set of muzzle flashes on the vid playback. "Confirmed. Just one."

Gunfire sounds over the radio. "We're engaged! Repeat, we are engaged!"

I stop trying to make sense of the shouts over the radio and blink my eye into scanning mode. The stairwell door isn't scan-shielded, and I verify that there's just one robot on the other side—a bigger version of the spiders we saw at SDF1, slowly creeping down the stairs, with some kind of large-caliber automatic weapon mounted to its chassis.

"One mech walking down the stairs," I say quietly to Jessica and Henderson, who have moved forward with weapons at the ready. Rich is hanging back with Varonfakis, looking nervously up and down the corridor. "How do you want to do this?"

"Tell me when it stops moving, sir," Henderson says.

My left eye scanner shows me the advancing robot in a glowing yellow outline, with the most radar-reflective objects and surfaces glowing the brightest. I can't get a specific readout on its weapon—probably missing its bar code; that's a common mercenary trick to make their weapons harder to trace. But the holes it's putting in the walls are pretty large caliber. I report this over the open radio channel for all the spacemen to hear.

"How close is it?" Henderson asks.

"Still at the bottom of the stairs," I say. "Stopped moving. Probably not going to get close to the door."

"Armored?"

"Yeah. Can't tell the composition."

"How big?" Jessica asks.

I check the size and range. "Not too big to fit inside a wormhole."

I think of a brown cartoon coyote and concentrate on opening a portal directly behind the robot, with no barrier so the mech will get sucked backward into the pocket.

It doesn't work.

"What's the problem?" Jessica asks. She's mentioned before that I get a certain look on my face when I use the pocket.

"Can't pull a portal," I say. "The mech must be touching the wall." I can only open the pocket facing me, and it has to be in midair; any solid object will stop portal formation. If that mech has a limb touching the wall behind it, I can't open the pocket big enough to suck it in. The best I could do is knock it off-balance, and I'm sure its targeting sensors can compensate for that.

"Why is that a problem?" Henderson asks.

"Long story," I say. "Henderson. If Dr. Chu pushes open the door, can you cover me while I zap the mech?"

"Sounds like a plan, sir." Henderson flicks off the safety on his weapon. "Tell me when you're set up."

I move to the left side of the doorway, the side that's going to swing open when Jessica pushes the door inward, and lift my EMP rifle. I brace the stock against my shoulder and aim it as well as I can at the robot's center mass as shown in my eye.

"Good to go," I say.

"On my mark," Jessica says, putting one hand on the door. "Three. Two. One. Mark!"

She slams open the door. Henderson lunges into the stairwell and ends up lying prone on the floor, firing up at the mech. I pull my trigger as soon as I see the red guide laser from my rifle painted on the robot, sending an invisible wave of electromagnetic disruption through it. The blast convulses all of its limbs in metal-grinding spasms.

Henderson stands, runs up to the robot as soon as the EMP blast hits, and slaps a yellow-and-black striped disk onto the side of the robot. A circle of orange sparks sprays from the disk as it cuts through the robot's armor, and the disk falls into its innards. A second later, an explosion topples the robot over onto its side, and then smoke puffs out of the opening cut by the perforator disk.

"Clear!" Henderson calls.

Jessica and I step into the doorway. She stops the door before it swings shut again. I turn to wave the rest of our team into the stairwell. Rich and Varonfakis push the gurney carrying Joey toward us.

The wall behind Varonfakis explodes in a shower of shattered plaster.

Henderson ducks out into the corridor and fires toward the source of the projectiles hitting the wall. Varonfakis joins him. Rich rushes past me into the stairwell, and I jump back to get out of the way. Henderson and Varonfakis follow him in, then kick the door shut just as more bullets strike it from the outside.

"Jesus Christ!" I blink my eye back into scanning mode. I see two pairs of spidery silhouette approaching from either direction. "We've got four more mechs, two on each side!"

"Rich, are you hurt?" Jessica asks.

Rich brushes some debris from his face and coughs. "I'm okay. Just got sprayed with debris."

"How's Joey?"

Rich checks the medical monitor bar fixed above Joey's chest. "Still stable."

"Good." Jessica steps off the stairs and comes over to where I'm bracing the door shut. "Kangaroo, take Joey and get him upstairs."

I stare at her. "What are you going to do?"

"Rich and I will stay here with the spacemen and defend this position."

"We'll what?" Rich says.

"I guarantee you're a better shot than Alisa." Jessica taps the radio button on her collar. "Gorski, what's your situation?"

I realize that we haven't heard any shooting noises over the radio for the last several seconds. Gorski's voice buzzes through.

"We've secured the top side of the stairwell," he says. "Tangos have retreated into the MTI lab. We're advancing now."

"You go up there and follow them in," Jessica says. "Don't waste time."

"But you—"

"We'll be fine," she says. "Your responsibility is Joey. Got that?"

I look down at the face of the sleeping child on the gurney. My face.

"Goddammit," I say, shoving my rifle at Rich and grabbing the handle of the gurney. "It's going to be a bitch getting this up the stairs by myself."

"So ask for help," Jessica says.

I blink at her, then squeeze my radio button. "Hey, uh, Gorski, can I get some help moving this gurney up the stairs?"

"I'm on my way," Alisa says.

"Great." I give Jessica a dirty look.

"Have fun with your new best friend," she says. "Rich! Get over here!"

CHAPTER THIRTY-FOUR

The Moon—nearside—Lunar General
2 days of not slapping Alisa Garro and counting

Alisa meets me at the bottom of the stairs, and we proceed up in total silence, for which I am supremely grateful. When we reach the top, we stop, and she checks in with the spacemen before opening the door into the hallway.

"Just clearing the last tango," Gorski says. "Wait one."

"Holding position." Alisa looks down at the gurney and frowns. "What are all these white flakes here?"

"Debris from the wall," I say. "Some mechs shot at us before we got into the stairwell."

"Is he injured?" Alisa leans down and taps at the medical monitor.

"Relax. Rich checked him out already."

"And now I will," Alisa finishes manipulating the controls on the monitor bar and exhales. "Okay. He's still stable. We've got time."

"By the way," I say, "was it your bright idea to not let him leave the Moon, ever?"

Alisa glares at me. "Joey's existence—*your* existence—is one of the biggest secrets the agency has. We couldn't risk any exposure—"

"He's just a kid," I say. "He doesn't understand any of that." I certainly wouldn't have, when I was five years old. "Did you even tell him that he can expect to have a weird crazy power someday?"

"I'm not discussing this now."

The radio buzzes. "Clear in the hallway," Gorski says. "Come on out, Doc."

Alisa unlocks the gurney wheels. "Let's go."

We wheel Joey into the corridor, then down past the spacemen guarding the area and toward the door of the lab. It feels like it's been several lifetimes since the last time I was here.

The treatment room is much more cramped now, with not only the MTI rig filling most of the room, but two spacemen in full body armor, three different disabled mechs in the corners, and machine parts all over the floor.

Both spacemen are kneeling on the ground, sorting through the debris. Several access panels on the back side of the MTI's main module have been pulled off, and I can see wires hanging loose from the exposed areas. It looks like components from the MTI have been mixed in with pieces that were shot off the mechs.

One of the mechs is glued to the back corner by a large wad of freeze-foam. It still has a sensor stalk sticking up out of the foam, twitching around looking for targets, but the congealed mass has pinned the barrel of its weapon against the wall.

"Are you kidding me?" I say as we stop the gurney at the foot of the chair. The spacemen have to stand up and move to let us in. There's not much room to maneuver in here. "Why were they taking apart the very expensive medical machine?"

"Stripping it for parts," Alisa says, kneeling to examine the MTI rig. "These robots couldn't carry the whole rig out in one piece. Dammit!" She touches the radio button on her collar. "Rich, I need you up here right now! You!" She points at the nearest spaceman, identified as SHIELDS in my left eye. "Go relieve him at the bottom of the stairwell."

Shields picks up his weapon and leaves. Alisa directs the other spaceman—a woman named Dumont—to help us lift Joey into the chair and pull the headrests close around his skull before lowering the transparent bubble over his head. Alisa attaches a monitor armband to Joey's left forearm, and a display lights up with his vitals.

"Did we get him here in time?" Dumont asks after moving the gurney out of the way.

"He's still alive," Alisa says, tapping at the controls behind the chair.

Dumont looks at me. "Is that a yes?"

I don't know what to tell her. "Talk to us, Doc."

"Fucking robots," Alisa spits. "We need to put this thing back together."

Rich runs into the room holding my EMP rifle and a medical bag. "What's happening? Oh." He looks around at the parts strewn across the floor. "Oh, that's not good."

"Sort out the MTI components and hand them to me," Alisa says, crouching down next to the nearest open panel.

"On it." Rich puts down his gear and starts picking up pieces.

I wave Dumont away from the rig. "Let's give them some room to work."

She nods and follows me into the observation chamber. "So how do you like that EMP cannon?"

I frown at her. "Really?"

"I'll bet it's not as satisfying as the FFG," Dumont says, hefting her freeze-foam grenade launcher. "There's no visible blast with that thing, right? This baby puts on a show. Did you see the mech I tagged in the corner?"

"Yeah. Nice work." I glance over my shoulder and do a double take. "What the fuck—!"

Dumont and I both turn around and raise our weapons.

Rich Johnson is backed into one corner of the room, aiming a pistol at Alisa Garro's head. She's standing up, with a med-sig collar around her neck, and I don't need to interpret the readouts to know she is not happy.

Rich's other arm is touching the back wall, and he's angled his body into the corner so I can't open a portal behind him big enough to suck him in. I'm just estimating whether I can open the pocket to yank his gun hand back when he speaks.

"I know what you're thinking, Kangaroo," he says, "but if you scan the room, you'll see that I'm holding a deadman switch."

I blink my eye into EM sensing mode and see radio waves pulsing between the collar around Alisa's neck and a small cylinder in Rich's left hand. There's no telling what he could have programmed the collar to inject straight into her arteries if he releases that switch.

"Okay, everybody," Rich says in a psychotically cheerful tone, "here's what's going to happen now."

"You are finished, Johnson!" Alisa shouts.

"Oh, absolutely, Dr. Garro," Rich says. "But I think I'll be much happier in my new job."

"I don't know *how* you think you're going to get out of here," I say, "but it is *not* going to happen, *Dick*."

"Now that's not very nice." Rich frowns at me. "And what are you going to do, Kangaroo? Zap me with an EMP? I'm not a robot."

Dammit. I lower my rifle and look at Dumont. "Please tell me you've got a spare firearm for me."

"Tail holster," she says, not taking her eyes away from the hostage situation. I do my best not to grope her as I pull a small machine pistol out of the holster at the small of her back.

"Dr. Garro," Rich says, "please get Joey out of the chair. You're going to carry him out of here."

He nudges Alisa forward. She stares at me. I stare back.

"What's the magic word?" she says, holding her hand in front of me where Rich can't see it. She flicks her wrist right next to Joey's head before reaching for the restraints around his chest. I do my best to keep a poker face when I realize what she's suggesting.

Oh, that is a bad idea, Doc. But I don't have anything better.

Joey's already got a breather mask on, so the lack of air inside the pocket won't be an issue. He won't freeze immediately after he goes in. Can we take down Rich in thirty seconds? Less than a minute?

"Quickly," Rich says. "We want to get Joey treated as soon as possible, don't we?"

"You could just stay here. Fix the chair, get it done sooner." I level my pistol at him, but it's an empty threat. My eye is telling me the transparency between this observation chamber and the treatment area is bulletproof. Which means it's also foam-proof. And if either Dumont or I makes a move toward the doorway—well, I'm pretty sure Rich doesn't want to kill Joey, but I also don't know how crazy he is.

"Kangaroo, you're also welcome to join us," Rich says, "but I must insist on you being unconscious during the trip."

"Thanks, I'll pass," I say. How else can we get to this guy, other than the insane maneuver that Alisa seems to be suggesting? "You do remember there are hostile mechs running around this hospital, right?"

"Oh, that won't be a problem." He grins. "The robots are my friends."

My head feels like it's going to explode. "*You're* Charlie Angel?"

"Well, yeah." The grin mutates into a smirk. "That's *obviously* a fake name."

My palms start sweating. "You've been in contact with Sakraida." If he knows where to find our former D.Int, we definitely want to take him alive.

Rich shakes his head. "I wish. He was very interested in my work here on the Moon, but he wasn't willing to meet in person." I blink my eye into lie-detector mode and see that he's telling the truth. "I'm just one of many middlemen in this transaction."

"*You* hired Scorpion," I say. Alisa's taking her sweet time undoing all of Joey's restraints. Good. "You know where she's going. You're taking Joey to meet her. She's got the other MTI rig, so you can treat him."

Rich shrugs. "That's certainly very plausible. Like I said, you can come along and find out."

"What about me?" Alisa asks, fiddling with the straps around Joey's ankles.

"I don't think Joey needs both of us looking after him anymore," Rich says. "He's a big boy now. Almost six years old, you know."

Both Dumont's and my radios buzz. "Kangaroo, what's your situation up there?" Gorski asks. "We've got more mechs headed your way. Be on the lookout."

Dumont twitches, as if she wants to turn back toward the door facing the hallway. "Commander?"

Goddammit. "Go. I've got this bastard."

She turns and takes up a guard position behind me, watching the hallway. I blink my eye through scan modes frantically. How is Rich identifying himself to the bots as a friendly? He's got a heat signature like the rest of us humans, he looks like an adult, it's got to be some kind of transponder signal—

"There's no need for you to die, Spaceman Dumont," Rich says. "Just leave now and you won't get hurt."

"She's not listening to you," I say. "And how the hell do you think you're going to get past all those marshals outside? And through the dome into space?"

Rich chuckles. "Who said we were going into space? Now here's what's going to happen," he says, taking fast steps forward until he's right behind Alisa, putting her between him and me, still with one hand on the wall. I hate it when my opponents know the limitations on how I can use the pocket. "Dr. Garro's going to pick up Joey and walk forward with him. I'm going to follow her."

He's in the other corner now, right on top of the freeze-foamed mech.

Rich touches his backside to the wall, taps some kind of control on his belt, and steps forward. I see a thin cable reeling out between his waist and the back wall. Solid matter to keep me from opening the pocket behind him. *Goddammit.*

"Kangaroo, you're going to walk in front of us," Rich says. "I'll tell you where to go."

"Sure you don't want to lead the way?" I ask. "I don't follow directions very well."

"No portals," Rich says.

Then I notice that the mech freeze-foamed into the corner has stopped twitching its sensor stalk. As if it's now receiving a signal telling it not to look for targets.

Of course! Rich and Scorpion and Clementine could have programmed these mechs to recognize them by sight, but he needs to protect his hostages, too. That dead man's switch isn't just preventing Alisa's collar from triggering; it's also painting a radius around him. A safe zone. A blind spot to all these killer mechs.

I blink my eye into radio-sensing mode to confirm. It's a very short-range transmitter. Rich doesn't want Alisa wandering too far away while carrying Joey. And that mech glued to the corner will start looking for a target again as soon as Rich moves away from it. Our small arms won't be able to touch Rich through his body armor, but the mech's artillery should do the job.

This is going to be tricky.

"Incoming!" Dumont shouts from the doorway. "I've got four—no, six mechs on this level and closing in!"

"Okay, it's time to go," Rich says. "Dr. Garro, would you please get Joey out of that chair?"

Alisa moves slowly, detaching the monitor from Joey's arm, then sliding both hands under Joey's armpits, eyeing me the whole time.

I can't signal her back with Rich looking right at me. I lower my weapon. I hope she'll understand what that means. *Your move.*

"You're forgetting one thing, *Dick*," Alisa says. "I have something very important that you need."

"And what do I need from you?" Rich asks, squinting down his gun arm at her.

Alisa tenses her shoulders and looks at me. "Now!"

Joey flies up out of the chair toward me. Alisa's stronger than I thought.

I make sure Joey's foot has cleared the chair. Then I open a portal right behind him, no barrier, as large as I can.

The vacuum sucks him backward into the pocket.

I hear two loud cracks.

Bullet holes appear in the observation window right in front of me. I close the pocket and bring my weapon up again.

Alisa's got Rich pinned against the wall. She has one hand closed around his left hand, keeping the deadman switch closed, and the other clamped on his right wrist, tilting his gun up at the ceiling. He's struggling against her, and they're standing right inside the doorway. I can't get a clear shot at anything.

"Dumont!" I call out, not looking away from Alisa and Rich.

"Here, sir," Dumont's voice comes from just behind my left shoulder.

"Freeze-foam, please!"

"Only one shot left." She braces one shoulder against the doorframe.

"Then you'd better not—"

She fires the FFG just as Rich twists his gun arm toward us. Rich and Alisa topple sideways. Dumont's grenade sails above them. Foam splatters across the back wall.

"—miss," I finish saying.

"Sorry, sir." Dumont drops the launcher and switches to her assault rifle.

"Fine. Plan B," I say. "As soon as you get a clear shot, shoot that switch out of his hand." I trust her to be more precise than I am with firearms.

"You mean his gun?" Dumont asks.

"I mean the radio switch. In his left hand."

"But the doctor—"

"That's an order!" I don't have time to explain this.

"Yes, sir." One good thing about using a military cover identity: people usually do what you tell them to.

I crouch and blink crosshairs into my eye, targeting the mech in the back corner. The overlay glows red, telling me I don't have the shot. It'll flash green when I do.

Timing's going to be crucial on this dance. All I can do now is wait. And hope Alisa's thinking the same thing I am.

"You're going to prison, asshole!" she shouts.

"Be just like old times," Rich grunts.

That's an odd response. His belt-wire is still attached to the back wall. I can't open a portal big enough to matter. Alisa's going to have to wrestle him down on her own.

She's not doing too badly so far. Guess living in Lunar gravity for so long is paying off. Rich tries to twist out of her grasp, but she kicks off the wall with one leg and throws him off-balance, slamming him back against the wall. "I will personally make sure the agency renditions you to a blue site on fucking Venus!"

Rich bends his right elbow and pulls his arm back. Alisa wasn't expecting that. He fires another shot just centimeters from her face, making her flinch. He uses the opportunity to lunge away from the wall, pushing her back against the MTI chair. She reaches back with her right arm to brace herself against him.

My crosshairs go green at the same time I hear a burst from Dumont's rifle. I close my fist around the trigger of the machine pistol I'm holding. It's on full automatic. I empty the entire clip into the foam around the stuck mech's weapon.

The foam shreds into a mist of bright orange fluff. The mech's artillery arm swings free and opens fire. I hear screaming and yelling.

I can't look. I hope Alisa managed to draw the mech's fire and then push Rich in front of her. I drop the pistol, dive forward to grab my EMP rifle, and fire it at the mech in the corner. I crawl forward and keep firing. I stand up and keep pulling the trigger until the battery indicator turns red.

I drop the discharged rifle and look at the mech. It's not moving. My eye doesn't show any power readings.

"Sir!" Dumont says behind me.

I turn around and see Rich Johnson's body on the floor, two large caliber bullet holes in his back, and Alisa clawing at the med-sig collar. The display's blinking all sorts of red alert lights. I use the butt of the EMP rifle to smash open the latch, then rip the collar away from her neck.

She gasps and falls to the floor. There's a series of puncture marks down the left side of her neck. And a lot of blood running down her right leg. I blink my eye into medical scanning mode. She's not doing well.

"Surgical, Kangaroo, get up here!" I call over the radio. "Now!"

Dumont kneels down and guides Alisa's left hand to cover the wound in her thigh. "Keep pressure right there, Doc. You got it?"

"Got it." Alisa clutches my shoulder with her other hand. "Joey."

"Yeah." I open the pocket, rotated, with barrier. Joey falls backward into my arms. He's cold. I hope that's just because he's been in hard vacuum for—less than a minute, right? I lift him into the MTI chair, checking him for wounds. Looks like Rich's wild shots missed.

The radio chirps. "We're on our way, Kangaroo," Jessica says. "These mechs aren't making it easy."

"Hurry!" I say, strapping Joey in and pulling the induction dome over his head and the signal collar around his neck. He appears stable—at least, nothing's blinking red or beeping loudly. "Alisa's injured, Joey's still unconscious, and we need to fix this chair! I'm leaving this channel open!"

I make sure Joey's secure, then crouch down next to Alisa. Dumont's kneeling next to the open access panel and connecting wires back together, following Alisa's directions.

"Kangaroo." Alisa points at a box on the floor beside me. Her other hand is pressed against her thigh. I see blood oozing through her fingers. "Give Dumont that pulse regulator."

I pick up the box and hand it to Dumont. She connects it to some wires, and a line of green lights appears along one edge and starts blinking in sequence. I hear gunfire and shouting over the radio. Alisa's breathing is shallow.

Get in here, Surge.

"Good," Alisa says. "Now plug the contact port into the first multilateral slot."

I recognize those terms from Oliver's various rantings, but couldn't tell you for the life of me what they mean or which parts they refer to. Fortunately, Dumont seems to know exactly what Alisa's talking about. She plugs in the box, and more lights appear on the control panel above us.

"You're a medic?" I ask.

"I'm a mechanic," Dumont says. "It's just a machine."

Alisa points at another part on the floor, and I grab it and give it to Dumont. "How long does Joey have? And how long is it going to take us to rebuild this rig?" It might go faster if we don't need to depend on Alisa's instructions. I blink up my data link and start an omnipedia search for MTI rig service manuals.

"Don't need to rebuild everything," Alisa says. Her heartbeat's fluttering. "Just need to ensure cardiovascular function."

"And how are we going to do that?"

"Stimulate vagus nerve." She points up at the control panel. "Diagnostic. Run."

I stand up and tap at the controls. Fortunately, they're pretty clearly labeled. A lot of red indicators appear when I run the diagnostic, but the MTI coils are receiving power. I hope that's the important part. I report this to Alisa.

"Good," she says. "Program victor-ten. Full power. Override safety."

I select those options and read the settings back to her. "Are you sure that's right?" Even without my eye sensors, I can tell her pupils are dilated. I don't want to push the wrong button here.

"Yes," Alisa says, staring off into space. "Run."

"Surgical, do you concur?" I ask over the radio.

"I don't know how those rigs are programmed," Jessica says. "What's Joey's condition?"

I check the readouts. "He's still breathing, but his heartbeat is slowing."

"We're almost there. Just hold fast."

Joey shivers. An entire bank of indicators goes red, and a high-pitched noise fills the room.

"Dammit!" I lean over the chair to make sure it's not a sensor malfunction. "He's not breathing! What do I do?"

"Run the program!" Jessica shouts. I hear more gunfire behind her.

Alisa's still staring into space, glassy-eyed. "Concur. Run."

Goddammit.

I hit the RUN button. The dome over Joey's head flexes, extends to fit against the back of his neck, and emits a low whine. The noise rises in frequency for a few seconds, then ends in a loud crack.

A shower of sparks explodes from the panel in front of Dumont. She falls backward. The control panel goes dark.

"What the fuck!" Dumont jumps to her feet. She's a little singed, but doesn't seem seriously injured.

"Maybe full power was wrong," I say, scrambling around the chair to get a better look at Joey with my eye. His heart rate is still slow, but it's steady now, and his chest is rising and falling. "No. We're okay. He's breathing again. We're good, Surge!"

"Don't call me Surge," Jessica says, not over the radio. I turn to see her entering the room followed by four spacemen. She grabs some equipment out of the bag Rich brought in. I step out of the way and let her examine Joey.

After a moment, she puts down her instruments and exhales. "He's stable. The stim-pulse must have overloaded whatever jury-rigging you did down there."

"Dumont did it," I say reflexively.

Dumont folds her arms. Jessica frowns at me. "My point is you didn't make it worse. We still need to treat the root cause, but this bought us some time." She turns and kneels down next to Alisa. Jessica examines the broken med-sig collar, then starts checking Alisa. "Dammit."

"I'll be fine," Alisa says.

"Shut up," Jessica says. "Kangaroo. Medkit."

I open the pocket and pull out a medkit. Then I check the inventory list in my eye and pull another one. I repeat until I've pulled all the medical supplies I have. It's not much, but Jessica doesn't complain. She just goes to work.

"Joey," Alisa says. "Help Joey."

"We can't," I say. "The machine's fried."

"That was a standard electroplasma pulse regulator," Dumont says. "We didn't reinstall any of the specialized components yet. We can replace the EPR and finish rebuilding the rig."

"Okay, well, let's get to—"

Joey screams like he's actually, literally dying. His eyes pop open when he takes a breath, and Jessica and I both scan him. I can't see into his brain, so I don't know what's going on there—with either his seizure-causing genetic disease or his five-year-old psyche—but he doesn't seem to be in pain. He's just afraid.

"Ali?" he calls. "Ali!"

Alisa reaches up with the hand that's not clutching her bloody thigh and touches Joey's arm. He reaches back with his own hand, closing it around her fingers.

"What's happening?" he cries. "Where are we?"

"It's okay, Joey," Alisa says. "It's going to be okay."

"I want to go home!"

"Soon, Joey." Alisa blinks and grimaces. My medical scanners are painting a lot of red flags over her in my eye. "Listen, Joey. I need to leave for a while."

"No!" Joey clutches her hand even tighter. "No! NO! NO!" He repeats the word over and over again, shaking his head.

"Kangaroo's going to look after you, Joey," Alisa says. "Right, Kangaroo?"

I put a hand on Joey's shoulder. He squirms, but he's still restrained, so he can't get away. The screaming continues. Jessica has now bandaged up Alisa's thigh, wrapped an IV cuff around her arm, and slapped some kind of gel-patch over her neck. I can't tell if any of those things is helping.

"It's going to be okay, Joey," Alisa says. "You're going to be okay."

I look at Jessica. "Please tell me she's going to make it."

She doesn't say anything. The medical scanner she's holding has a lot of blinking red lights on its display.

"Kangaroo?" Alisa says.

I let go of Joey and crouch down next to her. "I'm right here."

She grabs my collar and turns her head toward me. Her eyes are unfocused. My eye scanners are losing her heartbeat. Jessica injects Alisa with something, and her pulse quickens for a moment. But only a moment.

"You're the man, Kangaroo." She smiles. "Take care of yourself. And that . . . that . . ." She gulps in a breath. "Th-th-that's all, folks."

She starts to laugh, then stops.

Joey cries for a long time. So does Jessica.

CHAPTER THIRTY-FIVE

People are celebrating on the Moon.

It's five minutes before six o'clock in the evening, Zulu time, on July 21st. It's the precise day and time when the first humans to set foot on the Moon lifted off again in their flimsy little Lunar Module to return home, all those many years ago.

Through the window of the agency spaceplane, I see fireworks below, colorful starbursts over each one of the Apollo mission sites. My understanding is that the party on the Moon will continue for three more days: the entire duration of those first Lunar astronauts' return trip to Earth.

It's going to take Jessica and me just a few hours to land in Washington, D.C. But it's going to take me the rest of my life to deal with what's happened in the last few days.

Shackleton Crater is just another hole in the Moon now. Oliver tells me there's some pretty spectacular security vid of robots fighting each other, before too many self-destructing bots collapsed the entire crater. I'm not that interested. I've seen enough killer robots to last me a lifetime.

We lost Scorpion. Chances are she's on her way back to the asteroid belt. Doesn't matter. We'll catch up with her sooner or later. She can't fence all those stolen MTI parts without raising some red flags here and there. And she's too flamboyant to lie low for very long.

Gladys has been renditioned to a blue site somewhere on Venus. I'm sure the wardens will have some very interesting conversations with her.

Maybe the old hag will actually tell us something eventually. And we got most of that gold back. Bonus.

Richard Johnson, alias Charlie Angel, is dead. He might have led us to Terman Sakraida. He might at least have gotten us closer. Life's a bitch. The good news is, Sakraida probably hasn't managed to decrypt all those highly sensitive agency files he stole. All evidence indicates that Rich Johnson took the initiative to open his big mouth about Joey's existence, and Sakraida only knew as much about Project Genesis as Rich told him. That means we've still got time to hunt down Sakraida before he cracks the digital safe.

Alisa Garro is also dead. Her body is resting in a coffin in the cargo bay below where Jessica and I are sitting. She's going back to Earth at last. She'll be buried next to her mother. Jessica's going to deliver the eulogy.

I won't be attending the funeral. I'll pay my respects later. I've got work to do.

I pull out my red key to make a call.

Paul is not very happy when we meet. Probably because I presented an ultimatum—through Admiral Morris—that he had to come to the Eyrie for the meeting. But I didn't choose the location arbitrarily, or just to be a jerk.

This is as close to Earth as Joey can get. For now, anyway.

Nobody says anything for the first few minutes after Paul joins Morris, Joey, and me in the observation lounge. This part of the station is in zero-gravity, so there's a constant view of the planet through the large window, and I suspect Joey's fascination with the view is the only reason he's not bouncing around like a maniac.

There's a hurricane forming off the coast of Florida, and Joey is mesmerized. He's never seen large bodies of water before. He's never seen *weather* before.

Paul just floats there for a few minutes, one hand on the railing opposite the window, and stares at Joey. I can't quite tell from his face what he's thinking, but I have a few dozen educated guesses.

Finally, Morris pulls herself forward on the railing to approach Paul. "Lasher."

He nods at her. "Gryphon."

"Welcome to the Eyrie."

"You've redecorated."

"Funny."

Paul looks at me. "I just had a very long meeting at the White House."

"Did you get me a souvenir?" I've never been to the White House.

"The secretary of state had some choice words about your conduct on the Moon."

"*My* conduct?" I take a breath to calm myself. "State can suck my—"

"Stand down. The president's on our side," Paul says.

"I'm surprised we don't have a new secretary of state already," Morris says.

"We just got a new D.Int," Paul says matter-of-factly. "The president doesn't want to further destabilize agency leadership right now."

Now I'm getting angry again. "So State just gets away with conducting secret illegal medical experiments?"

"There will be consequences," Paul says. "Nothing public, and nothing right now. The other shoe drops after the election."

"Eighteen months is a long time for State to wheel and deal," Morris says. She's right. The new president won't be elected until next fall, and it'll be the following January before that person's inauguration takes place and any new cabinet appointments take effect. "People can forget a lot of things in a year and a half."

"We won't forget," Paul says.

"'We' meaning the three of us?" I ask. I'm not convinced we could out-maneuver State, if it ever came down to horse trading in the district.

"I mean all of the Intelligence, Operations, and Science Divisions," Paul says, his tone clearly indicating he thinks I'm an idiot. "Some of our people have been with the agency for decades. They're loyal to more than just the secretary."

"At least we've got an ace in the hole," Morris says, tilting her head toward Joey. He's followed the hurricane rotating beneath us and is now on the other side of the room.

I have to ask. "Do you—either of you—think State and Sakraida might have been—"

"Please," Paul snorts. "This was way above Sakraida's head. No, this is all State. Nobody else would have the hubris to even attempt something like—" He waves a hand toward Joey and grimaces. "Christ. He's tall for a five-year-old."

"Almost six," I say. "And he grew up in low gravity."

Paul turns back to Morris. "You're prepared to house him here? For the duration?"

"We're making arrangements," Morris says. "Dr. Chu's helping us with the gravity acclimatization plan."

It was my idea to send Joey to live on the Eyrie—Morris was betrayed by State as much as any of us, and she's got the resources to protect Joey here—but it was Jessica's idea to build a variable-gravity compartment for him in the Eyrie's rotating habitat ring.

His room will start close to the hub, at one-sixth gravity. Over time it'll get moved farther outward until he's adjusted to Earth normal gravity. That's the hope, anyway. Nobody's ever tried this before. Jessica's hoping that Joey's young enough that his body will deal with the changes as it grows normally.

I guess we'll find out in a few years whether it works. That's not the big question, of course. The big question is whether he'll also be able to use the pocket. We'll probably find that out in four to five years. Or maybe we won't.

I'm not sure which possibility I'm hoping for more: that he does have the pocket, which would make Science Division very happy, or that he doesn't, which would mean he might be able to live something approaching a normal life someday. Eventually. Hopefully.

"Have you cleared Garro's other assistant yet?" Paul asks.

"We're working on it," Morris says. "So far she's clean. The good news is, she had minimal contact with Johnson. They worked completely separate duty cycles."

"You make absolutely sure that nobody compromised her," Paul says. "Also, you'll need at least three more people to care for Joey."

"We don't need to rotate them off the Eyrie that often."

"I want two minders for Joey at all times." Paul gives Morris a stern look. "He's going to have parents, or at least the closest thing we can provide. God is my witness, that child *will* have some stability and normalcy in his life. Ops can help you source the personnel."

I seem to be getting a lot of lumps in my throat lately. And watering eyes. Maybe I should ask Jessica for another checkup.

"Does this mean you're going to start taking my calls, Lasher?" Morris asks.

Paul scowls. "I wasn't avoiding you. I simply needed to prioritize. You understand."

Morris nods. "Does this mean I'm higher on your priority list now?"

"What happened on the Moon is likely a bellwether of how last year's breach is going to play out," Paul says. "Sakraida's not going to come at us directly. He'll pull strings from whatever rock he's hiding in. He'll use other people to do his dirty work. We can find his weak links and exploit them."

"So am I in your top ten?" Morris asks.

"You never worked with Sakraida. You won't be able to recognize his patterns or habits. We're going to get a lot of data coming in after we co-opt SKR's robots in the belt. My analysts will help yours manage and review all that data. Ops and Intel will co-sign any operations pertaining to this objective."

"Top five?"

"Would you rather have a red key, Gryphon," Paul growls, "or just a vial of my blood?"

Morris smiles. "Lasher, I think this is the beginning of a beautiful friendship."

Paul turns his scowl on me. "You are a bad influence."

"What did I do?" I don't know if Morris is aware she's quoting an old movie. I certainly am, but it's fun to play dumb with Paul when nothing's at stake. I don't get opportunities like this very often.

"Kangaroo! Kangaroo!" I feel a tug on my shirtsleeve and look down to see Joey hanging off my arm. "There's flashes of light! In the clouds! Come look!"

"Excuse me," I say. Paul and Morris nod, and I push myself off the wall. Joey and I float back to the window, and I grab the railing there to stop us.

The hurricane off Florida is almost out of view, and we're seeing the huge bank of thick white clouds mostly from the side now. The sun's rising behind the weather system, putting the near side of the cloud mass into gray shadow.

"There!" Joey points to a lightning burst inside the dark clouds. "You see it?"

"Yeah, I see it, Joey." I'm starting to get used to saying his name. It's just a name, after all.

"What is it? Is it a fire?"

"No. That's lightning. Do you know about lightning?"

"Is that like making something weigh less?"

"Not quite. It's—" Boy, I don't even know where to start here. "That whole thing is a hurricane. Do you know about hurricanes?"

"Is it a wetter thing?" he asks.

"Weather," I correct.

"Yeah, weather. Like something that happens in atmosphere? Ali told me about weather, but she said we didn't have any on the Moon."

"That's right. Hurricanes are one specific kind of weather. They're tropical storms."

"What's a storm?"

This is going to be a long conversation. But I might as well get used to teaching him things.

After all, I might be doing a lot more of it in a few years.

"Hey," I say, "here's a fun fact. Did you know every hurricane gets its own name?" I blink up the latest Earth weather report. "Scientists start at the beginning of the alphabet and use a different letter for each hurricane name throughout the year. Looks like this is the eleventh this year. Do you know the eleventh letter of the alphabet?"

He moves his lips silently for a few seconds before answering, "K!"

"Yeah. That's good."

Joey points at me. "K for Kangaroo."

I hated that code name when Paul first assigned it. I've gotten used to it. And now I guess I'm stuck with it. I suppose I've gotten stuck with a lot of things.

All I can do is make the best of whatever comes next.

"That's me," I say. "Kangaroo."

We watch the storm until it drifts out of view, beyond the blue horizon.

ACKNOWLEDGMENTS

I am humbled by all the amazing people I've met who support me and my work. If I fail to mention you below, I apologize, but please know that I appreciate having you in my life.

First, last, and everything: I could not make good art without my beloved wife, who sustains me in countless ways. She always tells me what I need to hear, good or bad. She's the reason I don't give up when the going gets tough. And she's one of the best editors I know. (Pete thinks you're great!)

Thanks to my relentless professional editor, Pete Wolverton, who knows all about picking up the pace despite being in New York City. ("New York City?!" "Get a rope.") Thanks also to everyone at St. Martin's Press/Thomas Dunne Books who contributed to the development, production, or marketing of this volume.

Big ups to my literary agent, Sam Morgan, and all the other JABberwocks who negotiate on my behalf. I wouldn't be here without you. I can't wait to see where we go next.

Cheers to my beta readers—Carolyn O'Doherty, Fonda Lee, Sonja Thomas, and Vanessa MacLellan—whose keen insights showed me which paths to follow and what pitfalls to avoid during rewrites.

Thanks to Darla Myers for letting me use her snake names! (All snakes portrayed in this story are entirely fictitious. Any resemblance to actual snakes is purely coincidental and unintentional.)

Special thanks to Tinatsu Wallace for helping me brainstorm the "nursing home on the Moon" idea.

Secret thanks to Brian Ford Sullivan, Daniel H. Wilson, Sara B. Cooper, and Sean Berard for encouraging me to dream big.

Why, yes, there *is* a puzzle hidden in the cover image! Your mission, should you choose to accept it, is to first reflect upon the designs in both spacesuits, then use that information to complete this web address: __.kangaroo2.com (and thanks to Daryl Gregory for inspiring what you'll find there).

A general shout out to my #WriterLunch & #VanSushi cohorts: Alberto Yáñez, Alexis Radcliff, David Levine, Jessie Kwak, Laura Hall, Monica Villaseñor, Nadya Duke, Simone Cooper, and others previously mentioned. You make eating fun—and tax-deductible!

Speaking of food, I also need to thank my family for nourishing me in so many ways over the years: my mother taught me to love reading and learning, my father showed me how to build things, and my sister demonstrated kindness always. I wouldn't be the person I am without their positive influences.

I'm eternally grateful to everyone who helped launch *Waypoint Kangaroo* and who continues to spread good word of mouth about this series. If you care enough to have read this far, please consider telling two friends how much you enjoyed these books (and encourage them to tell two friends, etc.). Please buy from a local independent bookseller. Please suggest purchases for your public library.

Books can build community, and we are stronger together.

Finally, thank *you*, dear reader, for going on this journey with Team Kangaroo. I hope we'll meet again soon.